BLOOD
MARK

Praise for Blood Mark

A deliciously addictive fever dream of a mystery with a surreal beauty akin to a David Lynch film. I loved it!
—Jennifer Anne Gordon, author of
Beautiful, Frightening, and Silent
winner of the Kindle Award for Best Horror 2020

Featuring a fearless, badass heroine and plot twists that will leave readers breathless, J.P. McLean's Blood Mark *is a gritty, sexy, fast-paced thrill ride from start to finish.*
—E.E. Holmes, award-winning and best-selling author of
The Gateway series

An explosive new series that combines mystery and magic into a can't-put-down thriller.
—Eileen Cook, award-winning author of
You Owe Me a Murder

This edgy, intelligent, psychological thriller has tantalizing touches of Inca myth and will capture your soul from beginning to end.
—W. L. Hawkin, Author of
The Hollystone Mysteries

Praise for The Gift Legacy

" A profoundly intelligent story of a captivating young woman whose victories and struggles with a unique gift will grab your every emotion.
—Jennifer Manuel, award-winning author of
The Heaviness of Things That Float

" JP McLean possesses her own unique gift: the ability to bewitch her readers with her boundless imagination.
—Elinor Florence, Globe and Mail bestselling author of
Bird's Eye View and *Wildwood*

" A deftly crafted, impressively original and inherently compelling read from first page to last.
—Midwest Book Reviews

" Danger, suspense, and mystery all bundled into one perfect read.
—Urban Lit Magazine

" Riveting mash-up of urban fantasy, mystery and new adult—seamlessly woven together with a steamy love story.
—Roxy Boroughs, award-winning author of
The Psychic Heat series

" A superbly crafted fantasy thriller.
—Diana Stevan, award-winning author of *A Cry from the Deep*

" McLean's expertly drawn world is filled with intriguing characters and near-familiar settings that draw you into this compelling read.
—Katherine Prairie, author of the Alex Graham thriller series

" A well written, superbly executed thrilling read!
—Pat McDonald, British crime author

Titles by JP McLEAN

Blood Mark

The Gift Legacy

Secret Sky

Hidden Enemy

Burning Lies

Lethal Waters

Deadly Deception

Wings of Prey

The Gift Legacy Companion

Lover Betrayed (Secret Sky Redux)

BLOOD
MARK

JP MCLEAN

WINDSTORM
PRESS

Blood Mark
Blood Mark ~ Book 1
First Canadian Edition

Copyright © 2021 by JP McLean
All rights reserved.

ISBN
978-1-988125-56-5 (Paperback)
978-1-988125-57-2 (MOBI)
978-1-988125-58-9 (EPUB)
978-1-988125-59-6 (PDF)

Edits by Eileen Cook, Rachel Small, and Ted Williams
Book cover design by JD&J Book Cover Design
Author photograph by Crystal Clear Photography

Excerpt from *Secret Sky* copyright © 2018 by JP McLean

Cataloguing in Publication information available
from Library and Archives Canada

WINDSTORM PRESS
BRITISH COLUMBIA, CANADA
WINDSTORMPRESS.COM

For my family

Imperfection is beauty.

—Anonymous

1 | Jane

August 8

Jane Walker might have been the only person in Vancouver not afraid to be in a downtown alley at half-past midnight. Shadows clung to fissures and corners, morphing into nightmare shapes as she passed. A warm breeze stirred the scent of rotting garbage along with her gag reflex. Rescuing Sadie was getting old. One of these nights, Sadie's unique way of punishing herself would be the death of them both. And maybe Jane's bike.

She parked next to Ethan's Fat Boy in the hopes his reputation would spill over and protect her cherished Honda 500. But the caged bulb above the back door worried her. It bled a weak circle of light that pooled near the bikes. It was a toss-up whether it would draw attention or act as a deterrent. She said a prayer for the latter and removed her helmet. A slamming door punctuated a heated argument drifting down from a nearby apartment. She raked her long hair forward to hide the worst of the birthmark on her face then walked around the corner, bypassing the dregs of Riptide's nightly queue.

A bouncer she knew manned the door. His steady gaze slid sideways at her approach. Boos from the lineup he held at bay prompted him to inhale, emphasizing the girth of his chest. He flexed biceps larger than her thighs, tipped his chin, and let her pass.

She nodded her thanks and stepped inside. A cocktail of perfume and stale sweat assaulted her. Thumping music reverberated in her chest as she scanned the bar for Ethan Bryce and found him pouring shots. A seasoned bartender, he worked the room like a ringside bookie at an illegal fight, smiling with one eye and watching for trouble with the other.

"Thanks for calling," Jane said, pressing into the bar. "Where is she?"

Ethan held her gaze a moment longer than necessary then swiped his head to the left. Jane followed his line of sight to the dance floor, where her roommate swayed out of step with the music. Sadie had gone with tasteful tonight, wearing her LBD, as she called her little black dress. Her client must have been a high roller—unlike the 'roided-up jockstrap now keeping Sadie upright with a hand on her ass and a sure-bet smile on his face.

Jane strode through the dancers and stopped short of her. "Sadie?" she shouted over the music.

Sadie lifted her head from Jockstrap's shoulder and struggled to focus. "Narc?" She blew at a stray blonde curl. Jane winced at the nickname Sadie rarely used in public.

"You know her?" Jockstrap asked.

"Shurr. Tim, meet Narc. Dance with us." Sadie reached for Jane. Her mascara had smudged, leaving charcoal shadows under her eyes. It's what two lines of coke and a few too many vodka chasers looked like.

Jane took her hand. "Let's go home."

"She's with me tonight, honey," Jockstrap said, tugging Sadie's arm away from Jane. He looked down to Sadie with a smarmy smile. "Aren't you, baby?"

Sadie squinted up at him. When she looked back at Jane, sparks of awareness surfaced. She pushed against his chest. "I gotta go."

"You don't *gotta go*," he said, dragging her back. "Stay with me, baby. We're having fun, aren't we?"

"How about I bring her back tomorrow?" Jane said. "When she's not wasted."

Sadie stumbled as Jockstrap twisted to put himself between the two women. "I've made an investment here."

Charming, Jane thought, recoiling from his stale-beer spittle. She was quick in a fight and had the advantage of being sober, but Jockstrap had a hundred pounds on her and a hard-on with a destination.

She knew Ethan wouldn't tolerate her pulling a knife in Riptide, so she'd have to dissuade Jockstrap some other way. She looked to the floor. For Sadie, she'd expose her marks. Only for Sadie. An eyeful of ugly often gave her a split-second advantage. He was already wobbling—shouldn't be too hard to knock him on his ass.

She shifted the grip on her helmet, widened her stance, and drew in a calming breath. Then, in one swift motion, she swung the curtain of hair away from her face. "She's going home," Jane said, pressing upward into Jockstrap's personal space to ensure he got a good look at the thick blood-red birthmark that slashed an angle from her forehead to her temple. It looked like the work of a medieval battle-axe.

He shrunk back with a familiar snarl of revulsion. Already primed, Jane was ready to launch when a firm hand landed on her shoulder, halting her.

"Everything all right here?" Ethan asked, squeezing harder than he needed to. Jane felt a pinch of resentment at his interference.

Jockstrap's gaze darted to the figure standing behind Jane. Ethan wasn't big, but his reputation was. You didn't cross him unless you had generous sick-leave benefits.

Jockstrap's nostrils flared. He pinched his lips. Neither man moved. Long seconds later, Jockstrap faltered and blew out a deflating breath. His bravado and sure-bet attitude faded along with his hopes of getting laid. He released Sadie with a little shove. "Go on then," he said. "Take out the trash." He stalked away and called over his shoulder, "And it's Tom, not fuckin' Tim."

"Yeah," Jane mumbled, "not fuckin' Tom, either." With a shake of her head, Jane settled her hair back into place. She wrapped a steadying arm around Sadie's shoulder and turned her around, bumping into Ethan, who stood in their path.

"You okay?" he said, but his expression was a warning. She'd forced his hand and he didn't like that.

"Yeah. Watch my ride? I'll come by in the morning to pick her up."

"Jimmy'll keep an eye on her," Ethan said, before he swaggered back to the bar.

Ethan's faith in the stubble-faced panhandler who hung around the bar was a mystery to Jane.

She opened Sadie's purse and fished out her keys.

2 | Rick

Rick Atkins kept his back to the dance floor and gazed at Sadie's reflection in the mirror behind the bar. Not that Sadie would recognize him in glasses and a full beard, but vigilance had served him well to this point. He wouldn't tempt fate when he was so close to his endgame.

He watched the woman who called herself Jane flash her markings like a blowfish in the face of the predator shark who groped at Sadie. Jane had no inkling of the damage she was capable of inflicting. But not for long. Rick downed his beer and slinked out the door.

3 | Jane

August 9

Jane parked in Sadie's spot behind the Victorian house she and Sadie called home. The Kitsilano mansion had dodged the wrecking ball of the sixties but not the callous renovations of the seventies that left its old bones mutilated.

The pungent aroma of pot lingered in the hallway. Their new neighbour no doubt—his was the only other apartment on the basement level. Jane hadn't yet met him.

They descended a couple of steps and made their way down the dimly lit hallway to their apartment, Jane keeping a grip on Sadie's arm. They shared a small one-bedroom unit. First one home in the evening got the bed. She slipped her key in the lock and gave the door a shove, comforted by the heft of the steel against her shoulder. A door the landlord would never have agreed to if he'd had to pay for it.

Sadie staggered in ahead of her. Jane turned the lock and shot the two bolt locks. Thieves would find the sparse apartment a waste of their efforts, but the locks weren't to dissuade thieves. Jane set her helmet on the floor and heeled off her boots, careful not to dislodge her boot knife.

She helped Sadie to bed and tucked her under the sheet. The mattress and box spring rested on the floor beside a table lamp that Sadie had rescued from a dumpster. She was already fast asleep when Jane returned with two aspirins and a glass of water. Jane set them on the parquet floor, also known as the bedside table.

Back in the living room, she double-checked the bolt locks. She'd gotten a deal on the door from a demolition warehouse but would have paid full price if she'd had to.

She changed into her sleep pants and an old cotton work shirt and settled on the sofa, drawing a quilt up under her arms. Though she was glad to have Sadie safe at home, she hated leaving her bike downtown, regardless of Ethan's faith in Jimmy.

Her thoughts drifted to Ethan. He was the only man Jane could remember whose gaze didn't skitter to the left of her face when he looked at her. It was as if he didn't see her birthmarks, or that one anyway.

Port wine stains, the doctors had called them, though they hadn't shared with her that they'd never seen specimens so uniform. Or extensive. The stains strapped her body. When Jane was ten years old, her guardian had allowed her to be stripped and photographed. That small humiliation still haunted Jane—so much so that only Sadie had seen all the hideous birthmarks. A handful of men had gotten a preview—men who'd fooled her with sweet words and then cut her to the quick when they didn't have the fortitude to accept all of her.

The skin beneath the stains hadn't thickened with age, as the doctors had predicted, but the stains themselves had morphed into an intricate pattern. It looked as if the birthmarks had been applied with a blood-red rubber stamp in thick rows.

The only treatment available to rid her of the crimson stains was laser, a painful and expensive procedure not covered by any health insurance she could afford. And because the birthmarks were vascular, the doctors warned her that the treatment might not work. It could even make the stains worse.

That didn't sway Jane from her plan to attempt the removal process as soon as she'd paid off her Rebel. It wouldn't be long now. She'd begin with the biggest offender: the two-inch-wide red line that tracked across the left side of her face, from mid-forehead to her ear. Hiding that one from curious stares was the most difficult. Two of the others, one on the back of her hand and one on the top of her foot, posed seasonal challenges but were nothing gloves and boots couldn't cover.

Jane rolled over and gave in to the sleep that tugged at her. With the door bolted, the dreams could come. Not that she could stop them. They came when they wanted, without warning or apology. Vivid dreams that she could recall in painstaking detail, even when she didn't want to.

And when the dreams came, nothing could wake her until they'd run their course.

Visiting Dream

Jane finds herself in a hospital room. The young woman in the room is pacing. She's been in Jane's dreams before. Her name is Rebecca Morrow. Jane read it on an envelope in an earlier dream. That time, Jane had been in Rebecca's tiny apartment, where Rebecca had been all smiles, snuggling with a man who had a rumbling laugh. Jane doesn't know her or the man, which is unusual.

This time, Rebecca's demeanour is furtive, guarded. Her hair is long and in need of washing. She wears two hospital gowns, one open in the back and, over it, one open in the front. Surgical socks cover her feet. She's folded her arms tightly across her chest, pulling her shoulders into a hunch. Her circuit takes her from the wire-mesh-reinforced window to the bed to the open door.

Jane doesn't know why she's here with Rebecca. She scans the room looking for clues. Only a hospital bed and a padded chair furnish the space. No personal belongings. No warmth. No sharp edges. Austere. Jane senses it's a psych ward.

A kindly woman, short in stature and wearing a bright, busy smock, pushes a cart of linens past the door. Her dark eyes are ringed in blue and set in a deeply lined leather face. She acknowledges Rebecca with a warm smile.

Sometimes hairstyles or clothing reveal the dream's vintage, but Jane sees nothing to which she can pin a year or a decade. No disco hair, no visible tats or piercings.

When a nurse appears at the doorway, Rebecca freezes in place.

The nurse sounds as if she's speaking through water, her words indiscernible. This is a change from the dreams Jane had as a teenager. Back then, the dreams were silent movies.

With a jingle of keys, the nurse unlocks a door opposite the bed. It's a bathroom. She ushers Rebecca inside and supervises her use of the facilities. The nurse then guides her to the bed and hands her a small paper cup. When Rebecca reaches for it, the sleeve of the hospital gown rides up her arm, exposing white gauze bandages. A suicide attempt? The nurse doesn't take her eyes off Rebecca until she's washed down the pills with a few sips of water.

Jane wants to leave, but she's stuck in the dream. It will release her when it wants to and no sooner. Jane breathes deeply, forcing herself to control the sense of helplessness these dreams bring on.

Rebecca drifts into a drugged sleep. She tosses her head from side to side and incoherent words tumble out.

Jane watches Rebecca sleep until her attention is drawn to the doorway. A doctor, if the white coat is any indication, approaches the bed. The man's hair is short and gelled. He's handsome. Tassels adorn his shoes, and his fine wool slacks have sharp creases. He studies Rebecca's face while she sleeps, adjusts her blanket, then touches her cheek with his fingertips.

Jane woke with a start. Her dreams always ended abruptly. At least this one hadn't left her retching. Or screaming. Jane checked the time. Two o'clock in the morning; four hours before she had to get up. She rarely had a second visiting dream in one night. Relieved to have it done with, she rolled over and bunched up the thin pillow.

She thought about the doctor's gesture as she drifted to sleep. It felt off—inappropriate. Jane wanted to believe the doctor's caress stopped at Rebecca's cheek, but she wasn't that naive anymore. Her dreams had seen to that. People carried out unthinkable deeds in her dreams when they thought no one was watching. Dreams Jane wished she could forget.

4 | Rick

Rick breathed a sigh of relief when the HR police handed the random drug-testing kit to a colleague. He hadn't overindulged the previous night but knew it would take at least another thirty-six hours for the cocaine to clear out of his system.

He'd put in more time than any other program director and now, the hospital's chief of staff was retiring. For eight years, Rick had been passed over for promotion. The job was his due. He'd earned it and couldn't afford a positive drug test.

Rick's brother Michael had made partner in his investment firm three years ago, and he never shut up about it. Though Rick would have thought it impossible, his brother was more obnoxious now than when he'd bought their father a truck after being promoted to head up his firm's international division.

Mikey was a lousy big brother. He'd never been able to deal with Rick's success—a baby brother wasn't supposed to become a doctor, to have more in common with their father. He wasn't supposed to go to Europe to train at a renowned institute or be headhunted by Canada's pre-eminent psychiatric hospital.

Mikey often milked old school chums, including the hospital's CFO, for dirt on Rick's career, which he then selectively fed to their father. And worse, their old man fell for whatever gossip Mikey shared.

But the sun was setting on those days. When Rick was chief of staff at the most prestigious facility in the country, his father would see Mikey's jealousy for what it was. Chief of staff was the Oscar in his profession. When Rick had that in his fist, their father would have to concede that he'd made it, had outshone his brother. Then Mikey would have to pick at someone else's scabs.

"Dr. Atkins? Are you ready for rounds?" The new resident startled Rick out of his daydream. The rookie's enthusiasm nauseated him.

Rick collected the clipboard his unit clerk had prepared and turned toward the hallway. He called over his shoulder, "We'll start with D wing." A dose of the worst society had to offer should put a damper on the young doctor's zeal. Rick smiled at the rapid footfalls of the resident rushing to keep up.

Rick's thoughts turned to the chief's big office with the view of the manicured lawns and lush gardens. Perhaps he'd hire someone to redecorate. Make it into something more fitting.

5 | Jane

Jane woke at 5:30 a.m. and made a cup of tea. Then she adjusted the pillow and snuggled back into the warm spot on the sofa to check her phone. She'd had the ringer turned off. The last text had been the one from Sadie last night, a sunshine emoji in response to Jane's *RU safe?*

Sometimes, she resented protecting Sadie from herself, but the resentment never lasted. She'd known her since they were thirteen. They'd met at an all-girls group home on the day Jane arrived still wearing a hospital bracelet, a bandage where they'd removed the IV, and a suffocating cloak of shame and humiliation. She didn't remember much of those first days, but she remembered Sadie's kindness. Her acceptance of Jane, birthmarks and all, had brought Jane out of her shell.

They'd become inseparable and grew up protecting one another. No minor feat considering the group homes they'd lived in—and the neighbourhoods. Physical altercations were commonplace. You either learned how to fight or you became a punching bag. She and Sadie learned how to fight. And then they learned how to fight smart. Avoid or deflect whenever possible, but never, ever, run away. And never cry. Twelve years later, their symbiotic instinct remained strong.

She lifted her journal from the trunk that served as a coffee table. Sadie had suggested the journals back in high school, speculating that Jane's dreams might be triggered by food or something in her environment. Her journaling had become a habit, but the daily entries hadn't yet helped her find the triggers to her dreams.

At the top of a fresh page, she wrote, *August 8. Breakfast: banana and yogourt. Worked 7–4. Lunch: taco. Dinner: Mickey D's burger.* Jane lifted her pen from the page and paused. Though she'd normally record encounters such as last night's, she'd never put pen to paper about rescuing Sadie. She wouldn't risk hurting Sadie's pride. Not that Sadie was in the habit of reading Jane's journal—but given Jane's condition, she couldn't bank on privacy.

She finished the entry with *Saw Ethan.*

Ethan remained an enigma. Earlier in the summer, she and Sadie had run to Douglas Park to spar and practice their kicks. Ethan had ambled by, his skin slick with sweat. He leaned against a tree watching them until Sadie suggested he move along. Before he left, he had the cheek to correct her roundhouse stance.

A smile crossed Jane's lips as she remembered Sadie's hands going to her hips. Jane had looked to the ground to hide her amusement.

With typical Sadie sass, she'd taken the opportunity to demonstrate her kick. Sadie was aiming to break Ethan's nose, but the guy had skills. She ended up on her back in the grass looking up at him. As a peace offering, he'd invited them to Riptide for a drink, which was how they learned he worked there.

Jane had thought for sure he would have made a move on Sadie by now, but as far as she knew, he hadn't. She wasn't unhappy about that. She didn't think Ethan was gay, but he didn't come across as a monk either. Was Sadie interested in him? she wondered. An unusual man, that one. She stuffed the pen in the journal's coil spine and set the book back on the trunk, adjusting it so it lay exactly parallel to the edge.

Her tea finished, she slipped into the bedroom. Sadie didn't stir, but at some point in the night, she'd discarded her LBD in a heap beside the bed.

Their mismatched dressers sat side by side. Sadie's dresser drawers were askew, as if she'd left in a rush the previous night. Like their closet, Sadie's dresser overflowed with thrift-store finds that ran the gamut from tarty to tasteful.

Jane's dresser told a different story. Her bottom drawer held her journals and important papers. In the drawer above the papers was an old pair of motorcycle boots that she'd tired of having to dig out from under Sadie's clothing pile at the bottom of the closet. The top three drawers held clothes that Sadie called utilitarian. Jane didn't care. She wasn't a fashionista. Her clothes served only two purposes: camouflage for her birthmarks and protection from the elements.

She pulled out what she needed and clicked the door closed behind her. After dressing, she donned her biker jacket and took the bus downtown. She got off on Granville Street, and her anxiety ramped up with each step that brought her closer to the alley beside Riptide. The bar's facade suffered under the harsh light of day. The spackle job, which cast an enticing spell in the nighttime hours, revealed the building's crumbling cracks and grime. She turned into the alley and found Ethan's Fat Boy and, beside it, safe and sound, her Rebel. She exhaled with relief.

Jimmy stirred in his sleeping bag and opened his rheumy eyes. Jane knelt down and offered him a fiver. He accepted it with a toothless smile. She looked up to the fire escape that marked Ethan's apartment, across the alley. Though she'd never been inside Ethan's apartment, she knew where it was. Earlier in the year, he'd pointed it out to her when he'd shown her his Harley. He'd still be sleeping. She'd thank him later. She tugged on her helmet and eased her bike out of the alley.

A few blocks south, she parked on Beach Street, at the lower end of the fenced lot that housed Positively Plants. The nursery was the only garden centre in an increasingly dense downtown core with an abundance of postage-stamp courtyards and Juliet balconies that needed "a splash of green and a bit of colour"—Positively Plants' slogan.

Jane worked for the Bakker family, who owned the nursery. She had Nelson Leonard to thank for the job. He'd been Jane's caseworker and had set her up with the Bakkers a few years before she'd aged out of the system.

Without the nursery job she'd never have gotten her high school equivalency certificate, or GED, as it was commonly called. The special-ed class the school had dumped her into had been a joke. It seemed to Jane that a disproportionate number of system kids ended up there. After Jane refused to go back, Nelson helped her get a computer so she could continue classes online. She stuck it out. That was the deal she'd made with the Bakkers. She'd squeaked out a GED and kept the computer and the job.

Sadie hadn't been so lucky.

"Morning, Luc," Jane called, pushing open the glass front door. Humidity thick with the scent of lilies escaped into the street. Lucas was the Bakkers' eldest son and a horticulturist. He ran the business with the help of his sister, Anna, who was the one with the business gene. They'd formed a loose family with Jane, adopting her as one of their own.

"Hey, Joyce," Lucas called through the building's back door. "Could use a hand here."

Jane hated the name Joyce. But that was the name on her paycheque, the name the Bakkers had known her by when they'd hired her. Jane hadn't known then—and the Bakkers still didn't—that she'd been named after the Joyce SkyTrain station, where she'd been abandoned hours after her birth. Jane learned that little gem after she turned nineteen. At that age, the province could no longer keep the circumstances of her birth locked away from her. Nelson had warned her of the pitfalls of seeking that information, but Jane had stubbornly plowed ahead. She'd been an idiot—fell face-first into the fairy-tale trap of believing she'd been born to a teenage mother who would be all grown up now, married to Jane's father, and awaiting her long-lost daughter's contact with open arms.

Joyce Walker preferred her original name. Jane Doe. Or more precisely, Baby Jane Doe, the name given to every abandoned baby. She'd even given some thought to legally changing it.

Jane found Lucas loading a cart with nursery pots of cedar hedging. At the sight of her, he braced his hands against his back and stretched. "Windmore's truck will be here in an hour." He pulled the order from his pocket and handed it to her. "Pick the flowering specimens. Anna can start on the watering."

"Sure," Jane said. Windmore was one of their best customers. They specialized in landscaping new condo projects. They'd overplant lush show gardens during the frenzied sales period and then abandon them to bulldozers when construction started. She'd had to harden her heart to the task of selecting which plants she'd condemn.

With the order in hand, she headed to her locker in the staff breakroom, where she laced up her steel-toed shoes and snapped on her utility belt. Then she placed her curved pruning knife in one pouch; her clippers went in another. Finally, she grabbed her gloves and proceeded to the west end of the lot.

Forty minutes later, she wheeled a cart loaded with rhododendrons, azaleas, and hydrangeas to the street gate. In her early days at Positively Plants, the order would have taken her all morning to fill. It wasn't just a matter of finding the proper specimens—it was also heavy work that used to leave her aching after a full shift. Jane now credited the nursery for her power uppercut and a roundhouse kick with bone-breaking potential.

Lucas had a clipboard in his hand as he approached. "Find everything?"

"Yup."

Lucas had added a dozen one-gallon pots of needle grasses to a third cart. He carefully checked off Jane's selections against the order. They both looked up as Windmore's truck arrived. It coasted to a stop alongside the gate. Lucas rolled the gate open and shook the driver's hand.

"Joyce will help you load up," Lucas said, patting the driver on the shoulder before handing him the clipboard. Jane liked that Lucas didn't coddle her. He never had.

When the truck was loaded, the driver signed off the order and returned the clipboard without a glance at Jane. Instead, his gaze wandered into the greenhouse. He offered Anna a flirtatious smile, undeterred by the ring on her finger. Jane melted into the background, where she was most comfortable, and unconsciously tugged at the bandana she wore to hide her birthmark.

She walked back to the greenhouse and picked up the hose Anna had put down. Summertime watering at Positively Plants took the better part of two hours. It was mind-numbing work, but there was a certain satisfaction in the routine of it.

After she'd put away the hoses, she checked in with Lucas.

"Want me to do that?" she asked. He'd started culling the annuals to make room for the fall bulbs that would soon arrive.

"No. I need you to do deliveries. Two downtown and one out at UBC. Anna's got the paperwork."

Jane checked the time. "Okay. You want me to pick up some lunch?"

"Yeah. Get me whatever you're having. And something for Anna too."

Jane loaded the delivery orders into the company's Ford F-150 then poked her head back inside. "Back in ninety," she called out.

Lucas popped his head up. "Ninety? I'm starving over here."

"Snack on the parsley in edible herbs—it's about to bolt," she said, and scooted out to the truck. His trailing laughter put a smile on her face. He was exactly the kind of uncle she'd want.

Lunch-hour traffic clogged her route. She turned up the volume on the radio and drummed her thumbs against the steering wheel as she negotiated her way across the downtown toward her last delivery. She'd get takeout from a decent falafel place she knew of along the route back.

Jane pulled into a fifteen-minute delivery slot out front of the Department of Anthropology. The squat tan building reached out in several directions and was surrounded by neat gardens and manicured lawns. Hallowed ground. Untouchable. University had never been an option for troublesome system kids like her.

She checked the delivery slip. Nathaniel Crawford had ordered one of their more expensive orchids. Cradling the bloom, she headed to what she hoped was the main entrance. The place was deserted. A directory pointed her to the second floor.

A cubicle in front of Crawford's office was unoccupied, but the office door behind it was ajar. Jane adjusted her bandana and tapped on the door.

"Come in," called a man's voice from inside.

"Delivery for Nathaniel Crawford," Jane said, as she pushed open the door.

The man dragged his attention away from a computer screen and turned his chair around. Crawford didn't exactly fit the picture Jane had in her head of a professor. His smile broadened as he spotted the box in Jane's arm. He jumped up and walked around his desk, skirting Jane. She looked down at his surfer shorts and sandals. He peered out the door then swung it almost closed.

"Great timing." He pushed up the sleeves of a teal-blue rash guard. "The orchid is a surprise for my TA. She doesn't know it yet, but she's been accepted into the doctoral program. Set it here," he said, pointing to the corner of his desk. After Jane did so, he shifted the tissue paper and examined the long flowering stem. "Beautiful."

Jane gazed out the window to the mountains in the distance. She wondered if he found the view as distracting as she did.

The professor carried on talking as Jane took in the crowded office. "I had a hard time finding that one. She collects them, you see." Mounds of paper covered every conceivable surface. Floor-to-ceiling bookcases spanned two walls and were stuffed to overflowing and absent, even a nod, to aesthetics.

The professor smoothed the tissue paper back in place and walked behind Jane to the back of the door, where a windbreaker hung. As the professor rummaged through the coat's pockets, Jane's attention was riveted to the left of the door. Above the light switch hung a small print. Jane recognized it immediately. Hairs rose on the back of her neck. She took a tentative step toward it. The square black frame was no larger than eight inches, the print in the centre no bigger than three.

"Mesmerizing, isn't it?" the professor said.

Jane started, surprised to find herself inches away from the print. Her chest constricted. How had Nathaniel Crawford come to have a print of the pattern in her birthmark? She jerked her head in the professor's direction. He stood a few feet behind her and shifted his rapt gaze from the print to her face. "This is for you," he said, extending a ten-dollar bill. He held a pen in his other hand. "You need a signature, I expect?"

Unable to find words, Jane nodded. He wiggled the ten and Jane accepted it with a shaking hand. Inexplicably, she felt trapped.

"You all right?"

"Fine," Jane squeaked. She reached into her pocket and withdrew the delivery slip. As she did so, her gloves fell to the floor. Their heads nearly collided as they simultaneously bent to retrieve them, but the professor beat her to it.

"Let me," he said, mumbling an apology. He offered her a smile when he straightened and extended the gloves. Jane, still clutching the delivery slip in her right hand, reached for the gloves with her left. But the professor held fast to them. Jane saw, too late, that he was transfixed by the birthmark that stained the back of her left hand. He looked up at her, eyes wide.

Jane snatched her hand away. She saw his lips move but didn't hear the words. She turned to the door, swung it open, and ran.

Back in the parking lot, she jumped into the truck and peeled out of the driveway, narrowly missing an inbound vehicle. She cursed, swerved to the right, and stomped on the gas pedal.

Her heart thumped. Where had the professor gotten that print? Her birthmarks were unique. No one else had them. Jane's memory of being stripped naked and clinically photographed flooded back. Humiliation painted her face as red as it had been the day it happened. The day they'd allowed it to happen. She wanted to scream. There was only one way the professor could have a print of her birthmark: someone had gotten their hands on her old photos. What kind of person makes art out of a child's unfortunate skin condition? A pervert? How many other people had a piece of her birthmark hanging on their walls?

Jane pulled over on the side of the road and released her grip on the steering wheel. No matter how many times she buried that horrible day, it always resurfaced. And this time, she felt exposed and vulnerable, in addition to humiliated. She dropped her head to the headrest. After she took a few deep breaths, the nausea passed. She recited her and Sadie's mantra. "Look forward, never back." When she felt as if she'd regained control, she continued on her way.

At the rear of Positively Plants, she pulled into the small patch of broken asphalt Lucas called a parking spot. She held out her hand, pleased that the shaking had stopped. "Forward, never back," she reminded herself, and climbed out of the truck.

It wasn't until she caught sight of Lucas that she remembered lunch.

He looked up from the till expectantly. She pressed her hand to her forehead and spun on her heel. "Back in a minute."

She dashed across the street and around the corner to pick up sandwiches. On her way out of the deli, she nearly tripped over Buddy's wheelchair. As usual, he'd been zipping along at a fast clip, but he slowed to a stop when he saw her.

"Eh, Jaynee," Buddy said. She'd corrected his pronunciation of her name the first few times, but he kept right on calling her Jaynee. It didn't bother her. His perpetual happiness was infectious.

"Hi, Buddy. How's the missus?" Jane asked, keeping up their running narrative.

"Still in my dreams," he said, the words slurred. His cerebral palsy affected both his mobility and his speech. A wide smile uncovered teeth that appeared to be struggling to get out of his mouth, and when he laughed, his eyes—one brown, one hazel—sparkled.

Jane reached into her pocket and pulled out the ten-dollar bill the professor had given her. She folded it and pushed it into the donation can zip-tied to the side of Buddy's motorized wheelchair.

"You take care," Jane said. She crossed the street and strode back to Positively Plants. After she delivered the Bakkers' lunches, she began unpacking the newly arrived skid of chrysanthemums. She inadvertently sliced through the display box and had to hunt down a roll of packing tape to repair it. But when she discovered she'd dumped a bag of tulip bulbs into the bulk daffodil bin, she stopped pretending she could concentrate on anything other than the professor's print and begged off work for the rest of the day.

6 | Sadie

Sadie Prescott's head felt no better when she woke for the second time. The aspirins she'd downed on the first waking hadn't put a dent in her hangover. She pushed herself upright and took a moment to be sure she wouldn't throw up before she made the effort to stand. Her LBD lay like a puddle on the floor.

She padded to her dresser and rummaged through the top drawer until her hand found the smooth, cool glass of the micky bottle. After a few quick slugs, she replaced the cap and filed it away again. She took two more aspirins and a shower. By the time she was dressed, her headache had dulled to tolerable.

There were just enough coffee grinds left to make a small cup. She rinsed the French press with a swish of water. As she filled the kettle, her phone rang from the depths of her purse. She found it on the floor by the front door.

It was Cynthia. "I have a proposition for you."

"Not interested," Sadie said. Once a month, twice on occasion, was all Sadie could handle without wanting to drown herself. She dropped the purse on the trunk and returned to the kitchen to pour herself a bowl of cereal.

"I think you will be."

"Why are you phoning me?" Cynthia's gigs were handled online. At Cynthia's insistence.

"Because this one's different and there's a bonus in it for you. Stop by and see me."

Sadie hesitated. Cynthia had asked Sadie to stop by only once before. There had been a bonus that time too. Five hundred bucks. A "signing bonus," she'd called it.

"What's the bonus?" Sadie headed to the sofa, steadying her bowl.

"We'll talk when you get here. Thirty minutes?"

Sadie agreed and disconnected. She finished her Froot Loops then dumped out her purse.

Despite her efforts, she remembered most of the previous evening. She picked up the business card he'd given her. He'd become a regular client. Too regular. He'd thought they'd both benefit from cutting out the middleman. He was mistaken. She'd taken his card only to shut him up. Looking at it now, she wondered if Mr. Kristan, no initial, was his real name. He was at least twice her age and insisted she address him formally: Mr. Kristan. Sadie chalked it up to his predilection for teacher-student role play. Even that delusion he'd taken too far by asking questions of her as if he really believed she were a student. Sadie played along with a rehearsed list of subjects and complaints about course load, but she never divulged her real name. She was Chloe, and if a client pressed her, she'd whisper "Jennifer" as if it were a gift. She found a pack of matches, torched the card, and set it in her empty cereal bowl.

Cynthia Lee lived in a swanky downtown condo. Sadie parked in a visitor stall and presented herself to the concierge. With the push of a button, he released the lock on the heavy glass doors that granted access to the privileged.

Cynthia greeted Sadie at her door and turned back into the condo inviting her to follow. She strode barefoot down a short hall. Her yoga gear left no doubt about what was underneath. Though she was forty-something, she had the body of a toned twenty-five-year-old. The tantalizing scent of coffee drew Sadie forward. She gazed about the spacious condo that looked much the same as it had three years ago—sleek and modern with a whole lot of white leather and subtle lime-green accents.

"I'm having an espresso," Cynthia said. "Can I make you something?"

"Americano?"

"Cream and sugar?" Cynthia asked.

"Black."

"Have a seat." Cynthia swept her hand toward an armless tufted sofa and carried on behind a breakfast counter into the kitchen. Her shiny chestnut hair was cinched back in a high, bouncy ponytail and not a single strand stuck out of place. She spun the lid off a silver Illy can. "Mr. Kristan is quite taken with you."

Sadie took a moment to enjoy the view of Coal Harbour before she sat down. She pulled a shaggy cushion onto her lap and petted the faux sheepdog strands. "He probably says that about all the *students.*" Mr. Kristan had hired her every three months for almost two years now. Cynthia chuckled. She made a lot of money from men who fooled themselves into believing that undergrads weren't hookers. Of course, they weren't undergrads either. "Mr. Kristan only hires you."

A hiss of steam erupted from the espresso machine.

"Is that so?"

"Yes, and he has something special in mind."

Something special meant kink. Sadie didn't do kink. It helped her believe her own little self-deception that hooking was a sideline, not a career. Looked like it was time to dump Mr. Kristan no initial.

"He wants to cut you out," Sadie said.

"They all want to cut me out." Cynthia came around the counter with a cup and saucer and set them on the table in front of Sadie. She took a seat opposite and lifted a lipstick-stained espresso cup off its saucer. "They don't understand the game. Never have. Their egos want to think it's them and not their money we're interested in."

"I don't do kink. You know that."

"Mr. Kristan has somehow learned you work only one gig a month. Did you share that with him?"

Sadie thought back. "I may have. Don't see the harm. It reinforces the poor schoolgirl image."

"Maybe too much," Cynthia said. "He wants to buy out your contract."

Sadie frowned. "I don't have a contract."

"Mr. Kristan doesn't know that, and it's best if it stays that way."

"Why?"

"Because he's not offering enough. Yet."

Sadie's gut tightened. She'd been right. "I'm not interested. Cut him loose."

Cynthia set her cup back on its saucer. "Don't be foolish."

"He's getting attached. Too personal."

"And you're not a novice. Manage his expectations. I'll work him from my end and when he's ripe for the picking, we'll both get a bonus."

"How much is our *contract* worth?"

"I think I can get him up to a hundred K."

"And my take?"

"The usual."

Sadie's pulse quickened. She could do a lot with fifty grand. A new car, to start. Her old clunker had already eaten through a transmission and an alternator. But the reality of the deal soon set in. "He'll think he owns me, will want me at his beck and call. I'm not doing that."

"He wants to *save* you, honey. Get you out of the business. That's a winning lotto ticket with your name on it. Cash it in."

Sadie plucked at the pillow in her lap. "Give him a few freebies? Let him think he's done right by me?"

"Exactly," Cynthia said. "Be grateful for a month or three and then shake him off. I'll set you up with a new persona. Just make sure he doesn't learn enough to find you after we're done with him."

"I need to think about it." Sadie wasn't as confident as Cynthia about Mr. Kristan's motives. He didn't come across as the altruistic type, and a hundred grand seemed like a lot of money for a good deed.

"Don't take too long. He'll want an answer, and I don't want him shopping around."

Back in her apartment, Sadie gazed longingly at the tousled bed then checked her phone again. No time for a nap before her afternoon shift at Lodestones. She'd had to beg Angela to swap shifts and if she showed up late, Angela wouldn't do it again.

She ransacked her dresser for the restaurant's wait-staff uniform: black slacks and a white oxford shirt. The garments she found were a little creased, but they passed the sniff test. In the midst of applying mascara, she heard the apartment door open and poked her head out of the bathroom.

Damn! Shitty timing. "You're home early," Sadie said to Jane. She pumped the mascara's application wand in its tube and returned to the mirror above the sink. She didn't have time to apologize to Jane about last night, but she couldn't avoid it now. She owed Jane. Again.

Sadie applied a second coat of mascara, dropped her cosmetics back into her purse, and walked into the living room. Jane was sitting on the sofa staring into space with a frown pinching her lips. Sadie lowered herself to the sofa beside her.

"Just so you know," Sadie began, "I didn't ask Ethan to call you last night."

When Jane didn't respond, Sadie worried she'd messed up more than usual. "I'm sorry. He should have left you out of it and just called me a cab."

Again, no reaction from Jane.

Sadie picked at a loose thread. This was usually the point in the conversation where Jane told her that she'd always be there for her, no matter what. Sadie touched Jane's shoulder. "Did you hear me?" Sadie asked.

Jane swivelled her head. She had a distant look about her. "I'm sorry. What'd you say?"

Sadie cocked her head. Something was off. "What happened? Something at work?"

Jane shook her head. "No," she said, flashing a leave-me-alone smile.

"What's going on? Why are you home early?" Sadie asked. "And don't tell me it's nothing. Spill it."

Jane stared forward again. Sadie shifted impatiently beside her, conscious of the time.

"Remember me telling you about my guardian letting that photographer take photos of my birthmarks when I was a kid?"

"Yeah. Why?"

"I made a delivery out at UBC today. Some professor in anthropology. He had a print of my birthmark hanging on his wall."

"Ew." Sadie screwed up her face into a look of disgust. "Like a full frontal?"

"No. More like a block print. One perfect frame of the pattern." Jane drew a square around the wine stain on the back of her left hand. "Said he found it *mesmerizing*."

Sadie's disgust turned to curiosity. "Where'd he get it?"

Jane met Sadie's questioning gaze, and a vulnerability Sadie rarely saw leaked out. "I didn't ask. He saw my hand. Recognized it. I ran."

"Why? You're not a runner. You did nothing wrong."

"I don't know. He had this look on his face as if he'd caught me. It left me feeling filthy, repulsive. Just brought back a whole lot of shit I hadn't thought about in a while."

Sadie squeezed Jane's shoulder. "I'm sorry." She reached into her purse and pulled out a fifty-dollar bill. She'd have booked her a massage if she'd had the time. "Here. I got a nice tip last night. Blow it on something that'll take your mind off it."

"No," Jane said, refusing the bill. "It shook me up, but I'm fine. Besides, I'm not going out. I want to hide out here, take a bath, veg out. Maybe find something to binge on Netflix."

Sadie dropped the bill on the trunk. "In case you change your mind." She stood and looked down at her best friend. "Thanks for last night. And I'm sorry. I should have come home, you know, after."

"Yeah, you should have."

Sadie slung her purse over her shoulder and started for the door. "I'm off at eleven." She rushed out before Jane had a chance to remind her that she could cover their rent in a pinch. Sadie wasn't a charity case. She'd used the food bank a few times, but it always left her feeling as if she was taking from those worse off. Sadie could make the extra cash when she needed to. She pushed away the thought that she needed to most months.

At the end of her shift, Sadie trudged back to her car. The restaurant had been busy and loud. She soaked in the silence behind the wheel. As much as she disliked the fatigue after a long shift, and the disappointing pay, she was determined to keep her job. Though a thin veneer, it gave her the stamp of legitimacy. Without it, she was just a hooker, another "victim of the system."

Sadie refused to be a victim. She and Jane had made a pact to never again be at the mercy of the system. She'd do whatever it took to keep her end of that deal, even if it meant her self-respect took a hit once in a while. She could take it. And she was proud of what she and Jane had accomplished. She owned her car, even if it was a junker. Jane almost owned her bike, and they'd furnished their apartment without going into debt.

None of that had come easy. On minimum wages, it had taken Jane and her a year to save enough money for the deposit on the apartment that got them out of the rooming house on the Downtown Eastside. The novelty of not having to share their digs with rats and cockroaches hadn't worn off.

Sadie eased out of the parking lot. She thought about Cynthia, and Mr. Kristan's offer. That amount of money could change her life. She could make good on an old dream of becoming a hairstylist, maybe take a massage-therapy course, or learn bookkeeping—she was good with numbers. If she had a job that paid half decent, she could get out of the business for real.

But Mr. Kristan worried her. She'd been careful not to divulge anything that would compromise her identity, but he always wheedled her for more. He was falling for her. She could feel it. She also knew men with a disciplinarian streak could get possessive. And wasn't that exactly what he was doing by trying to buy her contract? What if he stalked her and learned where she worked, where she lived? He could do a lot of damage. He knew enough to get her fired from her job, and if the landlord learned what she did on the side, he'd freak and throw them out.

Sadie knew she should run in the opposite direction, but the promise of fifty grand held her back. If only she felt as confident as Cynthia did about shaking off Mr. Kristan when they were done with him. And she already knew what Jane would say. Regardless, she wasn't yet ready to walk away from Cynthia's proposal.

She parked behind their building and climbed out. Light leaked from their basement-apartment windows, signalling that Jane was still up. She unlocked the apartment door and called out, "I'm home." Jane lay on the sofa with her laptop on her stomach and her hand trailing on the floor.

Sadie kicked off her shoes and tiptoed to the sofa. "Narc. You awake?" Jane didn't stir. Sadie reached down, lifted Jane's computer, and set it safely on the trunk beside her journal. The laptop's screen had gone black. Sadie gently shook her sleeping roommate but got no response.

"Where are you tonight?" Sadie whispered. She pulled the tattered quilt up to Jane's chin. Few people understood Jane's rare form of narcolepsy, and fewer still the dreams she had when she couldn't wake. Horrifying dreams. A younger Jane had railed against the impotence she felt being subjected to the harsh injustices of her dreams with no way to intervene. Her early efforts to seek out the victims and offer sympathy to the neglected and abused she dreamed about were met with shoves, violence, and ridicule. But as disturbing as Jane's dreams were, worse still was how utterly helpless she was while dreaming.

Sadie headed back to the door and secured the bolts then took her purse into the bedroom. She returned to the living room wearing silk sleep shorts and a tiny top and found an open bottle of wine under the sink. "There is a goddess," she said, straightening. She poured herself a glass and checked on Jane one more time. When her roommate didn't wake with a gentle nudge, Sadie turned out the lights. "Looks like I get the bed again."

She mounded the pillows behind her and thumbed through her social media accounts while sipping her wine. She thought about Jane's journal—perfectly squared to the corner of the trunk. Jane had taken Sadie's journaling suggestion to heart, which meant something to Sadie. They'd been BFFs since the day Jane showed up at the group home with her green garbage bag in hand. Sadie had overheard their house mother talking to the social worker, who'd collected Jane from the hospital. Sadie remembered the house mother's disapproving expression, her haughty laugh. They thought Jane was a special kind of stupid, not only because she'd gotten herself pregnant, but because she wouldn't identify the father.

Gotten herself pregnant. Despite how much time had passed, those words still infuriated her. After Sadie saw Jane's narcolepsy firsthand, she knew the truth. Jane had been raped while comatose. Her diagnosis was narcolepsy with a kicker of cataplexy, which resulted in sleep paralysis. She'd been thirteen years old.

Sadie had begged Jane to go to the police, to do something about it, but she wouldn't. Jane didn't trust authority figures. Neither of them did. Jane never spoke of the rape, or of the abortion that had been forced upon her. And Jane never cried—she was freakish that way—and she always made sure she was home and behind a locked door before she dared close her eyes. Preferably a steel door.

"Don't look back," she said into the silence.

Sadie's phone chirped. Cynthia had sent a text. "Have you made a decision?" Sadie silenced her phone, downed the rest of the wine, and went to sleep.

7 | Jane

Visiting Dream

Jane is visiting Rebecca again. They're in a small office furnished with an overstuffed vinyl sofa past its prime and two armchairs. An ancient snake plant sits on the floor beneath a wire-mesh-reinforced window. Sunshine filters into the room through the grime on the glass. Another wall houses a bookcase with a built-in writing desk. Industrial linoleum flooring suggests Jane is back in the psych ward.

Rebecca's dark hair is clean and held back with a hairband. She wears a sweater and yoga pants. While Rebecca waits on the sofa, she picks at the edges of the bandages on her wrists. A box of tissues rests on a small round table in front of her. Every few seconds she glances at the camera staring at her from its mount in the hallway outside the office.

A man in a white coat breezes into the room and closes the door. Jane recognizes him as the doctor who caressed Rebecca's cheek in her most recent dream. He holds a file folder and opens it as he takes a seat opposite Rebecca.

"Dr. Ng is pleased with your progress in the group therapy sessions," the doctor says. Jane marvels that she can make out his words, even though his voice sounds as if it's coming from the bottom of a well. It's like someone has finally removed the cotton from her ears. "How are you coping with the meds?"

"Fine. Good." Rebecca's voice is soft, quiet.

"No more . . . *visions?*" the doctor says, as if unsure what terminology to use.

"No. None. When can I go home?"

"Let's make sure you're back on solid ground, first. Okay?"

"I am. I'm feeling really good."

"That's a great start. Are you ready to talk about your visions?"

"They're gone now. The details are . . . foggy. Mixed-up."

"Let's talk again in a few days." The doctor closes the folder. Rebecca lingers. "You may go," the doctor says, and his disingenuous smile feels like a slap.

After Rebecca leaves, the doctor stands and takes the folder to his desk. He pulls a filigreed pen from a drawer that also contains an ornate ivory letter opener. Over his shoulder, Jane reads his messy scrawl: *Patient employing manipulation. Uncooperative. Increasing meds.*

Jane lurched awake with a sharp inhale and froze. She scanned the darkness and slowly relaxed. She was home. Safe. The lights were out so Sadie had made it back. Jane rolled onto her side.

Her dreams finally had a soundtrack. But as much as she found the voices illuminating, she was glad her earlier dreams had been silent. She'd been spared the sounds of slaps and punches, of screams and crying. It had been bad enough seeing the begging without the dialogue.

She pulled up the blanket and found herself looking at the back of her left hand. She could understand how someone might find the design intriguing, someone who didn't know the source. Like the recipient of a blood diamond, for example, or someone who inherits an antique ivory chess set. Did the professor have an excuse?

Rebecca's doctor seemed particularly hard on her. *Tough love?* And who was Rebecca? What was Jane's connection to her? In her mind, Jane conjured up recent customers at the nursery, former teachers, old neighbours. Was Rebecca someone from the foster-care system? Jane couldn't place her and that bothered her. The people in her dreams always had a connection to her, no matter how tenuous.

What were Rebecca's visions about? They had to be bad for her to attempt suicide. For purely selfish reasons, Jane prayed Rebecca was telling the truth about her visions being gone—she didn't want to dream about Rebecca's next suicide bid.

8 | Rick

August 10

Rick pulled his Land Rover onto the gravel apron by the row of community postal boxes. He climbed out of the SUV and took in the familiar surroundings: the old chestnut trees across the road that shaded neat paddocks, the well-maintained stables. He took a deep breath, inhaling the hay-scented air, and retrieved the mail from his parents' box.

Back in the SUV, he flipped through the mail, discouraged by not one but two letters from real estate vultures. As if they sensed his parents aging, they were circling, waiting to claim the large Langley acreage. It was a prime parcel surrounded by others just like it, most of them owned by moneyed horse people who guarded their privacy. Elaine, his brother's wife, had practically drooled over the place the first time she saw it. She owned a horse and thought the house would be the perfect setup. Even though they'd moved to Victoria after Mikey's big promotion, she still had a horse and still coveted the place.

Rick removed the offending letters from the stack of mail and tossed them in the vehicle's centre console. He pulled back out onto Fifty-Sixth Street and turned down the long driveway to his parents' sprawling rancher.

He'd grown up here, so he knew every rock, every tree. He'd spent his summers painting the white rails and black fence posts that marked the property's perimeter. Every Saturday, one of his chores was mowing the considerable expanse of lawn around the house and outbuildings. Mikey was responsible for taking out the garbage and cleaning the kennels, which together took half the time of Rick's chores. Rick vividly remembered Mikey jumping on his bike and cutting in front of the mower on his way to meet up with his friends. Rick thought it unfair, but he wanted to please his parents, something his training had taught him was hard-wired into most kids. Sadly, his parents weren't the demonstrative type, and Rick could only guess whether he'd achieved that goal. It was likely why he'd never outgrown his need to please them. Rick had been making this weekly trip for nearly two years. His parents were aging badly. Arthritis had stolen his father's mobility, and with it, his veterinary practice. Macular degeneration had all but blinded his mother. It had taken them an insulting amount of time to take him up on his offer of help, but eventually they'd come around.

Not only did he collect their mail each week, he also brought groceries, their prescriptions, flowers for his mother, and occasionally, a bottle of Glenfiddich for his father. Rick did that, not their precious Mikey. Mikey didn't organize the yard maintenance or driveway repairs, he didn't line up the handyman who cleaned out the gutters, he wasn't around to help when a drain clogged or a tap needed a new washer.

Rick pushed aside his old annoyance and took the cut-off to the barn. His mother used to breed dogs. First Great Danes and then Shetland sheepdogs. They'd adapted the barn for her comfort as much as for the dogs'. She'd spend hours in there when the bitches were whelping. When his mother's eyesight began to fail, they'd shut down the business.

He checked the outer office and bathroom then opened the door to the kennels to make sure unwanted critters, human or otherwise, hadn't set up house. His parents hadn't been near the barn in a year. They'd never know if someone was squatting in it. Satisfied that everything was in order, Rick replaced the padlock, returned to his Land Rover, and continued to the house.

9 | Jane

Jane looked up from tugging on her boot when Sadie emerged from the bedroom. "Good morning."

"Is it?" Sadie rubbed her eyes then disappeared into the bathroom.

Sadie hadn't worked a gig the previous night, but her contempt for mornings was completely understandable. Mornings were when she had to look herself in the mirror and forgive herself for the night before. Her resilience was remarkable. She was like one of those inflatable punching bags—the ones with sand in the bottom that little boys loved to hit. She'd wobble, but she was never down for long, even if Jane had to help her up.

Sadie had learned early on in life that men were only good for cash, baubles, and entertainment. And punching. She'd been twelve years old and living in a car with her mom and her mother's boyfriend when she was taught that lesson. After her mother died of an overdose, Sadie was taken into care. Not one for rules or discipline, she ran away at the first opportunity. She found her mother's boyfriend on the street. He'd lost the car but welcomed her back.

And then he raped her.

Said he was doing her a favour. That she had to earn her keep. She did for a time but ended up in the hospital when one of his friends got rough with her. She went back into care and didn't run away again. At least not right away.

Jane hadn't known Sadie for long when she relived the night Sadie's mother's boyfriend raped her. Jane's dreams were silent movies back then. Months later, Sadie confided in Jane, and little by little, Sadie filled in the blank spots in Jane's dream.

So, Jane gave her space in the mornings. Space to forgive herself and get back up.

Jane rushed from the apartment. Only 6:45 and the sun already felt warm. The lights were out in Mrs. Carper's bay window. With any luck, her hearing aids were too. The landlord allowed her to park under the old crone's second-floor bay window, but another complaint and Jane's bike would be relegated to the space beside the dumpster.

"Feeling better, sweetie?" Anna asked, as Jane pushed open the door to Positively Plants. Anna stood behind the till preparing the day's cash float.

"Yeah. Sorry about yesterday. I can make up the time today if you'd like?"

Anna dropped the cash drawer into place. "No need. I'll take it out of your sick time."

Jane smirked. "I have sick time?"

Anna looked over the rim of her Dollar Store cheaters. "You really will get sick if you don't take some time off. You've got four weeks vacation saved up. Pieter can cover your shifts." Pieter was Anna's only child and currently between semesters at SFU. Some days, Jane felt like Pieter's younger sister. She'd worked alongside him most summers.

"I've got nowhere to go." She thanked Anna for the sick time then beetled toward the breakroom.

"Staycation," Anna called after her. "It's a thing. Look it up."

Jane changed boots, picked up her pruning knife and clippers, and stared at the empty space where her gloves should have been. She put on an old pair instead. Though there was a stash of gloves under the checkout counter, she didn't want to rehash the vacation discussion with Anna. When the time was right, Jane hoped to negotiate a payout for her vacation. She figured the balance after taxes would pretty much pay off her bike; one step closer to laser therapy to remove her hideous birthmarks.

Her attempt to slip unnoticed out of the breakroom failed.

Anna called her over. "Almost forgot. You had a visitor yesterday after you left." She reached under the counter and withdrew the gloves Jane had abandoned in Nathaniel Crawford's office. "The professor asked me to return these to you."

Jane mumbled her thanks and stuffed the gloves in her pocket. No cause for alarm. Obviously, he'd know where she worked. Jane turned to leave and looked back. "Did he ask for me by name?"

Anna creased her brow in thought. "No, but he did ask what it was. I didn't see the harm in telling him."

Jane's features fell.

"Oh dear. Did something happen yesterday?" Anna pulled back her shoulders with an air of indignation. "Was he inappropriate? We won't stand for that."

"No," Jane said, quick to reassure her. Customers willing to pay two hundred and fifty bucks for an orchid were scarce. Jane didn't want to be the one to kill that cash cow. "Not at all. I was just curious." Thankfully, Positively Plants stood between the professor and her.

By lunch hour, Lucas had already done the deli run. As a safety measure, they never left anyone alone on the shop floor, which meant Jane often ate lunch by herself in the breakroom. She didn't mind. She retrieved her sandwich from the mini-fridge and set it on the table along with her tea and the gloves the professor had returned.

All morning, Jane had been unable to shake the look on the professor's face when he'd seen her birthmark. What was it? Jane couldn't quite put her finger on it. Not revulsion—she knew that look too well. Recognition, perhaps? She cringed at the thought of her nude kiddy photos floating around the internet. Did the professor now know that she was the source of his *artwork*?

As she stared at the gloves, a slash of white caught her attention. She drew the gloves close. Nathaniel Crawford's business card had been stuffed inside one of them. *Call me* was written on the back.

Jane laid the card on the table and took another bite of her sandwich. What did the professor with a string of letters after his name want? Was it ghoulish curiosity? She thought back to what Sadie had said. She'd done nothing wrong. She hated that she'd run from him; it made her feel weak. She tucked his card in her pocket. She'd make the call, get some answers. But not from her own phone.

When her shift ended, Jane asked Lucas for the use of his office. "I'll only be five minutes."

"Take your time."

She closed the door, lifted the phone from its cradle, and dialled.

The professor answered immediately. "Joyce?"

"What can I do for you?" Jane kept her voice curt.

On the professor's end, a door closed with a solid thunk. "I'm glad you called. I'm—ah. This is awkward. I'd like to meet with you. Can I buy you a coffee?"

"I don't drink coffee," Jane said. "Where'd you get the print?"

"Well. That's what I wanted to talk about. How about a beverage of your choice? My treat. Somewhere neutral. Perfectly safe."

Easy answer. "No thanks." Jane wasn't some attraction for him to gawk at. "Who sold you the print? Did you buy it online?" She was keenly aware that she sounded like a cop.

"No one sold it to me. I mean, I didn't buy it. It was a gift."

"Who from?"

"A dear friend gave it to me."

"Then your friend's into child porn."

"I can assure you she's not." The professor paused. "Why would you say such a thing?"

Jane filled her lungs. "What's your friend's name?"

"Where'd you get the tattoo?" the professor said.

"It's a port wine stain."

"It's not."

"You have a PhD in medicine you forgot to put on your card?"

He chuckled. "I think I know what it is."

Like she didn't? "I don't get what kind of game you're playing, Professor, but I won't be a part of it."

"It's not a game. Please."

Frustration nipped at Jane's patience. "What is it you want?"

"I'd really rather meet in person."

"So you can what? Take a photo?"

"I just want a few minutes of your time."

"How about a trade? A few minutes of my time for that print."

"All . . . right. I suppose I can get another."

"You can get another? What's wrong with you? That's not *art*—it's a disturbing invasion of my privacy."

"It's not. I can prove it. Meet with me."

"I should report you to the cops." And she would if she thought they'd stop him and whoever was producing the prints. But the cops wouldn't do a thing, and he'd given her zero information. She wouldn't be a part of his sick game. And she sure as hell wasn't going to encourage him. "Please don't come by the shop again and don't call me. Goodbye, Professor."

As she set the phone back in its cradle, she debated telling Lucas and Anna. She decided not to. No one wanted a troublesome employee, less so one who'd just warned off a high-end customer.

Jane tossed the professor's card in the trash and called out, "I'm outta here." Lucas waved from the yard.

Ethan was on her mind. She owed him a thank-you and probably an apology. And if she was honest with herself, she wanted to see him and had the perfect excuse. She made one quick stop before parking next to Riptide. It was too early for a bouncer; the lineup wouldn't start until after eight. Inside, one of the regular servers acknowledged Jane's arrival with a tip of her head.

"Ethan in?" Jane asked.

"Office," the server said, indicating the hallway on the far side of the bar.

An old Stones ballad trickled from the speakers. Customers occupied a handful of tables. Low conversations mingled with the previous night's colognes.

Ethan had once mentioned that the bar had been recently renovated. Jane liked the feel of the place. Along one wall, opaque windows let in natural light. Steel tables and pale-wood chairs lent the space clean lines. Dim light shone downward from wall sconces spaced regularly around the room, and the underside edge of the long brushed-steel bar bled with the soft glow of a rope light. She had the impression the designer used these elements to keep eyes away from the ceiling, a black-painted recess hiding pipes, wires, and ducting. Proof that even the sleekest facade had something ugly to hide.

She walked down the hallway and knocked on the office door. "Hi," she said, when Connor answered. Connor was one of the bar's owners. His sun-kissed complexion and honest-to-god dimples dialled his true age back a decade. "Is Ethan here?"

"On the phone. Come in." Connor held the door open. The bar's office brought to mind a frat-house games room complete with dim lighting, mini basketball net, and cases of liquor. It was a postcard from the prerenovation version of Riptide. Jane's eyes widened at the view of the bar through the two-way glass, which looked like an ordinary mirror on the public side. She would never have guessed.

Ethan sat behind a battered desk tucked into a recess in the wall at the far end of the room. He'd propped his boots on the desk's extended file drawer and was holding a cellphone to his ear. Neat stacks of paper lined one side of the desk. When he saw her, he set his feet on the floor, slid the drawer closed, and held up a just-a-moment finger.

"Tell Ethan I'll be back in ten," Connor said, and he pulled the office door closed behind him.

Jane set her helmet on the sofa that sat between the door and the desk. When Ethan finished his conversation, she plopped a paper bag on his desk.

"What's this?" Ethan asked, setting down his phone. He wore a black Riptide T-shirt and Diesel jeans.

"A thank-you," she said. "For last night."

Ethan tilted his head. "Would that be for your bike's security detail? Or for preventing a brawl?"

"For Jimmy. I didn't need help with the jockstrap."

"Jimmy's my secret weapon. He's been sober almost a year now. And if you were as confident as you'd like me to believe, you wouldn't carry that blade in your boot."

"That? Just a little insurance." Jane was never without a knife. It had been a natural extension of her arm since her group-home days.

"Uh-huh," Ethan said. Still seated, he pulled the bag close and peered inside. "My favourite. You pay attention." His fine dark hair was short on the sides, long on the top. Hair that she imagined felt soft.

"One of my specialties," Jane said. "Speaking of which, Connor said he'd be back in ten. I'd better go. Don't want the boss to think you're slacking on my account." Jane turned to leave but Ethan grabbed her hand. The gesture made her start. She glanced down at his hand then up to his face.

Ethan held her gaze as he stood. Her heart thumped a happy beat. Dark flecks freckled his light-brown eyes. Eyes that still hadn't veered to the port wine stain on the left side of her face. Eyes that had never looked past or through her. He snaked a hand around her neck and pulled her so close their bodies almost touched. Up until that very moment, Jane had been certain his interest was in Sadie.

"I'd like to see you tonight. After closing."

Jane felt heat rush to her face. "I, ah, can't. Have to be at work at seven in the morning. Girl needs her sleep."

"Come back at nine, then. I'll take a break."

Jane was tempted, but then she stole a glance at the two-way mirror. Not here, and not before she cleared it with Sadie. Girl code. "Not tonight."

"Perhaps I can change your mind," he said, pressing up against her.

"You can try," Jane said, hoping like hell he would.

He bent and touched his lips to hers, unrushed. She let her eyes close, savouring the sensation, committing the rare event to memory. When he worked her mouth open, she nearly gave in and dragged him to the sofa. His tongue teased hers and pushed farther inside, searching, wanting more. Definitely not a monk. The man knew how to kiss. When he pulled away, reluctantly, she opened her eyes.

"Well?" he said.

"Ask me out when you've got a night off."

He smoothed her hair then brought a handful of it forward and released it slowly, watching the sable strands fall against her leather jacket. When Ethan stepped back, his absence left Jane unsteady. She shivered. A tiny smile curled his lips. He crossed his arms and leaned his butt against the edge of the desk. "I'll call you."

Jane felt a rush of embarrassment. She gathered her wits and bent to collect her helmet. If he was waiting for her to ask when he'd call, he'd be disappointed.

"Think of me while you're enjoying the sushi." She left without a backward glance, relishing that he'd be watching her all the way to the front door. What do ya know? she thought. A hookup might not be a pipe dream this year after all.

Back at their apartment, Sadie had Jane's laptop open, and laughter peeled out of its tin-can speakers. They shared a Netflix account, and the laptop's screen was much better than her phone's.

"Hey, Sade," Jane said, turning to lock the door. "You in for the night?"

"Yup. You?"

"Yeah." Jane set her helmet on the floor and pried off her boots. She headed to the kitchen alcove and set the kettle on the stove. She noticed yet another of Sadie's dirty cereal bowls in the sink. "Saw Ethan," she said, marvelling that the bowl had actually made it into the kitchen. She let the tap run until the bowl overflowed.

Sadie looked up. "Is he pissed about last night?"

"Nah. He's cool. Didn't think I could have taken down the 'roided-up jockstrap, though. That hurts."

"Jockstrap?"

"Your date at Riptide last night."

"Oh, him."

"Yeah, him," Jane said, and flopped on the sofa beside her. "Why don't you ever pick the scrawny ones?"

Sadie looked as if she were about to make a smart-ass remark when Jane's phone rang.

"Nelson?" Jane said, answering.

"The one and only," he said. "I was in the neighbourhood. Wanna let me in?"

"Sure. Hang on."

"Nelson's here?" Sadie asked. She closed the laptop. "What's he want?"

Jane shrugged. "Don't know." And because there was no buzzer to let him in, she hurried out into the hall to open the outside door.

Nelson Leonard had never quite let go of his head-banging days. Thumbing his nose at his balding crown, he wore his long greying hair in a thin ponytail at the nape of his neck. A perpetual scowl belied the softie underneath.

He greeted Jane using her preferred name. She'd always liked that about him. Of all the social workers she'd been assigned over the years, Nelson Leonard was, by far, the best. He understood her.

"Come in," Jane said, leading the way.

"Hey, Nelson," Sadie said. "It's been a while." She set the laptop on the trunk.

Nelson scanned the room with a practised eye. He'd provided a reference to their landlord and had been by a few times to check on them, but it was on his own time; they'd both passed out of the system closing in on six years ago. Nelson counted Jane among his success stories. She was the gold standard: GED and legally employed. But it was a qualified success—Jane was a twofer. She came with Sadie, and Sadie lurked around the edges of mainstream society.

Jane didn't have that luxury. She needed a legit job if she wanted to sleep behind a locked door, and despite what the law stated, her birth-marks limited her options. Sadie had ranted about the prejudice, but Jane refused to waste energy on threats and discrimination lawsuits. She had no stomach for the public eye.

"How're you ladies making out?"

"Now, Lenny, you know you're not supposed to call us ladies," Sadie teased.

"Have a seat." Jane gestured to the mismatched tub chair. She rushed to silence the kettle's whistle. "Can I get you something?"

"Thanks, no." Nelson sat and addressed Sadie. "You still working at Earls?"

"Lodestones," Sadie said. "Yeah." Jane took a seat beside Sadie.

"Good to hear. Thought any more about taking that hairdressing course?"

"Still saving," she said.

Nelson pressed his lips together and nodded. He could always smell a lie. "And you?" he said, addressing Jane. "Bakkers still treating you well?"

"Haven't fired me yet. Even got another raise."

Nelson lifted his eyebrows, which didn't erase his scowl entirely, but Jane took it to mean he was pleased. She gave herself a mental pat on the back.

"And you?" Jane asked.

"Same ol' shit," he said. "Never a shortage of cases." He pulled an envelope from his shirt pocket.

Jane recognized the logo. "Keep it," she said, raising her hand to him.

"You know I can't do that."

Jane crossed her arms. "It's not mine," she said, and pursed her lips.

Nelson tossed the envelope to the trunk. The top edge had been torn.

Jane glared at him. "You opened it?" She reached for the envelope. "Isn't that illegal?"

"I contacted them on your behalf. Gave them this address and your phone number."

"I asked you not to do that." Her discomfort teetered on the edge of anger.

Nelson sucked in a long breath. "It's been years, Jane. The director's done collecting your mail. You have to deal with that. If you don't want it, give it away. But deal with it."

Jane fingered the envelope's open edge, careful not to look inside. The guilt she felt about inheriting the Walkers' estate had never gone away.

"You were only two years old," Sadie said. "Even if you did start the fire, you couldn't possibly have known what you were doing."

She'd heard it all before, but the words didn't put a dent in her guilt. Jane, or Joyce as she'd been known then, had been found on the lawn that night long ago, clutching a spent match, delighted by the flames. Her adoptive parents had died in the fire.

"I don't even remember them," Jane said. The only photo she had of the Walkers was one where they were posing in front of the Sold sign on the lawn of their new home. A home with a yard that they'd purchased for Jane, their new daughter. A home far away from those who remembered the abandoned baby with the birthmarks who'd been speculated about in the papers. As a teenager, Jane had stared at the strangers in the photo willing a memory of them to surface. Any memory. None ever had.

Their expressions held all the hope and promise of a bright future growing old in their new home. But the house had burned to the ground. They had no family and Jane had once again become a ward of the court.

"Look forward, never back," Sadie said. "Isn't that our mantra?"

After Nelson left, Sadie heated a takeout dinner. Jane picked at her meal. Her attention kept returning to the envelope. The Walkers' money had come from the sale of their car and the little they'd managed to pay off on a mortgage they hadn't insured. Jane was about twelve years old when she learned about the estate. Back then, five grand had seemed like a fortune. Five grand. That's what the Walkers' lives were worth.

The Public Trustee had held the money until she was eighteen, and the government had added monthly orphan payments. But the money didn't go far. It paid for new cellphones and cellphone plans, internet service, clothes, shoes, and pocket money. She'd shared it with Sadie, since her friend didn't have the orphan payments. The Trustee had been pretty good about letting Jane have whatever she asked for.

When she aged out of the system, the funds that were left were sent to a private investment firm the Trustee recommended. It couldn't have been much, but she didn't know the balance. Somehow not knowing let her off the hook for spending the Walkers' money. It's why she never wanted the investment firm's statements. She didn't want to be reminded.

She'd vowed to repay what she'd spent, but after all this time, Jane still couldn't think of one thing she could do with the money that would honour the Walkers properly. A plaque on a bench? A contribution to a children's playground? Everything she thought of felt like a trivial gesture that would soon be forgotten. Some daughter she'd turned out to be.

Thinking of the fire had ruined her appetite. She took the envelope to the bedroom and slipped it into her bottom dresser drawer. She would deal with it, but not tonight.

Back on the sofa, thoughts of Ethan dragged her out of her mood. "Sadie?" she said. "Are you keen on Ethan?"

"How do you mean? Like dating him?"

"Yeah."

"I don't know. He's nice enough. Why?"

"I thought he had the hots for you."

"Nope," Sadie said. "I'm not convinced he likes chicks. Haven't you noticed? They flirt with him all night long and he never makes a move. Maybe he's got some ED going on."

"ED?" Jane said.

"Erectile dysfunction."

"God, I hope not," Jane said. "He kissed me tonight."

Sadie whipped her head around. "He did not!"

Jane nodded. "I don't think he suffers from ED. He felt pretty happy pressed against me." She fought a ridiculously wide grin.

"Did you do the deed?"

"Nah. He was working." Jane absently stroked the birthmark on her hand. How would Ethan react to the rest of her birthmarks? Would he be able to see past them as effortlessly as he had the track on her face?

"You know that mirror behind the bar at Riptide? It's one of those two-way mirrors, like on TV."

"You were in the office?"

"Brought him sushi to thank him for looking after my bike."

"Smooth move," Sadie said.

That night, Jane got the bed.

Visiting Dream

Jane stares down at the sharp-tipped snake plant. The chilled air raises goosebumps on her arms. She frowns. She's never felt the temperature in her dreams before.

She turns to her left and sees Rebecca Morrow sitting on the vinyl sofa opposite the doctor. Rebecca massages a tissue.

The doctor speaks. "Visions like the ones you're experiencing aren't as unusual as you imagine. They're coping mechanisms. Self-preservation, if you will. It's your mind's way of protecting itself—protecting *you*. If you really want them to stop, you need to open up about them, explore them."

"Nothing good comes from talking about it."

"I can guarantee you that's not true."

"You know what the kids on the Prairies where I grew up used to call me? Becky Bonkers. My father and even his mother—my ever-loving grandmother—told me I should be locked up. Just like my mother and her mother before her. That's what comes from talking about it."

The doctor inhales an arduous breath. "I'm sorry to hear that. But that was a long time ago. You're here now. Help us learn what you're coping with. Then we'll be able to address the underlying cause of these visions."

"When can I go home?" Rebecca asks.

"Do you not want to get better?"

"You're not listening to me. How many times can I tell you there is no underlying cause? If you want to help me, then help me cope with the visions."

"The visions aren't real, Rebecca. That you think they are is why you aren't getting better, why you can't go home."

Rebecca looks down to her tissue. A tear drops to her lap. "The vision I had yesterday was about you. You were maybe ten years old. You had an older brother you called Mikey. There were dogs. Lots of dogs. And puppies. I saw a painted sign." Rebecca pauses. "It was cut out in the shape of a dog. The name on the sign was Highland Breeders."

The doctor shakes his head. "That information is available on the internet. My father's vet practice, my mother's kennels. Lots of photos of Highland's dogs on there with my brother and me when we were kids. That you'd go to these lengths to defend your visions is troublesome, Rebecca. I want to help you, but first you have to help yourself."

Rebecca doesn't look up. She continues. "Your father had a shaving strap in his hand. There was a silver buckle on one end. He'd punished you for stealing from him. Something he'd found in your room. You had red welts in the shape of that silver buckle on your backside."

The doctor stills. Rebecca slowly lifts her head.

"Who have you been talking to?" the doctor asks, his voice hard.

Rebecca doesn't answer. She stands, balling the tissue in her hand. "The visions are real. If you can't help me, send me home. Please."

The doctor remains seated as Rebecca leaves the room. The door closes with a soft snick.

"Bastard!" the doctor spits out, and leaps to his feet. He yanks the phone from its cradle on the desk and punches in a number. "Talking to my patients is out of line!" The phone's coiled cord swings wildly. Jane can't hear the other side of the conversation. "Sure you didn't. Just like you didn't tell her the rest of the story, or have you forgotten who stole Dad's Scotch and hid it in my room?" The doctor's nostrils flare. "Don't. Just don't. This is so like you. You're an asshole, Mikey." He slams down the phone.

Jane's eyes shot open. She stared at the ceiling, her heart racing. Was this

Rebecca woman like her? Were her visions the same as Jane's dreams? Jane reached for her phone and typed *Rebecca Morrow* into Google. When the results populated, she went straight to the photos and swiped through them. Not one was of the Rebecca Morrow in her dream. Frustrated, she tossed the phone aside. She remembered the corded phone. Did institutions still use them? She bunched the pillow and rolled over remembering how she'd felt the chill of the doctor's office. "Who are you, Rebecca Morrow?"

10 | Rick

Rick swirled his glass of Ketel One and gazed out at the lights of Granville Island. A breeze cooled the rooftop patio of his townhome. A week ago, he'd had lunch with Vasul, his soon-to-be-retiring chief of staff. Rick knew him well. Over the years, they'd shared drinks, opinions, and commiserations. He didn't waste Vasul's time with hospital gossip. Heads of hospitals concerned themselves with larger issues. Rick sought Vasul's views on the latest controversy surrounding heroin-addiction research at the Crosstown Clinic. They debated the effectiveness of the province's latest rollout of mental-health initiatives. They brainstormed private funding ideas.

What they didn't talk about was Vasul's successor. The hospital board might seek Vasul's opinion, but it was the board that made the decision. After their lunch, Rick felt confident he'd proven his political prowess. And today, when his HR mole shared the shortlist with him, he knew he'd succeeded. His name was on it, as expected, but more telling was the three other doctors on the list. Two were insiders who Rick knew Vasul had little use for, and one was an outsider the board had thrown into the mix for appearance's sake. None of them had half of Rick's experience.

Rick tossed back the rest of his vodka. The board would meet with him before they announced their decision. He hoped they moved swiftly. He was bothered by the marked decline in his father's health. If the board delayed, he feared his old man wouldn't live to see his big day. He could already envision the smile on his father's face, could imagine the pride he'd feel knowing his son had reached the pinnacle of his profession. "Top of the heap," he'd say.

In many regards, he was just like his father. He'd chosen a profession that allowed him to help people, even those who couldn't afford it. He hadn't chosen the high life and fast money, like Mikey. And he hadn't made his father's mistake of having children he didn't have the time to raise.

Rick had given some thought to how his mother would manage after his father died. He knew his brother fuelled their parents' resistance to Rick's offers of help, but Mikey hadn't stepped up to fill the void. The financial wizard was happy to take their money and invest it, but he hadn't lifted a finger to make their day-to-day lives easier.

When his mother no longer had his father to be her eyes, she would reach out to Rick, he was certain. And when his father's harsh influence fell away, with Mikey at a distance, maybe she'd return to the softer, sweeter mother he remembered from his childhood.

Rick's life was at a turning point. Ahead, the prestige and challenge of his promotion, and in the not-too-distant future, the passing of a baton with the imminent death of his father.

Only one shadow hung over his head. One mistake he'd made twenty-four years ago that still haunted him. Soon, he'd be able to fix it. He just had to be patient.

11 | Jane

August 11

A bicycle courier rang the call bell and stood at the counter scanning the shop for assistance. Thankfully, Anna was closest to the till. Jane dragged the heavy hose back to the hose bib and turned off the water.

Anna approached with a skip in her step as Jane finished coiling the hose. "This came for you."

Jane looked at the cardboard Xpresspost envelope in her hand and furrowed her brow. "Who's it from?"

"The university," Anna said, beaming. "First a personal visit and now this? I think the young professor fancies you." Anna lingered, smiling expectantly. When Jane made no move to open the envelope, Anna's smile faded. "I'll give you some privacy," she said, and turned back to the till.

What was the professor's game? Jane took the envelope to the breakroom and ripped it open. Inside was a smaller white envelope. She took a seat at the table and opened it. The professor had stapled another business card to the top of the letter.

The sheet of paper had three URLs handwritten on it. Before the first URL, he'd written *Princeton University*. Before the second, *The British Museum*. And before the third, *National Geographic*. Written at the bottom was *Call me*. Jane flipped the paper over. It was blank.

She tipped her chair back. The professor didn't take direction very well. His persistence confounded her. She studied the URLs. They all had one word in common: *Inca*. As in, ancient Inca civilization? The professor had gone to some trouble to send this. Was he stalking her? She folded his letter and stuffed it in her jeans. Despite her efforts to not think about the letter, the URLs played on her mind all afternoon.

When Jane got home, she opened her laptop and typed in the first URL, the one related to Princeton University. She skimmed a few paragraphs about a student visit to Peru and scrolled through several photographs: the mist-shrouded mountaintop site of Machu Picchu; tiered emerald gardens encircling great, steep slopes; abandoned temples. Fascinating, but it wasn't anything she hadn't seen before, and what did it have to do with her?

She typed in the next URL and found herself looking at the British Museum's Inca collection. She swiped through photos of long-necked pottery, ancestor figures, offering bowls, and what looked like a necklace of knotted strings. This last photo was labelled *Khipus*. Why would the professor send her these links?

The final URL explained the knotted strings. The strings weren't jewellery at all but a method of communication. The type of knots and distance between them conveyed information, like an early version of a coded message. What was the significance of these URLs? Had she missed something?

She returned to the Princeton link and scanned the text and photos. Nothing leapt out. She revisited the British Museum page, paying closer attention this time. When she got to the offering bowl, she stopped swiping.

She magnified the picture and stilled.

Stamped into the side of the shallow silver bowl was a rendition of her birthmark.

Thoughts fragmented and scattered in her mind, each one too fragile to hold. Jane stared at the squat bowl for a long time. When her screen went black, she set her laptop on the trunk.

All her life, she'd assumed her birthmarks to be unique, hers alone— not that she'd wish them on anyone else. But this bowl proved otherwise. How she felt about that she wasn't yet sure. Did the professor have a theory?

Jane had accused his friend of being a pedophile. She'd threatened to call the cops. She blushed with embarrassment remembering her harsh words. No wonder he'd been so keen to get these links to her; they were defence exhibits.

Jane checked the time. She wanted Sadie's take on the Inca bowl, but it would be another agonizing hour before she was home from work. Jane changed into leggings and a long-sleeved tee, tied a bandana in place, and headed out for a run.

By the time she'd returned, her anxiety was under control, but her mind still raced with questions. If her birthmarks weren't unique, did other people have them? She pulled her computer into her lap but couldn't find a single photo of anyone with birthmarks like hers. She found an interesting article about patterns that repeat in nature and went down that rabbit hole but came out empty-handed. Nature, it seemed, hadn't repeated her marks, at least that she could find.

She jumped in the shower, and as she towelled off, she heard Sadie's key in the lock.

"I thought I should call him. Hear him out. What do you think?" Jane asked.

"You should definitely call him," Sadie said, examining the photos.

Jane did, and when the professor answered, she started with an apology and told him about the photos taken of her birthmarks years ago. "They said it was for medical research, but I don't really know. I wrongly assumed the print came from that photo session."

"That's the thing, Joyce. I don't think they're birthmarks. Not in the form you think they are. Would you meet with me? I'd like to explain."

Her curiosity piqued, she agreed to lunch the following day.

She'd barely finished conveying to Sadie what the professor had said when her phone rang.

"It's Ethan," Jane said, looking at the call display and grinning.

Sadie stood. "I'm going to shower. I smell like a fryer." She turned to Jane. "Use a condom."

Jane swatted her away and answered.

"I've got the night off," Ethan said. "Interested?"

That hadn't taken long. "Could be. What do you have in mind?"

"It starts with a ride. Grab your helmet. I'm outside."

Jane emerged from the side door and found Ethan astride his Harley at the curb. He'd raised his visor and didn't take his eyes off her as she strolled up to him. The intensity of his gaze stirred a longing low in her abdomen.

"Where we going?"

"You'll see. Get on," he said, scooting forward.

Jane secured her helmet, climbed on the rear foot peg, and swung her leg over. She glanced back at the old mansion and saw the curtain in Mrs. Carper's bay window drop back into place.

"You set?" Ethan said. He wore a bike jacket much like hers.

Ethan revved the engine. Jane cringed. She could almost hear the busybody's windows rattling. When Ethan nailed the gas, Jane snaked her hands around his waist. It felt strangely intimate and foreign. A shot of excitement bolted through her.

The evening sun warmed her back, its reflection blinding when it hit the mirrors. The Fat Boy was a more comfortable two-up ride than her Rebel. They continued east for another twenty minutes before they rolled into a private campground. Ethan drove past rows of RVs. Strategically planted columnar cedars and yews afforded each site some privacy. He turned down the last row along the edge of a heavily treed area and stopped the bike out front of a silver Airstream.

"We're here," he announced. Jane hopped off the back and stretched her legs. Ethan rested the bike on its kickstand and dismounted.

"This yours?" Jane asked. The rounded trailer had a dent or two in its silver skin and a faded awning tube mounted to its side. A barbecue was chained like a hostage to the hitch beside dual propane tanks.

"All twenty feet of her," he said, setting his helmet on the picnic table that sat a few feet away from the trailer's door. "Hey, Frank." Ethan waved to a neighbour seated in a lawn chair across from them. Frank raised a beer can in greeting.

"Come inside," Ethan said. He unlocked the door, pulled it open, and gestured for her to go in ahead of him.

Jane had seen plenty of Airstreams, but she'd never been inside one before. She mounted the stairs and stepped into the waiting heat. Directly in front of her sat a table between two benches. Tucked into the space to her right lay a tidy bed. To her left was the kitchen area, and at the far end, an open door through which she spotted a toilet.

"It's scorching in here. Let me get the windows open." Ethan guided her out of his path with a gentle hand. His brief touch sent delicious shivers through her.

"This is really sweet," Jane said. She took a few steps to her left and gazed out the window to the picnic table. A light breeze soon cleared the heated air from inside the trailer.

Ethan stripped off his jacket and tossed it on the bed. "I'll just be a minute." He stepped back outside and unfurled the awning. After he fiddled with the door, separating a screen door from its outer shell, he came back inside.

Jane dropped her jacket beside Ethan's and took a seat at the banquette.

Ethan bent to the fridge. "I'm having a beer. Can I get you something?"

"No," Jane said. "I'm good."

"You don't drink?"

Jane shook her head. A small lie. She did drink, but only on occasion, and only when she was home. Behind a locked door, preferably steel.

"Something else? Water? Soda?"

She took a glass of water. "How long have you had the trailer?"

"Three years. Took me a while to get this spot though." Ethan snapped the cap off a Corona. "Everyone wants a space in this row. It has shade, and Still Creek is right behind us. It can get pretty hot in the summer."

"A cabin in the woods," Jane said.

"That's what it feels like. One day I'll have an acreage somewhere just like this with a creek out back."

While he drank his beer, he talked about his plans to build a cabin someday. Through his guileless expression, she glimpsed the little boy he must have been. He made her feel special, as if he'd invited her into his secret world.

"How about you?" he asked. "Where do you see yourself in five years?"

"I'm not much of a dreamer." Her thoughts of the future didn't stretch beyond having her birthmarks removed. She didn't dare dream beyond that possibility. Besides, the money she'd need to accomplish that would devour any savings she might accumulate in the foreseeable future.

"You don't want to get out of the city one day?"

"I've only ever known the city, unless you count a grade four school trip to a farm in Chilliwack."

"Your parents never took you camping?"

Jane had known the circumstances of her parentage would eventually come up. It always did. It was the point that tested every friendship she'd ever had. She'd learned early on that people had preconceived ideas about kids raised in *the system*. Most assumed she was trouble, some sort of low-life, the product of drug addicts or alcoholics. She was labelled a "bad kid" by default because "good kids" didn't go into *the system*.

Ethan didn't seem like most people though, and if the truth was going to scare him away, she'd rather know now. She laid out the abbreviated version of her life: abandoned as a baby, adopted, orphaned, foster parents, group homes, tough kids, spit out of the system at nineteen.

During the telling, she watched for the signs—a syrupy smile, forced empathy, exaggerated pity. Sometimes body language gave away the judgy ones: a rigid back, a chin tucked in, crossed arms, as if creating a physical barrier would shield them from her.

Ethan didn't offer sympathy or platitudes. Instead, he studied his bottle of Corona. When he finally looked up, his gaze didn't falter. "Tough break. It's made you strong."

Jane mentally ticked a box. Her history hadn't fazed him. One down, one to go.

"Thought I'd barbecue burgers," Ethan said. "You okay with that?"

They ate late, outside on the picnic table, after the moon was up. Crickets chirped in the nearby bushes. "Where are your parents?" Jane asked.

"Mom died when I was a kid. Dad's around, but I don't see him much."

"Sorry. About your mom." What took her so young? Jane wondered.

When they'd finished eating, Jane took their plates into the trailer and set them in the sink. Moths beat their wings against the window screens. Ethan followed her inside with the condiments. She turned her backside to the sink, leaned against the counter, and watched him pull the curtains closed in the bathroom. The small space demanded an economy of motion, and he moved with practised ease. Of the two of them, he was in better shape, but she was no slouch. She'd always admired his toned arms, the smooth pecs beneath his T-shirt. He had no tats, or none that she could see. He spun around and pulled the curtains closed by the banquette. The only curtains that remained open were behind Jane, above the kitchen sink.

Ethan turned on her like she was prey. She didn't mind being the hunted tonight. He made her want to be caught. He pressed against her, holding her in place while he closed the curtains. He then rested his hands on the counter on either side of her.

She smiled up at him, an invitation. He leaned in to kiss her and, just as he had the first time, approached the task unrushed. Jane felt the heat of him at every junction between them: lips, thighs, hips. It had been ages since she'd had a man's attention, and Ethan was doing a very good job of making her want every inch of him. Still, a familiar fear lurked, holding her back.

Ethan ended their kiss. "Will you stay?"

"For a while," Jane said. "Not overnight."

A crease formed between his brows and then faded. "All right. I'll take you home." He paused, and a salacious smile played on his lips. "After." He pressed his lips to hers again.

She regretted not having that beer. It would have taken the edge off what was about to come. She felt him shift, lifting his hands from the countertop. One hand went to the back of her head, the other skimmed across her breast and slid under her shirt. Soon, he'd see the stained skin beneath his caresses. Just once, she'd like a man to stick around awhile after the unveiling.

Jane pressed her hands to Ethan's chest. It felt as firm and smooth as she'd imagined. As her hands ventured south, Ethan's lips froze. For a brief moment, she imagined he was enjoying her touch, but when her hands reached his abdomen, his entire body seized up. Something felt very wrong beneath Jane's fingertips. The skin was hardened in lumps and ridges. She tried not to react, but with Ethan playing statue, it was a tough sell.

She broke their kiss and sought his gaze. He met it as he always did, unflinching. He then stepped back from her, reached for the bottom of his T-shirt, and then lifted it over his head. Jane's gaze left his face and travelled down his perfect pecs to his ruined stomach. He'd been badly burned, and the scarring was extensive. She met his gaze again and recognized something familiar in his expression. Fear. Dread. Bravery.

Jane offered him a reassuring smile. "I'm not a runner."

"You sure?" he asked.

"Yup. You, on the other hand?" Jane said, raising an eyebrow. Jane had never in her life stripped in front of a man with the lights on, but Ethan made her feel brave. She followed his lead and stripped off her shirt, and before she lost her nerve, she reached behind her back, unfastened her bra, and took it off.

Ethan's gaze slid over her body: breasts, stomach, arms. He twirled his finger and she slowly turned around. Two thick red lines marred her back. When she again faced him, he drew her close and kissed her forehead. She felt his fingers rake the hair from the left side of her face, and then he brushed a kiss over the wine stain there.

"There are more," she said. Her breasts and belly had been spared, but the stains extended across her butt and marred her thighs and shins— even the bottom of one foot.

He licked the rim of her ear, sending shivers dancing down her arms. "I don't care."

She ticked the second box and reached for his belt buckle.

They stripped off each other's jeans on the five-foot hike to the bed. It seemed a mile away. When Ethan stood naked before her, Jane drank in his muscular physique as if she'd just crawled out of the desert.

His lips curled in a seductive smile. He tipped his chin toward the bed. Jane turned and when she did, he pulled her back to his chest. Holding her tight with a hand across her stomach, he pressed his erection into her back. His lips found her shoulder as he cupped her breast. An unfamiliar sensation lapped at her: she felt safe.

They eventually fell into the bed, though Jane couldn't remember the mechanics of it. But she remembered the rest with stunning clarity. The way Ethan kissed the length of the wine stains that ran diagonally across her shoulders and back. The feel of his feather-light touch on the stains across her butt and thighs. She never wanted it to end. It had been a long drought and she felt desperate for more. Too soon, he was inside her. Her doing, not his. She held on as long as she could, and then moaned with his name on her lips.

After he'd had his fill, they lay on their backs, side by side, staring up at the vinyl-covered ceiling. Eventually, Ethan rolled onto his side and propped himself up on his elbow. His fingers traced the stain on her face. He then moved on to the stains on her arm and her thigh. It felt wonderful to Jane. She never imagined anyone could be so accepting of her flaws.

"Roll over," Ethan said.

Jane complied and rolled onto her stomach, soaking up his fascination. She noticed a photo he'd tacked to the wall. "What will you do for work when you own your acreage with the creek?"

"Don't know yet," Ethan said, continuing his mission of tracing her stains. "Might open a dojo, maybe run boot camps."

"You could breed dogs. I dreamed of a kennel the other night. Highland Breeders, it was called. The dogs were so sweet, and the puppies—adorable."

"Highland Breeders? I hadn't thought of breeding dogs, but it's a great idea. An acreage would be the perfect setting. You like dogs?"

"Sure. Never lived anywhere where I could have one though. You?"

"Love them. I'll get one when I have an acreage."

"Who's in the picture?" Jane asked, tipping her head toward the photo. *Thanks for your support* had been written across the top with a Sharpie.

"They're dog handlers. I only know the guy in black on the right. The dogs visit sick kids and the elderly. Hospitals mostly."

She forced herself to focus on Ethan and not his touch. "How were you burned?"

"Car accident. I was twelve."

"You spend a lot of time in hospital?"

"Couple of months in and out for skin grafts."

"Must have been awful."

"Yeah, it was. Dad's never forgiven himself. You always had these marks?"

Jane recognized an exit line when she heard it. "Born with them. Port wine stains."

"One of the docs in the burn unit had one like that on his cheek," he said, twirling a finger near his face.

"I'm going to have them removed." Jane explained the laser procedure and that there was a risk that it might not work. Ethan's hand returned to the birthmark on her butt. "You committing my stains to memory?" Jane rested her head on her crossed arms.

"Something like that," he said.

"You missed one."

"Where?"

"Bottom of my foot." Jane crooked her right knee and bent the bottom of her foot toward him.

She felt the warmth of his hand examining the sole of her foot. "Nothing there," he said.

Jane laughed at her error and crooked her other knee. But no, the stain was on the bottom of her right foot, not her left. The left foot had the mark on top. Jane blamed the poor lighting. She rolled on her back and examined the underside of her right foot. She shot Ethan a confused glance then sat up and swung her legs over the side of the bed. She crossed her right leg over her left.

"That's not possible," she said, studying the bottom of her foot. She reached for her jacket and pulled her phone from the pocket. The flashlight confirmed the impossible. She checked the left foot and then the right again.

"It's . . . gone." She tried to remember the last time she'd seen it. "They never told me they might go away on their own." She poked at the skin where her mark used to be.

"They?"

"Doctors," she said. Doctors who'd repeatedly told her the marks were indelible.

"They don't know everything."

"No. They sure don't." She lay back down beside Ethan, who remained propped on his elbow. For the first time since she'd researched the expensive surgery, the risk that laser removal wouldn't work didn't seem quite so great. Her mind swirled with new possibilities. All her life, she'd wished the stains would miraculously disappear, and now the tail end of one of the many strips had done just that. Was it foolhardy to hope the rest would do the same?

What if the mark that had vanished reappeared tomorrow? What if it came back worse than before?

Jane reached for her clothes. "Take me home. Please."

Though Ethan protested, he kept his earlier promise.

On the back of his bike, Jane realized that she'd been so preoccupied with her birthmarks she'd forgotten about the third box: her narcolepsy. She'd tell him about her condition eventually, but not tonight. She couldn't think beyond the impossibility that a birthmark had vanished. And the depth of her desperation for the rest of them to do the same unsettled her.

Visiting Dream

Jane is jarred by raised voices. She's in a hallway at the psych hospital. The industrial linoleum gives it away. She sighs. Another dream. Directly in front of her is a door. It's ajar. The writing on the brass plaque reads Dr. A. Cohen, Department Head. She peeks through the crack. One of the two men arguing is the doctor who's been treating Rebecca. Jane has only a partial view of the other man. Dr. Cohen, she assumes. They both wear white lab coats.

"She's a danger to herself," Rebecca's doctor says. "Her suicide will be on our hands if we release her."

At the sound of squeaking wheels, Jane looks over her shoulder. Down the hall, a woman backs out of a closet pulling a rolling mop bucket. Jane is struck by the clashing bright colours in her blouse. When the woman turns toward her, Jane recognizes her from Rebecca's ward. The woman wheels the mop bucket in Jane's direction. Jane finds the woman's gaze disturbing, as if those dark eyes with the blue rings around them staring out from the kindly face can see her.

Voices pull Jane back to the doctors behind the crack in the door. "Rick. She's refusing treatment. And we need the bed. Either you sign her release papers or I will."

Jane raises a hand to the door and the air around it shimmers, like heat waves off pavement. She wants to get a better look at Dr. Cohen, and pushes against the door. The sound of a creaking hinge startles her.

Jane surfaced from her dream sucking in air. She examined her hand. In her dream, it had looked almost ethereal. And more startling, it had felt as if she'd actually touched the door, moved it. Ridiculous, she thought.

She adjusted her pillow. Another piece of the puzzle was solved. Rebecca's doctor's name was Rick. And now she knew another name. Dr. A. Cohen.

12 | Rick

The closer Rick got to news of his promotion, the more anxious he felt about the one thing that could spoil it for him.

He'd had a long time to sort through his options and devise a plan. He'd identified the weak points and eliminated them. He'd considered everything that could go awry and had put contingencies in place. Sadie was one of the contingencies. She would be useful.

It had been a few days since Rick made his request to Cynthia, and he'd yet to hear from her. She was probably salivating over his offer, devising lies to milk him for more money. Not that she'd see a dime of it. He'd made certain it was enough to get her attention. Her greed would ensure she made him Sadie's main source of income.

The chess pieces were in play. If the old woman was right, it wouldn't be much longer now.

13 | Sadie

After Sadie towel-dried her hair, she dressed in threadbare cut-offs and a tank top. She padded to the kitchen alcove and checked under the sink. At best, a half-glass of wine remained. The liquor store would still be open, and the night was warm. She slid into her sandals and headed out to stretch her legs.

She bought two bottles of cheap red and ducked into a Greek restaurant to order takeout. While she waited for her order, her phone rang. Cynthia again. She dismissed the call, not wanting to talk about that particular subject in public. A moment later her phone dinged, telling her Cynthia had left a message. It could wait until she got home.

Even though her meal was takeout, she left a generous tip—server ethics. She juggled her bags and headed back to the apartment. As she walked, she took in the quaint storefronts, tail-wagging dogs, and sleepy kids in strollers. Such a switch from her old Downtown Eastside neighbourhood. There, she'd have been dodging discarded needles, sky-high shopping carts, and ranting souls forgotten by the system.

She looked up as she approached Mrs. Carper's bay window. The woman's shadow lurked behind the gauzy curtain. "Hey, Mrs. Carper," Sadie called out, purely to disavow the woman of the notion she possessed invisibility superpowers.

She shifted her bags to get her keys out.

"I'll get the door!" came a man's voice from behind her.

Startled, she stepped back.

"I'm Andy," he said, slipping his key into the lock. "Your neighbour?"

Sadie shook off her surprise. "Thanks. I'm Sadie."

Andy held the door for her. His big smile revealed perfectly straight white teeth. He trotted down the stairs after her, his Nike flip-flops slapping the floor. Sadie once again shifted her bags to retrieve her keys.

"Let me," Andy said, offering to take a bag. He wore a short-sleeved button-down shirt over sleeve tats that extended to his wrists. An interesting choice, Sadie thought. Good boy on top, bad boy underneath? Sadie surrendered the heavier bag with an awkward smile and pulled her keys from her purse. She opened the door and turned back to Andy, who'd been peering inside the apartment. "Thanks."

"Yeah, no problem," he said, holding out her bag. Sadie dropped her purse to the floor and took it. The tendrils of another tat reached up his neck above his shirt collar. "Mrs. Carper tells me you have a roommate."

"Yeah," Sadie said, cursing the nosey body upstairs. "Jane. I'd introduce you, but she's not home."

"Another time," Andy said. He turned to his own apartment and disappeared inside.

Sadie felt a shudder of relief. She shut the door and set the locks then walked straight to the kitchen, unscrewed the cap from one of the bottles, and poured a glass. She swallowed a gulp. The encounter with Boy-Scout Andy had shaken her. Not Andy, but the fact that her mind had immediately gone to Mr. Kristan and the fear that he'd found her.

Sadie downed another gulp then topped up her glass. The moment she finished eating her takeout, she'd call Cynthia and sever ties with Mr. Kristan.

There was a soft knock at the door. Sadie rose to check the peephole. Andy again. The smell of pot wafted in as she opened the door.

"Sorry to bother you." He held a USB stick in his hand. "You don't happen to have a printer, by chance?"

"No," Sadie said. "Sorry."

"Do you know if anyone in the building has one? Mine's out of ink."

"No idea."

"Thanks anyway," Andy said, and he turned to leave.

"Hey," Sadie called after him. "Do you have a doob I can buy?"

"Just smoked the last of it. Do you vape?"

"Sure. THC?"

"Is there anything else?" he said, curling one corner of his mouth.

Sadie turned back for her phone and keys then locked up and followed him in her bare feet. His apartment was smaller than theirs. Just one room. To her left, three computer screens sat atop a glass-and-steel console. A mesh-screened office chair had been rolled off to one side. To her right, a rumpled bed lay pushed against the wall. Andy strode past an old-time gaming table and pulled the vape from a kitchen cupboard.

"Have a seat," he said, indicating a chair at the table. He checked the cartridge in the vape and then handed it to her.

Sadie took a hit and exhaled. "What's all the computer equipment for?"

Andy pulled out a chair, turned it around, and straddled it. "I code. Freelance."

"You work from home? Nice."

"You and your roommate—Jane, was it? Are you two a couple or what?"

"No," she said, laughing. "But you're not the first to ask."

They exchanged small talk, took turns with the vape, and half an hour turned into an hour, then two.

August 12

Sadie picked up her phone from the parquet floor and checked the time. "Shit!" She threw off the sheet and lurched to her feet. There was no time for a shower. Her head felt thick and heavy, her balance threatened, as she picked through the clothes on the floor. In the bathroom, she tugged a comb through her hair and fixed the makeup she'd slept in.

She could get used to a guy like Andy. He was sweet . . . and funny. He'd put his contact info into her phone under Handsome Neighbour. They'd ended up playing tongue tag, and she seemed to recall some groping, but she felt a spark of pride in the fact she hadn't screwed him. At least she didn't think she had; there were a few blank spots in her night, including how she'd gotten back home.

A blob of something brown clung to the buttoned flap of her oxford shirt. She picked at it with a fingernail and then dabbed at the underlying stain with a wet face cloth. Hardly noticeable, she thought, dropping the cloth in the sink. She dashed to the living room to find her shoes.

Jane's absence didn't dawn on Sadie until she was in the hall about to lock the door. Had Jane spent the night with Ethan? She opened the door again. Her Greek salad takeout container had been rinsed and rested on the drainboard. Nope. Jane's obsessive need to tidy up gave her away. She must have come home late and left early.

Berating herself, Sadie ran to her car. Even though Jane had made it home last night, Sadie should have checked on her, sent her a text at least. What if she'd accidentally fallen asleep at Ethan's? Jane's carefully constructed life revolved around control. She stayed under everyone's radar, managed her environment to the nth degree, and trained constantly. Sadie wouldn't last a minute under those conditions. Still, she understood Jane's motivation and should have had her back last night. That was the unwritten rule between them; Sadie watched over Jane when she was comatose, and Jane kept tabs on Sadie when she worked for Cynthia.

Sadie's sloppy parking job didn't even register as she grabbed her bag and raced for the restaurant's back door. Having arrived just in time, she slowed her step and smoothed the wet spot on the front of her shirt.

Employee cellphones were strictly forbidden on the floor. Once in the locker room, Sadie pulled hers out to text Jane and saw that she had a message from Cynthia *I'm awaiting your answer.* She dashed off a text to Jane with a question mark, and then replied to Cynthia: *Not interested.* She was about to drop her phone into her purse when it dinged. Jane had sent a heart emoji. Sadie sucked in a breath of relief, ditched her purse in her locker, and walked out to the floor.

14 | Rick

The Land Rover's touch screen lit up as Rick drove up Lamey's Mill Road. A text came in. Another failsafe had slid into place, but Rick felt no relief.

The mistake he'd made years ago had forced his hand, shone a light on a part of him he kept hidden in a compartment labelled *ugly but necessary*. He confided in no one. No one would believe him.

He'd had to think quickly to cover up Jane's birth, but he'd pulled it off and the hospital had been cleared. The investigation went away, as did the police. Regardless, the hospital brass asked him to sign an NDA along with a resignation letter. Fools. The NDA did more to protect him than them.

He'd never stopped looking for Jane. The private detective he'd hired eventually found the old woman who'd resigned from the hospital a week after Jane went missing. The old woman should have been more patient. She might as well have held a neon sign with a flashing arrow.

When Rick caught up with her, she admitted what she'd done. Seemed pleased with herself, cocky even. Boasted that Rick would never find the child. He could still see the smile on her weathered face. He didn't know it at the time, but that smile had been a dare, a venomous trap.

Even with the old woman's information, the private detective took a year and a half to locate Jane. Now, one way or another, he would neutralize the threat she posed. Twenty-four years of vigilance took a hard toll on a man. He was ready to be done with it and get on with his life.

15 | Jane

All morning, Jane fought off a bad case of nerves. Though Anna poked around as to her lunch plans, Jane kept her meeting with the professor to herself. Regardless, with a mother's sixth sense, Anna seemed to know. She hummed a happy tune from behind the counter and called out "Take your time, sweetie," when Jane headed out at noon.

They'd arranged to meet at an Italian restaurant on Hornby. Her choice had been Mickey D's, but she'd given in to his selection when he insisted on paying. The savoury scent of roasted garlic made her mouth water as she walked in. Sunlight streamed through tall, narrow windows. The professor was already seated in the dining room and waved to get her attention.

"I'm with him," she said to the hostess, and proceeded to his table.

His smile twitched as he stood to greet her. "Joyce," he said, exhaling. Cutlery tinkled on china and mixed with the quiet voices of diners at the surrounding tables.

"Professor."

He'd dressed the part today in a tweed blazer and chinos.

"Call me Nate, please. Have a seat." He motioned across the table, where a second menu waited on the white tablecloth.

"All right. Nate then."

"I wasn't sure you'd come," he said, laying his napkin on his lap.

A waiter hovered. "Water?" he asked, sliding a disapproving gaze to Jane's bandana. He filled their glasses, recited the day's specials, then backed away, excusing himself to get Nate's coffee order.

"Tell me about the woman who gave you the print."

Nate realigned his cutlery. "Her name is Dr. Ariane Rebaza. She specializes in Inca culture."

"Where'd she get it—the print?"

"In Peru. She has family in Lima. Studied there."

The waiter appeared like a ghost with a carafe, filled Nate's cup, and set down a tray with sugar and cream.

After the waiter slipped away, Nate said, "May I—" He paused and shifted in his seat. "Would you mind if I examined the mark on your hand?"

The price for answers, Jane thought, and extended her left hand. Nate squinted as he studied it, his nose inches away. "That's incredible." He reached into his breast pocket, pulled out a photocopy of the print from his office, and held it up beside her hand. "They're identical. See for yourself," he said, handing her the image. "Thank you for not insisting on having the print."

She glanced at the photocopy, but a careful study wasn't required. She'd been looking at the design every day for twenty-four years. A framed print would be overkill.

"Are there more?" he asked, indicating the bandana tied around her forehead.

"Yes. The doctors call them port wine stains. They're birthmarks."

Nate nodded with a finger pressed to his mouth. "I can understand why they think that. You've had them from birth then?"

"Yes." She frowned slightly. "On the phone, you said you didn't think they were birthmarks. What do you think they are?" Jane rubbed her sweaty palms on her jeans. She felt as if he were about to pull back a curtain, and that what lay beyond it might change her life. Whether it was for better or worse was still up for grabs.

"I'm not the expert Ariane is, but I talked to her. After I saw the mark on your hand." Nate looked down to his cutlery again, shifting the knife ever so slightly.

"And?"

He looked up. "Listen. I know how this is going to sound, but I wouldn't be here if I didn't hold Ariane in the highest regard. She's one of the foremost Inca scholars in the world." He sucked in a breath, as if steeling himself to rip off a Band-Aid. "She believes the marks are ritualistic."

Jane's frown deepened. "What does that mean?"

"She believes they were conferred as the result of a ritual. An Inca ritual."

Jane arched an eyebrow and waited for the punchline, but the professor's face remained solemn. She sat back in her chair, creating some distance between them. The man was delusional. What a letdown. Having lunch with him suddenly felt like a bad decision. Jane pulled out her phone to check the time.

"May I take your order?" The waiter had appeared soundlessly at their table.

"Would you give us another minute?" Nate asked. When the waiter was gone, Nate leaned forward on his elbows. "You saw the offering bowl? Do you know what it was used for in Inca times?" Jane shook her head. "Something precious was put in it and offered to a deity or a god in exchange for a blessing."

Jane snorted. "You're telling me these marks are a *blessing*? That's a hard no."

The professor raked a hand through his messy locks and hid a smile. "I don't imagine it feels that way. Still, I don't believe they're a coincidence. Do you?"

Jane toyed with her phone and thought about patterns repeating in nature that she'd read about in a magazine article. "I don't know what I feel." Disappointed, for sure, but did he have something else to offer?

Nate snatched his menu. "Let's order," he said, a note of anxiety in his voice. "Have you eaten here before?"

"No." The quaint restaurant was close to Positively Plants, and she'd walked by it countless times, but it was miles out of Jane's price range.

He skimmed the menu. "If you eat beef, their carpaccio is one of the best. The scampi is good. Lots of garlic, but good. Their Caprese salad is excellent."

Jane's eyes glazed over. She had no clue what carpaccio was, or Caprese. She searched for spaghetti and settled on something called spaghetti Bolognese hoping it wasn't a fancy name for spaghetti and fried bologna. She'd eaten her fill of that growing up.

After the waiter had collected their menus, Nate leaned in again. "Ariane is flying in from Peru. She wants to meet you."

Whoa. Jane recoiled. "She your girlfriend?"

"No. A good friend. We studied together in Cusco. In Peru."

"It's a long way to come." Too long. This Ariane wanted something. What?

"It is. What you have. It's very special. She's never seen the mark manifested on a person before. She's—she's anxious to meet you."

She's presumptuous is what she is, Jane thought, and she pushed back into her chair. "I'm not an animal in a zoo."

Nate quickly interjected. "No. That's not . . ." His voice faltered.

"I don't know. Her coming all this way? Seems a bit much. What does she want?"

Nate lifted his elbows from the table and sat back in his chair. "I don't think you understand how unique your markings are. That print"—he gestured to the photocopy on the table—"the original hangs in her family's home. In Peru. You present a once-in-a-lifetime opportunity for Ariane. She'd like to learn more about you."

"Study my birthmarks?"

"Yes. And you. She wants to solve the riddle of why you have them."

Jane left the restaurant with more questions than answers.

At nine thirty that evening, the outside temperature had cooled but the apartment hadn't. Jane stripped down to an old tank top. Her search for Dr. A. Cohen had left her frustrated. Cohen was a common name in the medical field. The *A* could stand for Alison, Abraham, Albert, and so many more. And that wasn't even considering the A.E. Cohens and T.A. Cohens. It was impossible. She heard Sadie's key in the lock and looked up from her laptop. "Hey. How was work?"

"Crap. As usual," Sadie said, throwing the bolt locks. "My feet are killing me." She kicked off her shoes where she stood and hobbled to the sofa. She plopped down next to Jane and sank into the balding velour. "Tips were decent though." She rolled her head toward Jane and a slow grin appeared. "So? How'd it go with Ethan last night?"

Jane sighed and smiled wistfully.

"Wow. That good?"

"Oh yeah. He's happily unacquainted with ED." Jane's smile faded. "But he hasn't called."

"He will." Sadie dragged herself off the sofa and lumbered into the kitchen. "Want wine?" She unscrewed the cap from the bottle and plucked a clean glass from the dish rack.

"No, thanks. There's something else. You know the birthmark on the bottom of my foot?"

"Uh-huh," Sadie said, pouring the wine.

"Well, it's gone."

Sadie swung her head around. "No shit?"

"Look," Jane said, bending her knee to show her.

Glass in hand, Sadie returned to the sofa. Her eyes widened. "When? Did you know that might happen?"

"Not a clue. I'm just glad it's gone, and fingers crossed it doesn't make a reappearance."

"I'll drink to that," Sadie said, lifting her glass. "And good riddance to the rest of them too."

"From your lips," Jane said, shooting a glance at the heavens.

Sadie pulled up her feet and settled into the corner of the sofa. "I met our new neighbour yesterday. He's a coder. You should see his setup."

"You were in his apartment?"

"Yeah. His name's Andy. Nice guy. Works from home." Sadie sipped her wine. "How'd it go with the prof today?" She leaned forward and picked up the photocopy of the professor's print from the trunk.

"I'm still trying to decide if he was putting me on."

"This the print from his office?" Sadie asked. Jane nodded. "Weird, isn't it? What'd he tell you?"

"He thinks I got the birthmarks from some *ritualistic* hocus-pocus."

"Seriously?"

Jane quirked a shoulder. "He has a professor friend who's flying in from Peru to see my birthmarks for herself."

Sadie's phone rang. She dug it out of her purse. "Shit. It's Cynthia. I've been ditching her calls. I'd better take it before she implodes." Sadie said hello then straightened. A look of alarm crossed her face. She ended the call and headed to the door.

"She here?" Jane asked.

"Yup. I'll get rid of her." Sadie left with the phone still in her hand.

Jane shook her head. Cynthia wasn't the *get rid of* type. Sure enough, moments later, she trailed Sadie into their apartment.

"Hello, Jane," Cynthia cooed. White capris and a flawlessly pressed sleeveless shirt gave the impression of crisp and cool on a sultry night. Sadie closed the door.

"Cynthia." Jane put effort into not disliking Cynthia. She reminded herself that the woman had, in a manner, helped Sadie. She'd offered her something safer and more profitable than what Sadie had been doing on her own. Cynthia's goons were old school. She'd been known to sic them on anyone who laid a heavy hand on her girls. That is, unless the john had paid for it.

Cynthia scanned the room. "It's a step up from the last place, but you girls could do better." Behind her, Sadie hollowed her cheeks as she crossed her arms. Cynthia looked pointedly at Jane.

Jane arched an eyebrow. "You're not still trying to recruit me?"

"That's not why I'm here, but as I've told you before"—Cynthia's gaze flitted to Jane's bare arms—"there's a high-end market for natural ink like yours."

"Natural ink?" Jane said, her tone skeptical. "Sounds almost wholesome." She found the concept hard to believe, and disturbing.

Uninvited, Cynthia perched on the edge of the sofa. "I'm here to ask you to talk some sense into your roommate."

Jane looked to Sadie, who'd flared her nostrils.

"I've been approached by a well-to-do client with a lucrative proposal," Cynthia said. "He's a regular, no rough stuff. He's offered to buy Sadie's way out of the business." Sadie started to speak, but Cynthia cut her off. "There's two thousand in it for you if you can talk her into it."

Jane furrowed her brow. "You want Sadie out of the business?"

"Not at all. I just want her to keep the client happy for a few months then make sure he tires of her. Afterward, she can shake him off."

Sadie chirped up from her post by the door. "The client has a saviour complex. He's gotten too close. Wants to know who I am, where I live, where I work. He won't be so easy to *shake off*."

Jane frowned at Cynthia. "That sounds like a very bad idea."

"I agree," Sadie said, shooting a dagger at Cynthia.

Unfazed, Cynthia continued. "At the rate you girls are going, you'll be collecting pensions before you work your way out of this cave." She swept a critical gaze around their apartment. "He's offering an express elevator to the top. All you've got to do is step inside."

"Sorry, Cynthia," Jane said. "I'm not talking Sadie into doing anything she doesn't think is safe."

Cynthia pressed her lips together. She stood. "He's offering more than you'll ever make in a year. Tax free. Cash. You want Sadie to turn that down?" She walked toward Sadie, who held the door ajar. "I'm keeping his offer on the table. And you'll take his next gig, or you won't get a gig."

Sadie closed the door and leaned her butt against it. "Sorry about that. Cynthia's not used to turning down money."

"You gonna take the guy's next gig?"

"I don't know."

"I can't believe she tried to recruit me again."

"Cynthia would try to recruit her granny if she found someone into corpses."

Jane laughed. "She's not all bad. Who's the client?"

Sadie pushed off from the door and returned to the sofa. "One of the teacher's-pet sugar-daddy set. Calls himself Mr. Kristan."

"He's a regular?"

"Yeah. Disciplinarian type, but harmless. Has a nasty scar on his face." Sadie drew a curved line on her cheek from her ear to her nose. "My gut's not wrong. He's looking for more than a professional relationship. As much as I like his money, I don't need the complication."

Visiting Dream

Jane is back in the psychiatrist's office. Rick's office. Rebecca is seated opposite him, her head turned to the side, staring absently past the dull snake plant and out of the window. Jane searches for her own reflection in the glass but can't find it.

The doctor has a pad of lined paper on his lap and a pen in his hand. "Our brains work in ways we don't fully comprehend, but still, visions like you're experiencing are well documented. They divert attention from an underlying issue."

Rebecca turns her head in his direction. There are no tissues this time, no tears. "Would you like to hear about the rest of my vision?" The doctor blows air out of his cheeks before relenting with a tip of his head. Rebecca looks back to the window. "After your father strapped you, he sent you to your room. Said you'd have no dinner. You lay on your bed listening to your family enjoy their meal. You brushed tears from your eyes at the sound of your brother's laughter. Long after dark, your mother came into your room. She brought you a peanut-butter-and-jam sandwich and stroked your hair."

Deep lines mar Rick's brow. "You couldn't possibly know that."

Rebecca once again turns to face the doctor. "You can't imagine how much I wish I didn't."

The doctor eventually looks away. He sets his pad and pen aside and walks to the window. "How often do you have these visions?"

"I sometimes go weeks without one."

"Is there a theme?"

Rebecca screws up her face. "A theme?"

"A common thread," Rick says, his back still to her. "Is it always children, for example?"

"No. I see animals too, and places."

"Places?" Rick says, and turns to face her.

"Bus depots, factories, parks, museums."

"In the past? Present?"

"The past. Always the past."

The doctor returns to his chair and crosses his legs. "I'll concede, I don't know what this is you're experiencing, but I'm prepared to help you. I'll let you go home on two conditions."

Rebecca inches forward. "What conditions?"

"First, you have to continue to see me. Once a week."

"I can't afford private sessions."

"Don't worry about the money. Second, you must promise that you'll call me if you feel the slightest urge to self-harm."

Rebecca nods and inches farther forward on the sofa. "Is that it?"

"You probably shouldn't talk to anyone else about your visions," Rick adds. "If you do, you're bound to end up back here."

"I never talk about my visions," Rebecca says.

The doctor plants his feet on the floor. "You need to understand that you are not well. I may not have answers yet, but I will. We'll work together to find a solution." He offers her a reassuring smile. The first such smile Jane has seen from the doctor. She doesn't trust that it's genuine. "In the meantime, I'll prescribe a sedative that should help, but if not, there are other treatments we can try."

Rebecca stands. "When can I leave?"

"Today. Give me an hour or two to organize your release."

Rick ushers Rebecca out of his office and closes the door. He remains still with his hand pressed to the back of the door. When he pushes off, he heads to his desk and phones the administration office. He directs them to prepare Rebecca's release papers.

Rick then opens a file folder containing the record of Rebecca's treatment. He flips to the beginning and runs his finger down each page, reviewing his notes, crossing out some sections. When he's done, he pulls out a fresh notepad and rewrites the pages eliminating the crossed-out sections. The new pages go in the file and the crossed-out pages go into the inside pocket of his sports coat.

He closes the file and leans back in his chair. "Incredible," he mumbles. He stares out of the window, unseeing. Moments pass before he sits forward. He opens the desk drawer and lays his pen inside beside the ivory letter opener. He hesitates. Something in the drawer catches his eye. He removes a photograph. It's a picture of two men with broad smiles. The younger man has his arm around the older one. They're standing beside a shiny pickup truck. Rick turns over the photograph and Jane reads the writing there: *Dad's new truck. Damn! It's good to be me. M.*

Rick's features harden. He tosses the photo in the trash can.

He leaves his office, and Jane follows him to the nursing station on Rebecca's ward. Waiting anxiously outside the glass doors is the man with the rumbly laugh whom Jane has seen cuddling with Rebecca in earlier dreams. Rick sees him too, and scowls.

Jane woke with a crushing weight on her chest. Rick was up to something; she felt it in her bones, and it felt bad. Rick's boss had directed him to release Rebecca, full stop. Yet he'd spelled out conditions for letting her go—conditions that might have been for his own benefit, not Rebecca's. And why was he covering his ass by rewriting her medical file?

Whoever this Rebecca was, Jane had to find her. Though neither Rebecca nor the doctor had mentioned narcolepsy, without a doubt, Rebecca's visions were just like Jane's dreams. And if Rebecca had been cured of them, Jane wanted in on it, regardless of her unease about Rick.

16 | Rick

C ynthia was sidestepping like a mambo pro and Rick conceded she
was good at the dance. Had she chosen a legitimate profession, she'd
be at the top of her game. Her reticence, she insisted, was because she
didn't want to lose "Chloe," but Rick suspected Cynthia was playing him
for more money. She'd come around. Women like Cynthia didn't leave
cash on the table.

He threaded more bait on the hook, suggesting they test the waters
with a three-month exclusive arrangement. A win-win. He'd get Sadie's
alter ego all to himself and Cynthia would reap a three-month extension
of paid gigs. As long as she could guarantee him unlimited access.

She took the bait. Three months was all Rick needed. Sadie would
be much more pliable when she learned her benefactor controlled her
purse. And if Sadie dragged her feet, he had other ways to ensure her
cooperation.

17 | Jane

August 13

E ven on her days off, Jane woke early. She stretched and crawled out of bed then padded to the bathroom. Sadie, who'd been allergic to mornings since seventh grade, slept soundly on the sofa.

Back in the bedroom, Jane pushed aside the towel they used as a curtain. Sunlight spilled into the room, highlighting drifting dust motes. She picked up her phone and journal and sat cross-legged on the bed.

The mark on the bottom of her foot hadn't reappeared. She still couldn't believe that none of the doctors she'd seen over the years had suggested they might go away on their own. She typed "do port wine stains go away" into Google. The answer was definitive. No. Other types of birthmarks faded, but not port wine stains; port wine stains grew more prominent. Could the doctors have been wrong about the type of birthmark she had? She examined the bottom of her foot. When had it started to fade? she wondered. She studied the other stains for signs of their impending demise but found none—they were as blood-red as ever.

Jane tapped her pen against the journal and refocused. With no extra cash floating around to hire a proper investigator, how was she going to find Rebecca Morrow? She'd struck out on Google. The online search services wanted money. Still, there had to be other ways to find people. Or people better at searching. At school, when she'd been assigned to write some boring paper, she'd go to the librarian. They were always eager. Maybe a librarian could help find Rebecca? And libraries were free. At the very least it was a place to start.

To narrow her search, she'd have to make some assumptions. She didn't know Rebecca personally, but she knew from past dream experiences that she had to be somehow connected to her. That meant the location in her dreams was probably Vancouver or somewhere in the

Lower Mainland. The events in her dreams took place prior to the tattoo craze but after the big hair of the eighties.

She found where she'd written Dr. A. Cohen's name in her journal and circled it. Beneath it, she underlined *department head* and added *psychiatrist*.

Jane wanted to drag Sadie with her to the library, but she didn't dare get between Sadie and her z's without a suitable bribe. She dressed and slipped into the kitchen, where Sadie's bag of coffee lay on its side, empty. Jane would have to make a coffee run. She grabbed her wallet and headed out.

Upon her return, Jane closed the door to their apartment with a hip-check. It shut with a bang.

Sadie stirred. "What the hell, Jane?"

"I brought you a treat." Jane held out a tray with a large Americano for Sadie, a spicy chai tea for herself, and a cinnamon knot the size of her head for them to share. Jane dropped the tray to the trunk and sat on the sofa, forcing Sadie to move her feet to make room for her. Jane twisted Sadie's coffee cup out of the tray.

Sadie glared as she scooted upright. "This better be good." She reached for the cup and took a sip, and her features softened. "What's up?"

"You're out of coffee."

Sadie's glare returned.

"Sorry. Couldn't resist. You're just such a party in the morning." Jane pulled her tea from the tray and tasted it. "My dreams are changing."

Sadie lowered her cup.

"They're coming every night, getting more intense."

"How so?"

"The voices are clear now. And I feel the temperature, as if I'm there—physically there."

"What's it mean?"

Jane shrugged. "No clue. I've been dreaming about this woman. Her name's Rebecca Morrow. She describes these visions she has. They sound so much like my dreams." Jane took another sip of her tea. "I want to find her."

"Don't. It'll only rip your heart out. Again."

"Not this time," Jane said. "This is different, not like when I was a kid. I'm not trying to offer sympathy. Rebecca is seeing a doctor. A psychiatrist. He's agreed to help her. They may have found a way for her to control her visions, maybe even stop them. If they have, I want to know how they did it."

Jane knew the labels put on people like her—psychic, clairvoyant, mind reader, oracle. Those labels didn't fit. She didn't see the future, only the past. And her dreams didn't help people, couldn't guide them to something better, or steer them from disaster. They were disturbing: a psychic leak that needed to be plugged.

"O . . . kay," Sadie said. "Who is she?"

"That's the thing. I don't know her—not personally anyway, which is strange because you know I'm always somehow connected to the people in my dreams. I must have met her, or someone close to her, but I can't place her. Not yet."

"Any idea where she lives?"

Jane shook her head. "Has to be close by, though, don't you think?"

"That's not a lot to go on. How are you going to find her?"

She took a sip of her tea. "How are *we* going to find her?"

Jane had to agree to do Sadie's laundry before Sadie finally caved. An hour later, they stood inside the Kitsilano Public Library. A scent memory hit Jane. "What is that? Kiddy sweat and old glue?"

"I hate libraries. They smell like school," Sadie quipped. She nudged Jane. "There's the help desk."

They started forward but were cut off by two girls who looked about five or six. Each girl had an uneven stack of picture books in her arms. They spoke in excited whispers as they dashed across Jane and Sadie's path. A stern *shush* followed them.

Jane and Sadie continued toward the desk. Sadie mumbled under her breath, "He doesn't look like any librarian I remember."

Jane had to agree. It wasn't just the beard stubble—it was the cleft chin, the studious expression, and the bed head. The man had not an ounce of nerd on him. He shifted his attention from a computer screen to Sadie as she stepped forward.

"Are you the librarian?"

"One of them," he said, smiling like a love-struck teenager. Sadie had that effect on men. They were helpless to resist her when she and her bouncy blonde curls decided to flirt. Within minutes, he'd escorted her to one of their computers and helped her sign into their system. Concierge service.

"I'll message this computer with a list of searchable sites," he said.

"Just click on the message when it pops up. Won't take a minute." He scooted his plastic chair back and it knocked into Jane. "I'm sorry," he said. "Didn't see you there." In Sadie's company, they never did.

The list of searchable sites was the gold Jane had been looking for. They started with Rebecca Morrow, typing her name into each of a dozen sites, guessing at a range of birth years and possible last known cities of residence. Few of the sites offered photos. They copied the results to an email and moved on to Dr. A. Cohen. His name returned several solid hits but nothing current. Again, they collected the results and emailed them to Jane's address. She sensed countless hours of follow-up ahead of her.

When they'd looked up all they could, they signed off the computer and headed back to the information desk. "Thanks for your help," Sadie said to the librarian.

"My pleasure." He handed Sadie his card. "Anytime." Jane knew without looking that his personal cell number would be scrawled across the back.

Returning to Sadie's car, Jane sighed at the impossible breadth of their search. "This is going to take way longer than I thought. Rebecca could have moved, or be dead, for all we know."

"Way to stay positive, Narc," Sadie said. "We've only just started."

Jane heard Sadie's *we*, and the thought of the upcoming search felt a little less bleak.

After Sadie left for work, Jane gathered her own laundry as well as Sadie's and headed up to the laundromat on Fourth Avenue. She was flipping through a vintage *Chatelaine* magazine when her phone rang. She recognized the professor's number.

"Ariane has arrived. Will you meet with her?"

Despite her misgivings, Jane was curious about this woman and what she could tell her about her birthmarks. She agreed to meet her at Nate's home the next morning.

Jane fell asleep on the sofa before Sadie got home.

Visiting Dream

Jane finds herself on the side of a highway, asphalt under her bare feet. A highway overpass looms to her left. Stars twinkle overhead and frogs croak close by. A transport truck thunders out from under the overpass. Her heart pounds and her nightshirt and hair are pulled into the vortex of air as it passes. Quiet returns, as does the frog song. A car whizzes past, and then another in the opposite direction.

She sees headlights in the distance and watches another vehicle approach. Its headlights sway gently, left and right, as if it's waltzing toward her. It's in the far lane, but she steps back, unsure if she's safely out of the vehicle's swerving path. The car speeds in her direction and she watches in horror as it careens off the toe of the overpass, flips onto its passenger side, and skids in a spray of sparks that light up the night. The sound of crunching metal reverberates through her. Through the centre overpass supports, she sees that the vehicle has spun around. Metal groans and then silence returns.

She checks for traffic and crosses to the median. A flame licks up the vehicle's exposed chassis. And then another. The flames feed on something dripping from the undercarriage. Jane runs toward the car as the flames flare. Startled by loud pops, she turns to see a transport truck hissing to a stop. The driver jumps from the cab with a fire extinguisher in his hands. But the flames are well fed and unwavering. Screams erupt from inside the car.

Jane rounds the wreckage and sees a figure emerge from the bent frame of the windshield. A man, staggering and covered in blood. He collapses feet from the vehicle. The truck driver aims the nozzle of the fire extinguisher at the blown-out back window. Flames dance inside and a child's head whips back and forth. His screams tear chunks out of Jane's soul.

The fire extinguisher clanks to the pavement and the truck driver reaches inside. It feels like an eternity passes before the truck driver pulls the child out. He lifts the child in his arms, races away from the vehicle, and then sets the child on the side of the road. Jane looks back to the wreck and sees a woman in the front passenger seat caught up in her seatbelt, hanging limp. Her body is engulfed in a sea of flames.

Jane stands above the child, whose screams have subsided into whimpers. His eyes roll back into his head and he stills.

The scream that woke Jane was her own. The child she'd dreamed of was Ethan. She bit into her fist, stifling her anguish. God, she hated these dreams. She listened for Sadie, hoping she hadn't woken her.

The car had been weaving. Had Ethan's father been impaired? Was the woman in the car Ethan's mother? She couldn't have survived that— no one could have.

18 | Jane

August 14

The next morning, Jane had difficulty shaking the dream. It felt like a vile hangover.

"You okay?" Sadie asked, taking her coffee to the sofa. She plopped down beside Jane, who'd wrapped her arms around her knees. "Bad dream?"

"Yeah," Jane said. "Ethan."

"I guess it was just a matter of time. Want to talk about it?"

Sometimes it helped to spill the details—kind of like pulling the plug in a sink full of dirty water. And Sadie was the only one she could tell. "He told me he'd been in a car accident when he was kid. That his father had been driving. But I saw the car swerving all over the road. His dad had to have been drunk or stoned. The car caught fire. If a trucker hadn't come by and pulled Ethan out, he'd be dead. And someone else was in the car. I think it was his mom." Jane shivered at the memory of the flames licking up the body.

"Does he talk about her—his mom?"

Jane sifted through their previous discussions. "No." She rubbed her face and shook out her hands. "I'm going to shower."

She braced her hands on the shower stall wall and let the warm water sluice down on her head. The morning-after-the-nightmare routine was always worse when she'd dreamed of someone she cared about. She took her time, burying her dream in the past by focusing on details that anchored her in the present. She and Sadie had the day off. Maybe they'd spar later, or follow up on the leads from the library. And she had an appointment with the professor to meet the woman from Peru. That would likely be interesting enough to chase the nightmare from her head.

By the time she'd emerged from the bathroom, releasing a cloud of steam, she felt better. She ate a piece of toast and, with the help of the pound of coffee Jane had picked up on her way home from the laundro-mat, talked Sadie into accompanying her to Nate's place.

The professor lived in Point Grey, a wealthy neighbourhood close to UBC's campus. Homes here were either maintained or bulldozed, and every inch of green space was manicured and planted to perfection. But parking was scarce. Sadie drove around the block twice before she found a spot.

Jane shook her hair into place as she and Sadie walked up Nate's front path. Though smaller than his neighbours' homes, his tiny bungalow was probably still worth seven figures.

"If this chick starts some mumbo-jumbo, I'm outta there," Sadie said.

"Yeah, I'll race you to the door." Jane reached out and rang the door-bell. "Remember what I said. No personal stuff. I'm curious about what they have to say, but I don't want them nosing around in my life."

Footfalls approached from inside. When Nate opened the door, his gaze jumped from Jane to Sadie and back again. "Hi, Joyce."

"This is Sadie. My roommate. I hope you don't mind. I asked her to come along."

"Not at all," he said, covering his surprise with good manners. "Glad to meet you, Sadie. Come in." He held open the door. The scent of cinnamon and something deep fried enticed them inside. "Follow me." His flip-flops slapped across the slate tiles in the foyer and down a hallway that led to the back of the house. They followed the smell of donuts to a compact kitchen.

A petite woman with a long ebony ponytail turned from the stove to greet them. She wiped her hands on an apron. Like Nate, she looked to be in her midthirties.

"Ariane Rebaza, this is Joyce Walker," Nate said. Ariane's warm brown eyes held Jane's as the women shook hands. Considering the pull of Ariane's curiosity, Jane was impressed by her steadfast gaze.

"This is my roommate, Sadie."

"What smells so good?" Sadie asked, as she shook Ariane's hand.

"A Peruvian favourite," Ariane said. She spoke with a Spanish accent. "*Picarones*. My mother insisted I make them for Nathaniel. They're his favourite *postre*."

Jane decided the smile Ariane offered *Nathaniel* was more than that of a colleague.

Nate motioned toward the table. "Have a seat." The retro chrome and Arborite table with its matching chairs would have looked at home in a 1950's sitcom. Jane and Sadie took their seats while Nate opened a kitchen cupboard and retrieved another cup and plate. He joined them and poured the tea. "I hope you like English breakfast." He handed Jane a cup and addressed Sadie. "Tea or coffee?"

"Coffee. Black, thanks."

At the stove, Ariane used a slotted spoon to remove the golden-brown donuts from a shallow pan. She laid them on a tray lined with paper towels.

Nate brought a pot of coffee to the table, poured a cup for Sadie and another for himself, and took his seat. "Thanks for coming."

An awkward silence hung in the air until Ariane approached with the Peruvian treats. She arranged two donuts on each plate and poured a pool of warm syrup over them. "Tell me what you think," she said, and took the last seat at the table.

Nate scarfed one down in three forkfuls. "Just as I remember," he said, with his eyes at half-mast, looking as serene as a junkie on the nod.

"Delicious," Sadie said.

Jane severed a piece with her fork, stabbed it, and swirled it in the sauce. The syrup didn't taste like anything she'd eaten before. It was sweet and spicy with cloves and cinnamon and a touch of citrus. "They're good."

Ariane smiled with pride. She took a small bite and chewed, seemingly testing its flavour. "Not bad."

Conversation around the table came in stilted fits and starts as it does when strangers try to make small talk. When everyone's forks quieted, Nate stood to clear the dishes. He returned with a tablet and handed it to Ariane.

"I'd like to show you something," Ariane said, and scraped her chair closer to Jane's. She tapped the screen and swiped through endless rows of photos before she slowed the scroll. She tapped on a photo and enlarged it. "You're familiar with these?"

It was a photo of the knotted strings. "Yes. Nate sent me a link. *Khipu* or something like that."

"*Khipus* when there's more than one. In Inca times, each of those strands would have told a story. Each knot, the distance between them, the colours—all meant something. They're coded communiqués. Runners would have carried them between commanders during battles or to facilitate negotiations. The *Khipus* in that British Museum collection have only recently come to light. We haven't deciphered them yet.

"But *Khipus* weren't the only artifacts discovered in that collection. They also found this." Ariane swiped to the next photo. It was a thin strip of richly coloured cloth that had been pinned to a board. A ruler drawn on the board beside the cloth indicated the strip was five feet long. "This piece hasn't been made public."

"What is it?" Jane asked.

Ariane swiped to the next photo. "Here's a close-up."

Sadie stretched her neck to get a look. "Damn."

The pattern in the strip of fabric was Jane's birthmark, repeated, just as it appeared on Jane's skin.

"I don't understand," Jane said.

"Though I can't be sure, I think I know what it is," Ariane said. "What it means."

"What?" Jane said.

"It's Inca and similar to a *Khipu*. It's a coded message."

"What's the message?"

"Good question," Ariane said. "When I first saw that piece in the collection, I recognized the design. A ribbon just like it is tacked to the doorframe of my family's home in Lima. Our ancestors are Inca. The house and the ribbon have been in our family for generations."

"Why is it tacked to a door?" Sadie asked.

"Our family's lore says it's there to ward away evil."

Jane pushed back in her chair. "You're telling me these birthmarks are some kind of message? Like an evil eye?"

"It's more than that. It's a blood mark. Anyone who tries to take your life pays with their own," Ariane said. "Look, I know this sounds . . . crazy, but your birthmarks are an exact replication. At least the one on your hand is. That can't be random."

"Not *exact*," Jane said, crossing her arms. She wasn't about to let Ariane label her like some specimen. "My marks aren't continuous like that ribbon. The width of them varies—"

Sadie butted in. "She's got strips all over her arms, her back, her—"

Jane kicked her under the table and Sadie cut her description short.

"Like I said, they're not the same."

"I think you'll find they are. If you've had them from birth, you would have received them in the womb. You would have been in the fetal position when that ribbon was wrapped around you."

Here comes the hocus-pocus, Jane thought. "You're right. That does sound crazy."

"It's an occupational hazard, I'm afraid." Ariane set the tablet down. "Forgive me if I'm being insensitive, but I'm curious. You have more marks under your headscarf?"

Jane raised her hand and smoothed the bandana in place, a reflexive gesture.

"Would you show us?" Ariane asked.

Showing anyone her marks was a rare event, but Jane found she didn't mind in this instance, even if Ariane was stretching the definition of plausible. She pushed the scarf into her hair and studied Ariane's reaction.

Ariane moved closer. "Fascinating," she said. "May I?" She raised her hand. Jane shrugged. Nate stood to get a better look. Ariane's touch was light, her fingers cool. "Exquisite."

"That's a first. People aren't usually so complimentary."

"Yes, I'm sure." Ariane settled into her chair again and Jane tugged the bandana back into place. "Perhaps if we knew more about your family, we could figure out why you have those markings."

"I don't have a family. I grew up in foster care."

"You don't know who your mother is?" Ariane asked. Jane shook her head. "Father?" Again, Jane shook her head.

"Have you tried to find them?" Nate asked.

"Yes. They don't want to be found."

"That's puzzling," Ariane said. "Because my theory is that your parents arranged for the mark to be placed on you. To protect you."

"Protect me?" Jane's laugh came out in a derisive sputter. "Then my marks must be defective. I could have used some of that mojo growing up. Took more than a few beatings. Don't suppose there's a return policy?"

Ariane hid a smile. "It can't be easy living with those marks. But they're intended to ward off death, not prevent bumps and scrapes."

Sadie shifted to the edge of her seat. "What did you say?"

"The markings protect her life."

Sadie looked to Jane. "That would explain how you survived the fire."

"What fire?" Ariane and Nate said in chorus.

Jane flared her nostrils at Sadie. She took a deep breath. "Six months after I was abandoned, a couple adopted me. I don't remember them. I'm told we lived in a two-storey house in Maple Ridge." A deep V formed between her eyebrows. Telling this story always felt like a confession of guilt. Jane focused on her crossed arms. "When I was two years old, the house burned to the ground. My adoptive parents died in the fire. It was classified as arson."

"She was found on the lawn, untouched," Sadie said, with an I-told-you-so air.

Nate sat back and raked a hand through his hair. "Ariane is right about your marks."

Jane looked up. "Or I was playing with matches," she said quietly. "And killed them."

"No," Sadie said. "You also survived the car accident. Or are you going to take the blame for that as well?"

Jane frowned.

Sadie plowed ahead. "Her foster parents drove off the Sea to Sky Highway. They drowned. Ja—Joyce was found in an air pocket in the back window."

"It was an accident," Jane said. Or a curse. A growing sense of unease straightened Jane's spine.

"The accident investigation said the car was cut off," Sadie said. "That's not an accident."

Jane glared at Sadie with a look that said *put a cork in it.*

Nate intervened. "How old were you?"

Sadie looked pointedly at the table but held her tongue.

"Five," Jane said. Sometimes the scent of warm chocolate chip cookies invoked gauzy memories of her foster mom, but her foster dad remained a shadow with no face. "Foster parents weren't beating down the ministry's door after that. Killing off two sets of parents has that effect."

"There's another explanation, if you're willing to hear it," Ariane said. When Jane didn't object, she continued. "Someone set the fire to kill you. When that didn't work, they bided their time and tried another approach, running you and your foster parents off the road."

"You just said if someone tried to kill me, they'd be dead. Are you trying to tell me several people want me dead? Because that's ridiculous."

"Not necessarily," Nate said. "They could have hired someone to do the deed."

Jane rubbed her arms against a growing chill.

"What kind of sicko wants to kill a little kid?" Sadie said.

"That's what we need to find out," Ariane said. "We need to find Joyce's parents."

"Well, good luck with that," Jane said.

"What would happen if Joyce were to have her birthmarks lasered off?" Sadie asked.

Jane darted a glance at Ariane.

"I don't know," Ariane said, quirking a shoulder. "I can only infer that without the ritual markings, she would have no protection from whatever, or whomever, she's being shielded from."

Jane thought about the mark that had disappeared from her foot. Maybe she shouldn't be so happy it was gone.

"Have there been other *accidents*?" Nate asked.

"No," Jane said.

"Could be that whoever it was learned what the markings meant," Nate said. "Gave up."

"Or died," Sadie offered, along with a hopeful smile.

"Or they're biding their time," Ariane said. "Waiting for another opportunity."

"That's terrifying," Jane said. "Thanks so much."

Ariane cringed. "My apologies. I'm simply thinking out loud."

"What about your MCFD file?" Sadie said to Jane. "Could be a clue about your parents in there. Nelson can probably get his hands on it."

"MCFD?" Ariane asked.

"Ministry of Children and Family Development," Sadie said.

"And Nelson?"

"Our former social worker," Sadie said.

"I've seen the file," Jane said. "There's nothing in it."

"It's worth another look," Ariane said. "Ask him. I also know someone who can help. Hunter Bishop. He's an investigator. Does research for me from time to time. He's used to my type of crazy."

Sadie snapped her head up. "An investigator?"

Jane shot a warning glare at Sadie, and Ariane caught it. "Something we should know?" Ariane asked.

"No. I'll call Nelson when I get home. Thanks for the donuts." Jane stood. "Sadie, you coming?"

Sadie stood, inhaling as if leaving were a hardship. "Nice meeting you."

Out on the sidewalk, Jane marched to the car, ranting under her breath. "Do you not remember me saying no personal stuff? That I didn't want them nosing around in my life? Ariane didn't come all the way from Peru to enlighten me. There'll be a price to pay."

Sadie threw her hands up. "The price is obvious," she bit out. "Would it kill you to give her some harmless details about your life—details she could get from old newspapers? That's hardly *nosing around your life*."

The previous evening's nightmare loomed in Jane's mind. "The harmless details aren't the ones that keep me up at night."

Sadie skidded to a stop. "You asked me to give up my day off to help you find this Rebecca woman, and I did. Ariane has a bona fide investigator who could probably find Rebecca in a heartbeat and what? You're too proud to ask?"

"You think I haven't thought about it? I have." Jane blew out a breath, and with it, her anger. "But how do I do that without telling them about my dreams?"

Sadie frowned. "I don't know." And then, without missing a beat, she added, "Make some shit up."

On the drive home, Jane called Nelson. He agreed to get a copy of her ministry file on the condition she agree to call the investment company and make an appointment to deal with the inheritance.

Back in their apartment, Sadie tossed her bag on the trunk. "I've been thinking about what Ariane said. About your birthmarks."

"What about them?"

"She said you would have gotten them when you were in the fetal position. Some of your birthmarks line up. Like the ones on your right arm."

Jane dropped to the sofa. She knew that if she bent her right arm, the birthmark that crossed above her biceps lined up with the mark on her forearm. She'd known it for years. Now she considered a new and disturbing possibility. "Coincidence?"

"There's only one way to find out," Sadie said. "Strip down and let's see."

Jane hesitated. Sadie made an impatient gesture with her arm. In her mind, Jane mapped out her birthmarks. She stripped down to her bra and undies and lay down knowing the answer even before she tucked in her arms and legs.

"Holy shit," Sadie said.

Jane uncurled and sprung to her feet, steadying herself. "Don't say it." She pressed a hand to her breastbone, holding back the anxiety that felt like heartburn.

"Ariane was right."

"No." Jane reached for her clothes and started tugging them on.

"Jane! This means something."

"Weren't you the no hocus-pocus girl?"

"Mumbo-jumbo, actually."

"Same thing." Jane zipped up her jeans and trotted to the kitchen. She paced back and forth in front of the cupboards wringing her hands. "It could have been the umbilical cord. An IUD. Maybe some weird thing with her womb," she said, wiggling her arm in the air.

"What if this explains the fire?" Sadie said. "Your birthmarks protected you. Just like Ariane said."

"Stop it. It's impossible. You sound as whacked as Ariane."

Sadie held up her hands. "Call me wacked if you want, but if those marks are disappearing, you'd better hope Ariane can figure out what they're protecting you from. Or who."

There had to be a rational explanation. There just had to. Because if Ariane was right, the implications were frightening.

Sadie's phone rang and she reached to answer it. "Now?" she said, and then checked the time. "Sure. I'll be there in half an hour."

"The restaurant," she said to Jane. "So much for a day off. But I'd better take every shift I can this month in case Cynthia gets pissy."

Jane held her tongue against an old argument that never went anywhere useful. It was hard to fight Cynthia's easy cash.

Sadie got ready for work and bustled out the door. Moments later, she rushed back inside. "Got a damn flat. Would you give me a lift?"

"Yeah, sure." Jane jumped up to grab her bike jacket and stuffed her credit card and some cash in her pocket.

Sadie found the spare helmet and grumbled as they made their way outside. "That flat's gonna cost me tonight's shift and the cab home's gonna wipe out another hour's pay. Shit."

"I don't mind picking you up," Jane said. "Text me when you're ready to leave."

Jane walked her bike out from under Mrs. Carper's window. For once the busybody wasn't keeping vigil.

They stopped in front of Lodestones and Sadie hopped off the postage-stamp pillion seat. Jane set the kickstand and dismounted.

"Want to come in?" Sadie asked. "I can comp you dinner."

Jane smoothed her hair over her birthmark. "Not tonight. I'm going to pick up some milk and then get a start on finding Rebecca. Need anything from the store?"

"No. I'll call you when I finish up." Sadie turned and walked into Lodestones. The sidewalk patio was packed with customers taking in the warm August evening.

Back home, Jane resumed her search for Rebecca Morrow. Ariane's words taunted her, but Jane had nothing worth protecting. If she had, she wouldn't have been abandoned at birth. And if her birthmarks were intentional, someone had made a cruel mistake.

19 | Rick

Rick raced up the driveway to his parents' Langley home. It was mid-morning. His mother had sounded uncharacteristically shaken over the phone.

"He fainted," she said, when Rick tore into the kitchen. "Don't let him tell you otherwise. Refuses to go to the hospital."

"Where is he?"

"In the living room."

Rick strode down the hallway. His father was an obstinate old bastard and wouldn't appreciate his visit.

The tirade began before Rick made it to the room's threshold.

"It was the goddamn carpet. I tripped. Haven't fainted in my life." Rick's father sat in one of the two wing-backed recliners, his canes propped up against the chair's arms. A round rosewood table sat between the chairs.

"Regardless, you took a tumble. Did you hit your head?"

His father's frown said no.

"Can you walk?"

"Obviously. How do you think I got in here?"

Rick folded his arms. "Then humour me. Stand up and switch chairs."

"Last I knew you were a psychiatrist, not an orthopod," he grumbled, but he grasped his canes with shaky hands and stood. "Your mother can't see. You should have known better than to come running out here. She gets a notion in her head . . ." His voice trailed off. "Satisfied?" he said, having travelled the four feet to reach the other chair. He was either putting on a good show, or he hadn't suffered a serious injury.

"You'll go to the hospital if the pain gets worse?"

"I'm not an idiot," his father said, settling into the chair. "I knew a thing or two about broken bones before you were born."

Exasperated, Rick sank into the chair his father had vacated. He'd probably had a spell of low blood pressure. Maybe when the old man wasn't so touchy about it, Rick would suggest a checkup. He might need a pacemaker.

Feeling her way around the door jamb, his mother shuffled into the room. "I can do it," she said defensively, holding up a hand to the men. Arms extended, she made it safely to the sofa.

"He'll be fine, Mom."

"Exactly what I told her," his father mumbled.

A long-overdue discussion hung in the air. Rick smoothed his hands on the damask armrests. "It's time you thought about bringing someone in to help out. Someone close by who could maybe do some cooking. One or two hours a day." Someone who could check on them and save Rick an unnecessary trip. A situation which was only going to get worse.

"We don't need anyone else poking around here," his father said. "You already have a gardener and a cleaner coming around at our expense. We're not royalty. We certainly don't have unlimited income."

"You're not destitute either. Surely Michael can free up funds to make your lives more comfortable." Rick had long known Mikey had talked his parents into investing with his firm in Victoria. He hoped they hadn't foolishly turned over their entire portfolio.

"Michael has done a marvellous job with our investments, hasn't he, dear?" his mother said.

Rick steepled his fingers. "Michael has a gardener, a cleaner, a cook, a personal trainer, and a driver. He's taking care of himself. You should too."

"Michael can afford it," his father said.

"And he needs the help," his mother chirped. "He's so busy with work. Spends far too much time in the office if you ask me."

Poor Mikey. Rick was sick of hearing about his brother's Big Job. A big job he'd inexplicably skyrocketed to after years of mediocre work, most of it in the firm's bullpen. Something hadn't smelled right about Mikey's sudden promotion to partner three years ago. Rick suspected he'd sunk to insider trading or a Ponzi scheme of some kind. Unfortunately, Rick's attempts to uncover the dirt on him had gone nowhere.

"You could also use the help," Rick said, but he knew it was futile. Next time his mother called in a panic, perhaps he'd suggest she call Mikey.

On the table beside him, Rick noticed a pale-blue triangle corner stapled to a document peeking out from under a newspaper. A legal document. "What's this?" he asked, pulling it out.

"Not your concern," his father said, waving at him to put it down.

"Power of attorney?" Rick quickly perused the document. "You're signing over power of attorney to Michael?" Heat flushed Rick's face.

"Well, it is his bailiwick," his father said.

"He's an investment manager, not a lawyer."

"At our age it's a smart precaution," his mother said.

"This was his idea?"

Rick's father leaned forward. "Much like it was your idea that we name you on our representation agreements for health-care decisions. I didn't hear Michael complain about that."

"Why would he? He'd never get here in time to make a medical decision."

"Stop it," his mother said.

"I hope you at least had it drawn up by a proper lawyer. Your own lawyer."

"That's enough," his father said. "This is our decision, not yours. Now put that down."

Rick shuddered to think of the control they'd handed over to his brother. One more insult. If they slid into dementia, Mikey would pick clean the bones of their estate. Rick wouldn't be surprised if his brother had already started.

20 | Sadie

S adie didn't like taking over another server's section, especially mid-service, but the hostess was experienced and diverted new diners to another section until Sadie had a chance to catch up. She picked up a water pitcher from the bussing station, donned a smile, and headed outside to the patio.

She turned right, did a quick assessment, and took an order from the four-top of women who'd finished their martinis. Sadie said she'd be right back with their bottle of wine, and then turned to the left side of the patio. She filled a few water glasses, promised to check on an order, and then approached the lone diner at a two-top. He had his back to her. She reached for his near-empty water glass and began filling it as she recited the waitstaff psalm: "Hello, my name is Sadie, and I'll—"

The diner glanced up from his phone.

Recognizing him, Sadie jerked back and spilled water across the table.

"Whoa!" Mr. Kristan said, shifting away from the water trickling dangerously close to his lap.

"What are you doing here?" Sadie's voice came out in a harsh whisper. Her heart slammed against her ribs.

"My apologies," he said, with a disapproving scowl. He shook out his napkin. "I didn't know you worked here." He lifted his water glass out of the puddle and dabbed at it as he darted a furtive glance around. Diners watched them with covert glances.

Sadie plastered a benign smile on her face and stepped back to the table feeling like a fly trapped in Mr. Kristan's web.

An awkward silence stretched on.

"You arrived on the back of that motorcycle?"

"My car had a flat."

"That was your roommate?"

She narrowed her eyes. "You didn't know I worked here?"

"Rest assured, I wouldn't be here if I had." He glanced at her nametag. "Sadie."

Shit! One more piece of her privacy slid into the trash. "No one uses their real name here." The deception was worth a shot.

"Is that so?" Another stretch of silence followed. "Listen. This is uncomfortable for both of us. I'll just . . . go," he said, rising.

"No, don't." The damage was done. His leaving without ordering would only draw more attention.

He resumed his seat. "Had you mentioned your employment here, we could have avoided this . . . situation."

Sadie raised her chin. "What can I get you?"

"Bring me your daily soup."

Sadie nodded and scooted back inside to enter his order. The hostess approached. "Everything all right?"

"Yeah, fine. Just clumsy." Sadie let out a sigh. "Gonna be a long night."

The hostess leaned in. "Hang in there. It'll be over before you know it."

If only, Sadie thought. "Hey, did that guy ask to be seated in my section?"

"No. Just wanted to sit outside. You know him?"

"I think I met him at a party or something. Did he come in alone?"

"Yeah." She glanced back at the hostess desk. "Duty calls. I gotta go."

The hostess walked away, and Sadie planted herself at the kitchen's service window, grateful Mr. Kristan had ordered the one item she could get her hands on quickly. When his soup order was up, she delivered it immediately. One of the four-top women glared at her. Shit! Their wine. She returned to the bar to place their order. While she waited for the bartender to get the wine, she loitered out of Mr. Kristan's sight, by the bussing station, where she could keep a discreet eye on her tables. The steam from the dishwasher was only slightly less nauseating than the smell of plate scrapings—cold fries, caramel, and the vinegary dregs of coleslaw—all dumped together.

She pressed into the bussing station's recess when she saw Mr. Kristan rise. He dropped some bills on the table and made his exit. Barely five minutes had passed since she served him. She collected the women's wine from the bar and headed outside to mock cheers. On her return trip, she glanced at Mr. Kristan's untouched meal and collected the money he'd left, surprised to see that he'd included a tip.

Still, Sadie's apprehension about Mr. Kristan's unexpected appearance persisted throughout her shift. What were the odds that out of all the restaurants in the city, he'd end up at hers? Her self-preservation reflexes were pretty well honed, but she found herself questioning her instincts. Was she overreacting? Or were there fifty thousand reasons clouding her judgment?

With her closeout finished, Sadie texted Jane to tell her she was ready to leave. During the short drive home, Sadie shifted her head from side to side scanning for a tail that wasn't there. After they dismounted, Sadie removed her helmet and shook off her paranoia.

Jane rolled her motorbike onto the gravel under Mrs. Carper's window and joined Sadie by the side door. "You look spooked. My driving scare you?"

"Never. Just thinking about getting the flat fixed."

She wanted to tell Jane about Mr. Kristan showing up at the restaurant but hesitated. He knew where she worked, but did he know where she lived? If he did, he knew enough that one call to their landlord would have them evicted. They'd worked so hard to get this apartment. She'd hate to be the cause of them losing it. That thought hung in the air for a moment, but she soon dismissed it. She was overreacting, being paranoid. She even felt a little foolish about it now that she was home. His showing up at the restaurant was just a coincidence. She didn't need to bother Jane with it.

Inside the apartment, Jane set her helmet on the floor. "I'm hitting the sofa." Given Jane's early hours, she took the sofa more often than not.

"Okay. The bathroom's all yours." Sadie headed to the dresser and took a swig of her vodka. As she undressed, she wondered if Jane might learn of Mr. Kristan's visit to the restaurant in one of her dreams. That was the thing about Jane. There was no privacy. Sadie's deepest darkest secrets were Jane's for the taking.

Sadie remembered the night she learned about Jane's dreams. It had been a few days after Jane arrived at the group home still dazed from the abortion that had been done *in her best interests*. Sadie had felt bad for her. Thinking she could use some cheering up, she broke into the pantry and pilfered a proper party. She'd stuffed cans of soda, an industrial-sized sack of chocolate chips, bags of potato chips, a solitary can of cocktail wieners, and a bottle of vodka into a pillowcase. She hid the vodka and offered Jane first pick of the loot. Everything else, save the vodka and the party wieners, made it to the other kids in the warren of bedrooms.

The following night, Jane sought out Sadie's bunk in the middle of the night and asked for a shot of vodka. Sadie hadn't told anyone that she'd stolen the liquor, but after Jane described Sadie's escapade in undeniable detail, Sadie admitted to it. Jane would have finished the bottle, but Sadie wouldn't let her. Barely a teen and Sadie was already familiar with a hangover.

From then on, they'd watched each other's backs.

21 | Jane

Visiting Dream

J ane wakes in an unfamiliar room. A richly coloured Oriental carpet covers the centre of a hardwood floor. Above the sofa hangs an abstract painting in tones of green. Opposite the sofa are two matching chairs and a coffee table. Beyond the chairs is a closed panelled door. Jane recognizes the ornate ivory letter opener that lies next to a sheet of paper on the table.

At a right angle to the sofa, a window offers a view of the street. Through the gauzy sheers, Jane sees an older-model truck parked close to the front walk. She recognizes Rebecca, who steps away from the truck's passenger door and makes her way up the walk.

A knock on the front door brings footsteps down a hall beyond the panelled door. Jane hears Rebecca and Rick exchange muffled greetings. Moments later, the panelled door opens and they enter the room. Rick's not wearing the white coat.

Jane can tell by Rebecca's familiarity that this is not the first time she's been in this room. Rebecca drops her purse and plops down beside it on the sofa.

"How was your week?" Rick asks, taking a seat opposite.

"Not good. Like I told you. The visions are back." Rebecca crosses her arms. "I need a refill on the prescription."

"I can't give you more Ambien. We discussed this." Rick picks up the letter opener. "The only way to manage your visions long term is to learn to control them."

Rebecca uncrosses her arms but only to push herself to the edge of her seat. "If not Ambien, then something else."

Rick raises his eyebrows. "Do you not want to get better?" His tone is condescending, as if he's talking to a child.

"You know I do."

"Then you need to commit yourself to doing the hard work. I will guide you. What were your visions about this time?"

"Not what you'd hoped. The hypnotherapy didn't work. I haven't been able to target my visions to any of the events you suggested. Not even close."

"Tell me." Rick settles into his chair with his elbows on the armrests. His attention is on Rebecca as he absently twirls the letter opener.

"You don't want to hear," Rebecca says, but Rick stares her down. Rebecca turns to the window. "My vision was of you again. You were being interviewed by a man with a British accent. Something about your dismissal from your residency in Canada. He said you'd displayed a gross lack of judgment."

"Ah, Dr. Chadwick," Rick says. He crosses his ankle over his knee. "Sadly, he was right." Rebecca jerks her head back around, surprise in her features. "My lack of judgment wasn't related to my competency as a doctor. I'd had an affair with the hospital director's wife." A shy smile crosses his face then vanishes. "Thankfully, Dr. Chadwick saw me through my residency and kept me on for a few years."

Rebecca's expression softens, but her hands remain fisted.

"Learn to control your visions, Rebecca, and they won't control you. You ready to tackle this?"

"More hypnotherapy?"

"I think that's the best course of action. This time, I'll be more specific." Rick sets the letter opener down on the coffee table and reaches for the piece of paper. He hands it to Rebecca. "This is a Rembrandt painting. Keep it in your mind while we work today."

As Rebecca gets comfortable on the sofa, Rick moves to a filing cabinet in the corner. He pushes a button and a CD spins behind a layer of glass. The sound of waves gently lapping at a distant shore fills the room.

Then Rick removes a folder and returns to his seat. He opens it on his lap and lifts a newspaper clipping.

Jane crouches to read the page beneath.

Patient X. Female.
Twenty-three years old. Good physical health.
Presents with visions, underlying cause unknown.
Patient describes historically accurate events to which
she has no obvious connection.

Rick speaks softly, taking Rebecca through relaxation exercises. On the page, below the typewritten lines, are handwritten notes:

The doctor who never gave up.
The doctor with the golden touch.
View from the Top of the Heap.

The statements read like book titles.

Who killed Kennedy? SOLVED.
What really happened in Roswell? SOLVED.
Every unresolved crime in history. SOLVED.

Every is circled several times.

Nobel consideration.

This line is encased in stars.

Goosebumps race up Jane's arms.

The doctor watches Rebecca carefully as his voice becomes a low drone, background noise, innocuous. "It's September 4, 1972," he says, and repeats it several times. "You're in Montreal, at the Museum of Fine Arts." Again, he repeats it. "You're in the Baroque hall looking at a Rembrandt landscape with cottages." After he repeats this, he adds, "Tell me, Rebecca, do you see the painting?"

Rebecca doesn't speak. Jane thinks she's fallen asleep, though that doesn't faze the doctor. "Keep your eyes on the painting, Rebecca. Follow the painting. Remember where it's taken. Remember."

As the doctor speaks, Jane straightens and reads the newspaper clipping. The headline reads "The Skylight Caper." Beneath the heading is a grainy copy of the Rembrandt he described, and three lines.

STOLEN FROM THE MONTREAL MUSEUM OF FINE ART
SEPTEMBER 4, 1972
NEVER RECOVERED.

The doctor sets the clipping back in the folder, stands, and returns the folder to the drawer. He silences the waves and returns to his seat.

He repeats Rebecca's name in ever louder refrains until she stirs. She blinks up at him.

"All done," he says.

Anger burned in Jane's chest as she woke on her own sofa. The bedroom door was closed. She focused on the ceiling while her heart settled. Rick was using Rebecca.

Jane picked up her phone, opened her browser, and typed *art theft Montreal Museum*. The first link produced the Rembrandt painting from her dream. The second link confirmed that the painting still hadn't been recovered.

Relief and disappointment clashed inside her. The Rembrandt was still missing, JFK's murder remained a mystery, and whatever happened in Roswell, New Mexico, continued to be speculation. Rick's self-serving ambition to solve the world's mysteries had been dashed, but the question remained: had he eventually taught Rebecca to control her visions? Maybe even stop them?

She was more convinced than ever that she needed to find Rebecca. Jane's dreams were growing more intense, and she dreaded the thought that she'd end up just like Rebecca: suicidal. But that wouldn't happen if she could control her dreams. Rebecca had the answers. She had to find her.

22 | Sadie

August 15

S adie made a cup of joe and scrolled through the morning updates on her phone. She smiled at a text from Handsome Neighbour. He wanted to get together later. She eagerly agreed and hoped her lace thong and matching bra were clean. A little surprise for Andy if things progressed where she hoped.

She was halfway to the door on her way to work before she remembered her clunker's flat tire. The bus was a poor but thrifty substitute. By 11:00 a.m. she was back at Lodestones settling in for the early lunch arrivals. She looked forward to 7:00 p.m. and the end of her shift, followed by an evening with Boy-Scout Andy.

But her date-night hopes crashed when she checked her phone on her break. Cynthia's Teachers' Pet app pinged with a request—Mr. Kristan. Sadie knew it wasn't a request at all but a command performance. Cynthia was well aware Sadie didn't take gigs until the end of the month, so it was a test. If Sadie didn't take it, Cynthia would make good on her word and freeze her out. How long had it been since she'd made it through a month without a cash infusion? She'd become far too dependent on the ready money and burned with resentment at how easily Cynthia pulled her strings.

So much for a tantalizing date with Andy. She texted him her regrets.

To Sadie's relief, Jane was out when she got home. In a rush, she plucked a short sleeveless dress from its hanger. She recalled that Mr. Kristan had complimented her the last time she'd worn it. After she fixed her makeup, she scratched a quick note to Jane telling her not to wait up, ordered a cab, and grabbed her purse.

23 | Rick

R ick handed over the second payment. His plant had settled in without suspicion, had already secured a key to Jane's apartment, and would dispose of her when the time came. Rick didn't mind spending money when it got him results. Or pleasure, which he intended to get from Sadie shortly.

Seemed he'd done nothing but bleed money since the day he met Rebecca Morrow. Finding the old woman who'd resigned from the hospital hadn't cost much, but getting someone to extract the information from her had taken a toll on his pocketbook. Initially, he'd resented paying for the information, which he dismissed as the ranting gibberish of someone pushed past the brink. He knew better now.

He'd had to borrow money to pay the investigator who located Jane. The man took his bloody time too.

He burned through more cash on his first attempt to eradicate the problem. When that failed, he saved up and tried again. After the second failure, he put proper stock in the old woman's warning. Keeping tabs on Jane was as close as he got after that. It wouldn't be long now though, and he'd finally put his mistake to rest.

He often thought about the night Rebecca showed up in his psych ward. His life, his career, would have unfolded much differently had another doctor been assigned to her. In hindsight, it was unfortunate Rebecca hadn't succeeded the night she slit her wrists.

24 | Jane

Jane was grateful for the monotony of the watering routine. She'd not been able to shake off thoughts of Rick's hypnotherapy treatment. Could she learn to seed her dreams? If she could choose what to dream about, she'd be free of the terrifying nightmares. She'd choose to dream about happy events in the lives of people not marred by trauma; dreams of birthday parties, Christmas mornings, and new puppies.

Controlling her dreams was the cure. Hope glimmered in the distance. And then she recalled her late-night Google search; the Rembrandt painting was still missing. Rebecca hadn't been able to track it to the thief's hiding place. She'd failed to control her visions, or at least that one.

During her lunch break, she found an email from Nelson with her ministry file attached. She opened the file and scrolled through the documents. Ariane's investigator would have to be a magician to find her parents using the scant info in her file. There was nothing in the collection of PDFs she hadn't seen before—except an opportunity. Could getting the professors' help finding Rebecca be as simple as adding a "mystery document" to her file? One that couldn't be ignored?

She opened her phone's note app and typed *Rebecca Morrow, psych patient, suicide attempt.* Below that she added *Rick, psychiatrist treating Rebecca Morrow, dismissed from Canadian residency for gross lack of judgment.* Then, *Dr. Chadwick. British psychiatrist.*

Satisfied with her cryptic note, she stripped the author and date properties from it, saved it as a PDF, and inserted it into the digital file that Nelson had sent.

Yes, she thought, nodding. This might work. And she wouldn't have to spill about her dreams. Even if the investigator didn't understand what the document was, or why it was in her file, he'd be curious. He'd check out the names, locate them. Jane could barely contain her excitement at the thought of being able to talk to Rebecca.

Sadie would be so impressed. Jane dug out Nate's business card and forwarded him the file. She felt as if she'd stepped back from the cliff's edge. Her dreams remained safely hidden.

When Jane arrived home after work, she found a note from Sadie, skimpy on details. She'd be late and Jane should take the bedroom. It was too early in the month for Sadie to be working a gig, so it must have been a date. With whom? Jane wondered.

She still had faith that one day Sadie would fall hard for someone worth getting out of the business for.

Jane flopped to the sofa and reached for her journal. She pulled the pen from the coil, and began the habitual routine she'd neglected the previous day. She scribbled *chai tea, Cheerios, buffalo chicken wrap* . . . and stopped, holding the pen aloft. What was she doing? These notes, this detailed record of her life, hadn't coughed up a single clue. Ever. How many years had she been recording her meals and activities hoping to find a trigger? Wasn't that the textbook definition of insanity?

She traded the notepad for her laptop. She wouldn't waste one more minute recording her daily food choices. The path to controlling her dreams started with finding Rebecca. Even if Rebecca had never learned to control her visions, it didn't mean Jane couldn't. And Rebecca would be someone to talk to; someone who understood. Unless she'd succeeded in killing herself. Jane prayed she wouldn't have a ringside seat to the event.

The evening passed without success, but Jane wasn't deterred. She headed to the shower, inspecting her birthmarks as she got undressed. There'd been no changes. She convinced herself she wasn't disappointed about that, and then Ariane's thoughts about the marks protecting her surfaced. She couldn't figure out Ariane's angle. The only explanation that made sense was that she was a zealot about her culture, actually believed the folklore.

After she towelled off, she found a voice message had come in. It was Ariane thanking her for the file, which Nate had forwarded. Jane felt a ripple of guilt over her deception but let it wash over her. She could live with a little guilt. It was better than exposing her dreams.

As she climbed into bed, her thoughts drifted to Sadie. Jane was curious about her date. Was it the librarian? Maybe it was Andy, their new neighbour. Sadly, neither the librarian nor Andy were good candidates. The librarian had been too eager, and Sadie had already been invited inside the neighbour's apartment, which meant he'd quickly fallen for her charms. Sadie toyed with the men who fell for her. Only someone who challenged her would hold her interest.

Jane fell asleep with Sadie in her thoughts.

25 | Sadie

M r. Kristan had been assigned a room at the Hyatt, one of several high-end hotels Cynthia insisted on to reinforce the image that her "students" were respectable, not "vermin from the streets." It was one of two features that had sold her on Cynthia's service: johns willing to pay two grand a gig, and the posh working environment. Mr. Kristan would expect her to be on time and well turned out because he often wanted her to keep him company over dinner. Sadie didn't care. He had her for four hours and could do as he pleased.

At the hotel, she collected the key card from the front desk. The card allowed her access to the elevator, but it wasn't to be used to enter the room. She knocked, as was the protocol. Mr. Kristan answered and held the door for her. Though she tried not to focus on the scar that cut across his cheek, it drew her eyes like a magnet. He'd scolded her for that scrutiny in the past. She quickly looked elsewhere. He wasn't dressed in his usual trousers and plaid sports coat. Instead, he wore jeans and an Under Armour jersey.

Normally, he'd inspect her from head to toe before admitting her, but not this time. He followed her into the room then took her hand and led her to the bed, urging her to sit. He sat beside her, toying with her fingers. Sadie frowned at his strange behaviour. Where was the disciplinarian? The man who found five flaws that needed to be addressed immediately?

"Thanks for coming," he said. Sadie's frown deepened. "I wanted to apologize for yesterday." He looked up and met Sadie's confused gaze. "Meeting you outside of this setting jarred me, as I'm sure it did you. It's important to me that you understand I was not aware you worked there."

"All right, Mr. Kristan," Sadie said.

"No. Not Mr. Kristan. Rick is the man who dined at Lodestones last night. Call me Rick."

Sadie hesitated. Was this his way of digging around for her real name? "Okay." He looked genuinely relieved, which surprised her. "You could have sent me a message through the website. Saved yourself some money."

"No. I wanted to see you."

"Why?"

He raised an eyebrow. "You mean besides the usual reason?" He chuckled as he patted the back of her hand and then stood. "Would you like a drink?"

"Sure."

"Vodka or wine?"

"Vodka."

He walked to the bar and dropped ice into two glasses. "Has Cynthia talked to you about my proposal?"

Wow. He knew Cynthia's name? Sadie had thought only the "students" knew who operated the Teachers' Pet website. "Yes. She mentioned it."

He unscrewed the cap on a bottle of Ketel One and poured a splash into each glass. "This game that we play in here is a distraction." He walked back to the bed and extended a drink to Sadie. "It's harmless, but it's a game I'm tiring of."

Sadie reached for the glass. "We can change the game." He must have turned the air conditioner on high—the room felt cold.

"I don't want to play games anymore."

"Then why do you want to buy out my contract?"

Rick pulled the rolling desk chair over to the bed and sat opposite her. "I enjoy your company. You're beautiful, funny. You're intelligent."

"Mr. Kristan—"

"Rick, please."

"Rick. I'm not looking for a boyfriend."

"And I'm not looking for a girlfriend. Romantic entanglements are complications I have little time for. I'm looking for an escort with discretion. Someone I can count on to accompany me without question."

"I can't be at your beck and call. I have a job."

"So I've learned," he deadpanned, then took a sip of his drink. "If you accept my proposal, you won't need that job."

Sadie smiled at the thought, but she'd long outgrown fairy tales. She looked down to her drink and poked at the ice cubes. "You want a mistress."

"A paid escort. Exclusive, of course. You'll have to sign an NDA."

Sadie considered the perfectly appointed king-sized bed with the soft, high-thread-count sheets. She smoothed her hand on the pristine white bed cover. "Sex?"

"Yes."

Sadie nodded. "For how long?"

"That depends. How much is Cynthia offering you?"

Sadie had checked with enough johns to know that Cynthia was paying her what she was due. She could trust her. Rick, on the other hand? "She wasn't specific."

He skewed his lower jaw and shook his head from side to side. "Don't play stupid, Sadie. It doesn't suit you."

Sadie shot him a glare.

"That is your name, isn't it?"

She stood, took her drink to the window, and gazed down to Burrard Street. He hadn't closed the curtains. Every lie she worked over in her head to deny that her name was Sadie sounded lame to the point of desperation.

"How much is she offering you?" he repeated.

Sadie answered to his reflection in the window. "Half."

He took a sip of his drink and lifted his feet to rest on the edge of the bed. "I hope your trust in her isn't misplaced. To answer your question, when our trial period expires, I expect you to be, as you put it, *at my beck and call*, for six months. After that, at my discretion, we make another arrangement. Does that work for you?"

"What trial period?"

"Ah, so she hasn't told you everything. She's already agreed to make you exclusive to me for the next three months."

Sadie frowned. Why would Cynthia want to delay the close of their deal by three months? "Did Cynthia remind you that I only take one gig a month?"

"Not anymore. You work as often as I need you. Hence *trial period*."

"I see." Sadie had misjudged how far Cynthia was willing to go to force her hand. "How often would you need me?"

"Weekly. Maybe more. I've a number of important social functions on the horizon."

Four times a month? Cynthia's plan was coming into focus. She'd reap a fourfold increase in Sadie's fees. For three months. On top of the buyout. How nice for Cynthia. "What do you mean by *at your discretion* we'll make another arrangement?"

"Exactly that. When the buyout period ends, I decide if we continue or not."

"And what if I don't wish to continue?"

"It's not your decision. If you agree to this, I'll own your contract. You're mine until I say so. You'll also be paid very well for your services. That's what you'd be agreeing to. Can you live with that?"

Not only had Cynthia screwed her over, she'd left out a few critical details. And it wasn't Cynthia who'd have to get rid of the guy after they'd taken his money.

Sadie swirled the ice cubes in her glass. "I won't agree to continuing at your discretion beyond the six-month buyout. I get a say or no deal."

"It's a lot of money for six months with no guarantee."

Sadie turned from the window with a smirk. "You telling me you're not a gambler?"

"I'm not a fool."

"Neither am I."

Rick planted his feet back on the floor. "All right. Well played."

"Then I'll consider it."

"Good."

Cynthia would answer for this. Sadie was no pushover. She was already working out how to use Cynthia's blindsiding to get more out of her. She thought about her and Jane's mantra: look forward, never back. She had at least fifty thousand things to look forward to.

Rick upended his drink. "Take off your dress."

26 | Jane

Visiting Dream

J ane finds herself in a dimly lit restaurant. Every table is full. Christmas wreaths hang from wall sconces, and laughter rides a chorus of "Santa Baby." Silver-painted pinecones adorn the tables. Jane is standing beside a frosted room divider. Behind her is a collapsible tray stand. Servers and bussers rushing about their business add a layer of confusion.

On the far side of the room, a hostess with menus in her arm comes into view. A couple trails behind her. The female half of the couple is Sadie. Jane recognizes her navy lace dress. Sadie's date pulls out her chair and then walks to the chair opposite, but the hostess blocks Jane's view of the man.

A waiter passes with a tray of food held high. The scent of rosemary tickles Jane's nose, and while she's considering if she's ever smelled anything in her dreams before, a young busser cuts in front of her. The girl places a platter of empty champagne flutes on the tray stand and scurries away.

Jane looks back into the dining room just as the hostess steps away from Sadie's table, and Jane gets a glimpse of her roommate's companion. Startled, Jane steps back, and the platter of champagne flutes crashes to the floor.

Awake, Jane blinked several times, stunned. Sadie's date was Rebecca Morrow's doctor. But not the fresh-faced Rick of her earlier dreams. Even from across the dining room she could see that he was older. And that scar on his face! He'd not had that before, and it was just as Sadie had described: a prominent white line from his ear to his nose.

As her racing heart slowed, two puzzle pieces fell into place. First, Sadie was the connection to her dreams of Rebecca. And second, Sadie referred to Rick as Mr. Kristan. Which meant Rebecca's doctor was Dr. Rick Kristan. That is, if he'd told Sadie his real name.

If only Jane had waited one more day before forwarding her MCFD file to Nate. One more day and she could have added Rick's full name to her cryptic note.

Jane's regret was quickly overshadowed by a bigger question: had she succeeded in seeding a dream? Or was it just a coincidence that Sadie had been on her mind when she'd fallen asleep?

She had to tell Sadie. She threw off her covers and padded to the living room. But it was only 11:30 p.m. and Sadie wasn't yet home. Disappointed, she returned to the bedroom.

Her thoughts soon returned to her dream. She remembered stepping back, feeling the edge of the platter against her butt. As impossible as it was, she felt certain she'd caused it to topple.

August 16

In the early hours, Jane woke to a crash outside the bedroom. She leapt out of bed and found Sadie trying to right the lamp she'd knocked over.

One look at her and Jane knew where she'd been, and it hadn't been a date. "He give you coke again?" Jane asked, struggling to keep the judgment out of her voice.

"Just a little," Sadie said. "Takes the edge off."

She was slurring her words, so it was more than coke, and it didn't look like just a little to Jane, though she wouldn't know. She'd never tried it—couldn't imagine giving up that much control. And there'd be no point talking to her about dreams until she sobered up.

"I'm up. You may as well take the bedroom," Jane said. "I'll be out of here early."

Sadie didn't protest. While Jane gathered some clothes for the morning, Sadie dropped into the bed and had passed out before Jane settled on the sofa. At least, Sadie hadn't gone to Riptide again after her gig.

But she'd picked a lousy night to get wasted. Jane was desperate to tell her about her Christmas dream and ask about Rick, but Sadie would be comatose for hours.

Jane woke groggy. The apartment felt stifling. She kicked at the sheet tangled around her legs and shoved it to the end of the sofa. She'd spent a restless, anxious night preoccupied with the Christmas visiting dream and the possibility that she'd successfully seeded it. Unfortunately, Sadie was the only one who could confirm this and she was out of commission. Again.

Frustrated, she dragged herself to the bathroom and splashed water on her face. When she straightened, she looked in the mirror and pulled her hair back. More than all the others, the stain on her face had defined a huge swath of her life. She couldn't count the number of times she'd wished the birthmarks away, but she'd never truly believed they'd vanish. Yet the one on her foot had. What if the mark on her face disappeared as well? Dare she hope? Or was it a foolish dream, like her childhood fantasy that she had real parents who loved her?

As she dressed, she considered what she might wear if she didn't have marks to hide. The idea of tank tops and shorts flitted across her mind, and then she chided herself for getting carried away.

She set the kettle on to boil and then, impatient for Sadie to rise from the dead, padded to the bedroom and creaked open the door. Sadie's head lay buried under a pillow.

Jane cursed and closed the door none too quietly. Returning to the kitchen, she took her time silencing the kettle's whistle. After she ate, she jostled the dishes in the sink as she washed them, and again when she put them away, banging drawers and cupboard doors.

After she finished her tea, she peeked in on Sadie one last time. She was still out cold and waking Sadie when she was hungover was a good way to lose an eye. Their conversation would have to wait until tonight. Resigned, Jane closed the bedroom door and left for work.

During her lunch break, she got a text from Ethan. He wanted to see her. The sight of his name lighting up the screen twisted her gut. The sound of his screams filled her head. It had been almost a week since their hookup, not that she'd been counting the days. She inhaled a cleansing breath. It wouldn't be the first time she'd have to pretend to not know something devastating.

When her workday ended, she jumped on her bike and drove to Riptide. She pulled into the alley behind Ethan's apartment and glanced at his window, three floors up in the red brick building, and caught a glimpse of him as he turned from the window. He'd been watching for her. She tamped down a bubble of excitement.

He met her at the front entrance barefoot and out of breath. She felt overwhelming relief at the sight of him—a product of her dream, and she kept it in check. He held the door open. "Hey," he said, reaching for her helmet. She stepped inside, sunblind in the dim interior. The air smelled of dust and old floor wax. He called the elevator, which protested with creaks and groans. She imagined a shackled old beast crawling down the ancient shaft.

"It'll be quicker to take the stairs," Ethan said, glancing at the small number panel above the elevator. It inched from eight to seven. "Come on."

Jane followed him into the stairwell and up well-worn treads to the third floor. The hallway they emerged into felt familiar. She'd lived in more than one apartment just like it, where the soundtracks of life leaked out from ill-fitting doors and mingled with the scents of a dozen different meals from around the globe.

"After you," he said, and closed the apartment door behind her. Just three steps in, she had a view of the entire studio apartment. Directly ahead sat a table and two chairs that looked as if they'd come from Riptide's prerenovation days. To her right lay a single captain's bed and a dresser. Daylight flooded in from a window in the kitchen and another near the bed.

Like his Airstream, his apartment was tidy and clean. It even smelled clean, or maybe the spicy scent was his aftershave.

"I like it," she said. Ethan came up behind her, and she turned in his arms. They kissed, and she indulged in a memory of their night at the trailer. It stirred a desire in her that loosened her natural inhibition. Her hands wandered.

Ethan pulled away. The surprise in his features melted into a sly smile. "Eager. I like that, but how about I close the blinds." He pulled off his T-shirt and led her to the bed. The sight of his scars brought back his screams to her mind. She chased them away. He walked to the nearby window and pulled the blind's cord. Half the room fell into shadow.

In the time it took her to remove her jacket and boots, he'd stripped down to his Calvin Kleins. She revelled in the freedom of Ethan's acceptance, a freedom that let him remove her clothes without fear of rejection. A freedom that let her forget the disfiguring birthmarks and enjoy the touch of his fingers, his lips, his body.

The first time he pushed inside her, she took the reins. She felt greedy, wanting her fill in case he changed his mind. The second time, he took her someplace she'd never been before, exploring, teasing, tasting, and, at long last, tipping her into ecstasy. Afterward, she snuggled in his arms, unwilling to open her eyes and end the moment. She'd never been happier.

She woke with a start.

"Hey, sleepyhead," Ethan said.

Jane shot upright, fuelled by a fear so deep it hurt.

"Whoa," Ethan said, shifting beside her.

"What time is it?"

"Almost eight. You fell asleep."

"I gotta go," Jane muttered, and tugged the sheet from her legs.

"No rush. Connor's covering me 'til nine. Want to go get a bite?"

Jane swung her feet to the floor and inhaled a calming breath. Sweat trickled between her breasts. How could she have let herself lose control like that? Stupid, stupid girl! "I gotta get home."

He pulled the sheet aside and sat up beside her. "You all right?"

"Yeah." She rubbed her face. Adrenalin receded in prickles under her skin. She'd screwed up, been careless.

"I thought you weren't a runner?" He turned his torso to face her.

"I'm not, it's . . . I . . . didn't mean to fall asleep." She forced a smile. He looked so concerned. It touched her. She rested her palm on his chest. "Sometimes I have bad dreams."

"Just now?" he said, holding her hand to his chest.

"No. Thankfully." She pulled her hand loose and looked to the floor for her clothes.

"Stay a little longer," he said, brushing her hair behind her shoulder.

"I can't. I'm sorry I wasted our night."

"Wasted?" He laughed and scooped her bra from the floor, dangling it in front of her. "You can waste my night any old time."

She hid a grin as she snatched it from his hands. While she dressed, he bit his lip and watched, making her insides melt. She kissed him goodbye and left his apartment already regretting her decision to leave. He waved from the window as she mounted her bike.

She drove home pushing the what-ifs out of her mind. She'd be more vigilant next time. God, she hoped there'd be a next time.

27 | Sadie

S adie stirred in her sleep, annoyed by the banging. It felt as if Jane were trying to pound nails into her skull. She pulled the pillow around her ears and drifted back to oblivion. When she eventually woke again, she had to pry her eyelids open. Her mouth felt like a well-used kitty litter box. She threw off the sheet and squinted at the sunlight streaking across the bed.

Rick had played her off against Cynthia, and she didn't like it. Mostly because he'd made her feel like a fool for placing so much trust in Cynthia. And more so because he was right.

Sadie wobbled upright, clutching the edge of the mattress. A small baggie of white powder winked at her from the floor beside her stiletto. He'd sent her home with a party favour. How thoughtful. Something to celebrate with later.

She stumbled to the bathroom and found the bottle of aspirin. The lid flipped to the floor and rolled behind the garbage can. She slurped water from her cupped hand to wash down the pills and then cringed as she caught a glimpse of herself in the mirror. Last night's mascara had glued her eyelashes together in clumps, and her eyeliner had smeared into bad-clown triangles under her eyes. What was left of the lipstick Rick insisted upon had migrated to one cheek. If he saw her now, he'd rethink that predilection.

Sadie waited for the water to run warm in the shower. Despite her colossal hangover, a smile bloomed. She'd come to a decision last night and remembered the exact moment with clarity. It was during one of her better orgasm performances. She'd be ditching Rick *and* Cynthia, but not until she negotiated a better deal.

Sadie found the toaster in the cupboard. Jane insisted on putting it away after she used it. Jane's tendency to have everything in its place drove Sadie batty. She figured it was in Jane's best interests to challenge her control issues. That's why she left the toaster out. And the cereal box. Or anything she didn't feel like putting away. It was Sadie's idea of aversion therapy. She'd read about it online. Like when someone was afraid of spiders. The cure was exposing them to big, hairy tarantulas. Sadie was providing Jane with tarantulas—helping her lighten up, chill on the control.

It wasn't that Sadie didn't understand what drove Jane's excessive tidiness. With Jane's narcolepsy and those damn dreams, her environment was critical: it was the one thing she had to control—the only thing she could control. Sadie didn't mind the steel door and double bolt locks, but Jane's need to micromanage their apartment felt suffocating at times.

Sadie's getting out of the business would be one less unpredictable element in Jane's life. Jane would be happy about that part, even if she didn't like the plan to get there. Though Jane had never judged her for how she earned her money, Sadie knew Jane worried about her safety. She couldn't fault her for that. Jane had been caught in the afterburner of her gigs more times than she wanted to think about.

"I take it you changed your mind," Cynthia said, as Sadie stood in her condo staring out at Coal Harbour.

Sadie turned around. "You were right. Rick is ready for a change. If we don't take his money, someone else will."

Cynthia cracked a confident smile. "Good. Then we have a deal."

"Not quite. He wants me for six months. That's going to cost seventy-five grand."

Cynthia's smile slipped. "It's taken me weeks to get him to a hundred. I don't think he'll go as high as one-fifty."

Sadie crossed her arms. "Seventy-five."

"You're overestimating your charms."

"I don't think so." It was Sadie's ass on the line, not Cynthia's. If Cynthia couldn't get him to go higher, then Cynthia could take a hit in her percentage for a change.

Cynthia leaned back in her white leather chair. "Something happened last night."

"Nothing you didn't know about. Seventy-five or no deal. And I want it up front."

"Half up front, and you don't get it until your trial period ends."

"That's not going to work for me." Sadie's trust in Cynthia had slid down a notch or two the previous evening. "And let's talk about this *trial period* you arranged."

"Yes? What about it?" Cynthia steepled her fingers.

"He wants me weekly during the trial period. That's four times what I agreed to when I came to work for you, and I have no doubt he'll want that pace to continue after the trial period."

"He was about to walk away. I had to be creative. I would have thought you'd be grateful I preserved the payout."

Sadie dropped a hand to her hip. What she'd *preserved* was an additional three months of increased income from Sadie, and to do it, she'd delayed the payout, which also effectively extended Sadie's commitment to Rick from six months to nine months. Cynthia knew Sadie would never have agreed to a trial period.

But Sadie wasn't stupid. She wouldn't jeopardize the payout. She just intended to get it sooner than Cynthia had planned.

"I want it all up front," Sadie said. "But I can wait until the trial period ends."

"I see. All right. After your trial period."

"Deal." Sadie let herself out of Cynthia's condo with a bounce in her step. She knew if Cynthia couldn't get Rick to meet the new price, Cynthia would bank on making up the difference over the next three months. But Sadie wasn't feeling particularly charitable where Cynthia was concerned. She jumped in her car and headed for work. The next time she saw Rick, she'd unleash her considerable charms and get him to reduce their trial period. Maybe even shorten it to time served.

28 | Rick

As delightful as his dalliance with Sadie had been, it wasn't enough to get his mind off his parents handing Mikey their power of attorney. Over a dinner meeting, Rick's lawyer confirmed what he'd suspected. Unless he could prove his parents were non compos mentis, they had every right to name Michael as their power of attorney. She reassured him that a POA didn't give Michael carte blanche. He still had to act in their best interests. But she didn't know Mikey.

Back in his townhome, he contemplated his options. He was fighting a war on two fronts: Mikey and Jane. He couldn't do both. He would put out feelers regarding someone to deal with his brother. The last crook he'd hired to get the goods on him wasn't worth his street cred. Not only had he failed to find the scheme Mikey had used to pry the partnership out of his firm, but he couldn't even dig up an affair. Mikey wouldn't know fidelity if it walked up, introduced itself, and shook his hand. And Rick didn't believe for a second that Mickey's phony wife hadn't stepped out.

One more reason not to marry. Other men's wives were easy bait—he'd had enough of them to know. Catch and release worked best. Married women were grateful for the attention and didn't make a fuss when you moved on. And if you targeted the right one, you could get some perks thrown into the deal. He had fond memories of a Paris vacation courtesy of Natalie, a well-heeled banker's wife. Sadie reminded Rick of Natalie. Curvaceous and daring, quick-witted and clever. Clever women were his weakness. He'd have to be careful not to underestimate Sadie. She was streetwise and cunning. He'd keep a tight rein on her. And after she'd played her part, she could crawl back to Cynthia.

29 | Jane

Jane laced her fingers and stretched her arms. She'd read as much about hypnotherapy as she could absorb in one sitting. Not that she'd been absorbing much. The possibility that she'd seeded her dream about Sadie in the restaurant at Christmastime hadn't been far from her thoughts all day. She'd crawl out of her skin if she didn't get confirmation one way or another, and soon. Sadie's shift had ended at six, almost an hour ago, and she still wasn't home. Jane was about to text her when she heard the scrape of a key in the lock.

"You're home!" Jane said, snapping her laptop closed.

"Ah, you missed me. That's sweet." Sadie offered a syrupy smile. She kicked off her shoes and trudged to the sofa, dropping her purse on the trunk. "The restaurant was rabid today."

"I saved you some KD. Want me to nuke it?"

"Sure," Sadie said, propping her feet on the trunk. "While you're up, bring me a glass of wine, would you?"

Jane trotted to the kitchen and pulled the bowl of KD from the fridge. She set it twirling in the microwave then poured Sadie's wine and walked it back to the sofa.

"Something's up," Sadie said, taking a sip. "Spill it."

"What? Don't act as if I've never made you dinner before."

"You left the drippy plastic wrap on the counter and the screw cap off the wine, never mind that the bottle's still out. And isn't that the empty Kraft Dinner box on the stove? The Jane I know would have broken out in hives walking away from that . . . chaos." Sadie waved her hand in the general direction of the kitchen.

"Hardly," Jane said, laughing. The microwave dinged, and she went to retrieve the KD. She made an exaggerated point of cleaning up before she returned with Sadie's dinner.

"Satisfied?" Jane said, sitting.

Sadie arched an eyebrow. "You talk, I'll eat," she said, taking the bowl.

"You were pretty wasted when you came home last night. Was it Mr. Kristan?"

"Yup." Sadie licked the fork.

"You sure you should be taking his gigs?"

"You're changing the subject."

Jane pulled a pillow into her lap. "Do you remember going to dinner with a client at Christmastime? White-tablecloth kind of place? You wore your navy lace dress."

"A dream?" Sadie asked, stacking noodles on her fork.

"Uh-huh." Jane smoothed the creases from the pillowcase.

Sadie's brow furrowed in thought as she chewed. "Yeah. Last December. It was Hy's. I was with Mr. Kristan."

Jane exhaled. She'd done it. She'd seeded a dream. "His name's Rick."

Sadie stilled. "How do you know that? I didn't know his first name until last night."

"Because Mr. Kristan is the doctor who was treating Rebecca Morrow. He's older now, but I recognized him."

"My Mr. Kristan? In your dream?"

Jane nodded.

"That's . . . disturbing."

"No! It's fantastic. In my earlier dreams, he was trying hypno-therapy, seeding Rebecca's unconscious mind with events and places. He thought if she could learn to control her visions, they wouldn't control her. And last night, I was thinking about you before I fell asleep." Jane felt giddy, as if she'd aced an important exam.

"You think that's why you dreamed about me?"

"Maybe he was onto something. Plus, this dream with you and Rick was different from the other dreams I've had of him, when he was with Rebecca. He's older now. By twenty years give or take."

"Don't you find that odd? A twenty-year gap in your dreams of this guy?"

"Not really. It's not like I can hypnotize myself—I'm probably just doing it wrong. I can't control the dreams, exactly, but maybe I can pick the subject. Last night is proof. I picked you!"

"Still, it's kinda weird that Rick's treating a woman you're dreaming about, a woman who just coincidentally happens to suffer from a con-dition similar to yours."

"Actually, it makes perfect sense. You're the connection I was missing from my dreams of Rebecca. I'm tied to you, you're tied to Rick, and Rick is tied to Rebecca. It's a direct line. So no, not that odd."

"Yeah," Sadie said. "Maybe."

"Maybe? Sadie!" Jane swung her pillow at Sadie's knee. "You're the glue between Rebecca and me. Thanks to you, I've got a lead on an actual doctor who might just hold the cure to my dreams. That's huge."

"You're right. That is huge," Sadie said, sounding unimpressed. "Can you stop dreaming about me now? Please."

"Humph. Your enthusiasm is underwhelming." Despite Sadie's blasé reaction, Jane collapsed back into the sofa brimming with good humour.

"I'd never have guessed he was a doctor," Sadie said, talking around a mouthful of noodles.

"Sure wish I'd known his last name before yesterday," Jane said. She explained how she'd planted the note with Rick and Rebecca's cryptic details in her ministry file and sent it on to Nate and Ariane.

"If Rick found a cure, I can try to weasel it out of him," Sadie said.

"No, don't. Not yet." Jane had considered that option earlier and dismissed it. "He's smart. He'd figure out that you know something you shouldn't. I don't trust him."

"You don't trust anyone," Sadie said, scooping the last of the noodles from the bowl. She stood and started for the kitchen.

"That's not true—I trust you," Jane said, dumbfounded by the sight of Sadie washing her bowl, a minor miracle that Jane dare not draw attention to for fear it would be the last time she'd witness the phenomenon.

She returned to her train of thought. "It's just . . . Rick is being weird about Rebecca—*was* being weird," she said, correcting herself. "When Ariane's investigator finds Rebecca, I'll get the answer from Rebecca herself. She'll understand, and if it turns out she trusts Rick, then I'll trust him."

Visiting Dream

Jane is in Rebecca's apartment. Rebecca is curled in a ball at one end of her sofa. A wineglass cloudy with fingerprints sits on the end table beside a half-empty bottle of wine.

There's a knock at the door. Rebecca looks up, startled. The knock repeats itself.

"Rebecca! Open up." It's Rick's voice.

Rebecca unfurls herself and stands. She corrects a wobble, steadies herself, and picks her way to the door. She checks the peephole before opening it.

"What are you doing here?" she says.

"What do you think? You missed your appointment. Didn't pick up your phone. I was concerned about your safety."

Rebecca steps back from the door and Rick walks in looking around with an attentiveness that suggests he's not been in her apartment before. His gaze lands on the wine bottle.

"You're self-medicating?"

"You have a better suggestion?"

"Why the no-show, Rebecca?"

"The hypnotherapy isn't working. The only visions I have are of you and they're—" Rebecca stops short, as if reconsidering her words. "I want them to stop."

"The visions aren't what? Rebecca."

"Did you hire someone to hurt your brother?"

Rick appears taken aback. "God no. Why would I hurt him?"

"You tell me. I saw you push an envelope of money across a table to a rough-looking man in a shithole bar. You gave him your brother's name and address. You told him where he works."

Rick nods, a thoughtful look on his face. "That's out of context." He leans in, softening his tone. "We talked about context the last time."

Rebecca's nostrils flare. She crosses her arms.

He tugs at the cuff of his sleeve. "Dad and I learned that Michael was being investigated for fraud. We hired that man to make sure the charges didn't stick. We were protecting him."

"I don't believe you."

"I've never lied to you."

"I want to see a different doctor."

Rick takes a step back. "I've pushed you too hard." He frowns. "I didn't see it. I'm sorry. Let's try something else."

Rebecca shakes her head back and forth. "No."

"Hypnotherapy is only one of many options, Rebecca. I thought it was a good place to start, but there are other treatments we can explore. It's too early to give up."

"I'm not giving up. I'm going to find someone else."

Rick looks to the floor and exhales loudly. "You sure you want to start all over? It'll be tough to convince another doctor that your visions are genuine."

"I convinced you."

"After you tried to kill yourself. You want to go down that road again?"

"Never again. But I am going to find another doctor, and David agrees with me."

Rick raises his hands to his hips. "You discussed this with your boyfriend?"

"Fiancé. And yes."

"I see. Well then, I guess you've made up your mind." He stuffs his hands in his pockets and stares blankly around the apartment. "If you'd like, I can put together a list of doctors. Talk to them. If you agree, of course."

"No. Thank you. I want a fresh start."

He tilts his head and offers her a disarming smile. "No harm in me sending you a few names. They won't discuss your case with me without your permission."

She considers his offer. "All right. Some names would be helpful. Thanks."

"You're welcome." He pulls his hand from his pocket. A small packet dangles from his fingers. "When you didn't come for your appointment today, I reconsidered your request. I brought you a mild sedative. How much have you had to drink?"

"Only one glass."

"Now who's lying?" Rick says with a smirk. He rips the top off the packet. "I'll leave you one dose. No more wine though. Give me your word."

"No more wine," Rebecca says, and she extends her hand.

Rick shakes one capsule into her palm and tucks the packet back in his pocket. "Good luck, Rebecca. I'll call with a list of names tomorrow."

After Rick leaves, Rebecca downs the pill with a gulp of wine.

August 17

An uneasy gasp accompanied Jane's waking. She calmed herself with deep breaths. She was no doctor, but she didn't think giving Rebecca a sedative when she'd been drinking was a good move. And was that the end of Rick and Rebecca's professional relationship? Had it ended without a cure? Jane hoped not.

She had to trust that the doctor knew what he was doing, and that Rebecca would be okay and get the rest she needed. Maybe once she'd rested, she'd give Rick another chance.

30 | Rick

The call came at dawn. Rick raced through the empty streets and parked in one of the spaces reserved for doctors.

Rick's mother hadn't accompanied his father in the ambulance. Her blindness was a complication the ambulance crew couldn't accommodate.

Rick had a brief discussion with the attending physician and then followed a nurse to a private room, where he stared down at a face as familiar as his own. His father's expression was peaceful, his skin pallid. Rick thanked the nurse then pulled a chair to his father's bedside.

"It's Rick, Dad. I'm here." Rick knew his father couldn't hear him. Knew he wouldn't survive more than a few hours. Remorse for his missed opportunity ate away at him while his father died.

The old man's breaths came in shallow puffs. He would never know about the most important promotion of his son's career, just days away.

"I should have told you sooner, Dad. I made chief of staff. Top of the heap, as you'd say."

Rick imagined his father's hearty handshake, his congratulations, a slap on the shoulder with an attaboy. He pictured Mikey in the room, because Rick would have made certain his brother was there to witness their father basking in Rick's glory.

An orderly arrived escorting his mother in a hospital-issue wheelchair. Mother and son sat on either side of the bed.

In time, numbness fell over Rick, cloaking his anger. Where the hell was Michael? He could have easily hopped on an early-morning flight. What a slap in the face for the old man that his favourite son hadn't made the effort to see him one last time. When Rick saw Mikey again, he'd be sure to mention it.

Hours later, Rick held his father's hand waiting for him to take another halting breath. When that breath didn't come, he laid his father's hand across the white sheet and caressed it one final time.

"He's gone, Mom."

31 | Jane

At Positively Plants, Jane moved through the watering routine on autopilot. On her lunch break, she volunteered for the deli run and crossed paths with Buddy. He slowed his motorized wheelchair as he approached and smiled a greeting. Whoever had shaved him had missed a patch on his neck.

"Hey, Buddy. Finished already?" She knew he worked the Pacific Centre Mall a few hours each day. Shoppers had money in their pockets, and Buddy's engaging smile earned him some of their change.

"Yep. Bin a good day."

"You headed home?"

"Lunch break," he said, beaming.

"Me too." Jane pulled a toonie from her pocket and dropped it in his can. "See you around."

"Thanks. Bye, Jaynee."

She stepped back as he pushed the knobbed control lever forward. If his chair were a car, he'd have had the pedal to the floor. A smiley emoji had been painted on the bright-orange donation can zip-tied to his chair. She called out after him, "Say hi to the missus." He raised his arm in response and sped away.

She watched his retreat then turned to open the deli door, but something caught her eye and made her turn back. Two figures had emerged from a convenience store alcove, hoods up, hands in the pockets of unseasonably warm jackets. They quickened their pace as they trailed Buddy. Jane hesitated, unsure of her instincts. She started after them, walking, not wanting to draw attention if she was wrong.

A red light halted Buddy's progress at the intersection. She was still half a block away when the two figures caught up to him. As soon as they split up, one on either side of his chair, she burst into a sprint. She'd seen the scam a dozen times. One would distract him while the other picked him clean. Lowlife sleazebags!

Buddy turned his head toward the man on his right, which meant her target was the man on his left, who already had his hand on Buddy's can. From twenty metres away, she could see the glint of something shiny working at the zip ties. With ten metres between them, she shouted a warning.

Both men jerked their heads in her direction. Desperation flashed in their sunken eyes and hollow cheeks. Meth heads. The one who'd distracted Buddy turned his back and stepped away, an innocent bystander. The other furtively redoubled his efforts to cut through the donation can's zip ties. Jane launched herself at him, hitting him with her shoulder. He staggered sideways, rocking Buddy's chair. The donation can clanked to the sidewalk and rolled to a stop against the light standard. Tires squealed off to Jane's right.

Quick to recover, the thief regained his feet and crouched in front of Jane in a fight pose, his blade in one hand. His eyes darted between Jane and the bright-orange can. Jane didn't give him time to make a bad decision. She opened her stance, pivoted, and executed a perfect roundhouse kick, knocking the blade from his hand with her steel-toed shoe. She spun on the rebound and threw her weight into a hit with the heel of her hand to the underside of his jaw. He fell backward and landed heavily on the road, stunned.

A police cruiser blipped its siren. Jane spotted it among the gridlocked cars jamming the intersection. She whirled around and found Buddy safe on the sidewalk. A neon-vested tow-truck driver crouched beside his wheelchair. The driver's truck sat abandoned in the road with its door ajar. Her relief at finding Buddy unharmed was tempered with unease: a police presence meant questions. Those interviews never went well.

She scanned the ground for Buddy's donation can and spotted it on the sidewalk by the light standard. As she strode toward it, she locked eyes with the would-be thief's partner, who'd slunk back to claim his prize.

He stood over the can and thrust his hand into his jacket pocket, jutting out a finger, or more likely, his meth pipe, in the hopes Jane would mistake it for a gun.

"Take a fuckin' hike," he said. His words whistled through missing teeth.

She stopped short and reached for her pruning knife. An addict frantic for a fix could be dangerous. "Buddy needs that more than you do."

"Not today," he said, and reached for the can.

Jane threw her knife with deft accuracy. It punctured Buddy's can and sent it spiralling out of the addict's reach. He looked up, glowering at her, and pulled his hand from his pocket. Not a pipe. A gun. His upper lip twitched.

Hesitation wasn't an option. Jane spun and tipped forward, dipping her left shoulder as she followed through with a back kick. But her kick landed in empty air, and the unexpected momentum sent her sprawling. She caught a glimpse of the addict's face frozen in a grimace and scrambled out of the way as he toppled over. Behind him stood a cop with a taser.

"Move away," the officer warned.

He didn't have to ask twice. She got to her feet and slipped into the milling crowd as more police cruisers arrived flashing their red-and-blues. Cops flooded the intersection like wasps from a kicked hive. The would-be thief lay moaning on the ground, his wrists already cuffed behind his back.

Jane found Buddy on the sidewalk still in the company of the tow-truck driver. Buddy's face was mottled red and white. Spittle flew from his mouth along with mangled words.

She took one of his shaking hands and crouched in front of him. "You okay, Buddy?" His mismatched eyes darted around her face. The sound of more sirens drew near. "They can't hurt you now."

The man from the tow truck repeated Jane's reassuring words. They stayed with Buddy, and Jane held his hand until a paramedic approached.

"See ya later, Buddy," Jane said, straightening. Looking around, she saw that the thief who'd come at her with a blade had recovered enough to sit up. He sat loose boned, eyeballs rolling around in their sockets, as another paramedic checked him over.

With a start, she realized she'd lost track of Buddy's can. She spun back to the light standard where the attacker who'd been tasered still lay, but the can was gone.

Clenching her jaw, she scanned the crowd for a glimpse of bright orange. When she finally spotted it, she sucked in a breath. It was in the hands of a cop who was speaking to a bystander. Her knife protruded like a murder weapon from the side of it. They turned as one and looked at her. Any thoughts she had of slipping away shrivelled up.

Moments later, the constable approached. He escorted her to the back of an ambulance, where a paramedic gave her a cold pack for her wrist and suggested she get it x-rayed. Her next stop was the back seat of the constable's cruiser. He took her ID, locked her inside, and walked away.

This was why she didn't like cops. They always assumed the worst of her. Guilty until proven otherwise, and people like her didn't see a lot of *otherwise*. She knew they'd be running a check on her. How much of her troubled history would they learn? she wondered. She hid from curious stares behind a veil of hair. Her wrist throbbed. Fear and humiliation mixed into a nauseating cocktail. She swallowed it down.

Close by, a car door slammed. Startled, Jane jerked her head up and locked eyes with the man who'd been tasered. He was rolling by on a gurney, and his glare left no doubt that if he hadn't been strapped down, he'd try to kill her again.

She dropped her gaze to her lap and the mark on her left hand. *He'd try to kill me again*, she thought, the words echoing. Had her marks somehow shielded her? She pushed the thought away. There probably weren't even bullets in the gun.

It seemed like hours before the constable returned. When he did, he had a partner in tow, the one with the taser. Together they questioned her, picking at the details of her version of events. They took their time, scratching notes, flipping pages. Their dogged questioning made her feel as if she were the criminal, and that was before they turned their attention to her blade. Their questions about her knife were edged with accusation.

They confiscated her holster belt and ended their interrogation with a promise to confirm with the Bakkers her explanation that she needed the knife for work. And no, they wouldn't return it.

"You're free to go," the cop said, handing her back her ID. She tucked it in her pocket, along with the constable's card, and asked him about Buddy. He couldn't tell her more than that he'd been taken to St. Paul's Hospital, a few blocks away.

Lucas materialized from the dwindling huddle of lookie-loos and walked her back to Positively Plants. He'd come looking for her when she hadn't returned with their lunch and had already heard most of the story from the sidewalk quarterbacks. But he hadn't heard about the gun and Jane didn't enlighten him. He and Anna would give her a hard time about it, and she'd had enough feedback for one day.

"It all went down so fast," she said, massaging her wrist. "I hope I didn't hit that guy too hard."

"Not hard enough if you ask me. Anyone who'd steal from Buddy doesn't deserve your sympathy."

"They're not evil, just addicts." Jane thought of the addicts she'd known when she lived in the rooming house on East Hastings. Desperation was a cold and ruthless friend.

Back at Positively Plants, Jane headed to the breakroom. Anna followed.

"It's not broken, see," Jane said, wiggling her fingers in evidence. Regardless, Anna was a mom through and through and pressed her to take Lucas up on his offer to drive her to emergency.

"St. Paul's is practically up the street," Jane said. "Besides, I need to walk off this adrenalin." She set out for the hospital, relieved to be free of their fussing.

In emergency, she explained what had happened. The nurse gave her a fresh ice pack and let her wait with Buddy, who was still there in one of the curtained examination rooms. His mother sat beside him. Jane introduced herself and learned her name was Mary.

"I can't thank you enough for coming to Dylan's aid," she said.

Jane shook off the uncomfortable praise and addressed Dylan, who she'd only known as Buddy. "You okay, Dylan?" His complexion had returned to normal.

He lurched back and forth with laughter, a wide smile on his face. "Yeah, you showed 'em, eh, Jaynee?"

"*We* showed 'em, Buddy."

Positively Plants was closed by the time Jane made it back. She sent Anna and Lucas a text with the good news about her wrist: It wasn't broken. She just had to keep it iced for a few days.

Then she jumped on her bike and drove home.

"Hey," Sadie said, sparing her a glance before looking back at her cellphone.

"You work today?" Jane sluffed off her jacket and draped it on the arm of the sofa. She took a seat beside Sadie. A dirty dinner plate sat on the trunk in front of her.

"Yeah." Sadie set her phone aside. "I brought chicken parm home if you want some. I already ate."

Jane examined her wrist. The bluing under her skin had blossomed.

Sadie saw it and sat up. "What happened?"

Jane rifled through her jacket's pocket and pulled out the nearly spent ice pack. "Couple of meth heads went after Buddy."

"Shit! Is he okay?"

"Yeah. Finally got to test out my roundhouse." She held out her wrist. "And my uppercut. FYI, it hurts as bad as the instructors said it would in the videos. But it's not broken." She and Sadie learned most of their moves through YouTube.

Sadie heated Jane's dinner and listened raptly as she unwound the story of the would-be theft. "He had a fucking gun?"

"Yeah, but you know how they are. He couldn't afford a fix, so he sure as hell couldn't afford bullets. The gun was just for show—a scare tactic."

"Sure. We'll just add 'show gun' to 'freak arson' and 'fluke car crash.' That works."

Jane absently stroked the mark on her hand. "Ariane's theory sounds like something out of a sci-fi flick. It's not as if the marks glowed or threw off sparks. They were just . . . there, like they always are."

"You gotta stop dismissing those birthmarks. Be grateful you don't have a bullet in you."

Sadie rounded the sofa and delivered Jane's plate. "The cops give you back your blade?"

"Nah," Jane said.

"Figures. Wouldn't be surprised if they tried to charge you with something."

"I hope not. I'm this close to paying off the bike," Jane said, lifting her hand, her thumb and forefinger not quite touching.

Jane stabbed a morsel and savoured the bite.

"You call the investment firm yet?"

Jane shook her head. "Nope." She'd put it out of her mind. Eventually, she'd have to look at the statement Nelson had dropped off. It had been years since she'd seen the balance. Maybe by now there'd be enough money to buy a small second-hand bus for an orphanage. Then again, a used bus seemed hardly a fitting tribute to the Walkers.

"Any luck finding that Rebecca chick?"

"Glaciers make better progress." Jane dipped another forkful in the marinara sauce and popped it in her mouth.

"Maybe you should reconsider asking the professors for help."

"No!" Jane nearly choked on her food. "I'm not telling them about my dreams." She'd sooner strip naked and prance down Granville Street. An involuntary quiver ran through her.

"You're overthinking it. They don't need to know Rebecca is from your dreams. Just tell them she knew your foster mom or something like that."

Jane looked down to her plate, poked at her food. Maybe Sadie was right. And no doubt the professor's investigator could find Rebecca faster than Jane could.

She washed their dishes, set them in the drain rack, and draped a perfectly aligned tea towel over top.

32 | Sadie

August 18

Sadie was back at the restaurant for an eleven-to-seven shift. She'd had to cancel a manicure to take it, but she wasn't turning down any extra shifts this month.

After she closed out, she found Cynthia's instructions on her phone and immediately regretted her earlier zeal. She'd had enough of smiling like she gave a shit, and now she had to keep it up for Rick. And more importantly, she had to pull off a performance that would convince him to cut short their trial period.

Sadie headed home to change, hoping against the odds that Jane would be out so she wouldn't have to deal with her disappointment. Luck wasn't on her side.

Jane turned from the sink as Sadie opened the door. "Hey, Sade."

"Hey. Thought you might be out with Ethan."

"He's working." Jane turned back to the dishes. "I already ate, but I can warm something for you."

"I'm not staying. Have a gig." Sadie scurried toward the bathroom. She had thirty minutes to get to the hotel.

"Another one? Man, Cynthia's keeping her word."

Sadie closed the door, stripped, and jumped in the shower.

"Take the bedroom tonight," she called, towelling off as she hit the bedroom. She was zipping up her skirt when Jane turned up in the bedroom doorway.

"It's not Rick Kristan again, is it?"

"Ah, no." Sadie hated lying, but she didn't have time to deal with Jane right now. Soon, though, she'd have to tell Jane that she'd made a deal with Cynthia.

"That's a relief. I dreamed about him again last night."

"Please don't tell me I was in it as well."

Jane laughed. "No. It was the younger Rick. There's something off about that guy."

Sadie cringed. "Is he abusive? Violent?"

"More like manipulative."

Sadie felt relief pulse through her. "Manipulative I can deal with—all johns have a bit of that going on." Sadie's phone dinged. "My cab's here." She stepped into her stilettos. "Don't wait up."

There was no answer when she knocked on Rick's door. She stood waiting. Was he playing some new game? She knocked again. When he failed to answer a second time, she took a chance and used her key card.

She found Rick passed out on the bed, shoes on and fully clothed. That was a first. An empty tumbler rested on the nightstand beside a dusting of coke.

She checked that he was breathing then walked to the bar and poured herself a drink. His dime, she thought, as she took a seat. She sipped her drink and watched him sleep. How had he gotten the scar on his face? she wondered.

When she finished her drink, she pulled out her phone and texted Jane. *I'm good here.*

"Who are you texting?" Rick said.

Sadie looked up in surprise. He hadn't moved or opened his eyes. "My roommate."

"Tell her you're busy."

"Of course." Sadie texted Jane *Later* and tucked her phone in her purse.

"Are you all right?" Sadie asked.

"You worried?" Rick opened his eyes and turned to her. "It's been a trying day."

"I can help with that," Sadie said, sliding into her role. She stood and sashayed to the foot of the bed, where she removed his shoes and then his socks. He watched her, his eyes at half-mast. She slid to the side of the bed and reached for his belt, but he waved her away and gestured at her blouse. She removed it and turned around to slowly unzip her pencil skirt. She'd worn the lace bra-and-thong set and was thinking of Andy as she shimmied out of it. She turned around.

"Keep the shoes on," Rick said.

The thought of seventy-five thousand dollars fuelled her performance. Rick didn't mention the buyout or Cynthia, but he wasn't himself either. His demands, like his hands, were rough. She'd be bruised come morning, and her scalp felt tender where he'd gripped her by the hair.

Afterward, she lay by his side stroking the greying hairs on his chest. "What happened today?" she asked.

"That almost sounds like you care."

His voice had a dangerous edge to it. Sadie held her tongue.

"My apologies," he said. "That was uncalled for."

"No. It's none of my business."

He stroked her arm. "I appreciate the sentiment."

"I have some news that might cheer you up."

"Oh?"

"I've decided to accept your offer."

He rolled his head in her direction. "You're prepared to leave Cynthia?"

"She's agreed to let me go. But how about we skip the three-month trial period?"

He slid his fingers through her curls, contemplating. "Cynthia won't be inclined to change our deal."

"Cynthia knows I only work one gig a month, and you've already paid for three. She's made her trial-period money."

"I'll talk to her. Perhaps I can change her mind," Rick said. "You'll need to resign from the restaurant. I won't work around someone else's schedule."

Sadie worried her lip. Lodestones was more than a job. When someone asked, she could say she was a waitress and hold her head up. She wasn't quitting the only proper job she'd ever had. She'd figure something out, find a way to work around Rick's schedule.

"And I need your phone number and address."

"After Cynthia agrees, I'll give you my phone number. Not my address." Jane would kill her if she gave him their address.

"You needn't worry about me dropping by. I'll send a driver when I want you."

She didn't agree to give him the address, but she didn't say no either. If he proved difficult to get rid of, then his having their address would be a problem. Then again, he already knew her name and where she worked. How difficult would it be for him to get her address?

Shit! Jane was going to go ballistic. Still, it wasn't as if Rick had a key to their apartment.

33 | Rick

Rick considered Sadie one of the few perks in an endless stream of spending. He'd set aside a stupid amount of money to eradicate the threat Jane posed. But nights like this made him wish his time with Sadie wasn't coming to an end. He was glad she'd been smart enough to give up on the name charade. Calling her by the wrong moniker was one less worry on his plate.

Cynthia had played right into his hands, allowing him to drive just enough of a wedge between Sadie and her so that he was the one who came out shining with integrity. And though he couldn't assess if Cynthia's lie of omission had caused it, he sensed a change in Sadie. Perhaps she'd figured out that he owned her now. But one thing hadn't changed: a couple rails of coke sparked her up as though she were born to be ridden.

34 | Jane

August 19

J ane had woken briefly when Sadie came home. She heard the shower
come on, rolled over, and went back to sleep.

Sadie was lying facedown on the sofa when Jane left for work.

She pushed through her morning watering routine begrudgingly
making allowances for her throbbing wrist. The adage about not doing
the crime if you couldn't do the time rolled around in her head, wagging
its finger at her. She wondered if the addict's jaw hurt as much as her wrist.

She'd like nothing more than to dismiss Ariane's notion that her
birthmarks were some kind of protection, but the incident with Buddy's
attackers and the gun kept getting in the way.

Hours later, when Jane arrived home after her shift, Sadie sat slumped on
the sofa in her restaurant gear. "You work today?"

"Four-hour shift," Sadie replied. "Brought a fajita home if you want
it. It's in the fridge."

Jane dropped her phone on the trunk and strolled into the kitchen
to warm the fajita. She was pulling it from the nuker when her phone rang.

Sadie glanced at the screen. "It's the professor."

"Maybe they found Rebecca! Put him on speaker," Jane said, rushing
to Sadie's side.

Sadie pushed the speaker button, and they bent their heads to the
phone.

"Jane?" Nate said.

"I'm here," Jane said. "Sadie's here too. You're on speaker. Has the
investigator found something?"

"Hunter hasn't, at least not yet, but I have. I got my hands on a copy
of the dermatology journal that features the photographs of you and your
birthmarks."

Jane lifted her head. "From when I was a kid?"

"Yeah. You mentioned it a couple of times. I wanted to put your mind at ease. It's a respected journal. Peer-reviewed. Strictly professional."

"You've got the journal there?" Jane asked.

"Ah, yeah. I'll send it to you."

"Would you get it now? I want to check something."

Sadie shot Jane a quizzical look.

"Sure. Hold on." A moment later, Nate was back. "Got it."

"Tell me if there's a mark on the bottom of my right foot."

They heard the sound of paper flipping. "Here it is. No. No mark on the bottom of either foot."

Jane's shoulders slumped. "You must have the wrong journal."

"I'm looking right at it, Jane. It's definitely you."

Jane drew her eyebrows together. "Is there a mark on the top of my left foot?"

"No. No mark on either foot. Top or bottom."

"Then it's not me," Jane said. She reached down, pulled the running shoe from her left foot, and tugged off her sock. She furrowed her brow and shot a look at Sadie. "That's not possible."

"What's not possible?" Nate asked.

Jane quickly removed her other shoe and sock and glanced at her feet. The stains were gone from both of her feet.

"What's happening?" Jane whispered. Her stomach clenched.

"We'll call you back," Sadie said, and she disconnected Nate's call.

"This is unbelievable," Jane said. "I know I had a mark on the bottom of my right foot. Top of my left. I'm not insane. Please tell me you remember."

"No question. But they're not there now."

Jane sat back, dazed. "I should be happy about that. Right?"

"Right. Happy." Sadie curled her lips around her teeth.

Jane jumped up and rushed to the bathroom. Moments later she returned, tugging her shirt back into place.

"The rest of them still there?"

Jane nodded, distracted. "The mark on the bottom of my foot could have been fading for a while—it's not like I ever checked on it—but not the mark on top. That one was definitely there when I was at Ethan's."

"I'm just going to come right out and say this," Sadie said. "Mumbo-jumbo or not, something disturbing is happening. Port wine stains don't just vanish. Call the professor back. Tell him what's going on."

Thirty minutes later, Jane and Sadie were once again walking up Nate's front path. He met them at the door and silently ushered them into the kitchen.

Ariane leaned back against the counter, her arms crossed. She wore her hair in the same slick ponytail. "Joyce, Sadie," she said, greeting them.

Jane paused. The name grated on her, and one personal detail wouldn't kill her. They'd earned it. "Call me Jane. Please. Joyce is the name of the SkyTrain station where my mother abandoned me."

"All right."

Nate suggested they sit. "Can I get you something?" he said, as they took the seats they'd occupied the last time they sat in his kitchen. No one took him up on his beverage offer.

"May I see the journal?" Jane asked.

Nate reached to the counter behind him and grabbed the journal. He held it out to Jane. She noticed he had two copies. She flipped slowly through the pages. It was the first time she'd ever seen the photos that had haunted her.

"I don't understand why these pictures don't show them," Jane said. "But I'm not mistaken. Sadie can back me. I had birthmarks on my feet. Prominent ones, and now they're gone."

"Fascinating," Ariane said. "The fact that they're vanishing from your skin, from that journal," she said, pointing, "may explain why we've never seen evidence of that mark on a person before. Maybe on humans the mark was never meant to be permanent."

"Are you for real? Vanishing from a journal?" Ariane really had drunk the folklore Kool-Aid. "Doesn't it make more sense that those marks were just not very pronounced back then?"

A look of concern crossed Ariane's face. "When did the first mark disappear?"

Jane pressed her lips together and quirked a shoulder. "It's not like I take roll call."

"It would be good if we knew how fast they're disappearing," Nate said.

"Why?" Jane asked.

Nate looked to Ariane, who answered. "If they continue to fade, the rate at which they're disappearing will help us determine how long you have until they're all gone."

"And if they all disappear?" Sadie asked.

"Then Jane's protection will end," Ariane said.

Jane rubbed her face. She felt like a rat trapped on a conversational sticky strip.

"The timing could be important," Ariane said. "Jane, do you remember when the first one vanished?"

Jane dropped her hand to her lap. "I noticed the one on the bottom of my foot missing a few days ago. The one on top must have vanished today sometime."

Ariane frowned in concentration. "Do you have a birthday coming up?"

"Yes, at the end of the month." Jane felt a pinch of anxiety. "How did you know?"

"Call it a hunch," Ariane said.

"I bet that's it," Nate said. He looked to Ariane. "Doesn't give us much time."

Sadie looked up from the journal.

"Time for what?" Jane asked.

"To find out why you have those markings. There's no question they're Inca, and I believe your parents arranged for them to protect you from something or someone. It's vital we learn what or who before the marks disappear altogether."

Jane crossed her arms and shook her head. "See, that's where you lose me. If my so-called parents were so keen to protect me, why did they abandon me? Why!" The question had echoed through every moment of her life, and there was a time when she'd cared, but she was so done with it. Her parents hadn't spontaneously combusted. They could have left a note, sent a letter. They could have given her up for adoption—that, Jane could have understood.

"I don't know," Ariane said. "They paid a price to get those markings. Maybe giving you up was the price."

"Yeah, that just makes it worse. First off, what kind of parent would agree to any of that? Marking their kid like this? Abandoning them? And second, why? It makes zero sense. I'm no one special. I have no money, nothing of value. I'm no threat to anyone."

Sadie crossed her arms and pinched her lips. Nate watched her with curiosity. Jane silently willed Sadie to keep her mouth shut about the dreams. Jane might have to concede to Ariane's theory about the marks protecting her, but her marks weren't connected to her dreams—Jane's parents hadn't stuck around long enough to know about them.

Ariane looked down to her hands, which were folded on the table. "I can't tell you why, Jane. I wish I could. The only thing I know for certain is that someone went to extreme lengths to protect you. They must have known someone meant to do you harm. I believe those marks have already saved your life. Once in the house fire and again in the car accident."

"Something you want to say, Sadie?" Nate asked.

Sadie wouldn't meet Jane's gaze. "Someone tried to shoot her a couple of days ago."

Nate's and Ariane's heads swivelled to Jane, who stared wide-eyed at Sadie in disbelief.

"It wasn't a big deal," Jane said. "Some meth heads tried to rob a friend of mine. I stopped them. The gun was just a prop."

"A cop tasered the guy," Sadie added.

"That makes three," Ariane said. "The *coincidences* are piling up."

Sadie closed the journal and addressed Jane. "Maybe she's right. Unless you've got some other bizarre explanation for what's happening."

Ariane chuckled. "Bizarre is normal for me. I grew up steeped in superstition. Our family lore goes back countless generations and unashamedly hints at otherworldly events. It's why I chose this area of study. The unexplained calls to me."

"I don't know," Jane said. "My marks are disappearing, and I'd like to know why, but I'm having a hard time fitting my situation into your Inca lore."

"It's a lot to absorb," Nate said. "But don't dismiss what Ariane says. We wouldn't need scholars if all the world's mysteries were solved, now would we?"

Jane and Sadie exchanged a glance.

"Is there something else?" Ariane asked.

"Tell them," Sadie mumbled.

Jane's nostrils flared. Her expression hardened into a furious glare aimed at Sadie.

"Tell us what?" Nate asked.

"It's nothing," Jane said. She scooted back her chair and stood. "It's late. We should go."

"Please," Ariane said. "If it's anything that would help us solve the riddle."

"It's not," Jane said. "It's private."

"I'm not wrong about this," Ariane said. "Those marks are protecting you. For now. It would serve you well to know why. And from what."

"Thanks for the warning," Jane said.

The moment Sadie closed the car door, Jane turned on her. "What the hell, Sadie?"

"I'm sorry." Sadie started the engine. "I just thought—"

"You didn't think. It was bad enough you added fuel to their little theory and told them about the gun. But you were going to tell them about my dreams. How could you? You're the only one who knows. The only one I trust." Jane thrust her seatbelt into place. In the uncomfortable silence of the trip home, Jane questioned Sadie's loyalty for the very first time.

"You can have the bedroom," Jane said, sliding the second bolt lock into place.

"All right." Sadie poured herself a glass of wine, took it into the bedroom, and closed the door.

Jane dropped to the sofa. She felt wounded. How could Sadie bring up her dreams to Nate and Ariane, people they barely knew? She glanced at the medical journal on the trunk. Nate had insisted she take it.

Jane changed for bed and lay on the sofa staring at the ceiling. She folded the edge of the sheet and pressed it with her palms. Sadie had closed the bedroom door without saying good night.

Maybe she'd been too hard on her. Jane felt terrible about the tension between them. Tension she'd caused. Her world didn't feel right without Sadie in it.

Jane tossed the blanket aside and padded to the bedroom door. She tapped. "You awake?"

"Uh-huh."

Jane opened the door. "I'm sorry I yelled at you."

"I know. It's okay." Sadie sat propped up against the wall behind the bed with her wineglass in one hand and her phone in the other. "I'm sorry I told them about the gun."

Jane sat on the edge of the bed. "I hate it when we argue."

"Me too." Sadie set down her phone. She ran her finger around the rim of her glass. "I love you, Narc. You know that. I'd never hurt you, but you've got your head up some serious ass on this one. I know you don't want to hear it, but you need to woman up and tell Nate and Ariane about your dreams." Sadie held up her hand, stifling Jane's protest. "Hear me out. You dream some crazy shit. Except it's not crazy because the shit in your dreams is real—it's happened. But it's shit you shouldn't know."

Sadie met Jane's gaze. "Maybe that's why you've got those birthmarks. Why you need protecting."

Jane looked down to the blanket and traced her finger around an old stain. "My dreams can't be the reason. My parents couldn't possibly have known before I was born that I would have these dreams. And except for you, no one knows that I dream about them. The last person I confided in was a boy named Adam, and that was in grade five. He shoved me into a mud puddle when I tried to console him about something I saw in a dream."

Sadie smiled a knowing smile. "Yeah, boys want to be tough guys."

Jane looked up from under her lashes. "I told him I thought his old man was a bastard."

"Uh-huh. And you wonder why he shoved you into a puddle?" Sadie took another sip of wine. "Still, if Ariane is right, someone wants to get rid of you. You've had three near misses. I think you need to take Ariane's warning seriously."

Jane looked down to the mark on the back of her left hand. "You think these marks protect me?"

"You got a better theory?"

"How about they're port wine stains. Regular old birthmarks."

"You're pushing back awfully hard. Why? Your birthmarks are disappearing. From a fucking journal."

"Come on. You know that's impossible."

"Impossible? Like your dreams? The two are connected. And deep down I think you know it."

Jane pulled her legs up and hugged her knees. She knew she was fighting to keep her dreams away from Ariane's theories, but that was because not fighting meant that her dreams were deadly—someone wanted to kill her because of them. And that thought made her feel as if she were choking. "Can I have a sip?"

"It's yours," Sadie said, passing her the glass.

Jane tasted the wine. "What if Nate and Ariane are the people I need protecting from?"

Sadie stilled. "I hadn't thought of that."

Jane took another sip and picked at a loose thread on the hem of her sleep pants. "Oh no." Her scalp prickled. She shifted and yanked up her left pant leg.

"What?" Sadie asked.

"More of my birthmark has disappeared."

"Really? Show me."

Jane twisted her leg to show Sadie the newly clear skin on her lower left leg.

"Incredible. Shit, Narc."

"My whole life, I've wanted these ugly birthmarks to disappear, and now, bit by bit, they are. It's hard not to be happy about that. I wish I'd never heard Ariane's theory about the marks being some kind of mumbo-jumbo protection."

Sadie jumped out of bed. "Where's the journal?"

"On the trunk."

A moment later, Sadie returned, flipping through the pages. She stopped and looked at Jane. "Not mumbo-jumbo." She turned the journal around and put it under Jane's nose. The mark on Jane's lower left leg was no longer visible in the journal.

"On the upside," Sadie said, crawling back into bed, "if all your marks are gone by your birthday, you'll get to wish for something different this year."

Jane swallowed a gulp of wine. "Or whoever I need protecting from might get their wish instead."

35 | Rick

Rick's thoughts were often of his father in the days before the funeral. Though he remained saddened that his father would never know about his promotion, he set aside the regret. Regret was a useless emotion. He accepted the situation for what it was: a lesson. He understood now that he'd put far too much value in his father's opinion of him.

He pictured his father with the canes he needed to get around after arthritis had crippled him. He'd died a husk of the man he used to be. Rick had felt the sting of the strict disciplinarian's belt more often than any child should.

Rick's mother was coping well considering she was burying her husband of fifty-two years. Her macular degeneration had almost blinded her in recent years, but she'd always been blind in other ways: blind to the abuse his father inflicted in the name of discipline, blind to Michael's lies.

So blind she happily jumped at Michael's insistence that the funeral be a rushed affair so that precious Mikey could be back in Victoria for a critical meeting that wouldn't survive his absence. What an ego. Not even their father's death rose above Mikey's self-importance.

When Rick pulled into the parking lot of Henderson's Funeral Home, Michael's Mercedes sedan was already taking up a spot. Though Mikey could afford a hotel, he—along with his Barbie-esque wife and their adult children—had been freeloading with their mother. Rick had relegated contact with his mother to phone calls after his brother's family's occupation.

Rick steeled himself before getting out of his SUV. For his mother's sake, he'd have to be the Teflon man today and sluff off whatever garbage Mikey threw his way. He fortified himself knowing their father's power of attorney had turned to ashes on his death. Rick emerged from the SUV and headed inside. Barbie had her arm around his mother. Michael stood to the side, engaged in a conversation with an old friend of their father's.

"Elaine," Rick said, approaching his sister-in-law. Elaine immediately dropped her arm.

"There you are," his mother said, as Rick gave her a hug.

"How you holding up?" Rick said, moving her away from prying ears.

"Good. Elaine's keeping me busy, filling the freezer. I'm going to miss them when they leave."

"Yes. You have a big adjustment ahead. But I'm close by. I'll help you get through it."

Michael walked around Rick's blind side. "We'll both help you through it, Mom," Michael said, butting into their conversation.

"How're you doing, Rick? Haven't seen you out at the house. You should come by. Have a drink."

"I've been busy."

"I'm sure. Still, it'd be good to catch up. Raise a toast to the old man."

Rick glared at him. Mikey never stopped playing the game, always trying to come off like Mr. Congeniality, the reasonable one.

"I wish you two would make amends," their mother said. "I need both my boys right now."

She didn't need Mikey—hadn't for quite some time. And with Dad's influence gone and Mikey living at a distance, the family dynamics were about to shift.

Poor Mikey.

36 | Jane

August 20

Anna swept into the greenhouse and waved to get Jane's attention. "Buddy's here with his mom. He's looking for you."

"Be right there," Jane said, wiping the sweat from her brow. The late-blooming perennials had arrived, and she'd been dodging customers to get them on the shelves. She adjusted her bandana and followed Anna to the front desk.

Buddy's mom, Mary, stood off to the side.

"Hey, Buddy. How ya doing?" A large gift box sat in his lap. Jane felt touched, and at the same time, her heart sank at the sight of it.

"Good. Thanks. This is for you. Fer helpin' me."

"Ah, Buddy, I can't—"

Mary stepped forward, fidgeting with her purse strap. "Dylan insisted I bake them for you. They're his favourite."

"I helped."

"He did," Mary said, smiling at her son.

Jane looked back to Buddy, relieved that he hadn't spent money on an unnecessary gift. "You baked something for me?" She knelt to open the box. "May I?" Buddy beamed, rocking in his chair. Jane lifted the lid to find a tray of pastries. "Butter tarts!" Her face split into a smile. "They're my favourite too. Thank you."

Jane lifted the box from Buddy's lap and set it on the counter. She leaned down and kissed him on the cheek. "That was very thoughtful, Buddy. I'm glad you're okay."

"Thank you for all you did, Jane," Mary said. "I'm so grateful."

"Anyone would have done the same."

"*Anyone* wasn't there. You were." Mary reached out her hand, looking for purchase, and settled on Jane's forearm. She patted it then quickly withdrew, settling it once again to worry her purse strap.

"She's fearless, this one," Anna said, sounding like a proud mother. Jane flushed. Anna turned to address Mary. "Let's go for a coffee sometime soon. It really has been too long."

"You know one another?" Jane asked.

"We met years ago. In the maternity ward," Anna said, and her smile ebbed.

"I'll be in touch," Mary said. "We won't keep you from your work. Enjoy the tarts. You ready, Dylan?"

Before Buddy and Mary had reached the intersection, Jane and Anna had each scoffed down a tooth-achingly sweet and runny tart, made just the way Jane liked them.

"Mary called you Jane," Anna said.

"Yeah. I don't usually go by Joyce."

"But Joyce is a beautiful name."

Jane stared out the window. "Someone at the hospital named me after the Joyce SkyTrain station. It's where I was abandoned. I prefer Jane."

"Oh, sweetie. All these years? Why have you never mentioned this?"

Jane swept imaginary crumbs from the counter. "I'd already been working here awhile when I found out." Back when Nelson Leonard had suggested the job at the nursery, he'd told Jane that if she wanted the job, he'd have to give the Bakkers some background on her, including her scrapes at the group homes. The Bakkers had hired her anyway, willing to give her a chance. She hadn't been keen to cause them to rethink that decision by making trouble over her name. But looking at Anna now, Jane realized she'd misjudged them. They would have understood.

"I should have said something. I'm sorry. Speaking of 'all these years,' I didn't know you knew Buddy's mom."

Anna exhaled a heavy weight. "Not very well. Our sons were born on the same day at St. Paul's. Should have been the happiest day of her life. Turned into a vigil instead." Anna reached out to straighten a stack of flyers. "Every time I see Dylan, I think of Pieter. It could just as easily have been my son," Anna said, with a mournful shake of her head. "I'm so blessed."

"Buddy's lucky to have such a great mom. So is Pieter." Jane pushed the tart box in Anna's direction. "Have another."

At the end of the workday, Jane retrieved the tarts from the breakroom and headed home to find a note from Sadie saying she'd taken a shift and would be home after seven.

Feeling bold, Jane texted Ethan. *Miss you.*

He answered right away. *Swing by the apt. I don't start til 8.*

Jane's heart leapt. She took the fastest shower of her life, brushed her teeth, and skipped out of the apartment. She parked next to his Harley, and her heart melted at the sight of him staring down at her from his window. Shirtless. Oh yeah, she wanted a piece of that.

He pulled her inside the apartment and had his lips on hers before the door closed. "I missed you too," he said, when he finally pulled away, breathless.

She stared into his light-brown eyes and dared to hope she was more than a booty call. She'd never felt drawn to a man the way she felt drawn to Ethan. It frightened her as much as it excited her. She tucked the scary part away and concentrated on the present—the hard-bodied man unbuttoning her jeans as he slowly walked her backwards to the bed. They peeled off each other's clothes, leaving a trail of garments in their wake, and sank into sheets that smelled freshly laundered. He'd changed the bedding for her. His attention to detail was impressive, and it wasn't just about the fresh sheets. He took his time, exploring every inch of her, finding erogenous zones she didn't know she had. And he steadfastly held the lead this time, not letting her rush ahead like she desperately wanted.

When he'd finally wrung every ounce of ecstasy from her, they collapsed in a spent heap. Jane closed her eyes and savoured the moment.

"What are you smiling at?" Ethan said.

She turned her head. He'd been watching her again. "This chemistry between us. It's . . . hot. You are amazing."

"It is pretty hot—and I am amazing," he said, wagging an eyebrow. He laughed as she swatted at him. He pulled her into his arms, and she curled into him. He trailed his fingers over the mark on her biceps.

"I noticed more of your birthmarks are gone."

Jane stretched her leg out and looked. "Yup."

"Strange, isn't it? Have you asked your doctor about it?"

She should have said that strange wasn't the half of it. She should have told him what was going on. But fear had her in its grip once again. What would he make of Ariane's theories?

"Yeah, strange," Jane said.

Ethan shifted under her shoulder. "You know what else is strange?"

Jane turned her head to look at him. "What?"

"You froze up harder than a cue ball when I mentioned your missing birthmarks."

"Did I?" Jane's gaze slid to his chest. She contemplated how much she could tell him without scaring him off. "I heard a theory the other day about why I was losing them."

Ethan tipped his head. "Go on."

"It's bizarre really, but I guess it's one way to explain disappearing port wine stains." Jane stroked his chest, gathering her thoughts. "The pattern in my birthmark isn't unique," she started, and then she told him about the ribbon tacked to the entrance of Ariane's family home in Peru and the museum's offering bowl. She finished with Ariane's conclusion that the marks' protection would end when the last mark vanished.

"Sounds like something from the brothers Grimm. Who is this Ariane woman?"

"She's a colleague of a customer from work. The customer is a professor at UBC. He saw the mark on my hand and recognized it."

"You sure he's a real prof? 'Cause that theory of why your marks are disappearing is a little far out there," Ethan said.

"Yeah, but he does have an office at UBC with his name on the door." On her phone, she pulled up the museum's website and showed him the Inca offering bowl.

"Huh. I still think this theory sounds like a dark fairy tale, but it'd be incredible if it were true, wouldn't it?"

Jane nodded. "Yeah, incredible. But it would mean someone out there is sharpening an axe with my name on it."

"They'd have to get through me first," Ethan said, as he rolled on top of her. He settled between her legs and found his way inside her again.

"Guess I don't need to ask where you've been," Sadie said, looking up from thumbing something into her phone. Jane looked at her quizzically as she set her helmet on the floor.

"It's the sappy smile," Sadie said, shifting her gaze back to her screen.

"This is not a sappy smile," Jane said, laughing. Buddy's box of butter tarts lay open on the trunk.

"You're right. It's more like a 'I'm so glad Ethan doesn't have ED' smile." Sadie put her phone away. "Seriously, Narc. You look happy. It's good to see. Where'd you get the tarts? They're really good."

Jane heeled out of her boots and sat beside Sadie. "Buddy's mom baked them."

"Nice."

Jane pulled the pastry box close. "Did you already eat dinner?" She plucked out a butter tart.

"No, but I'm good with these." Sadie leaned in and helped herself, moaning her appreciation around a mouthful of flaky pastry.

"How about I go to Safeway and pick up some chicken wings and greens?"

"If you're going to Fourth Avenue just swing by Mickey D's and skip the stove."

"We eat takeout way too often. For the same price, we can eat for two nights. Three if we keep stuffing our faces with these tarts."

"Killjoy," Sadie said, and reached for another pastry.

Thirty minutes later, Jane was in the kitchen spicing up the wings. After getting them into the oven, she joined Sadie on the sofa. "You were pretty quick to brush off your gig with Rick the other night when I asked," she said, and joined Sadie on the sofa. "Did something happen?"

"Nah. Rick is manageable. It's Cynthia who's pushing my buttons."

"She doesn't like being challenged."

"She went behind my back. Offered him a deal. He's got me all to himself for three months. She didn't even ask my opinion."

"Well, her opinion was pretty clear." Jane queued up an episode of *Black Mirror* on the laptop. "You change your mind about taking him up on his buyout offer?"

Sadie's gaze drifted. She rubbed her phone against her bottom lip. "It's seventy-five grand, so yeah, I'm thinking about it. I'm thinking about a lot of things."

Jane whistled. "Seventy-five grand? What are you going to do?"

Sadie gave a noncommittal shrug.

Jane imagined the doors that kind of money could open for Sadie— one final gig to end them all. But the tug of hope soon faltered. As much as she wanted Sadie clear of the business, it wouldn't be because of a john. That was way too *Pretty Woman*. And this particular john made Jane uneasy. "You think you can dump him when you need to?"

"That's the seventy-five-thousand-dollar question." Sadie grabbed her phone and thumbed out a message. "Rick asked me about you."

Jane snapped her head around. "Me! What the hell, Sadie?"

"It's not what you think. He saw you drop me off at the restaurant the other day. He was on the patio. Didn't know I worked there. Saw your birthmarks," she said, twirling a finger to indicate Jane's face. "Was curious."

"What'd you tell him?"

"Not much. That we're roommates. That the marks are port wine stains."

"Weren't you worried he was getting too close? Now he knows where you work, that you have a roommate—"

"And my name."

"Shit." The apprehension Jane had felt about Rick escalated.

"He saw it on my nametag. Not sure it's a big deal. We could be spending a lot of time together in the next few months. Now I won't have to worry about tripping up."

"No. You just have to worry that he knows your name and where you work." Jane didn't add that he now knew about her as well.

"I can't change it, Narc."

"You sure he didn't know you worked there?" Jane asked. Sadie shrugged. "You think he's stalking you?"

"I'd considered that, but I don't think so."

"I hope you're right." Jane wasn't so sure. "Seems weird, doesn't it? Rick on one side of you, me on the other, you in the middle."

Sadie raised an eyebrow. "That doesn't sound awkward at all."

Jane laughed. "I didn't mean literally."

"Maybe this is how it's supposed to be. How we get close enough to ask him about a cure for your dreams."

Jane's face lit up in alarm.

Sadie raised a hand. "Don't worry. I won't say a word without your say-so." Her attention diverted to her vibrating phone. She exhaled in disappointment. "Andy can't come out to play."

They balanced dinner plates on their laps while *Black Mirror* played out on the computer. When they'd both finished eating, Jane picked up their dishes and took them to the kitchen.

"Sadie," Jane said. "That night in December at Hy's—do you remember a tray of glasses falling to the floor shortly after you were seated?"

Sadie looked up at the ceiling, squinting into the past. "Yeah, I do. Felt sorry for whoever caused it. They probably had their pay docked. Why are you asking?"

Jane hesitated. "I think it was me who knocked them over. They were champagne flutes."

"You're shitting me."

"It's happened before. A few dreams ago, I touched a door and it moved."

"Jesus, Narc. Are you sure?"

"No. I mean, it was just a dream, right? But I swear. I backed into that tray of glasses. I could feel the edge of it right here," she said, pointing to her butt. "And the door? It creaked when I touched it." She examined her right hand. "It felt solid under my palm. How is that possible?"

"You're asking me? How is any of it possible?"

A deep furrow knitted Jane's brow. "Do you remember Mrs. Nicols, our science teacher in grade nine? Remember she talked about the butterfly effect?"

"Vaguely. Something about how a butterfly flapping its wings can cause a hurricane halfway around the world?"

"Something like that. What if me upsetting a tray of glasses or opening a door caused something in history to change? Something big?"

"Like what? Someone didn't get their champagne so didn't turn into a raging alcoholic and ruin some kid's life?"

"Exactly."

"That was sarcasm, Narc. A joke." Sadie leaned back into the sofa. "Shit."

"Yeah. Shit." Jane's thoughts rolled back to something she'd said to Ariane. *I have nothing of value.* Unless she was the butterfly flapping its wings. Maybe her dreams *were* valuable.

"Perhaps it's time you told Ariane and Nate about your dreams," Sadie said, as if reading her thoughts.

Jane looked over at her. "Are you really going there again? You know how I feel about that. I'm not telling anyone about my dreams." But for once, she wondered if she should.

August 21

"Good morning, Jane," Anna called.

A smile spread across Jane's face at the sound of her name. Her real name, as far as she was concerned. "Morning," she said, and headed to the breakroom to change. After she'd finished her watering routine, she went in search of Lucas. She found his office door closed and hesitated. His door was seldom closed. Rather than interrupt, she headed to the orchids to find Anna.

"Lucas's door is closed," Jane said.

"The police are here. They're grilling him about your knife."

"Oh. Guess they didn't believe me."

"I had no idea it was illegal to carry a concealed knife," Anna said.

Jane knew. "I wouldn't call my pruning knife concealed. The holster protects the blade, is all." Her boot knife? Now that was concealed. The environment she'd grown up in had taught her it was best to be prepared and to hell with legalities.

Jane followed Anna to the front desk. "How long have they been in there?"

Anna checked her watch. "Twenty minutes."

"Seems like a long time to ask if I use a pruning knife for work."

Jane and Anna turned to the sound of the office door opening. Voices drifted out. Jane backed away behind the picked-over seed stand. Lucas kept up an easy banter with the uniformed cops as he walked alongside them.

"There you are," Lucas said, blowing Jane's feeble cover. "You remember Constables Hewitt and Zhou?"

"Hello again," Jane said.

"They're here to confirm a few details around the incident with Buddy. You didn't tell me one of his assailants had a gun."

"What!" Anna said.

"He didn't have time to use it," Jane said, mollifying Anna. "Besides, the guy's an addict. He wouldn't have wasted money on bullets."

"That kind of thinking will get you killed," Zhou said. "Not only was the gun loaded, it had been fired. Lucky for you, it jammed. Next time, stand down and give them what they want."

Jane stilled. Swallowed.

"Did you bring my knife back?"

"We'll get you another," Anna said.

The officers thanked Lucas for his time and left.

"What else did they ask about?" Jane said, watching the officers approach their cruiser. They'd left it in the no-parking zone.

"Nothing I wouldn't have expected. How long you'd worked here, your address."

"They ask if I caused you any trouble?"

"They might have if I hadn't told them you've been an exemplary employee. You earned that, Jane."

Jane. Her frown melted. "Thank you." She turned before her eyes sprang a leak, and strode back to the waiting late-season bloomers.

Visiting Dream

Jane hears a doctor's name being called over an intercom. She spots Rick standing at a bustling nurses' station in his white coat, furiously scribbling on a chart. A man in scrubs sits behind an array of monitors. Acute Care is emblazoned on the wall behind him.

Jane gazes around the ward. Bold numbers above wide doorways identify the patient rooms. Through the rooms' glass walls, Jane has a clear view of the patients. She already knows she'll find Rebecca in one of them.

She takes a step and stops then looks at the floor. The cold linoleum sends chills up her legs despite what looks like heat waves rippling up from her bare feet. She rubs her arms and resumes her search. In the third room, she finds Rebecca.

Even though she's unconscious, she's strapped to the bed. Wires extend out from under her blanket and a needle snakes from her arm to a hanging bag of clear liquid. Another suicide attempt?

Jane's attention is drawn back to Rick.

"Absolutely no visitors," he says. "We don't know what or who set her off." He hands the chart to the man behind the monitors. "Transport her to us as soon as she's stable. We'll be waiting for her."

"Will do. The police sent someone to talk to you. Ask at reception on the first floor. They'll show you where they parked him."

"Thanks. Take care of her," Rick says, and he walks briskly out the door.

Jane jerked awake. She puzzled over the timing of the dream. Had Rebecca's suicide attempt followed Rick's visit to her apartment, where he'd given her the sedative, or had months passed?

Jane raised her arm and gazed at her pale-blue nightshirt. She'd been wearing it in her dream. She remembered rubbing her arms and feeling the soft cotton. Had she always worn her nightclothes in her dreams? She couldn't remember ever being aware of her clothing before.

She closed her eyes but couldn't shake a deep foreboding.

37 | Rick

August 22

Betty, the woman Rick had found to help his mother adjust to living alone with blindness, had been remarkably efficient. It had taken her only two days to assess the house and make the necessary changes. Better still, his mom seemed to like the woman and agreed to have her check in regularly and take her out to shop and socialize.

Rick took advantage of one of those planned outings to search his mother's papers and learn just how far Mikey's influence had seeped. He dropped the mail on the kitchen table and strode to his father's office. Lucky for him, his parents hadn't joined the paperless movement. Also lucky for him, his father wasn't very inventive about where he hid the key to the file cabinet.

A quick perusal of the bank statements indicated someone had set up regular payments to the utility companies as well as a bank credit card. On the second and fourth of each month, their government pension cheques were deposited. On the fifth of the month, Mikey's investment firm deposited a modest stipend. There wasn't much left after the bills were paid. He knew his parents were frugal, but they'd been living like paupers. Why? And where was the rest of their money? Surely they hadn't invested the sum of it with Mikey.

Rick came across the phone bill, which listed several long-distance numbers. Looked like his mother phoned Mikey's land line every few days. The credit card statement outlined his mother's expenditures: groceries, hairdresser, and a handful of local shops whose names he recognized.

His mother's new will was a surprise. It hadn't taken her long to take care of that detail after his father's death. More of Mikey's influence no doubt. He scanned the details. Mikey had been named sole executor. Naturally. How many times had his father explained his decisions with

Michael's the oldest, or *Michael's the financial expert*? Rick fumed at the affront, but took comfort seeing that the estate was still destined to be split equally between the brothers.

Behind the new will was a power of attorney. He should have known his mother would have one. It was identical to his father's, naming Mikey. A stinging reminder.

Where were the investment statements from Mikey's firm? Or any other firm? Rick moved on to the desk and then the closet. He found nothing. Now that he thought about it, he couldn't recall having seen any such statement in the two years he'd been collecting their mail. Had the financial phenom directed the statements to himself? That had to be a conflict of interest. And if his mother's positive assessment of how well their assets were doing under Mikey's stewardship was based on Mikey's opinion, then she needed a wake-up call. Rick would have a forensic audit done as soon as he got his hands on those statements.

Rick returned to the kitchen and flipped through the mail, filtering out the junk and flyers. A large manila envelope from a RE/MAX realtor with a Victoria address drew his curiosity. It was personally addressed, so not the usual bulk mail, vulture approach. He eased it open. Inside, he found a property assessment for the family's Langley home. The cover letter was addressed to Mikey and his mother, per his brother's recent request.

Damn him! He was gearing up to sell the place and would probably siphon the proceeds into his company's hands. And without a word to Rick.

Mikey had his fingers everywhere. Who else was influencing his mother? He picked up the land line and scrolled through the recent calls. RE/MAX showed up twice. So had Marlin Travel. What was that about? he wondered.

He heard a car approach. Betty emerged from his father's Lexus and walked around the car to help his mother out. She kept a hand on his mother's elbow as they made their way to the door that Rick held open.

"Hello, Mom," he said, and kissed her cheek.

"Have you been waiting long?" she asked.

"Just got here. How are you, Betty?"

"Never better. I'll let you two visit and go finish the laundry." Betty scooted past them and disappeared to the back of the house.

Rick guided his mother to a chair. "Marlin Travel called while you were gone."

"You don't need to answer the phone, dear. The machine will pick up."

"You planning a trip?"

"Betty suggested a change of scenery for a few weeks. We're considering Palm Springs."

"That's a wonderful idea." And a trip to Palm Springs would give him time to find the investment statements he was certain had to be in the house somewhere.

38 | Sadie

Sadie padded on autopilot from the bedroom to the bathroom to the kitchen. Jane's clean cereal bowl rested under a towel in the drain rack. A pinch of guilt surfaced. She should have been more forthcoming with Jane about Rick's offer. At this point, even if Cynthia didn't agree to reduce the trial period, she'd already accepted the deal. She could drag her feet about giving Rick their address, but what was the point? Jane wouldn't be happy about it, but it wasn't as if Sadie were bringing the business into their home. She'd never expose Jane to that risk.

Sadie took her coffee and a bowl of Alpha-Bits to the sofa. All she had to do was convince Jane that Rick having their address was a harmless necessity. Seventy-five grand in her bank account would be a good start. So would convincing her that she could ditch the guy when she had to. And if not, they could find another apartment. Hell, Sadie would have the funds to pay out their lease *and* pay a new security deposit. It would be nice to be the roommate with the cash reserve for a change.

But moving wouldn't get rid of Rick, she reminded herself. He knew where she worked, and she wasn't giving up her job, regardless of what Rick wanted. She considered asking her boss for some kind of leave of absence. Or maybe she could apply for a job at one of the company's sister restaurants—somewhere Rick wouldn't find her.

None of those options appealed to her; pulling a disappearing act would mean looking over her shoulder for years. No, she'd rather take a page from Kate Hudson's movie about how to lose a guy in ten days and transform herself into precisely the type of woman Rick didn't want. Sadie had acting chops. She could do clingy, needy. She imagined he'd get pretty tired of her calling him at work, showing up uninvited. He'd hate it if she fell in love with him, and she could definitely fake that, or tell him she was pregnant—oopsie! Yeah, she could get rid of the guy when she needed to.

Her phone buzzed. "Cynthia," Sadie answered.

"Rick has renegotiated. You'll get sixty, tops."

"The deal is seventy-five."

"*Was* seventy-five. He dropped two-thirds of the trial period. It's over at the end of the month. Seems he's anxious to take over."

Sadie smiled. "That's between you and Rick. My deal is with you and it's *still* seventy-five."

"I suspect you had something to do with Rick's request, but I'll tell you what. I'll pay sixty now, the other fifteen, when you're back in the stable."

"You can hold back ten."

Silence stretched on so long Sadie thought she'd blown it.

"Fine. But this ATM is closed. You won't see a penny before the trial period expires. And exactly six months after it expires, if you don't take a gig from me, you'll forfeit the holdback. That's my final offer."

"But you'll pay me for the trial-period gigs, right?"

"What part of 'not a penny before the trial period expires' was unclear?"

"My rent's not going to pay itself. I'll need some cash."

"You should have considered that before you sweet-talked your john at my expense. Final offer. If you don't want it, I'll sell him someone else."

"He wants me."

"I can be very persuasive, but sure. You can take that gamble."

Shit! She was inches away from more money than she'd seen in her life. The thought of losing it made her ill.

"Deal," Sadie said.

Cynthia didn't say goodbye.

Sadie headed to Kits Beach that afternoon and spread out a beach towel. Since agreeing to the deal with Cynthia, she'd been working out how she'd pay her half of this month's rent. Regretfully, she'd spent most of her gig cash paying down her credit card debt. She'd been working her ass off at the restaurant with extra shifts, but it wasn't enough. She'd have to fit in even more shifts and pray that Rick's growing appetite didn't collide with them.

It wouldn't be for long, she reminded herself. In a matter of weeks, she'd be in a different tax bracket—not that she'd be paying the tax. Her mind whirled with thoughts of the baubles she could buy. She'd already earmarked the first couple of thou for Tommy Bahama sunglasses, a

Coach bag, and a killer pair of red-soled Louboutins. Maybe two of each, she thought, scrolling through the online catalogues.

She swiped away from her shopping sites with a sigh and pulled up Kwantlen College's course offerings. Baubles were fun, but if she was serious about getting out of the business for good, she needed to get serious about another line of work. Becoming a hairstylist used to appeal to her, but waitressing was making her rethink a job where she had to stand on her feet all day. She bypassed the massage-therapy courses for the same reason and drilled down into the bookkeeping offerings. The idea of working from home, like Andy, appealed to her, as did that of setting her own hours. She downloaded Kwantlen's PDF application form and started filling it out.

She'd been baking in the sun for an hour when her phone pinged. Handsome Neighbour had invited her for a drink on Fourth Avenue. *Love to,* she replied. She shimmied her dress on over her bikini and packed up her beach bag. She wondered if she'd have time for Andy between her classes and Rick. It would be a shame if she had to give him up.

Browns Socialhouse was a twenty-minute walk away. Andy sat with a sweating glass of beer at one of the tables on the sidewalk patio.

"The elusive Handsome Neighbour," she said, pulling out a chair.

He eyed her over the top of his sunglasses. "What's got you in such a good mood?"

"I'm always in a good mood. Where you been?"

"In front of the computer. Where else?"

A server stopped at their table and took Sadie's order.

"What are you working on?"

"An app I developed. It's taken me a while to get the bugs out but it's clean now. Just finished testing it. It's going to be my ticket."

"Then shouldn't we be drinking champagne?" Sadie asked.

"I said it's gonna be my ticket. I haven't sold it yet. Got a few interested parties though."

He pulled his chair up beside hers and showed her how his new app worked. "You just tag the person you're looking for by inputting their phone number right here, hit this key, and the app zooms in on their location. Bingo!"

"Handy. But a little stalkerish, don't you think? Is it even legal?"

"Sure it is. The tech's already out there. This is just a slicker interface. I'll send you a download link. Share it with your roommate and try it out. Tell me what you think."

After a couple of drinks, Andy said he had to take a meeting and left with a promise they'd get together again soon. Sadie downloaded the app to her phone and input Andy's number. His little red dot moved east on Fourth Avenue. Probably headed back to his apartment, she thought. Next, she input Jane's number and the app found her right where she expected: at work. She sent Jane a text with the download link.

On her way home, Sadie dropped by the Kitsilano Wine Cellar. This time, she bypassed her usual section of ten-dollar specials and headed to the shelves where the prices hovered around twenty. She selected one red and one white and walked home feeling like an heiress.

Jane wasn't home. Sadie put the white wine in the fridge and checked Andy's new app. Jane's little red dot was travelling toward the university. Maybe the app really was Andy's ticket. She wondered if Jane's trip to UBC meant Hunter had found someone from her MCFD file.

Feeling too lazy to make a proper meal, she poured boiling water over a cup of ramen noodles. Her phone dinged as she slurped down the last of them. Cynthia had sent through details for a gig with Rick. Tomorrow at 6:00 p.m. Dammit! She'd agreed to take Angela's afternoon shift tomorrow. On a slim prayer she'd gotten the day wrong, she checked her schedule, but no, she hadn't.

Turning Cynthia down wasn't an option, which left finding someone to cover her restaurant shift. She phoned the people whose numbers she had, but not one of them could take it on such short notice. With no other option, she phoned the hostess desk. Employees willing to swap shifts left their names on a list in the locker room, and she needed that list.

Marcel picked up. He was one of the supervisors and the last person she wanted to talk to.

"It's Sadie, Marcel. I'm looking for Kim." Kim was the hostess who should have answered the phone.

"Kim called in sick. What can I do for you, Sadie?" The impatience in his tone suggested he'd had to fill in for her.

"I need the swap list. Could you send it to me?"

"It's on the bulletin board."

Supervisors tolerated staff swapping shifts but didn't encourage it. "I'm at home. Could you just take a photo of it and text it to me?"

"We're short-staffed, but the moment I get a break, I'll do that."

Sadie thanked him but knew it would be hours before he got back to her. If he got back to her. The longer she delayed the less chance she'd have of covering the shift.

She grabbed her keys and drove to Lodestones. Marcel looked up from the table chart and acknowledged her with a nod.

On her way to the staff lockers, she stopped by the server station at the bar. Everyone she asked was either already working or not able to take the shift. She carried on to the lockers and snapped a photo of the list.

Back in her car, she dialled every name. They all turned her down. She rubbed her temples. Marcel wasn't stupid. If she phoned in sick, he'd fire her ass, and it would be one more strike against swapping shifts. And reneging on Angela would be a shitty thing to do. Angela was hosting some kind of shower.

She couldn't even quit without giving two weeks' notice. Well, she could, but she'd be kissing waitressing goodbye; the company that owned Lodestones owned dozens of restaurant chains. If she didn't give notice, none of them would hire her, and another restaurant wouldn't hire her without a reference. Sadie cradled the steering wheel. She was fucked.

And not just because she needed the cash this month. Having a real job separated her from the business and provided a safety net. Without it, she'd be walking a tightrope with Cynthia holding one end and Rick holding the other.

A hooker.

Maybe Marcel could help her. She caught up with him as he hurried back to the hostess desk with an armful of menus.

"I need your help," she said, keeping pace with him. "I've swapped shifts with Angela tomorrow night, but something's come up that I can't get out of."

Marcel stuffed the menus in the cubbyhole beneath the hostess stand. "We don't cover swaps and you know it."

"Come on. Do me a favour. It's not Angela's fault."

"If I start the practice of covering swaps, everyone else will expect the same. I can't do it."

"I won't tell a soul, promise."

"You just asked everyone in here and on that list if they'd cover for you. They'll know."

"Damn it, Marcel. This is important."

"So's your job. Cancel whatever else has come up." He turned to the elderly couple who'd arrived and plastered a smile on his face. "Table for two?"

Deflated, Sadie stepped back. As Marcel showed the couple to a table, she ran through some numbers in her head. The cost of the bookkeeping course, her half of the rent, her cellphone, credit card, spending money. Could she really do it? Set herself up in a different line of business? A legitimate one that paid better than waitressing and didn't have her on her feet all day. Or her back.

Sadie sucked in a breath and smoothed her dress. It would be. If she was careful, she could pay for all that and more. And when would another opportunity like this come around? She'd sacrificed her pride for a lot less money. She could do this. Jane was always offering to help with the rent. This month, Sadie would finally take her up on that offer.

With her courage bolstered, she walked back to the staff room and cleared out her locker. She scribbled out her resignation and slid it under the supervisor's locked door. No going back now. Look forward, she repeated to herself.

On her way out, she found Marcel back at the hostess desk.

"My resignation is under your door."

Marcel's head shot up. "You're quitting?"

"I don't want to, but like I told you, I can't work Angela's shift tomorrow. You'll need to cover it."

"So you're leaving without notice? Don't do that. We can't give you a reference if you don't give us two weeks."

"It can't be helped. I'm sorry. I gotta go." Sadie turned her back and strode out the door. The safety net vanished. She was on her own now. Her new life had just begun.

39 | Rick

Rick walked out of Vasul's office numb to the core. He found his way to his office, collected his jacket, and told reception to reschedule his appointments for the coming week.

Their lack of surprise infuriated him. They'd known. Everyone had known. The board hadn't even had the balls to meet him face to face. They'd pawned off the job of telling him on Vasul. Ever the politician, Vasul insisted he'd volunteered, wanted it to be a friend who broke the news. Some friend.

Rick sat behind the wheel of his Land Rover struggling to comprehend the board's decision. They'd given the chief of staff's position to an outsider from Ontario. A neophyte. One whose remarkable insight would magically take the hospital in new directions. Was there a family connection he'd missed? A romance he'd not known about?

He'd been so certain. Eight years he'd put in. Five years in the top spot until he retired was all he wanted. He'd kissed more ass and taken on more pet projects than any of the others, and this was how they repaid him?

He turned the key in the ignition and headed to his townhome. Distance was what he needed. From the hospital, from the board's careless decision. From the visions of his father's disappointment and Mikey's smug smile that were burned into his retinas.

40 | Jane

Jane arrived at the anthropology building's parking lot. Ariane had called her at work saying she had news.

Helmet in hand, Jane walked up the front steps passing a flurry of book-laden academics on their way out. She kept her head down behind a curtain of hair as she made her way to the second floor. Jane knocked on the office door.

Ariane called, "Come in." Her ebony hair was pulled into a ponytail, as usual. The woman turned from the window, arms crossed. "Have a seat. Nathaniel will be here any minute."

Jane slid into one of the two wooden armchairs. She searched the desk for a suitable place to rest her helmet. Not finding one, she set it on the floor. How he could work with the clutter of papers on the desk confounded her. She itched to straighten it.

"What's your news?" Jane asked. "Did Hunter find someone?"

"Let's wait for Nathaniel," Ariane said. Her smile fell just shy of genuine. The coolness that wafted off her was new, and troubling.

"More of my birthmarks have cleared up."

"I know," Ariane said. "I've been tracking them in the journal."

"You still think they'll be gone by my birthday?"

The office door opened and Nate bustled in. "Got here as quick as I could." He crossed in front of Ariane and dropped his satchel on the wide windowsill. His armful of papers landed atop a stack on the desk.

As Nate settled into his seat, Ariane reached for a file folder on the desk. She pulled out a sheet of paper and handed it to Jane. "What's this?"

Jane stared at a copy of the cryptic document she'd inserted into the ministry's file. A guilty flush crawled up her neck. She set the sheet back on Nate's desk.

"Why did you add that note to your file?" Nate asked.

Jane looked down at her thumb and picked at a hangnail. "How'd you know?"

"Hunter isn't keen on wasting his time," Ariane said. "He checked the file's authenticity. IT isn't your strong suit."

"Who are they?" Nate asked, picking up the paper. "This Rebecca Morrow, Rick no last name, and Dr. Chadwick?"

"I don't know," Jane said.

Ariane huffed. "You know their names."

"I do, but I've never met them."

"You must have some reason for adding their names to your file," Nate said.

Jane looked up and met Nate's gaze. She clamped her mouth shut, unable to bring herself to tell them. Jumping off a cliff wasn't on her agenda for the day.

Nate and Ariane exchanged a look, and then Nate tipped his head to her.

Again, Ariane opened the file folder. She pulled out a photocopy of a black-and-white photograph and handed it across the desk to Jane.

Jane stared into the unsmiling face of an austere woman in some kind of traditional outfit. "Why are you showing me this?"

"Have you seen her before?" Ariane asked.

Jane shook her head. There was something familiar about the woman, but Jane couldn't place it. "No. Who is she?"

"Are you certain?"

Jane studied the woman's face. "If I've seen her before, it was in passing. I don't know her." She set the photo on top of the nearest pile of papers.

"Her name's Maria Yupanqui. After you left Nate's the other day, I spoke with my grandmother. Told her I'd seen your markings. She reached out to the old families. They sent me that photo. According to Maria's sister, Maria emigrated to North America in 1980."

Jane frowned. "What does that have to do with me?"

"The Yupanqui family is of Inca heritage, a family once known to possess an offering bowl. One that bears the same mark you do. Maria may have known how to use it."

"Great! Let's ask her."

"Maria left Peru in disgrace. The family disowned her. That photo's old, but it's the only one they had of her."

"Can Hunter find her?"

"He's put out feelers but doesn't expect a hit. The parameters are too large. Likely a dead end. Which brings me back to the names you added to your file. Will they help us narrow the search for your birth parents?"

Jane shook her head. "They won't. I'm sorry." The names would only help them find Rebecca. Frustrated, she slid back to wondering how she could get them to find Rebecca without revealing her dreams. She should have prepared better. What was it Sadie had suggested? Telling them Rebecca was a friend of her foster mom?

Ariane chewed her lower lip. "There is something else my grandmother told me. The old families came to the same conclusion we had. Those marks you bear are protecting you. But not for long. Your time is running out."

"Doesn't mean someone's out to get me."

Ariane tucked her hands in her pockets and turned to the window shaking her head.

Nate opened his mouth and closed it again.

"Look," Jane said, feeling awkward. "I know you have a mystery to solve, but—"

Ariane spun back around. "I have nothing to solve. I know what those marks mean. If you want to ignore it, that's up to you. If you want to ignore that your marks are being erased from the journal, from history, that's up to you too. I won't tell you I'm not curious to know more, but why aren't you? Someone already tried to kill you. Three times. You want to ignore that, go ahead. But denial or ignorance or whatever you want to label it won't stop what's happening. Someone wants to silence you."

"Why!" Jane shot to the edge of her seat. "That makes no sense. I'm no one. I have . . . nothing." But even as she said it, she pictured a butterfly and knew she was lying to herself, to everyone. Her sense of self-preservation was incredibly strong where her dreams were concerned.

"It makes sense to someone," Nate said, his calm voice defusing the tension in the air. "The people you mentioned in your note. Who are they to you?"

Jane regained her composure and settled back into her chair. "They're nothing to me. Sadie knows Rick. His name is Dr. Rick Kristan. I knew only his first name when I wrote that note. He's a psychiatrist."

Nate dug around in his pile of papers and unearthed a scratchpad. He made a notation. "Sadie's his patient?"

Patient. The word echoed in Jane's mind, tugging at a memory. She shook it off and returned to Nate's question. "No. She dates him.

Casually." Jane felt the burn of Ariane's glare and looked away. Every word out of her mouth was a bomb that could blow up in her face.

"Who's the other doctor?" Nate asked. He riffled through the papers on his desk.

Doctor, patient. Jane frowned as her thoughts tumbled back to a dream. Rebecca, the patient. The hospital. Jane reached for the photograph Ariane had showed her. Of course. The woman had been in her dreams. She worked at the hospital. On Rebecca's ward. Jane's thoughts tunnelled. Not a coincidence.

"Chadwick," Nate said.

Jane blinked. "What?"

"The name of the doctor? In your note?"

"Oh. Yeah. Rick worked with him in London. England, I think."

"You think?" Nate asked.

"He had a British accent."

"You've talked with him?" Ariane asked. Her tone veered into accusatory.

"No, I just heard his voice."

Ariane looked to Nate. He pressed his lips together.

Nate tapped his pen against the scratchpad. "Help us understand why you're being so elusive. Have we done something? Said something to make you mistrust us?"

Mistrust was Jane's default setting. "No. It's private, that's all. Something personal."

Ariane inhaled an impatient breath. "Who is she to you?" She pointed to the picture that sat in Jane's lap. The silence that followed felt like a stamp on her indictment.

"You've got to trust somebody sometime," Nate said.

No, I don't. She put down the photograph of the woman from Rebecca's hospital ward on the closest pile of paper and stood. She snatched her helmet from the floor and started for the exit. Neither Nate nor Ariane tried to stop her.

The black-framed print of her birthmark, to the left of the door, confronted her. A challenge. Her step faltered. She looked to the door. If she opened it, she'd walk away with her secrets intact. How much insurance would that buy her? Her birthday was less than two weeks away. What happened after that?

A decision lay before her: the door or the print. Was the risk of exposing her dreams worth the possibility it could end the threat? Or lead to a cure? To her parents? Would she regret never knowing? Flight or fight?

Jane had her answer: she wasn't a runner.

She dropped her gaze to the floor. "You won't believe me."

"Give us a try," Nate said.

Jane cradled her helmet and turned around. "I didn't lie to you. I've never met Rebecca or the others in that note. They have nothing to do with my birth parents."

Jane looked up. Ariane arched an eyebrow. Nate appeared expectant.

"I dream of them," Jane said. She stood tall, bracing for their condemnation.

When none came, she continued. "My dreams aren't like other people's. They're a window to the past."

Ariane's eyes widened. Nate's head tilted.

Here it comes, Jane thought. The guffaws, the dubious scowls. But no, their expressions remained open, curious.

"What does that mean?" Nate asked.

"I see things that have happened in the past to people I know. Things I couldn't have known. Things I couldn't have seen."

Ariane, still wide-eyed, took a step back and crossed her arms over her stomach. "You've dreamed of the people you named in your note?"

"Yes. And the woman in that picture." Jane gestured to the photo on the desk. "She worked in the hospital where Rebecca was a patient. A psychiatric hospital. Rick Kristan was a doctor there."

Nate picked up his pen. "Which hospital?"

"I don't know."

Nate gestured for Jane to sit. "Tell us about your dreams?"

Jane sat back down and pulled the helmet into her lap. "I dream of people. Always people."

"And you know them?" Ariane asked.

"Not necessarily, but I'm connected to them somehow. Kids I went to school with. Their parents. Teachers. Friends. People I meet in passing."

"What prompts the dreams?" Nate asked. "Is it just seeing them, or do you have to touch them, or touch something that belongs to them?"

"I—I don't know. It's not having something of theirs, for sure. And the dreams don't come immediately after seeing or touching them. It feels random."

"What happens in your dreams?" he asked.

Jane sucked in a breath and exhaled slowly. "Things no one wants others to see. Abuse. Neglect. Violence. Manipulation," she added, thinking of Rick. "Sometimes it's an embarrassing moment, a lapse of judgment. But my dreams of Rebecca are different. It's like they're evolving."

"And you're certain these events actually happened?"

"Yes."

Ariane's gaze drifted as she turned toward the window. Was she questioning Jane's sanity? Regretting her decision to travel all the way from Peru?

"Every time?" Nate asked.

"I don't check anymore. But a few nights ago, I dreamed of Sadie. When I asked her, she remembered the evening in my dream."

"Why is it important to you that we find Rebecca and her doctor?" Nate asked.

Jane lowered her gaze to her helmet and flicked at a crusted spot. "Rebecca has visions. They sound like my dreams. She tried to kill herself because of them. That's how she ended up in the psych ward." Jane took a breath. Bad things happened in her dreams. Not for the first time, she desperately hoped Rebeca's suicide wasn't an upcoming attraction. "I worry about what's happened to her. Rick was helping her learn how to control the visions, to cure her. If he did, I want to know how."

Ariane's voice came out flat. "There is no cure for what you have."

Jane and Nate stared at Ariane's back.

She turned around, her arms hugging her torso, her expression solemn. Had Jane offended her? "What you have is not a disease. The old families would call you *un testigo*. A Witness. There hasn't been a Witness for a hundred years."

"A witness to what?" Jane asked.

"Injustice. The truth. In the old days, the words of *un testigo* were held sacred."

Jane grunted. "Not anymore. No one wants to hear what I dream about, trust me."

Ariane narrowed her eyes. "This is why you are marked. You've witnessed something. Someone's trying to silence you because of it."

Jane shook her head. "I've never seen a crime worth killing over, and even if I had, I don't tell anyone that I dreamed of them. Not since grade school."

"Perhaps the dream has yet to happen."

"That's even more reason to find a cure. I want the dreams to stop!"

Ariane scowled. "Witnesses don't squander their ability—they nurture it, use it to restore justice."

"Justice? There's no justice for victims too embarrassed to admit they've been abused or raped or ripped off. They don't want a spotlight. They want to forget."

Ariane lowered her arms. "Then you find a way to make it right."

"There is no way. You can't prove an old man was pushed down the stairs when he's fallen so many times before. It's not like I have a camera. And if a woman with a dislocated shoulder is too afraid to tell the hospital her husband did it, the cops sure as hell won't listen to me. You have no idea how horrifying it is to watch an adult whale on a kid. To hear the whimpers, the begging. I'd do anything to stop that."

"It can't be easy. But if I could do what you can, I'd be there for them. I'd be present. And I'd seek retribution."

"You think I haven't tried? I've been beaten up, spit at, and shunned for my efforts."

Jane looked to Nate for relief. He had none to offer.

"What if we find this Rebecca woman and she's not cured?" he asked.

"Then I'll be bitterly disappointed," Jane said. "And I'm afraid of what might happen. The dreams are getting more frequent. More intense."

"What do you mean?" Nate asked.

"For a long time, my dreams were like old black-and-white movies. I could see lips moving but couldn't hear anything. A while ago, the voices became indecipherable mumbles. Now the voices are as clear as yours. I can feel the temperature in my dreams and pick up scents. The dreams are in colour. I can touch the clothes I'm wearing. It's as if I'm actually there."

"But you're not," Ariane said, and her tone felt like a pat on the head. "They're just dreams."

"Not just dreams. Not anymore. I moved a door. Knocked over a tray of glasses."

Nate stared at her. "That's not possible," he said. "Is it?" he added, addressing Ariane.

Ariane had grown still. "No."

Jane's hackles shot up. "You think I'm lying to you?"

"No," Ariane said. "But you must be mistaken."

"I'm not."

"There's no mention of this in our lore."

"You think your lore explains everything?" Jane said.

"It's not just the lore—what you're suggesting is scientifically impossible."

"I'm not suggesting it. It happened."

There it was. It had taken a while, but a dubious scowl had surfaced on Ariane's face.

Nate appeared more thoughtful. "Einstein's theory of special relativity?" he said, in a thinking-out-loud tone. "The fourth dimension?"

"No," Ariane said, crossing her arms again. "Even if a person survived travel at light speed, they could only move forward in time, not back."

"Weren't you the ones who told me all the world's mysteries weren't solved?" Jane said. "You asked me to trust you. You're going to have to trust me too. I'm not mistaken."

"She's got a point," Nate said. He leaned back in his chair, contemplative. "Maybe we need to set aside what science tells us and consider an element the theory doesn't account for. She's not travelling in physical form. It's her consciousness that's travelling."

"Not if she's interacting with the physical world," Ariane said. "Her body in some form has to be going with her."

Jane flared her nostrils at Ariane's use of *if* but let it slide.

"Does Sadie ever see you when you're in one of these dream states?" Nate asked.

"Sometimes."

"That would be an interesting observation," Ariane said. "We need to set that up as soon as possible."

"What? Watch me sleep?"

"We'll monitor your body. Heart rate, brain waves. If your body is in some way changing when you're dreaming, we can get irrefutable proof." Ariane looked at Nate. "How I'd love to silence the skeptics for a change."

"Whoa," Jane said. Putting her on display when she was at her most vulnerable? Not happening. "I'm not letting anyone hook me up to machines and watch me sleep."

"If you're travelling to the past, and we can prove it, it would revolutionize science."

"How about you stop saying *if* and just take my word for it," Jane said.

"This is bigger than you, Jane," Ariane said. "If you're physically moving things in your dreams—in the past—you're changing history as we know it. Do you have any idea how far reaching, how dangerous that is?"

Now it was Jane's turn to be skeptical. "It was a tray of broken glasses. *Dangerous* is a bit of a stretch."

Ariane rubbed her face with her hands. "You're wrong," she said, pushing her hair back. "What if someone cut themselves on that glass, needed stitches, and instead of meeting the person they were supposed to have children with, they fall for a doctor at the hospital? Children who were supposed to be born—who were born—wouldn't exist. Whatever those children did or would have done in history is gone.

"What you have to understand," she continued, using her hands for emphasis, "is that everything in this world is connected through time. The chair you're sitting on wouldn't exist without an infinite web of events that occurred many years ago: a viable oak seed landed in fertile soil; sufficient rain and sunlight fell to nourish it; someone harvested the wood; an architect designed the chair; a carpenter built it; a buyer purchased it; a shipper delivered it. The list goes on."

Ariane took a breath. "If any one of those events is altered, you might find yourself sitting in a chair made of maple, or no chair at all. Every single event in time is connected to and dependent on an infinite number of other events in history. Change one of them and you change the world. That's why it's dangerous."

Jane thought of the butterfly flapping its wings. "Then finding a cure is critical because I'm not mistaken. And it's getting worse. It's just a matter of time before I accidentally break something important."

"I'll call the old families together. Tell them what's happened. Seek their advice."

"Tell more people?" Jane felt a pinch of panic and whipped her head back and forth. "Hell no. I don't tell anyone about my dreams. No one. And you can't either."

"You don't need to fear ridicule or judgment from the old families," Ariane said.

"I learned to deal with ridicule and judgment when I was seven. That's not why I don't tell anyone about my dreams." She pinched her brow. She'd come this far—she might as well go all in. "Do you know what narcolepsy is?"

"Yes," Ariane said.

"Cataplexy?"

"Paralytic sleep," Nate said.

"When I'm having these dreams, I'm unable to wake up. Unable to move. I'm paralyzed. The apartment could fall down around me, and I wouldn't know it."

"Damn," Nate said.

"That's why I don't tell anyone. I won't leave myself vulnerable like that. Ever. You can't tell anyone else."

"The old families may be the only ones who can help. I can keep your name out of it."

"No," Jane said. "There's another way. Find Rebecca Morrow."

Visiting Dream

Jane shivers. She's not dressed for the wintery weather. She looks at her feet. They're bare, and her body shimmers. This transparent glow is new.

This time, she knows where she is. She recognizes St. Paul's emergency entrance. Ambulances occupy two of its four bays. A man dressed in a parka flings handfuls of salt on the sidewalk. Nearby, patients wearing heavy coats over their pyjamas huddle against the cold under the building's overhang. Cigarette smoke drifts in Jane's direction.

A taxi pulls up and parks in one of the empty bays. A woman opens the back door. She swings her legs out and clutches the armrest, hoisting herself out. When the woman stands, Jane recognizes Buddy's mom, Mary. She's heavily pregnant and as ill-prepared for the weather as Jane is, with slip-on shoes and a coat draped over her shoulders.

It's icy and there's nothing for Mary to hold on to. On impulse, Jane steps toward her, seeking out a path where the asphalt is clear of ice. The frozen pavement drills spikes up through her feet.

A Jeep pulls up behind the taxi and slides to a precarious stop, inches from the taxi's bumper. The taxi driver bolts out and yells at the other driver.

Jane has made it to Mary's side. She feels substance beneath her grip as she grabs hold of Mary's elbow. Mary looks to her arm. Jane's confusion is echoed in Mary's face.

A man emerges from the driver's side of the car, apologizing to the taxi driver. He slips on the ice and catches himself on the door. Keeping a hand on the vehicle, he shuffles around the back of the car to open the front passenger door.

Despite Mary's confusion, she steps away from the taxi and follows the pressure on her elbow to the safety of the overhang.

Jane looks back. She doesn't immediately recognize Anna's husband until she catches sight of Anna emerging from the passenger seat. Anna's husband helps her out and steadies her.

The emergency room's doors swish open. Jane escorts Mary inside as shouts erupt behind them.

Violent shivers accompanied Jane's awakening. Her feet ached and her body was a relief map of goosebumps.

Not all the goosebumps were because of the cold—she'd seeded her dream again. She'd eaten one of Buddy's butter tarts before going to bed and had been thinking of him when she fell asleep. It couldn't be a coincidence.

More and more she felt convinced that Rick was onto something. She just needed some guidance, a little direction. Controlling her dreams was within reach. She could feel it.

She rolled onto her side and pulled her knees to her chest. Her thoughts turned to Mary navigating the ice. Not that Mary would have fallen, but Jane was glad she'd been there. Would there be ripple effects in history as a result of that small gesture? she wondered.

41 | Rick

R ick stared past his reflection in the living room window and out to the lights of Granville Island. The Ketel One had sharpened his anger. Resentment drifted around him like a bad smell he couldn't shake off.

The board "appreciated his dedication," Vasul had said. Hoped he'd understand their need for a "fresh face" to represent the hospital.

He didn't. What he understood was that the board had screwed him over. Vasul had had the temerity to defend the neophyte. Said she "made up in vision what she lacked in experience." Her funding initiatives were "breaking new ground," he'd said.

What went unsaid was that Rick would have to report to her, follow her questionable lead. Did the board also expect he'd pull her ass out of the fire when she embarrassed them and made front-page news for a colossal newbie fuckup?

Rick walked back to the bar and splashed another shot of vodka in his glass. Was Mikey already gloating over the board's decision? Perhaps Rick should be grateful his father hadn't lived to see the day. At least Rick wouldn't have to endure his maybe-next-time platitudes again, though no doubt his mother would add something about it "not being a competition." Tell that to Mikey. God he was sick of coming in second.

He took a sip and considered his options.

Early retirement was a possibility though an unpleasant one—he'd invested more heavily than he'd anticipated to fix the mistake he'd made with Jane. Hence, his financial cushion wasn't as comfortable as he would have liked.

He could resuscitate his private practice, though he wasn't keen to step on that roller coaster again. Maybe he'd seek a consultancy position. His CV was impressive: recruited from a two-year stint in London into the largest criminal psychiatric facility in Ontario. From there, a number of small but forward-thinking hospital appointments across the Prairies, followed by a supervisory position in BC in one of the country's pre-eminent psychiatric facilities. He'd made program director in record time. Any headhunter would see that the board had made a critical error passing him over.

The idea of a couple of months off appealed to him. He'd already booked a trip to Europe. Perhaps he'd leave early, take Sadie along with him. She'd be entertaining and easy enough to dispose of when he'd had enough.

Hell, maybe the hospital board had just cleared the path for him.

42 | Jane

August 23

Ever since her second mark vanished, Jane had started taking roll call on her birthmarks every day in the shower. Frame by frame, the film strip was disappearing. She now had no marks south of her butt. At the rate they were clearing up, she no longer doubted they'd be gone by her birthday.

Ariane had been right about that. She'd been right about so much. Could she also be right about someone wanting her dead because of something she'd witnessed in a dream? The idea felt absurd. She grabbed a towel. The worst offenders in her dreams never knew she'd witnessed their crimes—crimes that didn't rise to the level where her knowing about them would call for her premeditated murder. Unless Ariane was also right that the dream was yet to come. But even so, as she'd explained to Ariane, she was powerless to prove anything anyway—couldn't prove the crime had happened.

Her thoughts drifted to the previous night's dream of Buddy's mom. Ariane would consider Jane's intervention tinkering with history, but how could she not step up? Helping Mary navigate the ice had been instinctual. What if instead of witnessing tragedies, she was supposed to prevent them?

She wished she'd asked Anna more questions about Mary and the day their sons were born. If Buddy's condition had been caused by Mary's falling on the ice, had Jane changed the course of his life? She bubbled with the possibility. If this was what Ariane's justice and retribution looked like, she was all for it.

When Sadie got up, Jane would talk her into a run to the park. Now that she'd actually used one of her kicks to defend someone, she felt she owed it some practice.

She'd finished her tea by the time Sadie opened the bedroom door.

"Morning," Jane said. Sadie answered with a grunt and disappeared into the bathroom.

Jane rinsed out the French press and made Sadie a cup of coffee.

"What's the story on this app you sent me?" Jane said, when Sadie plopped down beside her. "I can't find anything about it on the internet."

"It's Andy's app. The new tenant?"

Jane nodded. She still hadn't met him.

"He developed it. It's pretty cool. He gave it to us gratis."

"What's it do?"

"Stalks your friends," Sadie said with a laugh. After Jane installed it, Sadie tagged herself and showed her how it worked.

"He says it's legal and the technology is out there, so I guess it's not as creepy as it seems. What'd you learn from the prof yesterday?"

Jane wrinkled her brow. "You knew I met with him?"

"Saw your little red dot heading out there on Andy's app," she said, and then stalled. "Maybe it is a little creepy."

"A *little*?" Jane said, thinking it would be every stalker's wet dream. "Ariane's investigator nailed me on the note I slipped into Nelson's file. They grilled me about it."

"What'd you tell them?"

"Everything." Jane recounted the events and her decision to tell Nate and Ariane about her dreams and the narcolepsy. "I hope that wasn't a mistake. Ariane seems a little too keen to tell people about it."

"I wouldn't worry. Who's going to believe her? Besides, I like her and Nate. I don't think they'd screw you around. I'm glad you told them."

"Look forward, right?" Jane said. "You want to go for a run to the park?"

Sadie declined Jane's workout offer. She said her nails would revolt if she didn't get a mani-pedi.

Jane checked the time. It was early to phone Ethan. But thirty minutes later, when she heard the roar of his Fat Boy, she was glad she'd taken the chance. She joined him on the sidewalk in front of her building, where he was bent over his bike securing his helmet. He caught her admiring the view and pulled her into a kiss. She could have stayed in his arms for hours but pushed away from him before her libido dragged him to her bed.

They started for the park at a jog. Ethan's gait soon turned to a run. "Beat you there," he said, then sprinted ahead, showing no mercy.

She found him posing with his back against a tree as if he'd been waiting for hours. "Don't pretend you're not sucking wind, Ethan. I can see your chest heaving." With her hands on her hips, Jane walked off her exertion in slow circles.

Sparring with Ethan wasn't the smooth tai-chi-style dance it had become with Sadie. He challenged her every move, countered her every kick. More than once, he connected with an arm or a leg and each time he did, he followed up with a self-satisfied grin.

It was the grin that finally shook Jane out of her fantasies about doing the nasty with him. Instead, she began studying his form for the moves that projected his intentions.

When she scored her first hit, she mimicked his annoying grin. He stepped up his game, and she countered. He was heavier, stronger, but she was quicker. They were a good match for sparring.

Finally, exhausted, they lay on the grass and caught their breath.

"I had a chance to use my roundhouse a few days ago," she said, panting. "You know Buddy? The guy in the wheelchair with a smiley face painted on his donation can?"

Ethan shook his head. "Don't think so."

"Huh. I thought everyone knew Buddy," Jane said, and told him about the incident with the would-be thieves. She rolled her wrist. "Just like new," she said, showing Ethan where the colour had started to fade from purple to green and brown.

On the walk back to Jane's apartment, Ethan talked her into following him on her Rebel to his place for lunch. It didn't take a lot of convincing. Jane met his suggestion with cheerleader enthusiasm.

Ethan slipped the chain on the apartment door and raced to close the blinds, shedding his clothes along the way. Turned out lunch was not the meal on Ethan's mind. His hunger for her was an aphrodisiac. Ethan had given her something no one else could. For the first time in her life, she felt sexy and attractive. It pumped her full of confidence and courage.

Ethan left a trail of kisses on her stomach as he pulled her underwear off. When he crawled back up her body, he cupped a breast and then he was inside her, driving her hard and taking them both where they needed to go.

Afterward, she lay in his arms, luxuriating in the ease she felt being naked in Ethan's company. Whatever this was between them, she never wanted to lose it.

Ethan broke their postcoital daze. "More of your marks are gone. A lot more."

"Yeah. Ariane thinks they'll all be gone by the end of the month."

"Ariane? The loopy professor from Peru?"

"That's her. Maybe not so loopy though. She was right about the marks clearing up." Jane pulled up her knee and brushed her hand over the newly cleared skin on her leg.

"Why the end of the month?"

"It's my birthday. I turn twenty-five on August 31."

He nodded, and Jane knew he'd remember. "Tell me again her theory about the marks."

Jane repeated what she'd told him before. When she'd finished, he wore a deep frown.

"I looked up port wine stains," he said. "None of the articles I read said anything about them clearing up. If anything, the marks get more pronounced over time." He grazed his thumb over the mark on her shoulder. "What's happening to you isn't normal. Maybe you should see a doctor."

"It was doctors who told me these were port wine stains. I'm not so sure anymore."

"Didn't you tell me your marks were photographed? Published in some medical journal?"

"Yeah. Nate found the issue for me."

"I always thought the research published in those medical journals had to be factual—accurate."

"Guess not."

He shifted and looked down at her. "You don't believe Ariane's Inca ritual bullshit, do you?"

Jane looked away. If Ethan thought the idea of a ritual was bullshit, what would he think of her dreams? She had to find a cure. She just had to. "It's pretty far out there. And I do plan to see a doctor. I know his name—I just don't know where he works. Ariane's investigator is looking for him." And it couldn't be soon enough.

After she left Ethan's, Jane prowled the downtown streets looking for Buddy. She rode past his usual haunts and then cruised into the West End to see if she could spot him there but had no luck.

Disappointed, she headed home, all the while wondering if helping Mary navigate the icy hospital parking lot had impacted Buddy in the slightest. His cerebral palsy could have been caused by any number of events besides his mother slipping on ice and falling.

She parked her bike under Mrs. Carper's window. As much as she hoped she'd changed Buddy's fate for the better, Ariane's warning lurked in the back of her mind, a gnawing fear: had she also changed history?

Jane's stomach growled as she fit her key into the apartment's lock and opened the door. The shower was running. Jane checked the time. Sadie would be late for her shift. Nothing new there.

She set her helmet on the floor and wandered into the kitchen. The bathroom door opened while Jane had her head in the fridge. She pulled out a loaf of bread and the last of the deli ham. Not enough for both of them, but Sadie ate her meals at the restaurant when she worked.

At the click of high heels on the parquet floor, Jane turned from slicing her sandwich.

Sadie stopped midstride. "Hey. Didn't know you were home." She snapped shut the small clutch she held. A clutch that Jane knew held no ID. The one Sadie used when she worked a gig.

"I thought you were working a swap shift at the restaurant tonight."

"Ah, no. Have a gig." Sadie said it casually enough, but she wouldn't look Jane in the eye. Her white sleeveless shirt had a plunging V in the front. She tugged at the hem of her grey pencil skirt.

"You look great," Jane said, smiling through her disappointment. She didn't relish another night of waiting to pick up the pieces of Sadie's self-respect.

"Thanks. Listen. It's good you're here. I've got something to tell you."

Jane took her plate to the sofa. Sadie perched on the armrest.

"I've taken Cynthia up on Rick's offer."

Jane hesitated. "It's a done deal?" She lifted the top of her sandwich and pushed a slice of tomato back in place.

Sadie nodded. "Our trial period has officially started."

Jane replaced the slice of bread and licked her finger. "So you've got an out? If this trial doesn't work out, the deal's off?"

"I'm not going to blow the trial."

"You've worked more gigs this month than you have all summer. Is that the pace you'll work when Rick owns your contract?" Jane took a bite.

Sadie dismissed Jane's remark with a wave of her hand. "Cynthia lied. There is no contract. I thought you knew that."

Jane set her plate on the trunk. "But that's the thing, Sadie. There will be a contract with Rick. He'll have paid for it. He'll own you."

"He can think he owns me, but he won't. I'll shake him loose as soon as I can."

"I hope you're right." Jane had a feeling it wouldn't be quite that easy. She returned to the kitchen and poured herself a glass of water.

"I am. Just think! Very soon now, Cynthia will be out of my life. You've been waiting for me to sever that tie for years."

Jane forced a smile. Took a sip of water. "God knows you'd be safer out of the business, but without Cynthia's goons, there's no one between you and Rick. That's not smart. You told me yourself this guy was trouble, that he was getting too close."

"Jesus, Jane. I thought you'd be happy for me."

"I am, or I will be when you make it out. You're not there yet. Do me a favour," Jane said, as she walked back to the sofa. "Don't give up your job at the restaurant. This deal could still blow up. And even if it doesn't, that job is your independence."

Sadie pursed her lips. She avoided Jane's glare. "I can't do both."

Jane came to a stop. "You quit your job?"

"I told you. I'm all in. You need to wrap your head around that because I can't be around you if you're trying to make me feel like crap about it. One last gig, Jane. One last client. One. And he's paying a shit-load of cash. That's a new life for me."

"That's great. If the money materializes." Jane set her glass on the trunk and sat down.

Sadie stood. "Do you have to be so negative? This is my big break and you're dumping all over it."

"He's in my dreams, Sadie. That's not usually a good sign."

"He's only in your dreams because of me. I'm the connection. Isn't that what you said?"

It was, but still . . . "This feels different."

"You're just afraid I'm going to blow your shot at a cure."

Jane jerked her head back. "That's not it at all!" Did Sadie really think she was that selfish? "It's just . . ."

"Just what?" Sadie said. She had a hand on her hip.

"I think he may have caused Rebecca to overdose."

"You think or you know?" Sadie's skeptical tone gave Jane pause. Sadie doubted her, and that hurt.

"I can't be sure. I saw him give her a sedative, and in the next dream she'd overdosed again. I just can't tell how much time passed between the two dreams."

"So his sedative and her overdose might not be connected. You said she was suicidal. It makes more sense she tried to off herself again than it does her doctor tried to kill her."

Jane frowned. Sadie was justifying her decision. A bad decision. "You're telling me you trust him now?"

"Why not? He knew my name. It wouldn't have taken much for him to find me if he'd wanted to, but he didn't. I shouldn't have been so paranoid."

Jane leaned forward. "You should have followed your instincts."

"That's easy to say when you're sitting on an inheritance, Jane. Must be nice to be you. Some of us aren't that lucky."

"My *inheritance*?" Sadie's words knocked Jane aback. Sadie had never thrown that in her face before. "A couple grand isn't enough to cloud my judgment. Can you say the same?"

"*A couple grand?* You ought to read your mail, Jane."

Jane felt a stab of betrayal. "You went through my papers?"

Sadie's phone dinged. "That's his driver."

Jane frowned. "Wait a minute!"

A horn tooted twice from the street.

Sadie smoothed her skirt. "I gotta go."

Jane jumped up, alarmed. "Is that him out there?" She raised her voice. "You gave a john our address!"

"Loosen up, would you? It's only his driver. Rick gave his word—he'll never show up here."

"Sadie! How could you?" Jane felt heat rise up her neck and flared her nostrils. "You promised."

"And I have a once-in-a-lifetime offer. It's not a bank balance that'll sit around waiting for me to decide if I want it. If I don't take his offer now, it's gone."

"He's buying you, Sadie."

"News flash, Jane: someone buys me every month. This is no different. Just a bigger paycheque. And if you can't live with it, then maybe it's time we went our separate ways."

Sadie blew out the door leaving Jane with her mouth open.

Jane dropped to the sofa. Sadie had torched their friendship without a backward glance. After all they'd been through, how could Sadie think so little of her? Did she really believe she'd maliciously stand in the way of her big payday? The pain in her chest grew until she thought it would crush her.

She walked to the bedroom and opened the bottom drawer of her dresser.

Visiting Dream

Jane is back in Rebecca's world. She recognizes the scents and sounds of the psychiatric hospital. Her body shimmers in the shadows but the shimmer washes out under the lights. She follows raised voices to a reception area that sits in front of double doors.

Rick and David, Rebecca's fiancé, are squared off. Close by, a security guard stands ready.

"There's nothing wrong with Becca. She wouldn't even be in here if she hadn't taken the pill you gave her," David says. His hands are balled into fists by his sides. Jane pictures the pill Rick slid out of a small packet into Rebecca's palm.

Rick's hands are on his hips. "Prescribed her," he says. "Judiciously, which, I'll remind you, the ombudsman confirmed after your complaint."

"Becca wouldn't try to take her life. She was getting better."

"Clearly, she did, and she wasn't." Rick inhales an impatient breath and clasps his hands in front of his chest. "I know this is difficult. It's not easy to accept that someone you care about wants to harm themself, but that is the case. This is the best place for her right now."

Jane sidles up to the double doors with the windows and peers through the glass. There's not much to see—a corridor lined with offices and another set of doors at the far end.

"She was looking for a new doctor. She didn't want to see you anymore."

"I can't discuss Rebecca or her treatment, but rest assured, she has a voice in here. She can speak for herself."

"She was afraid of you."

Rick looks to the floor and shakes his head. "The reason Rebecca is in here is because she stopped treatment. You had a part to play in that. If she'd taken the pills as prescribed—"

"She would never have taken an overdose!" David's face is flushed.

"You may want to believe that, but the toxicity levels in her blood the day she arrived in emergency tell a different story. Deluding yourself won't change the facts. Rebecca needs help."

"I have a right to see her."

"No. You don't. You're not a blood relative and you're not her spouse. You didn't even cohabitate."

"Please. Let me see her. It's been three months." The sense of loss in David's expression makes Jane's heart ache for him.

"She's fragile. We can't risk a setback." Rick nods to the security guard. "Goodbye, David." The security guard steps in front of David as Rick waves a security card across a pad mounted on the wall beside the double doors. A lock releases with a click. He pushes the door open and Jane rushes through behind him.

He walks straight to one of the office doors and knocks. The door isn't fully closed.

A woman's voice calls out, "Come in."

Behind a steel-and-glass desk sits a woman in a white lab coat. She stops tapping on her keyboard and looks at Rick over the top of her glasses.

"David Banner again?" she asks. "Does he know?"

"If he does, he's keeping quiet about it. He's going to be a problem. Doesn't want to accept that she needs to be here."

"Still no improvement?"

"None, and until we can get her back on meds, I don't see it happening. She tells anyone who'll listen about these visions of hers."

"I heard. Any further violent outbursts?"

"No. She seems to have settled down."

"Good. Let's hope it lasts. Make a record of David's visit. If you think it's necessary, we'll involve legal, get a restraining order."

The woman must be Rick's boss. He exhales as if the weight of the world is on his shoulders.

Jane slips out the door and heads down the hall looking for Rebecca, but another set of double doors bars her way. Behind her, someone approaches with a stack of linens piled so high Jane sees only a mop of dark hair over the top and stockinged feet in sensible shoes beneath. The woman taps the ID badge she wears on her hip against the security pad and the door opens.

She's humming as Jane follows her into the ward. The woman and her stack of linens disappear into a closet beside a dispensary window. Chairs in groups of two and three are spread throughout the large, bright room. An upright piano sits in one corner.

Jane heads for the corridor and searches for Rebecca in the patient rooms beyond. She finds her in one of the few rooms with a closed door. Through the door's window, she sees Rebecca curled on her side in the single bed. She's not sleeping. Her fingers trace shapes on the sheet.

Jane pushes the door lever, but her hand has no heft to it. She turns at the sound of approaching footsteps. Rick's white coat flaps out behind him. He opens Rebecca's door with his security card and Jane follows him inside. The room is spacious, as if it were made for two beds, not one.

"Did you bring paper?" Rebecca asks, sitting up. "You promised me." She's wearing an oversized shirt and leggings.

"I never break a promise," he says, and produces a notepad. "Did you have another vision?"

"I did, but that will cost you more than a notepad." Rebecca's smile is disingenuous, a challenge.

Jane walks across the room to a narrow writing table set against a window. The lawn outside is green and the trees are in full leaf.

"Give me a hint and I'll see," Rick says.

"Your brother's having an affair," Rebecca says. "Has David come by?"

Rick narrows his eyes, skews his jaw. "Group meets in an hour. It'll be good for you to get out and see Dr. Ng and the others, don't you think?"

A quick knock on the door is followed by the release of the lock. The door opens and a woman's voice announces, "Fresh linen."

With a start, Jane stares into the face of the woman she saw in Ariane's photograph—Maria Yupanqui.

"Shall I come back?" Maria asks in a thick Spanish accent.

"No, please, stay and visit," Rebecca says, reaching out her hand to Maria.

"She's got group in an hour," Rick says.

Maria's forehead folds into a furrow, and she looks across the room to where Jane is standing, almost as if she can see her. Jane checks her shimmer, but it's barely there.

Rick follows Maria's gaze and frowns. He turns to Rebecca. "I'll see you tomorrow."

Rebecca stands, and Jane stares wide-eyed as she smooths her hand over an unmistakable curve. A baby bump.

With one final glance in Jane's direction, Rick leaves. The steel clang of the locking door ripples up through the dream.

The clang was still reverberating in Jane's mind when she woke. Rebecca was pregnant. And they were keeping David from her. Why? David was no threat.

She fought against a rising tide, not wanting to think the worst of Rick but no longer able to ignore the disturbing truth. He might have found a cure for Rebecca, but at what cost? David thought Rick had caused Rebecca to overdose. Jane thought so too. She suspected Rick had given her just enough of the drug to get her back under his control. He'd manipulated her, risked her life, the life of her baby. For what? Another stab at glory?

Her thoughts turned to Sadie. Rick had manipulated her too. With money. Jane looked in the bedroom. Two in the morning and Sadie wasn't home. She checked her phone. Nothing. And Ethan would have called if she'd turned up at Riptide.

Though she was still hurt by Sadie's careless jibes, and furious at her for giving Rick their address, she put her anger on pause. If anything happened to her and Jane hadn't checked on her, she'd never forgive herself. She sent her a text and waited.

With each minute that passed, Jane's unease grew. She was ashamed to realize that Rick's manipulation extended beyond Rebecca and Sadie; she'd allowed herself to be manipulated as well. In her desperation for a cure, she'd been giving Rick a pass on his abhorrent behaviour. Not that she could have stopped him, but she could have tried harder to stop Sadie from taking his deal. A done deal, she reminded herself. A situation Jane could have prevented if she'd opened her damn mail.

Twenty minutes later, Jane's text remained undelivered. Sadie had turned off her phone.

43 | Rick

Though the board hadn't officially approved Rick's leave, he hadn't been back to the hospital since the day Vasul had so carefully explained why they'd stabbed him in the back.

He pulled up to the row of mailboxes in Langley but found his mother's compartment empty. Betty must have collected the mail. He'd have to find a way to discourage that.

Rick walked through the house and followed voices to the backyard. "There you are," he said, spotting his mother and Betty on the patio loungers.

"Rick, dear," his mother said, and swung her legs to the side.

"Don't get up." Rick bent to kiss her cheek then handed her the flowers he'd brought.

"I'm sure they're lovely," she said.

Rick turned to Betty. "You're looking well."

"Thank you. Can I get you a drink? Your mother and I are enjoying a bourbon."

"A bourbon?" Rick blinked in disbelief. The woman was being paid to look after his mother, not join her for cocktail hour. "Yes, thank you."

"I'll be right back," Betty said. She set her drink on the table and reached for the flowers. "Let me put those in water while I'm up."

The moment the back door closed, Rick turned to his mother. "About Betty—"

"Isn't she wonderful? I've been waiting to tell you—Betty and I are all booked for Palm Springs. We leave day after tomorrow."

Rick frowned. "That was fast."

"Betty found one of those last-minute deals," his mother said, smirking like a proud co-conspirator. "Got a terrific price."

Rick noticed a glossy brochure on the table beside Betty's drink and picked it up. "Is this the place you're going to in Palm Springs?"

His mother's unseeing eyes grew wide. She groped for Rick—or more precisely, for the brochure he'd picked up.

"What is this?" Rick said. He read from the front page. "*Retirement living in the province's capital.*" Photos on the cover depicted smiling seniors posing over candlelit dinners, pushing their faces into the wind on sailboats, and teeing up on a golf course.

"Just something I'm considering," his mother said.

Inside the brochure was a map of Victoria with a red flag identifying the property, which was close to the harbour. Close to Mikey.

"You're moving?" Rick said.

"I'm considering it, yes."

Michael had her power of attorney—he could sell the house and buy it himself at a bargain-basement price. Rick felt his blood pressure rising. Mikey's wife had always wanted to live here. When Mom died, they'd move in and bring Elaine's horse. How convenient. He had to find a way to stall the sale, at least until he could figure out a way to stop Mikey from taking everything.

"Remember what Dr. Lewis said? He advised you not to make any major decisions for a year."

"Dr. Lewis isn't blind and living alone in a big old house."

"He didn't want you to make a decision out of grief that'd you'd regret a year from now."

"I don't need a year. The house is too big for me. I don't want to spend all my money paying other people to take care of it. The apartment in Victoria is close to Michael and Elaine. I can take my meals in a common room and there'd be company for me. I could see the grandkids anytime I liked."

Score another one for Michael. "What about all your friends here in Langley? You don't need to be in a rush to sell. Give it a few months, at least."

His mother reached over and patted Rick's arm. "I'll be fine."

"Of course you will," Rick said. But he couldn't let the house fall into Mikey's hands. "Will you talk to me before you list it? I might be interested in buying the place."

"You? Why would you want to live way out here? Your life's in the city."

"I suppose I'm attached to the place. It's sentimental."

"It's four walls with dated décor and I'm told it needs a new roof. Nothing to be sentimental about."

Why was she discouraging him? "You haven't already sold it, have you?"

"No, it's just . . . Well, I know you didn't get that promotion you'd been hoping for. And you've got that beautiful townhome in the city. You shouldn't have to worry about a mortgage at your age."

Rick's temper flared. "I see Mikey's been busy feeding the rumour mill. Guess he thinks he knows my finances as well as yours!"

"Don't be like that. If it puts your mind at ease, when I return from Palm Springs, I'll check with you first if I decide to sell. How's that?"

"I'd rather you heeded your doctor's advice and wait a few months." Rick blew out a breath and calmed himself. "Listen, while we have a few moments alone, I'd like to talk to you about Michael."

"What about him?" Her tone was already defensive.

"I know he looks after some investments for you and Dad." His mother started in with a protest, but Rick cut her off. "I'm not being critical. You told me he's doing a good job and that's great. But I know you also had investments with a few banks. I don't know which banks, and with Michael over in Victoria and Dad gone, I'd like to keep an eye on them. Make sure the banks aren't trying to take advantage of you."

"You needn't worry. Your father and I simplified our finances a while ago. Michael takes care of everything for us now and it's so much easier."

Rick pressed a hand to his forehead. The situation was worse than he'd imagined.

His mother continued talking, rattling on about how difficult she found it to stop using *us* and *we*. Rick interrupted her ramble. "Do you think that's wise? Putting all your eggs in one basket?"

"I'd rather have my eggs with Michael than some stranger. He and your father built the portfolio together. It'll do me for the time I have left."

"You have plenty of time left," Betty said, returning and resettling into her lounger. She handed Rick a drink. "The painters called. They're all lined up. They'll start the day we leave."

"Painters?" Rick said.

"To freshen up the place," his mother said. "They're going to paint the whole house while we're gone. Isn't that wonderful?"

The paint job wasn't to freshen up the place—it was to get it ready to sell.

"And Rick, dear. Thanks for your concern, but you don't need to worry about me. You've got enough on your plate. It's time you took care of yourself."

Indeed, he thought. He'd take care of himself. He'd just have to go through Mikey to do it.

44 | Sadie

Sadie fumed in the back seat of the town car. Jane's reaction had infuriated her. Sadie's one big opportunity and Jane couldn't bring herself to be happy for her, to support her decision. Jane wouldn't be so keen on waitressing if she'd had to work a single shift in a restaurant. Was minimum wage all Sadie was worth in Jane's eyes?

Jane and her damn rules. Maybe it really was time for Jane to learn how to live with her condition, for them to live their own lives. Sadie would soon have the money for her own place.

The limo pulled up outside the Sutton Place Hotel. The Sutton wasn't on Cynthia's roster of hotels, she noted. The driver bid her a good evening as a uniformed doorman opened her door.

With each click of her stilettos, she shook off a piece of her foul mood and settled into her role. The hostess at the Boulevard Kitchen & Oyster Bar escorted her to Rick's table. He stood, kissed her cheek, and seated her: a perfect gentleman on a dinner date. The illusion was safe under the cloak of respectability in an upscale place like Boulevard.

Sadie spread her napkin on her lap. A chilled martini, twin to Rick's, arrived at their table.

"To us," Rick said.

"To new beginnings," Sadie said, and touched her glass to his.

When the appetizers had been cleared away, he asked, "What's bothering you?"

Sadie furrowed her brow. "What do you mean?"

"You're tense. Distracted."

So much for Sadie thinking she'd done a good job masking her annoyance with Jane. She smoothed her napkin. "It's nothing. Just an argument with my roommate."

She redoubled her efforts to bury her agitation as their meal trickled out. Each dish resembled a work of art to be admired before its consumption. Rather like her, she thought, noticing an admiring glance or two as Rick escorted her to the elevators after their meal and then up to his room.

The perfect-gentleman illusion tumbled away behind the closed door. He pulled a small baggie from his pocket, laid out four lines, and inhaled two. "Those are for you, but only when you're wearing nothing but those shoes."

She made a show of disrobing. He liked that. She bent to the coke. Afterward, he insisted she sit in one of two brocade chairs separated by a small glass end table. He poured vodka over ice and brought the drinks over.

"Not yet," he said, as she reached for one. He nodded for her to sit back, and he touched the cold glass to each nipple. The shock of it chilled her to the core. "Better," he said, and then let her take the drink. He sat across from her and admired her assets while they finished their drinks.

The game he played might have changed, but the rules were the same: he held the reins. It didn't faze her. She was used to it. Most of her gigs were men like Rick. Their need to be *the man* made her job easier. She could be a good pet, or bad, for a few hours.

"Is your phone still off?" he asked.

"Yes." She'd turned it off in the restaurant when he asked her to do so.

"Good. I don't want any interruptions. Come here," he said, as he unbuckled his belt.

Rick took his time, savouring her ministrations. She suspected Viagra. When she'd finally sated his appetite, they moved to the bed and she lay beside him, propped on her elbow.

Rick stroked the underside of her breast. "Tell me about the argument with your roommate."

"She's not happy that I gave you our address."

"That hardly seems like enough to cause an argument."

"It shouldn't have been. I also told her I quit my job."

Rick's fingers paused. "Good girl. I'm pleased to hear it."

"We've never argued like that before." Sadie found herself opening up to him about their fight. It felt good to cleanse it from her system. She'd made the right decision taking Rick's offer. She refused to beat herself up about it any longer. No second thoughts. Jane might think he was dangerous, but Sadie was strong and street savvy. She could handle him.

So what if she let him play his silly power games? They were harmless.

She'd done nothing that wives and girlfriends across the country didn't do every night. The difference was that Sadie got paid well for it.

Besides, Sadie knew the truth about power; the one who held it was the one who could walk away. When she had his money in her account, for once in her life, she'd be the one doing the walking.

"Sounds like Jane is afraid you might leave her. She's trying to keep you in the box she's defined for you."

Sadie wondered if that was true. "I don't think it's intentional."

"Even friendships as long-lasting as yours can become toxic over time. The Jane you describe is needy. Needy people don't do well on their own. These rules she's set up keep you close to her. Tell me, does she keep tabs on you?"

"I suppose." In truth, they kept tabs on each other, but wasn't that what friends did?

"Do you think that's healthy?"

Rick's rapid-fire second-guessing made Sadie feel as if she'd lost her footing. "You're the professional. What do you think?" But the instant the words left her mouth, she knew she'd screwed up. She'd have to think quickly.

Rick shifted so he was looking at her. "Why would you say that?"

Sadie bit her lower lip and walked her fingers across his abdomen. "You're a psychiatrist, aren't you?"

"Who told you that?"

"No one," she lied, scrambling for cover. "I looked it up."

"I see," Rick said. He got out of bed and poured them another drink. "It is indeed my professional opinion."

Sadie sighed.

"Why don't you skip the drama and stay the night."

"Cynthia wouldn't approve."

"Cynthia or Jane? Because I think we're beyond Cynthia now, don't you?"

Did he know Cynthia charged extra for all-nighters?

Rick handed her a tumbler.

"How did you get Cynthia to agree to this hotel?" she asked. "It's not one of her usuals."

"Cynthia's proving to be quite flexible. I suspect it's because she knows it's in her best interests to keep me happy. As it is in yours. Stay the night."

This time it wasn't a suggestion.

45 | Rick

August 24

Rick left a fifty-dollar bill on the bedside table. A tip. Sadie had earned it. He'd showered and dressed but she hadn't stirred. Reaching down, he twirled a blonde curl around his finger. He'd miss her, but he couldn't keep her. Not now.

He'd done a lot of thinking in the hours after she climbed off him. She'd told him more than she was aware of. Only Jane could have connected the Kristan persona to his profession, which meant Jane was close to learning who he was and getting more dangerous. He would have to act sooner than he'd anticipated. He'd known keeping Sadie close would pay off.

And getting Jane under his control sooner would open a window of opportunity he hadn't considered before. Now, instead of simply fixing the mistake he'd made, he might be able to take Mikey down as well.

Andrew would kick up a stink, and Rick would have to delay his travel plans, but the potential payoff was huge.

He'd have to move quickly, though.

He'd never believed in serendipity before, but how else could he explain the incredible convergence of good fortune before him? Not only did he have the time and the right people in place, he now had the perfect location.

He dialled Andrew from the back seat of the cab. "There's been a change of plans."

46 | Jane

Jane paced their small apartment, cursing that she couldn't sleep in. Where the hell was Sadie? Andy's stalker app had proven useless. She'd texted her a warning about Rick, but like the message she'd sent yesterday, it remained undelivered.

The last time Sadie had pulled an all-nighter, Jane had found her in their old rooming house on East Hastings. She'd sought out familiar company in which to drown her self-loathing. It barely qualified as a step up from passing out in an alley. Jane had half a mind to leave her there if she'd done it again. She was tired of picking her up and dusting her off only to repeat the routine in another month. Keeping Sadie upright made Jane feel better, but it wasn't helping Sadie. If she was honest with herself, it had never helped.

Rick sure as hell wasn't Sadie's ticket out of the business. People didn't change. She couldn't guess his angle, but no doubt he had one, and saving Sadie wasn't it. The money had blinded Sadie. It had always been her Achilles' heel. When she had it, it vanished into consignment shops and nail salons. She spread it around like candy, getting high on the gratitude, but it never bought her the dignity she so desperately needed.

And now Sadie resented Jane for the Walkers' inheritance—money Sadie knew damn well Jane hadn't known about until last night. She felt the sting afresh remembering Sadie's words. Yesterday's fight hadn't been like any of their others. Sadie had gone too far. She'd broken Jane's trust on every level. And giving Rick—a john—their address was something Sadie couldn't undo. Jane would never feel safe wondering what he was up to, knowing he could find them.

She dressed for a ride. Her Honda 500 was the one sure cure for a toxic mood. Where she was going she didn't know, but she needed out of the city. Traffic, thick with commuters, held the speed she craved in check. It wasn't until she hit the on-ramp to the Sea to Sky Highway that she was finally able to crank up the horses and let her Rebel run.

The tug of the wind washed over her, cleansing her. She remembered the first time she ever donned a helmet. It was a turning point in her life: when she pulled down the visor, she was safely hidden from the stares of strangers. That feeling of freedom never went away.

Dodging sleepy sedans, she wove through the wind's caress, got lost in its tendrils. When she saw the sign for Cypress Mountain, she took the exit, laying her bike low through the road's sharp switchbacks. She bypassed the lookout with its views of Vancouver far below and kept climbing. When she reached the top and could go no farther, she slowed and circled the ski resort's empty parking lot.

The air felt cooler on the mountain, smelled sweeter. She stopped the bike and pulled out her phone, hating that the ride hadn't swept away her concern for Sadie. Jane's texts had been delivered. Sadie must have turned on her phone, but she hadn't responded, and Andy's crappy app still couldn't find her.

Jane wound her way down Cypress Mountain and continued north. The stretch of Sea to Sky Highway from Vancouver to Whistler was one of her favourite escapes. She followed the curves and took in the vistas, not turning around until she passed the old Britannia Mine Museum. She stopped at a picnic area, where she stretched her legs and dawdled by the water's edge.

Her birthday was a week away. She couldn't imagine not celebrating it with Sadie, but she wasn't ready to forgive her. She wasn't ready to move either, but Sadie's carelessness had set those wheels rolling. Maybe Sadie was right: maybe it was time Jane moved out.

Loneliness crept over her as she cruised back to the city. She headed for Riptide. Day drinkers occupied a scattering of tables, their conversations louder than the music. She spied Ethan behind the bar. He looked up as she approached, and a slow smile curled his lip.

He scanned the room and waved a server over. "Take over, would you?" He caught Jane's gaze and jerked his head toward the end of the bar. Jane paralleled his path and they met at the end. Without a word, he relieved her of her helmet and stepped down the hall digging keys from his pocket. He unlocked the office door and held it open for her.

"Connor not here?" she said, stepping inside.

"He'll be here later." Ethan closed the door and set down Jane's helmet on a table beside the sofa. He sauntered up to her and raked the hair back from her birthmark, studying the stain as he had that first night in the trailer. His eyes slid to her mouth. He kissed her, a slow sensuous tasting that had Jane wishing they were back at his apartment. She felt his arousal pressing against her and broke off the kiss.

"Kinda feels like we have company," she said, nodding toward the two-way mirror. She knew the people in the bar couldn't see their intimate embrace, but she felt self-conscious.

He looked at the mirror as if he'd suddenly remembered it was there. "Ah, you get used to it." He took her hand and led her to the sofa. "Something's off. What is it?"

"Sadie and I had a blowout." As Jane searched for the right words to explain, it occurred to her how hard she had to work to keep the fact that Sadie was a prostitute out of the conversation. Without that piece of intel, the argument sounded trivial. "She's seeing a man. Rick Kristan. He worries me."

Ethan toyed with Jane's fingers. "Sadie's questionable taste in men isn't new. What makes this Kristan guy different?"

"He's twenty years older than her, for a start. And I think he's been stalking her. He showed up at the restaurant where she works." Worked, Jane thought. Past tense.

"You think he'd hurt her?"

Jane wanted to scream YES! "He has the potential. He's already manipulating her."

"How so?"

"Money. Drugs."

Ethan's hand stopped moving. He furrowed his brow. "For sex?"

"No!" Jane replied, horrified that she'd almost told him yet knowing her slip-up wasn't entirely innocent. It was a product of her frustration. "Forget I said that. I have no right to judge her. I'm just angry she can't see how messed up this guy is."

"I'm sorry," Ethan said. He pulled Jane close, and she snuggled into him, letting go of her anger.

"I have news," he said. "I called a real estate agent today. Told her it was a ways off, but she's going to start sending me listings for acreages."

Jane listened as Ethan told her about his plans for the future, and her spirits lifted. He trusted her with his dreams, and she didn't take that lightly. Trust was a gift.

All too soon, he returned to work. Jane sat at the bar with a glass of ginger ale, and they stole moments together as customers came and went.

At four o'clock, her phone vibrated against the bar. It was Ariane. Jane slid from her stool. She called down the bar to Ethan, "I gotta go."

He lifted his hand from the beer tap and waved.

Jane answered before she pushed open the door. "Have you found something?"

"Yes and no. A woman named Rebecca Morrow was a patient at Wild Rose Psychiatric Hospital. It was near Banff, Alberta."

"Was?"

"It's now a long-term-care facility."

"What happened to Rebecca?"

There was a pause. "She died, Jane. I'm sorry." Ariane cleared her throat. "The death certificate indicates the cause of death was suicide."

"No!" Jane's hopes for a cure turned to ash and scattered. She slumped against the building feeling hollow.

"There's a grave marker for her in the Canmore Cemetery. And there's something else. There is no doctor or psychiatrist, not even a psychologist, named Rick or Richard Kristan. Not in Canada, not in England."

"I don't understand," Jane said. She'd heard him called Rick in her dream. That had to be his name. He'd also told Sadie it was Rick. And Sadie was certain his surname was Kristan.

"Could you have misheard his name?" Ariane asked. "Or did you see it in writing?"

"No, I heard it, from two sources. But not his last name." Jane paused. She'd been an idiot. The man was a john. He wouldn't use his real name. "I may have got his surname wrong."

"Okay. I'll have Hunter take another look at the Richards. I'm sorry about Rebecca."

"Yeah, me too." Jane stared at her phone's screen until it went black. Whoever Rick was, he hadn't cured Rebecca. And Rebecca hadn't learned to live with her visions. Could Jane be headed for the same future?

She pushed off from the wall and walked toward her bike. Her thoughts turned to Buddy as she strapped on her helmet. If preventing Buddy's life-altering injury was the only good thing that came out of her terrible dreams, maybe that was enough. It had to be. She wondered again about her purpose—it might not be Ariane's version of justice or retribution, but she could dial 911 within a visiting dream even if the victims couldn't. She could lock doors and hide weapons.

Possibility trickled into the hollow space inside her. She headed to Positively Plants. It wouldn't be the first time she'd turned up on her day off, and Anna might be able to give her some answers about Buddy and his mom.

Anna stood in the orchid section beside a pinched-nosed man who appeared torn between choices. Her hand rested on her hip, and she radiated uncharacteristic impatience. When she saw Jane, she waved to get her attention. "Pieter is here. He was asking for you." The smile in Anna's voice was missing. Jane was tempted to blame it on the customer, but Anna's complexion was drawn, and shadows had moved in under her eyes.

"I'll go find him," Jane said, and scurried away. She'd return after Anna completed her sale and convince her to go home and get some rest. Jane could cover the few hours until closing.

She searched for Pieter in the greenhouse and then spotted Lucas as she headed outside. "I'm looking for Pieter," she said. "You seen him?"

He furrowed his brow. "Breakroom, as always."

As always? What had Pieter done to end up in the doghouse? she wondered. "Thanks," she said, and did an about-face before she got snagged in his foul mood.

She swung into the breakroom and stopped short. Confusion gripped her. What had happened to their breakroom? A floor-to-ceiling partition had cut the room in half. Neither Lucas nor Anna had said a word about a renovation. The table where she'd eaten her lunch for the past eight years had been replaced by one a third the size. And where was the mini-fridge?

From behind the partition, she heard the sounds of a children's television program. She drew close and poked her head around the corner. A man with his back to Jane sat in a wheelchair watching a cartoon on a flat-screen TV. The woman who sat near him lowered her knitting needles and smiled. "Hi, Joyce. Look who's here, Pieter."

Jane lurched off centre, as if she'd stepped into one of her dreams. She'd never seen the woman before. What were these people doing here?

"Are you all right, dear?" the woman said.

"I'm sorry . . . I'm interrupting." Jane backed away, unable to piece together what lay before her.

"Nonsense. Pieter's been asking for you." She set her knitting aside and angled the man's chair so he could see her.

Jane froze in place.

A smile of recognition lit up his face.

She couldn't breathe. The Pieter she knew was trapped inside a body she didn't recognize.

And she knew without a doubt that she was responsible.

Jane checked the scream in her throat and stilled the hand that wanted to fly to her mouth. "I'm so sorry." Jane looked away from him. She turned and rushed for the door. The woman called out to her, but Jane didn't stop. "What have I done?"

In a daze, she found herself at the front counter. Anna approached.

"You're limping," Jane said.

"No worse than usual. You leaving already?"

"What happened?"

Anna cocked an eyebrow.

"With Pieter! What happened to him?"

Anna's eyes hardened. "What's gotten into you?"

"The day Pieter was born. Tell me." A well-worn forearm crutch rested against the counter.

"It's hardly the—"

Jane grabbed Anna's hand. "The day Pieter was born. You met a woman named Mary. She had a son the same day. His name's Dylan but everyone calls him Buddy."

"Are you on drugs?" Anna shook Jane's hand off.

"Please, Anna." Jane felt her heart thudding in her chest.

"I don't know who you're talking about, Joyce. As for Pieter, you know the story."

Joyce? Jane paused, and then backed away. She left Anna where she stood and ran to find Lucas. She cornered him in the yard and forced a casual smile. "Humour me, Lucas, please. Tell me why Pieter's in a wheelchair. What happened?"

He tilted his head and frowned. "That's not something you forget. What's going on?"

"Lucas, I'm begging you." Her voice cracked. A scream gathered in her throat as her sanity unravelled.

"All right. A taxi rolled into Anna's car at the hospital. She got knocked down by an open door. Hit her head, lost consciousness. Her leg got trapped under the wheel. By the time they got her out and into surgery . . . well, you saw Pieter."

Jane stumbled backward.

"You gonna tell me why you needed to hear that again?"

"I'm sorry," Jane said. She turned and bolted straight past Anna and out to the street.

She made her way home but didn't remember the drive. She locked the apartment door. Sadie wasn't there. Good. She had no time to worry about her. She had to fix what she'd done to Pieter. To Anna.

Sleep. She needed to dream and quickly. She strode to the cupboard where Sadie kept her wine and poured herself a full tumbler. Gulp by gulp, she forced it down and then refilled it. She drank the second helping in the same fashion, and drained the bottle with the third refill. Buddy's butter tart box lay on top of the recycling pile. She pulled it out, took it to the sofa, and lay down, boots and all, clutching the box to her chest.

"I'm sorry, Pieter, so sorry." She gripped the box and held Buddy's image in her mind, willing herself to focus, praying she could seed another dream. "I won't interfere this time. I'll make this right, I promise. Forgive me, Buddy," she said. Guilt turned her stomach to acid as she repeated the refrain, over and over, vowing to fix the horrible mess she'd made.

Visiting Dream

Jane is in Rebecca's room in the hospital. Something about being here makes her angry, but she doesn't know what.

Rebecca is here, and so is Rick. The door is closed. Jane looks down to her boots. She's fully clothed, and her body looks like a shadow.

"You lied to me," Rick says. He stands between Rebecca and her with his back to Jane. His hands are pushed deep into the pockets of his lab coat. "There was no affair! How am I supposed to trust you when you lie to me?"

Rebecca sits on the edge of her bed, gazing at Rick's shoes. She worries her bottom lip. She's further along in her pregnancy than she was in the last dream. Jane stands in the void where the second bed would have been.

"You lied too. I know David has been here. I want to see him."

"His influence is detrimental."

Rebecca peeks up with defiance in her face. "To me or to you?"

"The last time you saw him, you tried to harm yourself."

"That's a lie."

"It's what the police report says."

Rebecca's gaze falls to her lap. She caresses the curve of her belly. "You could have killed the baby."

"The doctor assured you the baby is healthy, perfectly fine."

"The doctor wasn't a pediatrician. Let me go. Please."

"Give me what I want, and I will." Rick takes his hands from his pocket. He removes the safety cap from a syringe.

"I can't. I told you. You're the focus of my visions, not your brother." Tears track down her face.

"Then change the focus. I know you can do it. You just need the proper motivation."

Rebecca lifts her head. "Please—" Her gaze shifts beyond Rick to land on Jane, and her eyes widen.

Jane checks her body. It's no longer a shadow, but not quite solid. "Can . . . can you see me?" Jane asks. Her voice sounds like a faint echo.

Rebecca squints, focusing on Jane's lips. Jane repeats her question. Slowly, Rebecca nods.

Rick turns. Confusion clouds his features. "What the—who—how'd you get in here?" His nostrils flare as he steps toward Jane, needle in hand. His face hardens.

Instinctively, Jane reaches for her boot knife.

Rebecca shouts, "Run!"

Rick lunges for Jane.

Jane ducks the needle and slashes a crimson line across Rick's face. She slips out of his reach as he stumbles past her, stunned.

Jane stands before Rebecca, who is now on her feet. Her expression is a mix of fear and wonder. She reaches a hand to Jane's face, and Jane feels the warmth of Rebecca's fingers on her cheek. "She said you'd come, but not like this."

Jane glances over her shoulder. Rick holds a hand to his wound. Blood drips from his fingers. He glares at Jane.

"Go!" Rebecca whispers. "Now."

Jane pinches her eyes closed, and in her mind, she screams at herself to wake up.

Jane blinked. She was awake. She'd interrupted a dream. As she marvelled at the revelation, it registered that she was gazing up at an unfamiliar ceiling.

47 | Rick

Quiet!" Andrew hissed.

"If getting her here didn't wake her, my voice sure as hell won't," Rick said.

Andrew straightened and hiked up his jeans. "What is this place? Some kind of kennel?"

Rick reached into Jane's boot and removed her concealed knife.

"Whoa!" Andrew said. "You knew she had a weapon and you didn't think to mention it to me?"

"It was a guess."

Andrew narrowed his eyes. "Didn't look like a guess."

Rick stepped around Andrew and out of the kennel, motioning for Andrew to follow. Rick then secured the latch with a padlock and pocketed the key.

"You're making a mistake," Andrew said, looking at Sadie's roommate, comatose on a thin mattress on the concrete floor. "A clean fentanyl overdose wouldn't raise a flag. But this?" he said, shaking his head and gesturing around the space. "This is a conviction in the making. I'm not taking the hit for you."

"A short delay is all this is, and I've made careful adjustments to compensate for it."

"I believe *I've* made the adjustments. All you've done is block the windows and hang soundproofing."

And install a modified cage, but Andrew didn't need to know that. "You've been well compensated."

"You changed the plan. Increased my risk of exposure."

"Unless you plan to introduce yourself, she can't identify you."

"I want the rest of the money you owe me."

"You'll get it when I'm in Europe, as we agreed."

"No. Pay me what you owe me now. Otherwise, I'm out."

"I don't think you want to piss me off, Andrew. Send me proof that she's still alive after I arrive at my London hotel and then take care of her. You see what she's like. Getting her downtown and pumping her full of fentanyl will be child's play. Burn this place to the ground and no one will ever connect her to it."

48 | Jane

August 25

In the near dark, Jane pushed to a sitting position. Her heart thumped a tattoo she felt in the pit of her stomach. She was in a cage. The thin padding she sat on took up most of the five-by-eight-foot cell. The walls, fabricated with metal welded in a two-inch grid pattern, were bolted to a concrete floor and stretched to the ceiling. It was a kennel, she decided, spotting two silver dog bowls mounted low in the narrow end wall that was also the door. Big bowls. Must have been made for Great Danes or mastiffs. A bottle of water rested in one of the bowls.

The space was tall enough that when she stood, she couldn't touch the top of the kennel. Beyond the walls, quilted packing blankets hung from the ceiling and blocked any view she might have had. She examined the squat plastic box in the corner of the kennel and lifted its lid. A toilet.

She shook the grated walls. They held firm. The door to the kennel wouldn't budge. She poked her fingers around the edge of the doorframe and confirmed the padlock was secured with a key and not a combination.

And she knew without a doubt who held the key.

How had he gotten to her? She'd been in the apartment after the terrible shock of finding Pieter in a wheelchair. Had she forgotten to lock the door?

She patted her pockets and lifted the mattress. Her phone was gone. She reached down for her knife. Gone. A wave of panic chased her back to rattle the metal grate. She hip-checked the cage door, but it was pointless. She was trapped.

What did he want from her? Was this some twisted payback for cutting him?

Had he taken Sadie as well? "Sadie! Are you in here?" No one answered. She sat down and hugged her knees. Hours later, she rolled onto her side and drifted to sleep.

When she woke, she convinced herself that her cocoon was a lighter shade of grey. Daytime? She looked to the door. The water bottle remained in one of the dog dishes, but something else now sat in the other one. He'd been here. She shivered at the thought of him anywhere near her while she slept.

It was her boot knife and with it, a tourist map of Victoria. She slid the boot knife back where it belonged. He'd been a fool to return it, and he wasn't a fool, so why'd he do it? She opened the map and a photograph fell out. A printed label on the back identified the man in the photo as Michael Atkins. Another printed label was stuck to the map:

You have only one job. Kill Michael Atkins.

He'd circled two addresses, one marked *home* and one marked *office*. At the bottom of the note, he'd added another printed label:

I'm armed at all times. Don't be stupid.

Michael? Could this be Mikey, the older brother Rebecca had mentioned? Had to be. Which meant Atkins was Rick's real surname.

Did he plan on letting her out of the cage to kill his brother? A disturbing thought chilled her. She'd cut him in a dream. Had he figured that out? Did he imagine she could kill his brother in a dream?

Jane called out into the emptiness, "I know who you are." Silence answered.

"People are looking for me," she said, but were they? Not Sadie. Not after their fight. She'd be avoiding Jane for a few days. Ethan wouldn't even know she was missing yet, and who knew how long it would take Ariane and Nate to figure out something was wrong. She had to hope Anna and Lucas would raise the alarm when she didn't show up for work. She never missed work. How long until the police acted on the information? For the first time in her life, she desperately wanted to see a cop.

Ariane had been right, Jane thought, looking at the blood-red stain on the back of her hand. Someone did want her dead; she wasn't naive enough to think Rick would let her go after she'd served her purpose. But how did he know who she was?

Jane held on to the hope that Ariane was also right about her birthmarks protecting her. Rick couldn't harm her as long as they remained. She tried not to dwell on her looming birthday.

Within an hour of waking, she had to use the toilet. As if it were possible, the action left her feeling even more vulnerable.

Hours drifted by. Jane's stomach grumbled. She cracked open the water bottle and drained it. It satisfied her hunger for a time.

The quilted padding hanging outside her cage pooled on the floor agonizing inches beyond her fingertips. She moved the dog bowls and stretched her arm through the holes, but she couldn't get close enough to touch the fabric. She extended her reach, first with the empty bottle and then with her knife, but the risk of dropping her only weapon tempered her efforts.

The water ran through her and she had to use the toilet again.

She then used her knife to pry at the welds that secured her cage, but they held, and she wasn't willing to crank harder and risk breaking her blade.

She counted the two-inch squares, gaining a new perspective on the life of prisoners. How did they survive the monotony?

She prayed for sleep, but not to harm Michael. Armed or not, she was going after Rick, and she had to do it while she still bore the marks. He didn't know her very well if he thought she'd walk away from a fight.

At one point, she thought she heard someone beyond the blankets. She called out and strained to hear, but the moment passed and monotony drifted back in.

Visiting Dream

Jane is back in Rebecca's hospital room. It's dark outside. Rebecca wrings her hands and mumbles to herself. She keeps up a steady pace walking from the window to the door and back again. Jane's body shimmers, not that Rebecca notices, being as preoccupied as she is. Jane hides in the corner's shadow.

Rebecca turns at the sound of a lock releasing. She races to the door and stops short, expectant. Jane reaches for her knife.

Maria Yupanqui steps inside and ushers David in behind her. Rebecca and David are in each other's arms in seconds.

"Shh! You must be quiet," Maria warns. Her back is to Jane. "You have only a few minutes," she adds, then closes the door behind her.

Emotions ricochet around the room: joy, despair, love, regret, longing. Rebecca and David never stop touching. She holds his hand to her abdomen and they both shed tears.

Jane stays by the door, knife in hand. David leads Rebecca to the bed. They sit and speak in quick, conspiratorial voices, making promises they can't keep.

Jane feels torn. She's itching for Rick to make an appearance, but not now. Maria has arranged a miracle, and Jane wants this precious moment to last as long as possible.

But the moment scatters with the sound of racing footfalls in the hallway. With the click of the lock, Rick rushes in. David leaps up, holding his arms wide to protect Rebecca, who cowers behind him.

The doctor lunges, and they both go down at Rebecca's feet. Rebecca screams. Jane lurches forward gripping her knife as the two of them writhe on the floor, intertwined. Jane dances around the blur of limbs, hesitant to act and accidentally harm David.

An alarm sounds in the hallway. A white-clad elbow thrusts back and jams forward. David's hand snakes out and grips Rick's shoulder. Rebecca screams again and then she's on her knees, clawing her way to David and shoving at Rick's shoulders.

An orderly rushes into the room with a security guard on his heels. Jane stumbles backward, into the corner.

Rick pushes to his knees, holding his side. His white coat is smeared with red. "Restrain her!" he shouts, grimacing in pain.

The security guard climbs over Rick and pulls Rebecca off David. He shoves her down on the bed face-first and none too gently. Her hands are covered in blood. She's still screaming for David, who lies still on the floor.

The orderly helps Rick to his feet and escorts him outside. On the bed, Rebecca continues to resist the security guard.

Another orderly arrives with a nurse, and the security guard holds Rebecca still until the nurse can deliver an injection. Within moments, Rebecca is limp, and soon she's removed from the room.

Jane is left alone with David. Having watched the horror unfold before her, she feels weak. Her body has lost its shimmer, its substance. David hasn't moved and Jane fears he's dead. She still hasn't seen a weapon.

She forces herself to leave the room and follow the commotion to the dispensing window. Behind the protective glass, a scrub-clad orderly rummages through a tray of medical supplies. She hears Rick demand the orderly leave him and attend to the man on the floor in Rebecca's room. The moment the orderly departs, Rick pulls off his lab coat, rolls it in a ball, and heads in the other direction. Jane follows him.

"That way," he says, as he opens the door by the piano. A squad of uniformed police rush in. When they pass, he leaves and races down the hall. Jane trails him into his office. She sees him remove an ivory letter opener from the coat's pocket and wipe the handle on the garment. It's the same ornate letter opener she's seen in his possession before.

He then stuffs both the coat and the letter opener in a briefcase behind the door. Another lab coat hangs from a hook. He rips it from its hanger, pulls it on, and heads back in the direction of the ward. Then he ducks into the men's room, where he carefully washes his hands. When he emerges, his coat and his hands are stained afresh with blood. His own. Jane watched him press his coat into a weeping wound on his ribs.

"I know what you've done," Jane says, and she can hear her voice echo in the hallway.

Rick stops and searches the hall through narrowed eyes.

Jane woke in a rush of adrenalin. Rick killed David.

She should have stopped him. She clenched her jaw, angry that in her hesitation, she'd failed David. Failed Rebecca. She kicked the cage wall in frustration.

Jane's slashing Rick's face wasn't the reason he'd gone after her—David's murder was. He'd heard her. He must have known she would dream of that moment. And so what? She couldn't *restore justice*, despite Ariane's beliefs. Rick would surely have destroyed that letter opener. It would be her crazy-town word against his professional word. No contest. No threat. So why take her? Was this all about Rick wanting to destroy his brother?

Rick was narcissistic and delusional. And he had his hooks in Sadie. Jane had to find a way to warn her.

49 | Rick

Rick sat at his father's desk flipping through the mail he'd collected. Though he wasn't certain at which point in the past Jane would select to get rid of Mikey, he anticipated he'd sense when the deed had been done. There were sure to be signs around the house, changes he would notice. Grief left a mark.

He'd given some thought to the fallout. If Michael died before he married Elaine, his kids would be gone. Good riddance. If he died later in life, a few of his investors might feel the impact. His parents' grief would be unfortunate, but otherwise, Rick couldn't think of a single negative repercussion. Regardless of when Mikey met his demise, Rick would end up the sole heir. And if Mikey died early enough, he wouldn't be able to poison their parents against him.

He tossed the junk mail in the trashcan. The painters presented an inconvenience he'd have to work around. The two men had started in the bedrooms. They seemed innocuous enough. He'd explained to them he'd be working from the house for a few days. They'd agreed to check in with him at the beginning and end of each day. He didn't want any surprises.

He watched Jane on his laptop. She mesmerized him. When she slept, she looked perfectly normal. Whether she was in a narcoleptic state or not, he couldn't tell by observation, but if he had to enter her kennel, he'd verify to make sure she was truly comatose and not just sleeping.

She hadn't stirred when he slipped into the barn to deliver his instructions. Parting the soundproofing blankets, he noticed that the hair she used to hide her marks had fallen away in her sleep. He couldn't help himself. He'd lifted the soundproofing above her head to get a closer look at her face. Seeing her markings from afar all these years hadn't prepared him for the deep-blood-red shade of them.

She looked remarkably the same as she had the day he first saw her. The day she'd slashed his face. It was as if time had stood still for her. Back then, he'd mistaken her facial birthmark for a tasteless tattoo, an act of teenage defiance. It wasn't until the old woman confessed that he'd learned what the mark really was. It was his fault that she bore it, though not his doing. That alone would be enough to stir her contempt. But before her marks were gone, she'd learn to loathe him.

Returning her knife had been a risk, but he knew what was coming; he'd lived through the events she was only now experiencing. He'd been armed since the day she cut him, all those years ago.

Andrew thought Rick's preparations were overkill—that she was harmless—but Rick knew better. Until her birthmarks were gone, he'd handle her from a distance.

50 | Sadie

S omeone pounded on the door. "Housekeeping!"
Sadie pried her eyes open. The light hurt her head. A fog lifted, and memories of the previous evening rolled in. Sadie pulled the sheet over her head.

The bedside phone rang, once again pulling Sadie out of sleep. She lifted the receiver.

"Checkout time was an hour ago. Would you like to book the room for another night?"

"No," Sadie mumbled. "Give me twenty minutes."

She crawled from the bed and splashed water on her face. If she'd known she was staying the night, she'd have packed her travel kit. Thankfully, the hotel had disposable makeup-removal wipes. She rinsed her mouth and ran her fingers through her curls. If she kept her distance, it was enough to pass as presentable. When she returned to the bed for her clothes, she found Rick's fifty-dollar bill. He was good to her that way. If she didn't go home with a tip, he'd usually leave her some coke.

She took a cab home and breathed easier seeing Jane's Rebel was gone. Why did Jane have to be so negative? This time, Sadie was going to stand her ground. If she let Jane ruin this opportunity for her, she'd always wonder what might have been. She headed straight for the bottle of aspirin in the bathroom. From there, she dropped into bed.

It was late afternoon before she stirred. She padded to the kitchen and put the kettle on. A bottle of wine stood empty on the counter. Her bottle of wine. What the hell, Jane?

She peered into the living room and saw a tumbler on the trunk. A sniff of the contents confirmed it was the dregs of the wine Jane had helped herself to. Sadie frowned. It was very unlike Jane. Had she been numbing herself after their argument? Drinking to oblivion was usually Sadie's role.

She put her feet up on the trunk and checked her phone. She shouldn't have been surprised there was nothing from Jane, but it was unusual. Jane always checked on her. Perhaps her silence was a measure of how bad their argument had been. Sadie had her own regrets about their fight—she felt like a shit for having gone through Jane's papers. She shouldn't have done that, and she would make a point of apologizing. Still, she had to stay strong or Jane would talk her out of the deal.

Sadie headed to Fourth Street just before Jane was due home. She wasn't yet ready to deal with her. She sat on the outdoor patio at her favourite Greek restaurant and ordered a beer. Andy had gone quiet, and she couldn't find him or Jane on his app.

It was after nine when Sadie made it back to the apartment. She was relieved to find Jane's Rebel was still gone. Jane was probably with Ethan, avoiding Sadie as much as Sadie was avoiding her.

At midnight, Sadie took the bed. Jane was definitely avoiding her. She broke down and sent her a text. *Still friends?*

Sadie drifted off to sleep before she got an answer.

51 | Rick

Rick checked the time. It had been almost twenty-four hours since Jane arrived. He walked up to the soundproofing blankets. "Do you have news for me?"

"I know who Michael is," Jane said. "Or should I call him Mikey?"

"I'm sure it doesn't matter. Just get the job done."

"You expect me to do that from in here?"

"Are you hungry?"

Rick drank in the silence. He then dropped an energy bar to the floor, lifted the curtain slightly, and kicked the bar up against the side of the cage. "Consider that a gift. You'll have to earn the next one."

52 | Jane

After the exterior door closed, Jane heard the soft thunk of a car door. He was gone. And so was any hope that he might not expect her to kill his brother while in a dream. She thought of the colossal damage that had been done by simply helping a woman cross a patch of ice. Killing someone would cause unfathomable ripples through history.

The *gift* he'd left was an energy bar. He could have dropped it in one of the bowls, but instead he was making her work for it. She crouched and, using both hands, reached several fingers through the cage's small squares to manipulate the three-inch bar through a two-inch opening.

When at last she'd pulled it inside, she examined the package for tampering. He wasn't done with her yet, so she didn't think he'd poison her, but he might try to drug her to sleep. After carefully unwrapping the bar, she held the packaging to the light. Seeing nothing that looked like a pinhole, she devoured the bar. Moments later, her stomach cramped. It felt as if she'd swallowed a baseball, and she had to fight to keep it down. When the pain passed, her stomach started rumbling again.

With her back against the cage, she pulled the knife from her boot and skimmed the blade across her thumb. He would kill her when he got what he wanted. It terrified her to think he'd do it when she was paralyzed. The only way to survive was to kill him first. The thought of it sickened her. She'd finished many fights, broken someone's nose once, blackened a few eyes, but could she go so far as to take a life?

If she could, she'd have to seed a dream to find him. Her anxiety ratcheted up another notch. She wanted to believe she could seed her dreams—she'd done it before with Sadie and again with Anna and Mary—but doubt leaked in. What if those seedings had been flukes? It hadn't worked every time.

Her thoughts turned to Sadie. Rick had used Sadie to get to her. When he was done with Sadie, he'd probably kill her too. Jane was the only one who could stop him.

She tucked her knife away and lay down. Her anxiety rose like bile. Once again, she thought the energy bar would come back up. Killing Rick might save Sadie and her, but the impact on history would be massive. And unpredictable. Still, she had to try. Her dreams were their only hope.

She pushed away the negative thoughts and turned to the practical considerations. Slashing a bare throat was easier than going through fabric for a fatal stab to the groin or an armpit. Regardless, she'd have to find him when he was alone, without witnesses. And her body would have to be more solid than a shimmer.

She thought back to the time she'd slashed him. Her body had been solid then. She'd been angry, furious that he'd threatened a pregnant woman, someone weaker, vulnerable. Someone he'd locked up. Just as he'd done to her. If anger was what she needed, she was ready.

There was more chance of finding him alone in the house where he'd been treating Rebecca than at the hospital. Her stomach growled. She closed her eyes and pictured the room with the Oriental carpet and hardwood floors. Sleep felt miles away. She rolled over and tried to get comfortable. She imagined the CD player, Rick's chair, the sofa where Rebecca lay. Rebecca must have been devastated to lose David. Had his death been the final blow for her?

Visiting Dream

Jane wakes in Rick's boss's office, the one with the steel-and-glass desk. She's angry about being here instead of the room with the CD player.

Rick's boss sits behind her desk. Rick sits in one of the guest chairs. In the other chair sits a suited man with a dour expression. The fluorescent lighting washes out Jane's shimmer.

"We're in cover-your-ass territory," the man in the suit says. "How the hell did David Banner get past security, never mind into a patient's locked room?"

Rick's boss sits unnaturally straight in her chair. "His name was added to Rebecca Morrow's list of approved visitors from Dr. Atkins's computer," she says. "But Dr. Atkins was with me at the time it was added. It's date-stamped."

Jane can't tell if she's lying.

"What does security say?" the man asks.

Rick's boss adjusts a piece of paper on the desk in front of her before meeting the suited man's pointed gaze. "With no cameras in nonpatient areas, the only thing security can confirm is that there was no unusual activity on this floor the day David Banner's name was entered into the computer system." The woman starts to cross her arms and thinks better of it. "There are only two possibilities. Either someone broke in and security didn't catch it, or someone on staff is responsible."

The man in the suit snorts and shakes his head. "Terrific. The murder is bad enough, but the breach of our computer's security system is where we're vulnerable and, in all likelihood, liable. Sure as hell someone will blame that breach for David Banner's death."

The dour man's face has reddened. He turns to Rick. "Have you shared your password with anyone, Dr. Atkins?"

Rick snaps back in his seat. "Certainly not. And if I'm away from the computer for more than five minutes, it locks automatically."

The man tips his chin. "What's IT's explanation?"

"They have nothing," Rick says, leaning in. "Our internal investigation needs to start with Maria Yupanqui." He taps a determined finger on the wooden arm of his chair. "She's the one who escorted him to Rebecca's room."

"Maria Yupanqui is a psychiatric care aide," the man says. "It's her job to escort visitors. We take that route and the public will think we're looking for a scapegoat."

"We've already started a security audit," Rick's boss says.

"Good. I want every doctor to perform an integrity review of their patient files."

"Absolutely."

"The final matter concerns Ms. Morrow," the man says, addressing Rick. "David Banner's family has retained a lawyer. We'll have to settle to keep the incident from growing legs. Thankfully, his murder isn't Ms. Morrow's first physical altercation, but it's imperative the hospital is clear of any further public fallout. I trust you're prepared to declare her unfit to stand trial?"

"I am. Have the police concluded their investigation?"

"Forensics confirmed her prints are on the murder weapon they found hidden in her mattress, so yes, they're moving forward with the charges."

Jane's chest felt painfully tight as she surfaced from her dream. Only one person could have planted that evidence.

And if losing David hadn't been what drove Rebecca to kill herself, being charged with his murder surely would.

She rubbed her sternum. Jane felt certain Maria was responsible for getting David's name on the visitor list. Rick knew it too, which put Maria in Rick's crosshairs. Maria had befriended Rebecca, tried to help her. Had she planned to work with David to get Rebecca out of there? Sadly, whatever escape plan they might have had lay in ruins now, and they were both in danger. Jane studied the mark on the back of her hand. If only she could extend her protection back in time to safeguard them.

She knew for sure now that Rick's last name was Atkins. If Jane was a Witness, as Ariane had said, then she had to right Rick's wrongs, seek retribution for Rebecca and David. But how? Frustration and impotence were all she had to offer. And which of Rick's growing number of wrongs was she supposed to set right?

53 | Sadie

August 26

Sadie woke late and Jane was still gone. It didn't look as if she'd even been home. Either that or her compulsion to tidy-up had taken a much-needed break, she thought, looking around at the pile of dishes that hadn't miraculously cleaned themselves. Sadie pulled a bowl from the cupboard and thumbed through her phone while she ate.

Finding no response from Jane, she texted her again. Argument or not, they were still each other's oldest friends. She loved her regardless of their fight. *You with Ethan?* If Jane was staying with Ethan, she would've had to tell him about her narcolepsy.

Had she taken Sadie's get-a-life words to heart? Was she all right? An unexpected wave of sadness washed over her. Jane had stepped outside her safety zone. If she was following through on making her own life, then Sadie would be on her own. Even more reason for Sadie to hold her ground and make sure she kept Rick and Cynthia happy. At least until she had his money in her bank account.

Had Jane dreamed about him again? She knew that the people Jane dreamed of were often nasty pieces of shit. Rick hadn't met that bar. At least not yet. Perhaps when she could afford her own investigator, she'd learn more about him.

When lunchtime rolled around and she still hadn't heard from Jane, she knocked on Andy's door hoping he could fix his damn app and find her. He wasn't home.

By nine o'clock in the evening, Sadie had grown tired of Jane's silent treatment. She jumped in her car and headed to Riptide. She found Ethan in the office and was momentarily sidetracked by the activity in the bar behind the two-way mirror.

"What can I do for you?" Ethan said. His tone landed somewhere between *take a hike* and *don't come back.*

"I'm looking for Jane. She staying with you?"

"No. Said she's taking a break."

She furrowed her brow. "What do you mean?"

"Said you two had an argument and she needed some space. Apparently she has some decisions to make and can't make them with me distracting her."

"Jane said that?" Sadie hadn't meant to sound as though she didn't believe him, but she couldn't imagine those words coming from Jane. Jane wasn't a runner.

He pulled up a text from Jane on his phone and showed her. It was pretty much word for word.

"What the hell did you two argue about?" he asked.

"Roommate shit." Pretty bad roommate shit.

"Really? Nothing more?" Ethan didn't even try to mask his skepticism.

"It's between Jane and me." And it was more serious than Sadie had imagined.

"If she's not back soon, you and I are going to have another talk."

They both started as the banker's lamp on Ethan's desk toppled to the floor and smashed.

"What the?" Ethan said. He hesitated before approaching the broken remains, and then reached to unplug the cord.

"That was . . . weird," Sadie said, frowning. She pictured the tray of broken champagne flutes from Jane's dream and slowly gazed around the room looking for . . . what? Jane's ghost?

Ethan straightened. "Where'd she go? D'ya know?"

"No. She's never gone off like this before."

Sadie brushed off his dirty look and left him sweeping up the mess.

Back at their apartment, she texted Jane. *Please come home.*

54 | Rick

Taking care of Jane's job at the nursery had gone smoothly, but Rick hadn't known Jane and the bartender's relationship had progressed to the point where she might stay with him. Sadie had once again proven her worth. Thanks to Sadie's text, Rick had been able to ward Ethan off.

He checked Jane's phone once again. Sadie was softening, reaching out to Jane. He'd have to address that, but not until Sadie got the message that Jane had taken their argument very badly.

55 | Jane

J ane had been awake for what felt like hours, but without a clock it was
difficult to track time. She'd close her eyes for a while then open them
to get a sense of the changing shades of grey, but the shifts were too subtle.
It was daytime, but morning or afternoon was up for debate.

Earlier, she'd run through some of her and Sadie's sparring routines.
It helped fight the monotony and build her courage for what lay ahead,
but it drained what little energy she had.

She lay down, and her thoughts turned to Richard Atkins, or Rick
Kristan, as Sadie knew him. If Jane wasn't mistaken, he'd been a gig of
hers for two years, maybe longer. He'd been planning this moment for a
very long time.

Was there any significance to the name Kristan? she wondered. She
remembered asking Sadie about the spelling a while ago. It was an odd
spelling. She imagined the letters as she drew them with her finger on the
concrete floor. Then she drew out Atkins. The realization hit her with a
dull thud. Kristan was an anagram of R. Atkins. He'd probably patted
himself on the back for that.

Jane's hunger hadn't abated, but her stomach no longer rumbled. If
something were to happen to Rick now, she'd starve to death. It disturbed
her to find herself hoping he'd come back, and soon. The thought of
Mickey D's fries would have made her mouth water if she weren't so
parched.

She tried not to think about the act of killing and concentrated on
the where and when of it. The further back in time she went, the more
impact Rick's death would have on history.

Then again, maybe she didn't have to kill him. What if all she had to
do was prevent him from meeting Sadie? And if she could stop Rebecca's
and Rick's paths from crossing, maybe she could save Rebecca some
suffering as well.

The possibilities lifted her spirits, but the feeling didn't last. Visions of Pieter surfaced. He was the embodiment of Ariane's warnings. Changing history had unexpected consequences—dangerous consequences. Like, where would she wake up if she succeeded? Not in the kennel, for sure, but would she recognize her life? Sadie? The Bakkers? The risk was too great. There had to be another way.

She'd been drifting in and out of sleep when the door beyond the blankets opened and footsteps approached. Jane sat up.

"Do you have news for me?" Rick asked.

"My dreams don't work that way. I can't direct them."

"Sure you can. How else do you explain finding me?"

"I need a connection. Sadie's my connection to you. I have no connection to Michael Atkins."

"You're a bright girl. You'll figure something out."

An arm reached between the overlapping blankets and a bottle of water dropped into one of the dog dishes. "You'll get something to eat when you give me results."

"And if I do what you ask, what happens to me?"

"You walk out of here."

She stifled a cynical snort. "I need something to eat. I'm too weak to do what you want."

"Nice try, but you're not there yet."

"I'm not going to kill your brother."

"Suit yourself, but if he doesn't die, you will."

That wasn't true. A defiant smile bloomed. "You can't hurt me."

"Not yet. But when those marks of yours are gone? Let's just say you'd be wise to take care of Michael before they disappear entirely."

Jane's smile slipped. "How could you possibly know about my birthmarks?"

"Yes, how could I?" His footfalls faded and the door closed.

Jane felt a chill and reached for the bottle of water. As she twisted the cap, she noticed the mark on the back of her hand was gone.

Visiting Dream

Jane wakes in the dim hospital corridor in front of Rebecca's room. She peers through the small window. The room is void of furniture except for the bed. The moon shines outside her window. Rebecca is curled in a ball on the bed. Jane tries to open the door, but her hand is too ghostly. Her frustration mounts. Why is she here if she can't help the woman?

Voices draw her down the corridor. A security guard and a scrub-clad nurse stand in the doorway to the dispensing room.

"There she is," the nurse states, looking toward Maria, who's just entered the ward.

Maria has sensed Jane's presence before. Maybe she can help. Jane takes a chance and sweeps toward her.

"Hello," she says.

Maria's step falters. She quirks her head in Jane's direction but quickly corrects and continues toward the nurse.

"Strictly by the book," the nurse says to Maria, and her voice is a warning. "Bathe her and get her back to her room."

Maria nods, and she and the security guard start down the hallway to Rebecca's room. Jane follows. When the guard unlocks Rebecca's door, Jane enters behind Maria and slips into the shadows. The guard waits by the open door.

Rebecca sits up.

"It's all set," Maria says, helping her to her feet.

Rebecca sighs. "Thank you." A frown crosses her features as her gaze passes through Jane, who's standing in the corner.

Rebecca stills. "Is she here?"

"Yes."

Jane checks her shimmering limbs.

"I won't let that bastard hurt you," Rebecca says in Jane's direction.

The guard shifts. "No talking," he says. "Let's go."

Jane woke momentarily confused. Her surroundings quickly informed her: she was Rick's prisoner. Disappointment set in with the realization she'd fallen into a dream without seeding it to find him.

She pondered that she was becoming more present in her dreams. She not only shimmered, but Maria and now Rebecca could sense her. Something she hadn't considered before struck her: Rebecca was also a Witness. Maria must have known that. Maybe that's why Maria was helping her. Did something in Maria's Inca heritage help her sense Jane?

She recalled Rebecca's promise. *I won't let the bastard hurt you.* Did Witnesses protect one another? She wished she could talk to Ariane.

A light beyond her cage had been left on. She pulled a stainless-steel bowl from the kennel door and used it as a mirror. Her arms, shoulder, and face still had their markings.

56 | Rick

Night was closing in. His mother had called twice. Why? Had she been in touch with the painters? Perhaps they hadn't been as agreeable with his presence as he'd thought. He'd blame work for why he hadn't picked up and return her call in the morning.

She should have been pleased that he was watching over the painters, strangers to whom she'd given free rein of the house. So far, they'd shown no interest in the barn, but he'd keep an eye on them. He couldn't risk them suspecting it was occupied, let alone have their curiosity stirred by the modifications he'd made.

Rick estimated it would be two more days before Jane became hungry enough to do his bidding. He considered calling Sadie to help him pass the time, but that would mean going back to his townhouse, and he didn't care to leave quite yet. He wanted to be at the Langley house when signs of Mikey's death showed up.

Then he'd deal with Jane. What she knew about David Banner's death, and Rebecca's, could ruin him. The threat she posed had messed with his life long enough. After her marks were gone, whether or not she'd dealt with Mikey, she had to be put down.

57 | Sadie

August 27

The next morning, Sadie finally heard from Jane. *Need some space. Don't know when I'll be back.*

Sadie texted back, *I'm sorry we argued. Where are you?*

An hour later, Jane still hadn't responded. The conversation vacuum left Sadie feeling lost. She couldn't even get excited about spending the day at the beach or shopping downtown. Her day-off hot spots had lost their appeal.

Though she was happy that Jane had broken away from her stifling routine, she missed her. When had they turned into that old married couple who hadn't spent a night apart in years? Sadie rehashed their argument. Had their fight really been bad enough for Jane to take off and not tell her where she'd gone? Was she behind a deadbolt, somewhere safe? Had she lost more of her birthmarks? Surely she'd come home before her birthday.

Unable to relax, Sadie got dressed and headed to Positively Plants. She'd met Anna and Lucas a number of times. They'd know where Jane had gone and when she'd be back. She stopped at a corner store and picked up a box of Cracker Jack, a treat for Pieter if she needed to soften Anna up.

"She's taken the vacation time she had coming," Anna said.

"But . . . she wasn't going to do that." Sadie knew Jane's plan was to pay off her bike with a vacation payout.

"Well, she did. All four weeks. Didn't even give us notice so we could line up a replacement."

Four weeks? Their rent was due before then. Sadie felt a twinge of panic. She didn't have the funds to cover the rent, and Cynthia sure as hell wasn't going to cough up a dime before her trial period ended.

"If you'll excuse me," Anna said, and grabbed her cane. "Pieter shouldn't have sugar, but he loves Cracker Jack. Thank you."

The idea that Jane would leave Anna and Lucas in the lurch seemed unlike Jane. Very unlike Jane.

58 | Rick

Rick closed his laptop and drove down to the barn to pay Jane a visit before the painters arrived to complicate his day. He noticed he'd left the light on—a dangerous oversight. He'd have to be more careful.

"Do you have news for me?" he asked.

"I found your brother."

"Is he still breathing?"

"He wasn't alone."

"That doesn't answer the question."

"You want me to kill him in front of spectators?"

"I don't care how you do it or who watches. Just do it."

"How did you learn about me?"

"You don't know?" When Jane didn't respond, he gave her the answer he gauged would break her spirit the quickest. "Sadie told me. She's been very helpful."

"I don't believe you."

"Tell yourself what you need to. Tick tock, Jane."

The sound of a vehicle passing in the direction of the house sent Rick's heart racing. Damn it! He started for the door and left Jane begging for something to eat. He'd take her water tonight, but she'd get no more food until she'd done what he'd asked.

Rick parked beside the painters' van. They were already inside. He found them setting up in the living room.

"Good morning," he said. "You're getting an early start."

"Hope that's not a problem," the older of the two painters said.

The younger one added, "You were down at the barn or we would have checked in."

"Yeah. Saw a racoon on the roof last night," Rick said. "Wanted to make sure it wasn't making itself at home. In future, phone me if you're going to be here early."

"Ah, sure," the younger one said.

Rick made himself a coffee, collected his phone, and settled into a lounger in the backyard. He called his mother and apologized for not returning her earlier calls.

"I appreciate you checking up on the painters, but it's not necessary," she said.

"You can't be too careful."

"You're far too busy to be driving out there every day."

"I'm happy to do it. How's Palm Springs?"

59 | Jane

Jane beat herself up for wasting an opportunity. She should have come up with a better lie to get Rick to hand over something to eat. Anything. She'd never been so hungry. How long could a person live without food? she wondered.

There was no way Sadie would have told him about her dreams or the narcolepsy. Yet, somehow, he knew about both. She'd had arguments with Sadie over the years, though none as bad as the last one, and even when they were at odds, she'd never once told anyone, let alone a stranger.

Then again, Rick wasn't a stranger to Sadie, was he? And Sadie *had* given him their address, something else she swore she'd never do. Would Sadie betray her deepest secret? She, more than anyone, knew what Jane had suffered at the hands of pigs who knew she couldn't defend herself. Sadie wouldn't do that.

Not intentionally.

Rick excelled at manipulation. Sadie might not have known she'd given him the information until it was too late.

Jane had to stay strong. She refused to let Rick come between Sadie and her any more than he already had. He was lying to her, just as he'd been lying to Sadie. Would Sadie figure it out before he forced Jane's hand? The possibility that killing Rick might result in Sadie and her never meeting frightened her.

Anxiety roiled her stomach. If she and Sadie hadn't found each other in that group home, it's possible that neither one of them would have gotten out. And worse, Jane would retain the memories, as she had with Buddy, but Sadie wouldn't. Anna and Lucas hadn't remembered Buddy, and now that she thought about it, neither had Ethan. Sadie might never know Jane existed. She might even be lost to the streets.

If Jane took Rick's life, she risked Sadie's life too. There had to be another way to get out of this damn cage. If only she could get a message to Sadie, to let her know that they were in trouble, but how?

Jane lay on her side and pulled her knees to her chest. She pushed away the doubt she felt about her ability to seed her dreams and set her mind on Sadie. She pictured her blonde curls, her endearing smile, her confident strut when she knew someone was admiring her. How Jane wished she could feel even an ounce of Sadie's confidence now.

Jane rolled over time and again. She used her arm for a pillow until it went numb and then lay on her back while boredom ate away at her sanity.

Visiting Dream

Jane wakes in the office at Riptide. Ethan taps at a computer. Elated, Jane steps toward him. *Ethan?* she calls, but he continues tapping, undisturbed.

She hears a knock at the door.

"Come in," Ethan says.

The door opens and Sadie steps inside.

Sadie! Jane shouts.

"What can I do for you?" Ethan says.

Jane frowns. Why is he being so cold?

"I'm looking for Jane," Sadie says. "She staying with you?"

"No," Ethan says. "Said she's taking a break."

I did not! Jane yells, but they're deaf to her. Frustrated, she looks to her shimmering form. It's not solid enough for them to see her.

"Said you two had an argument and she needed some space. Apparently she has some decisions to make and can't make them with me distracting her."

No! Jane shouts. *That wasn't me!*

Ethan pulls out his phone, scrolls through it, and then hands it to Sadie. Jane rushes up behind her and reads over Sadie's shoulder the text—a text Rick must have sent—from her phone. Damn him!

"What the hell did you two argue about?" Ethan asks.

"Roommate shit."

"Really? Nothing more?"

Jane is encouraged by Ethan's tone. He knows something's not right.

Jane stands in front of him and cups his cheek. *It's me, Jane.* But he doesn't react. Anger fuels her frenzy to be heard. She searches the room and spies the banker's lamp. In desperation, she swings for it. Her palm connects. It teeters and then topples to the floor in a satisfying crash of glass.

"What the?" Ethan says, approaching the lamp as if it might bite him. Jane shouts his name.

Sadie bunches her forehead. "That was . . . weird."

Ethan looks back to Sadie. "Where'd she go? D'ya know?"

She's right here, Jane whispers. Disheartened, she watches Sadie leave.

The frustration Jane felt in her dream clung to her when she woke. And then it hit her that it had worked! She'd seeded her dream—for all the good it had done.

60 | Rick

August 28

Rick drove to his townhome in the early-morning hours, something he wouldn't have had to do at such an inconvenient hour if the painters weren't mucking up his day.

He'd been careful to make certain Jane's battery and SIM card were out of her phone at all times. He strolled down the path from his house to Granville Island and sat on a bench outside the Granville Island Hotel. From there, he reassembled her phone and sent Sadie one last text from Jane. Satisfied with Sadie's response, he removed the SIM card. If the police ever investigated Jane's death and traced her movements, they'd find she'd never left Vancouver.

Back in his father's office in Langley, he watched a documentary while he monitored Jane on his computer.

When the painters finally cleared out for the day, he drove to the barn.

"Do you have news for me?" he asked, approaching the sound-dampening barrier.

"Michael knows about Rebecca."

"He's still alive?"

"He has a file with her name on it."

Rick hesitated. What could his brother possibly know? "He's got nothing."

"Maybe. But why keep a file if he has nothing? And who gets it when he's dead?"

"You think you're being clever?"

"Just thought you'd like to know."

"The only thing I want to know is when you've done what I've asked you to do."

"It would be easier if I weren't so hungry."

"Consider the hunger motivation. Unpleasant, but it won't kill you. Not yet."

"What happened to Rebecca?" Jane asked.

"I was too easy on Rebecca. I won't make the same mistake with you. No one's missing you, Jane. I suggest you get busy. Time's on my side and I have nothing to lose."

He parted the curtain and dropped a water bottle in the dog dish. "Sweet dreams."

61 | Sadie

Sadie woke with a clear head and a luxurious feline stretch. Her sobriety, on the heels of too many wasted nights, felt cleansing, empowering even.

Then her thoughts turned to Jane, and Ariane's theories. Her Zen moment fizzled. Had Jane told Nate and Ariane where she was going? The Jane she knew would have, but the Jane who was angry with her was acting out. She wished she'd paid more attention. If Jane had told her Nate's surname, she didn't remember it. Nor could she remember which department he taught at. UBC was huge. She'd have to drive to his house if she wanted to talk to him. Perhaps she'd do that later today.

Jane had never taken a vacation before, other than a few days off here and there. She'd sure pissed Anna off. Normally Sadie was the one making the rash decisions. Hopefully Jane still had a job to come home to.

She'd thought she'd have heard from Cynthia by now. It had been days since her last gig with Rick. Was he out of town? she wondered.

Jane couldn't have picked a worse time to take off. This month was the one time Sadie would have actually taken her up on her standing offer to cover the rent. Now, she'd have to ask Rick for a cash infusion. If he didn't come through, she'd be left with the uncomfortable option of grovelling at Cynthia's door.

Amateur mistake, she thought, berating herself. She should never have agreed to delay her regular payments. Knowing any cash Cynthia provided would come with a hefty premium, she composed a text to Rick. *Jane is still AWOL and the rent's due. I have some creative ideas for how I might earn some extra cash if you're game.* She hesitated for a moment. Sidestepping Cynthia was a risky move. But Rick was familiar with the business. He'd be smart enough to know what Sadie was doing and keep it from Cynthia.

She exhaled, hit send, and traipsed to the bathroom. Her gaze fell on the cup where Jane's toothbrush should have been. Sadie hadn't noticed it was missing before, but naturally she'd have taken it. Out of curiosity, she padded back to the bedroom and opened Jane's top dresser drawer. It was empty. She opened the next, and the next. All her drawers were empty. She'd cleared out everything. Even her old boots. For the first time since Jane had left, Sadie wondered if she ever intended to return.

Had their argument really been that bad? Sure, she'd given Rick their address, but Jane still had her deadbolts. And yeah, she'd told Jane she couldn't be around her if she was going to be so negative about Rick's gig, but Jane had to know she didn't mean it. Not like this.

In a daze, she walked to the kitchen and paused, surveying the mess that had accumulated. Dirty dishes competed with takeout containers for counter space. The Froot Loops box stood open beside the jam jar that was missing its lid. It had rolled to the floor when Sadie's hands were full, and she'd forgotten about it. She scooped up a discarded clamshell pack and opened the cupboard under the sink. The garbage was overflowing. With a sigh, she dropped the plastic package back where she'd found it and put the kettle on to boil.

Back in the bedroom, she dressed, bewildered by Jane's empty drawers. How could Jane have carried everything she owned on the bike? Her duffle bag wouldn't have held it all, and she couldn't have juggled the duffle plus whatever bag she'd loaded the overflow into.

She was still puzzling it out when the kettle's whistle dragged her back to the kitchen. After her first cup of coffee, she pulled the last clean bowl out of the cupboard. While she ate, she thumbed through her messages. Jane was still maintaining radio silence. Their fight had entered epic territory, and the silence hurt worse than the fight. Sadie texted her. *Are you okay? Please call me.*

With her bowl in hand, she returned to the kitchen sink contemplating the impending cleanup. Breakfast bowls lined the back counter. She tried to lift one of the spoons from its bowl and found it stuck fast to a dried puddle of sugary milk that had soured and smelled like vomit.

Her resolve to clean up the kitchen watered itself down to a solid commitment to deal with the garbage. After her second cup of coffee, she picked the counter clean of containers and hefted two bags out to the steel bin behind the building.

She found Mrs. Carper standing in front of the dumpster looking like an airline passenger waiting for a flight attendant to lift her bag into the overhead bins.

"Can I help with that?" Sadie asked.

"Would you, dear? That lid is so darn heavy, and my arthritis is acting up."

Sadie dropped one of her bags to the pavement and lifted the lid.

"I don't mind telling you, I'm happy to see your roommate let that bike go." The frail woman pushed her bag over the lip of the bin.

Sadie frowned. "What are you talking about?" She tossed in her own bag and reached for the second one.

"She sold it, didn't she?"

"No. She's just away on vacation." Sadie tossed her second bag into the bin and lowered the lid.

"I must be mistaken, then," Mrs. Carper said, sounding disappointed. "Thought I'd seen the last of that bike when she posted the For Sale sign."

Sadie wiped her hands on her jeans. "What For Sale sign?"

"On the bulletin board by the mailboxes. And then a few days ago, I saw that young man from the apartment downstairs drive it away."

"Andy?" Sadie said. There was no way Jane would sell her bike. Mrs. Carper's marbles had to be loose.

"That's him. The manager is none too happy with him. Broke his lease. Said he had a new job in Toronto."

"He moved out?"

"Showed up with a U-Haul. Couldn't have had much to move. Was out of here in an hour."

Sadie escaped Mrs. Carper's gossip and marched to Andy's door. She banged on it, but he didn't answer. Had he really moved out? Without telling her? Ignoring her texts was one thing, but this was taking ghosting to a whole new level, Sadie thought, returning to her apartment.

She tried to open his app but got an error message. She opened his last text. It had been a week since she heard from him. Some Boy Scout he'd turned out to be. So much for thinking he was a nice guy.

Dejected, she found herself standing in front of the mound of dirty dishes on the counter. One more cup of joe, she thought, and then she'd tackle it. She reached for the kettle and knocked over the new bag of coffee she'd left open on the counter. "Shit!" She jumped back to avoid the coffee grinds that spewed across the counter and onto the floor. She stepped out of the grinds and shook off her foot.

Her phone dinged. Rick had answered her. *Tempting as your offer is, I'm swamped. Cynthia owes me a favour. Call her.*

Could he really be that naive? "Screw him." She slung her purse over her shoulder and headed to the coffee shop on Fourth Avenue. On the way, she texted Jane again. *You were right about Rick. As soon as I have his money, I'll dump his ass and get out of the business. That's a promise.*

62 | Rick

Rick felt disappointed in Sadie. Sitting on the bench outside the Granville Island Hotel, he considered sending her a couple thou to keep her happy but soon dismissed the idea. He had to stop thinking she was anything more than a prostitute. She was Cynthia's problem, not his, and he'd outmanoeuvred them both. Neither one would see the payday they imagined. A well-timed anonymous tip to the proper authorities would take care of that. A smile formed as he thought of Sadie in her stilettos, naked. Maybe he could squeeze in another night with her.

His smile faded as thoughts of Jane crept in. She'd lied to him about Mikey having a file on Rebecca. Rebecca had been dead for years—long before Rick moved back to BC. There was no way Michael could know about her.

Jane was stronger than he'd anticipated. She'd gone four days with only one energy bar. The hunger had weakened her, but she hadn't given an inch. And though she continued to test him and scheme, her time was running out. When her marks were gone, so were her options.

63 | Jane

Jane lay on the mattress examining the newly clear skin on her forearm but couldn't muster an ounce of panic about it. Fatigue had set in. Her thoughts scattered easily. It took tremendous effort to concentrate on connecting with Sadie. She prayed she wouldn't find her when she was with Rick because she was no longer sure she wouldn't kill him, if only for the satisfaction.

Rick hadn't fallen for her story about Michael having a file on Rebecca. Jane had misjudged him. She'd thought the threat of a secret file might buy her a meal while he searched for it. But no, he was following through on his promise. No more food.

The outside door opened, and Jane thought she heard the clinking of keys. Footsteps approached.

"Any news?"

"Ethan knows something isn't right about my *vacation*."

Rick laughed. "Not anymore. After you begged for his understanding, he told you to take all the time you needed."

Defeat overwhelmed her. That sounded like something Ethan would say.

"Ethan isn't making waves, and neither is Sadie."

Jane fought a surge of despair. "You don't know that."

"Oh, but I do. You know that new neighbour of yours? Andrew? You know him as Andy. He works for me. And that little app of his? It controls Sadie's phone. And I have yours. They're not looking for you."

His words hit Jane with a thud. "That's a lie," Jane said, but there was no conviction in her voice. He'd been meticulous in his preparations, taken care of every detail. Jane had thought his planning had begun two years ago, when he sought out Sadie, but she'd been wrong. He'd been planning this since she slashed him.

"In fact," Rick said, "your departure is bringing them closer. You left

Sadie in quite the financial bind. I wouldn't be surprised if she and Ethan hook up. She'd screw anyone for a buck."

Jane flared her nostrils. She took a measured breath. "Why are you baiting me? Isn't starving me enough?"

"Apparently not. You seem to think there's a knight in shining armour waiting to rescue you. There isn't. The sooner you accept that, the sooner you give me what I asked for."

"You must think I'm an idiot. Even if I get rid of your brother, you won't let me go. Not with what I know. I watched you stab David Banner. I'm guessing you killed Rebecca Morrow. You torched my adoptive parents' home, ran my foster parents' car off the road. How many others have you killed?"

"Do you think anyone's going to believe your rantings? You're known to police. You have a reputation as a troublemaker. Your room-mate's a prostitute. You have no proof of anything. You're not a threat to me, Jane. Do what I ask, and I'll open that door. You can walk away."

"I need food. I don't have the strength to kill a cockroach like this. Give me something to eat."

The curtains parted and a bottle of water dropped into the dog dish. "When you give me what I want, you'll eat, and not a moment before."

Jane closed her eyes at the sound of the door swinging shut. He would not win this fight. She wouldn't give him that satisfaction. And he was wrong about the knight. She had two of them: Sadie and Ethan. She rolled over, determined to find a way to connect with one of them.

Visiting Dream

Jane wakes in the bedroom of her and Sadie's apartment. The bed is in its usual dishevelled state, as is Sadie's closet, but why are Jane's dresser drawers askew? She peers inside. They're empty. Rick's taken her things. What must Sadie think?

Jane leaves the bedroom, searching for her, but she's not home. From the state of their living room, it looks as if a dirt devil's blown through and the kitchen was ground zero. The cupboard door under the sink hangs open. The garbage bin is gone. Dirty dishes line the counter. An open bag of coffee lies where it fell, as do the grinds that have spilled to the floor. In them is the outline of a footprint. Sadie must have been standing there in her bare feet when the bag tipped over. Does she know they own a broom?

She wants to laugh, but an image of Rick surfaces. Thoughts of what he's done to their friendship stir the anger she can barely control. Jane toes her boot into the grinds on the floor. A frown forms as she stares at the path she's just cleared through the coffee. An idea emerges. She steps to the counter and looks down at the spilled grinds on it. Her hand shimmers with heat waves. With a tentative finger, she draws a line in the grinds. Excitement flitters in her empty stomach. She takes a moment to think and then writes *Kristan = R Atkins*. Pleased, she steps back.

The thick letters are clear as can be. Sadie can't miss the message. Relief dances on the edge of Jane's anxiety.

She turns to the sound of a key in the lock. Sadie appears with her keys in one hand and a pizza box balanced in the other. Shopping bags dangle on the arm holding the pizza. Sadie tosses the keys to the trunk and slips her purse off her shoulder onto the sofa as she walks past. Jane fists her hands as Sadie makes her way into the kitchen.

Without a downward glance, Sadie drops the pizza box on the counter. Jane watches in disbelief as the coffee grinds scatter out in a puff from beneath the box.

Jane woke with a curse on her lips.

64 | Rick

Rick puzzled over the voice message left on Jane's phone from a woman who called herself Ariane. The name was unfamiliar and the message was simply "Call me." There was no such woman in Jane's contacts. Call display showed that Ariane had called from Nathaniel Crawford's office. It took only one phone call to get Ariane's full name. Ariane Rebaza. A quick Google search turned up her work as an Inca scholar. Rebaza was a Peruvian name. As was Yupanqui. Rick's instincts told him that was not a casual coincidence. What business did a Peruvian-born Inca scholar have with Jane? He would have traded an energy bar for that information had Jane not proven untrustworthy.

He reviewed Jane's communications with Crawford for mention of the Rebaza woman and came up empty. Jane didn't save voice messages, so he couldn't check those, but her text and email histories were intact. He soon learned that Jane had sent Crawford her government file. He was pleased to find that Jane hadn't known enough about him to do any damage—not even his name. Still, he'd do some research on Ariane Rebaza before he answered her.

He opened the kennel's video feed. The mark on Jane's face hadn't faded. She lay on her back with the knife in her hand. Her early attempts to keep active had fizzled out. Her body would be in full ketosis at this point, converting fat first and then cannibalizing muscle to get the energy it needed. But she wasn't in any serious danger yet.

He closed the laptop and headed to the barn.

"Do you have news for me?"

"How many times a day do you think I dream?"

"As many as you need, I would imagine. I can give you something to help you sleep."

"Nothing you give me would make me dream. I told you before, I don't control them."

"So you say, but that's another lie, isn't it?" She had no smart-mouth retort. "I'll take your silence as a yes. Your friend Ariane tried to reach you. She and Nathaniel are taking a trip to South America. She thought you'd like to know."

"Now look who's lying," Jane said.

"Your marks will be gone soon. If you want to get out of here alive, you'd best do what I ask sooner rather than later."

"Who told you about my marks?"

"A meddlesome nobody."

"A nobody? You put a lot of faith in a nobody. How do you know it's true?"

"I'll make you a deal. You tell me about Ariane Rebaza, and I'll answer your question. You go first."

"Okay. She's the girlfriend of a professor I delivered flowers to at UBC."

"That tells me nothing."

"What else do you want to know?"

"Why is Ariane contacting you?"

"Don't know. Maybe she wants to order flowers."

He'd been right to think he'd get nothing useful out of Jane. "Nathaniel Crawford is the professor you mentioned?"

Jane mumbled in the affirmative.

"Why did you send him your government file?"

She paused. "He thought he might be able to find my birth parents."

That brief hesitation signalled another lie, and her vague answers suggested there was something more to their relationship. He'd treat Ariane Rebaza and Nathaniel Crawford with care.

"Well?" Jane said. "Who's the nobody you've put so much trust in?"

"Her name is unimportant, but unlike you, she spoke the truth. She warned me that those marks of yours rendered you untouchable, that anyone who tried to harm you would die. I didn't believe her, of course, but then you survived the house fire, and later, the car accident."

"And yet . . . you're still alive," Jane said. "Which means you didn't do it yourself. You hired some loser to do it for you."

"Yes, fortunately I took a hands-off approach. The *losers* as you call them, dropped dead within hours of their futile attempts."

"I'm curious, Rick. Where do you shop for someone willing to kill a child?"

"Deal's done," Rick said, dumbfounded by her audacity. "You answered my question, I answered yours. Good night, Jane. Go take care of business."

65 | Sadie

August 29

That's an hour I'll never get back, Sadie thought, examining the damage to her manicure. She pulled the plug from the sink and dried her hands on the tea towel. When Rick's money came in, she'd buy a dishwasher. Not that Jane ever complained about doing dishes, but Jane didn't get manicures either.

Wondering where Jane had gone was getting old. It wasn't like Jane to hold a grudge this long. Not with her, anyway. If Jane didn't return by her birthday, it would be the first time they hadn't spent it together since they were thirteen years old.

Sadie pushed against an eerie feeling. She sensed a dark cloud closing in around her. It wasn't just the epic argument with Jane. It was Rick's lack of enthusiasm and Cynthia's silence. It was Jane leaving Anna in the lurch. It was Andy vanishing, not that he was any prize. It was Mrs. Carper telling her Andy had bought Jane's Rebel. Most troubling of all, the parade of weird events had been set in motion after Jane's marks started disappearing.

Sadie couldn't dismiss the feeling that something was amiss. At the same time, she didn't know what to do about it.

Thinking Jane might have contacted Ethan, she took the gamble he wouldn't hang up on her and called him. She pictured the look on his face when the lamp in his office hit the floor. Strange how that lamp had tumbled off the desk. Something else to add to the weirdness parade.

"Hello," he answered, clearing his throat.

She'd woken him. "It's Sadie. Sorry to wake you." She dropped onto the sofa.

"You heard from Jane?"

She propped her toes on the edge of the trunk. Her pedicure was still in good shape. "No. I was hoping you had."

"She's ghosting me."

Sadie frowned. It was one thing for Jane to ghost her, but Ethan? "She wouldn't do that." Sadie knew Jane considered the practice cowardly. She was all about being upfront with people.

"I've got a lengthy list of unanswered texts that disagree with you. If that's all—"

"Jane sold her Rebel."

Ethan went quiet, but he didn't hang up.

"The neighbour upstairs told me she had it for sale. Said the tenant down the hall from us bought it. Jane didn't say a word to me about it."

"That must have been one hell of a fight you two had."

Sadie looked away from her toenails. "Did Jane mention anything to you about wanting to sell her bike?"

"Nope."

"Her boss at the nursery told me she's taken all of her vacation. Four weeks."

"Four weeks? I thought she'd only be gone a few days."

"Yeah, me too. I was trying to figure out where she might have gone with all that time. Did you guys ever talk about taking a road trip?"

"No. But if she's on the road, she probably traded the Rebel for a cruiser. Listen, I gotta go."

"Will you let me know if you hear from her?"

"Sure," he said, and the phone went dead.

Sadie stared at the screen. A sense of loss rippled through her. Her best friend had abandoned her. Once again, she checked their joint bank account. It had thirty-four dollars in it. She had three days to come up with twelve hundred dollars for their rent, and another couple hundred to cover her phone, the car insurance, the power bill, and whatever else came out of that account. Selling her old clunker wouldn't come close to covering it.

She wished she'd never given up her waitressing job—not that it paid enough to cover her expenses, but the manager might have given her an advance in a pinch.

With no other option, she left a message for Cynthia. Rick might have negotiated exclusive access to her, but Cynthia would have no qualms skirting the fine print to slip her a gig. Sadie would have to settle for less than her usual fifty percent. She'd be on her back until the rent was due.

She tossed her phone to the trunk and walked to the bathroom in search of nail polish remover. Chipped polish made her feel trashy, and she couldn't afford a manicure right now.

Back on the sofa with a wad of acetone-soaked cotton, she let her thoughts shift back to Jane. She had a hard time believing she'd sold her Rebel without a word. And even though Ethan's suggestion that she'd traded up for a cruiser sounded reasonable, Jane loved that Rebel. Sadie couldn't quell the wrongness she felt about Jane selling her bike.

She thumbed through her messages. The last one from Jane was two days ago. Since then, two of Sadie's texts had gone unanswered. It hardly qualified as ghosting. Sadie typed another text. *I miss you. Will you be home for your birthday?* She hated that she came off sounding so needy, but the place felt too quiet. And if she was honest with herself, she was lonesome.

Besides, if Jane's birthmarks were gone, Sadie wanted to see what she looked like. As long as she'd known her, people had condescended to tell her beauty was unimportant. Those people had never had to turn away from awkward stares or ignore the taunts from kids who should have been friends. They'd never know how it felt to be told some carefully crafted lie that really said they were unsuitable for a job because the marks on their face would put the customers off. When Jane's marks were gone, she'd be free. Sadie wanted to be a part of that.

Would Jane be vulnerable when her marks were gone? In some kind of danger? Given Ariane's belief that Jane's marks disappearing might put her at risk, she and Nate would probably appreciate knowing she'd taken a vacation.

That she'd told no one about.

Possibly with a new bike. Also that she'd told no one about.

She checked her phone one more time then slung her purse over her shoulder. Until she heard from Rick or Cynthia, she could either continue cleaning the apartment or get out and do something to ease her mind about Jane's silence. She headed to Positively Plants. Someone there might have seen Jane's new bike. Knowing for a fact that she had a new ride would help settle the eerie feeling Sadie couldn't quite shake.

Sadie walked past the unattended front counter and into the greenhouse, where she found Lucas wheeling a cartload of stoneware pots.

"Hey, Lucas," Sadie said, matching his pace. "We met a while ago. I'm Jane's roommate."

"Jane?"

"I mean Joyce."

He nodded and slowed his cart to a stop. "Sadie, right?"

"That's it. I know Joyce is away on vacation, but did you happen to see her new bike before she left?"

"Nope. Wasn't aware she'd bought a new one. Check with Anna though. She may know more," he said, and once again set his cart in motion. "She's in the office."

Sadie thanked him and headed to the office. She knocked on the doorframe. Anna looked up from the computer.

"Sorry to bother you again, but I was wondering, did you happen to see Joyce's new bike before she left on vacation?"

"No, didn't see her at all. She texted her request for vacation. Didn't even talk to us."

Sadie frowned. Texted? "Have you heard from her since she left?"

"No. I suspect she knows we're not too happy with her."

"Thanks," Sadie said.

She left the nursery and drove straight to Riptide. Ethan was behind the bar pulling beers.

She leaned in. "Got a minute?"

"Come back at nine."

"It's important," she said.

He stared at her while he filled a jug, as if considering whether what she had to say was worth his time. When the jug was full, he handed it to a server. "I'm taking five," he told her.

Sadie followed him into the office. The door closed, silencing the noise from the bar.

"What is it?" Ethan said.

"Have you heard from Jane?"

"I already told you—"

Sadie stopped him. "That's not what I meant. Have you actually *heard* her voice? A phone call?"

His scowl dropped. "Nope. Nothing but texts."

"Me too. And I just talked to her boss at the nursery. Jane *texted* them her vacation request."

"That's odd," Ethan said, frowning.

"Odd I could live with. Something doesn't feel right about Jane taking a vacation, or about her selling the Rebel."

"What did you two argue about?"

"Did Jane ever mention the name Nate to you? Or Ariane?"

He furrowed his brow. "That the woman from the university? The one with the theory about why her birthmarks are disappearing?"

"Yeah. Maybe not a theory." She turned for the door.

"Wait! Where you going?"

She called over her shoulder. "I don't have Nate's phone number, but I know where he lives. I'm going to see him."

She left Ethan midprotest with a promise to call if she learned anything.

During the drive to Nate's, Sadie checked her panic. Ariane had said that as long as Jane had her birthmarks, no one could hurt her. So Jane was okay no matter where she was, at least until her birthday.

There was no answer at Nate's. She scribbled a note on an old parking ticket asking him to call her right away and then headed back to her car.

Her phone dinged. Rick wanted to see her. Tonight.

Seeing his name set off a wave of guilt. Learning that a john had their address was probably what had triggered Jane's rash actions. The apartment was Jane's safe place and Sadie had exposed it, not that she'd had a choice. Sadie said a little prayer that Jane was simply hiding, reestablishing control.

Unless she isn't came the thought that Sadie couldn't silence.

As she pulled away from the curb, ice crystals formed in her stomach.

66 | Rick

Rick checked into his room at the Sutton Place Hotel. He might not get the information he wanted out of Sadie, but he would at least have a good time trying.

He'd spent his afternoon reviewing the published work of Dr. Rebaza and the professor. The professor wouldn't be an issue, but Ariane Rebaza presented a challenge. Not only did she appear to be respected among her peers, but her research on Inca rituals left open the possibility that some of those rituals continued in secret to this day. Though not critical, it would be prudent to know what she'd discussed with Jane.

Sadie arrived promptly, and she'd worn the strappy red dress he'd asked for. Obedient? Or had she come running because she wanted to wring more money out of him? Either way, she'd be eager to please him tonight.

"You look exquisite," he said, greeting her at the door. "Come in."

She set down her clutch and walked to the window while he poured two vodka rocks. "How are things with your roommate? Has your argument blown over?"

"No."

"She's pouting?" Sadie offered a shrug as he handed her a tumbler. "Are you worried about her?"

"I suppose."

He pushed a curl away from her temple. "Have you tried reaching out to her friends? Maybe she's contacted them."

"I've spoken with a few people. No one's heard from her."

He pressed his lips together and nodded. "Classic passive-aggressive behaviour. She's punishing her inner circle. You need to speak with someone further out, a casual friend or a colleague."

Sadie stood in uncharacteristic silence, sipping her drink.

"Do you know anyone you could talk to?" he asked, prompting her.

Her reticence to answer his questions was curious. "Earlier you'd mentioned someone at the university?"

"No. I . . . ah . . ." Sadie furrowed her brow. "I'm sure I didn't."

"Of course you did. How else would I know?"

Sadie took a deep breath and donned a fake smile. "We're not going to talk about Jane all night, are we?"

He raised an eyebrow, reminiscent of their earlier games, and glared down at her. "Do I have to remind you? We'll do whatever I say."

She looked to the floor. "Of course."

"Finish your drink," he said, in a tone she was more familiar with.

Sadie dutifully upended it, and he relieved her of the glass. He left her standing by the window and took a seat in one of the brocade chairs. "Let's start with you on your knees, shall we?"

He finished his drink while Sadie got busy doing what she did best. He watched her work with a twinge of regret. What had she said? Something about dumping his ass as soon as she had his money? He'd miss having her around when he was in London. Or at least her talent.

When he'd taken his pleasure, he directed her to make them another drink. Afterward, he had her strip and then lay out a few lines of the blow he'd brought. She'd be much more pliable with a kicker of coke in her.

He settled on the bed with his back to the headboard, and she bent to the lines. "Come here," he said, extending his arm. She crawled in, and he stroked her back until the drugs had taken her to her happy place. "I'm surprised you don't remember mentioning the university professor. You've piqued my curiosity. How did Jane come to know someone so far outside her circle?"

Though it took her a while, and a few more prompts, she finally mentioned Nate—not Nathaniel—by name. But she shut him down with bullshit answers when he pushed for details, and she never mentioned Ariane. How much would it cost him, he wondered, to have Andrew troll through the doctors' email accounts?

"I need to ask a favour," Sadie said. She propped herself up on an elbow, offering him a view meant to tantalize. "I hate to ask you again, but Cynthia hasn't answered my calls and she hasn't paid me all month." She circled his nipple with her fingertip. "Could you spot me a few grand? It's just until Cynthia loosens up."

Poor delusional Sadie. Her messages hadn't been delivered to her greedy madam. He'd cut Cynthia out of the loop two gigs ago.

"I just dropped two hundred thou into Cynthia's account, so I'm a little strapped." Sadie's finger stilled. "How about you take what's in my wallet." He'd planned to give it to her anyway—a final tip for her stellar services.

"You will, however, have to finish earning it," he added.

67 | Jane

Jane's prison grew dark as another night approached. A chill fell over her at the first tugs of sleep. She'd find Sadie again tonight in her dreams. She simply had to. The mark on her biceps was the latest to disappear. Only the mark across her shoulder and the one on her face remained. That bought her two days. Maybe. That's how long she had until she'd be at Rick's mercy, a quality Jane knew he didn't possess.

Rick hadn't delivered any water all day. Every time she stood, she had to hold on to the cage to keep her balance. She changed positions to fight the lethargy. Every tick and groan of the building felt like a gift for her sanity. The sounds kept her grounded.

She closed her eyes, but her efforts to visualize Sadie were interrupted.

"You're late," she said, before Rick could ask what had become his trademark question.

"Yes, I apologize. Sadie kept me out late. Unlike you, she was quite keen to tell me about your friend Nate. And Ariane."

He'd called him Nate, not Nathaniel, as he had before. Jane fought against the growing despair, fearful that Sadie had turned on her. But that's what he wanted, wasn't it?

He parted the packing blankets and dropped a bottle of water into one of the dog dishes. "Oh, I almost forgot. Ethan came through for Sadie. Paid more for her services than I ever have. She must have worked hard for it."

"He wouldn't do that."

"No? The text he sent to thank her was rather explicit. Seems he's looking forward to seeing her again. All of her. That's a good sign for a budding relationship, don't you think?" His footsteps faded with his parting jab, and she heard the door close.

Helplessness overcame her. She gave in to the despair. Tears rimmed her eyes. She didn't want to believe him, but doubt ebbed into her thoughts. Had he poisoned Sadie and Ethan with text messages they thought had come from her? She curled into a ball of misery. Sobs she felt powerless to stop soon racked her body.

He was fighting a psychological battle with her that felt dirtier than any physical fight she'd ever experienced. He wanted to break her, to lead her to the point where she'd kill for him to stop him from tormenting her.

She couldn't let that happen. She had to be smarter than him. Stronger than him.

"You're not a quitter," she said out loud. She sucked in a deep breath, and then another, putting an end to the sobs. He might have poisoned her relationship with Sadie, and with Ethan, but she couldn't dwell on that.

The new conviction had barely formed when his taunt echoed: *A good sign, a budding relationship*. She pushed down the thought, but it popped back up. *A good sign*. Something about those words niggled at her. What was it?

She wiped her nose and concentrated on where she'd heard those words before. It was in a conversation. Was it Sadie? Ariane? No, but it was a woman's voice.

Rebecca! In one of Rebecca's visions, she'd seen a sign. Shaped like a dog, she'd said. It was Rick's mother's kennel. The cage! That's where she was being held.

The kennel had a Scottish name. Jane ran through the dog breeds she thought were Scottish, but nothing tweaked a memory. Scottish Highlands was close. Highland Kennels? Not quite. And then she got it: Highland Breeders!

Hope brought fresh tears. She rubbed them away. "No crying," she said. She rolled over and once again set her mind on Sadie.

Visiting Dream

Jane is in the kitchen of their apartment. It's dark outside. She hears the shower running. The dishes have been washed and lay under a tea towel in the drain rack. She stills, fearful that she's looking at her own handiwork, but then she spots coffee grinds stuck to the backsplash.

One of Sadie's stilettos masquerades as a tripping hazard behind the sofa. The matching shoe rests five feet away, closer to the bathroom. Her red dress lies in a crumpled heap outside the bathroom door, which remains ajar. It looks as if Sadie started stripping at the front door, dropping her clothes in a beeline for the shower.

The water turns off and Jane hears Sadie talking to herself. "Fucking Cynthia. Should have known." Jane peeks through the cracked bathroom door. Sadie lifts her head at the sound of her phone pinging. Her makeup is only partially removed, as if she'd made a few careless wipes at it. Sadie marches out of the bathroom buck naked and wobbling as she blots her hair with a towel. Jane looks past her into the bathroom and smiles as an idea comes to her. She stands in front of the fogged-up mirror and draws on the anger that cramps her insides. Her hand shimmers. She writes *Send help 2 Highland Breeders*. She then draws a heart and signs it *Jane XO*.

She exits the bathroom and pulls on the door handle to preserve the steam. Sadie is seated on the sofa with her feet on the trunk. She thumbs a message into her phone, but Jane doesn't reach her in time to read it. Sadie jumps up, phone in hand, and heads to the bedroom.

No, no, no! Jane says, as Sadie opens a dresser drawer.

Go to the bathroom. Hurry, she says, but Sadie continues to tug at one garment after another. She finally settles on a teddy and sniffs it before stepping into it.

Bathroom! Now! Jane shouts. Sadie heads for the kitchen. She pulls a bottle of wine from beneath the sink and pours herself a glass. She takes a sip then recorks the bottle.

Dammit, Sadie! Jane says, but Sadie ignores her and settles on the sofa.

Jane drifts to the bathroom and peeks through the crack in the door. Her message to Sadie is almost gone.

Sadie's phone pings again. Jane returns to stand behind her. This time she's able to read the text.

It's from Ethan. *Swing by my apartment.*

Jane feels as if she can't breathe. His message is the second in a string that started with *I'm off. Ping me.*

Jane surfaced from her dream feeling numb. It isn't true, she told herself, knowing that it was. It isn't what it seems was the next lie she told herself. Ethan might have given Sadie rent money, but he wouldn't sleep with Jane's best friend. He wouldn't do that to her. Would he? Would Sadie?

68 | Rick

Rick watched the digital feed from Jane's kennel again. He hadn't been mistaken; Jane was crying. At long last, he'd gotten through to her. It was about bloody time. He felt hopeful, and wasn't that a pleasant change. He touched the scar on his cheek. Jane had the ability—maybe now she finally had the motivation.

Once again, Rick rewound the footage, and a smile crept across his face as he watched Jane fall apart all over again.

69 | Sadie

August 30

Sadie cracked an eyelid at the ping of her phone. She groaned and pulled the pillow over her head and then drifted back to sleep.

"Piss off!" she said, when the phone started ringing, waking her once again. It quieted and then pinged one more time to tell her she had a voice message. Sleeping after that proved impossible. She sat up and steadied herself. A construction crew had taken up jackhammering in her head. She stood and zombie-walked to her dresser. The flask she pulled out had only a dribble in the bottom. Not nearly enough hair of the dog, she thought, upending the bottle anyway.

Avoiding the mirror, she used the bathroom then tipped two aspirins into her palm and cupped water into her hand to swallow them. She splashed water on her face and rested her forearms on the edge of the sink.

Anger seeped out of her pores. Anger at herself for getting wasted. Again. Anger at Rick, the pompous prick, for not spotting her enough to cover the rent. And most of all, anger at Cynthia for ripping her off. Two hundred thou? Looked like Cynthia had exceeded her goals of getting him up to one-fifty—or had it been two hundred all along? Sadie had been a fool to trust her, and that stung. Cynthia would hear from her, but not until her hangover buggered off.

She traipsed to the kitchen, stepping over the red dress she'd shed on her race to the shower last night to scrub Rick off, and filled the kettle. She cringed at the thought of getting a steady dose of him over the coming months. But that was the deal she'd made. She didn't have to like it, but she wouldn't renege on it. "Don't look back," she said, and headed to the bedroom to grab her phone. She turned her thoughts to the future and the money that would open new doors for her.

The missed call had come from an unknown number. At the sound of Nate's voice, the bubble of hope that it might have been Jane calling burst. The professor would be tied up with lectures until lunch. She saved his number and checked the time. That meant she had two more hours to get the worst of the hangover behind her.

She made a coffee as she thumbed through her messages. Nothing from Jane, but Ethan's text reminded her she'd agreed to drop by his place today. She couldn't remember why; she'd been wasted last night when she agreed to meet him. Maybe he had some news. Sadly, her drunken bravado hadn't made allowances for a hangover.

But Ethan would have to wait. Her first priority was setting Cynthia straight. The conversation wasn't going to be easy. No doubt she'd tell Sadie that Rick lied about the two hundred thou. Then she'd play the loyalty card: would Sadie believe Cynthia, who'd pulled her off the streets, or a john?

Sadie tried to figure out what Rick had to gain from lying about how much money he'd paid. He must know she'd check with Cynthia. Then again, he'd played her off against Cynthia before. Did he benefit from a rift between Cynthia and her? Sadie couldn't imagine an upside for him. He sure as hell wouldn't risk a visit from Cynthia's enforcers.

Still, Sadie would be cautious. Cynthia was granting Rick favours, like using the Sutton and allowing him direct contact—keeping him happy until payday.

Sadie steeled herself. She wouldn't let Cynthia get away with it. As far as Sadie was concerned, Cynthia owed her another twenty-five thousand dollars. She finished her coffee and headed back to bed.

The construction crew had cleared out of Sadie's head by her second waking. She dressed and, after eating a bowl of cereal, phoned the professor.

"Have you heard from Jane?" she asked. He hadn't, and Sadie told him what had happened since their argument. "I don't mean to sound paranoid, but she loved that bike. And maybe she is hiding out and doesn't want to speak to me, but I've got to find her. Just to make sure she's okay."

"Let me get a pen," Nate said, and then he asked her to repeat the details and the dates on which they'd occurred. He promised to get back to her after talking with Ariane and her investigator. Sadie felt enormous relief knowing he was on it.

Then she gathered her courage and phoned Cynthia.

"Sadie? Are you okay?" Her concern sounded genuine, but it was bogus—Cynthia's way of reminding Sadie not to contact her by phone.

"We need to talk. Today."

Dead air hung between them.

"All right," she finally said. "I'll be expecting you within the hour."

Twenty minutes later, Sadie took a deep breath and knocked on Cynthia's door.

Cynthia looked Sadie over from head to toe, and then beyond her into the corridor. "Come in," she said, turning into the condo. Her perfectly smoothed hair swung in a thick sheet down her back. She pointed toward the sofa. "Have a seat."

The cold leather creaked as Sadie sat. Cynthia stood before her and crossed her arms. "You're angry," Cynthia said. "Why?"

"You have to ask?"

"Humour me."

"Rick's paying two hundred for my contract, not one. Not one-fifty. You owe me twenty-five grand."

Cynthia tilted her head, her expression neutral. "I see. When did he mention this?"

"Last night."

Cynthia dropped her arms and turned for the kitchen. "Can I get you something to drink?"

"You lied to me."

Cynthia pulled two espresso cups from the cupboard and proceeded as if Sadie hadn't spoken.

"Why?" Sadie asked.

Cynthia scooped grinds into the handled filter and tamped them down. "How did you hear about yesterday's gig?"

"The usual way."

Cynthia looked up. She raised an eyebrow.

Sadie answered with impatience. "You pinged me. Rick sent his driver. The usual."

"Where did you meet?"

"Why the questions? You know where we met."

"I'd like to be certain."

"The Sutton."

"Right. Of course." Cynthia continued with the coffee-making routine. When the machine stopped sputtering, she came around the kitchen counter and offered Sadie a cup. "Black, right?"

Sadie took it, puzzled by Cynthia's measured reaction. "Are you going to deny he's paying two hundred?"

"No. If that's what he told you, then that's what he's paying."

"And you'll pay me the additional twenty-five?"

"Absolutely. I'm sorry for the confusion."

Sadie pinched her forehead. "As easy as that? What the hell, Cynthia? Why'd you lie to me?"

"I didn't. It appears Mr. Kristan is playing games with us."

Sadie sagged into the sofa. Well, it wasn't as if she trusted Rick, but she was disappointed. "Is this deal going to fall through?"

"Not to worry. I'll handle Mr. Kristan," Cynthia said, and the way her lips curved into a confident, cruel smile left no doubt she would. Or her enforcers would.

Before Sadie left the condo, Cynthia transferred two grand into Sadie's account—an advance. She handed her another grand in cash. "Get yourself a new phone. My treat. And that's not a suggestion."

Sadie got behind the wheel of her car and dropped her head to the headrest. Cynthia thought Sadie's phone had been compromised, though she wouldn't give her specifics until she knew for sure. If it had been, it was probably because of Andy's stalker app. What a pain in the ass. She felt bone-tired, weary of the bullshit and lies. She just wanted the deal to go through, do her time, and then she wanted out.

At least Cynthia had been reasonable. Sadie had been prepared for a whole lot of denial and accusation and instead had come out with another twenty-five grand plus a cash advance.

She picked up a new phone and had the saleswoman swap out the SIM card so she could keep the same phone number. She then drove straight to Ethan's apartment. He buzzed her in, and she took an aging elevator to the third floor.

"Hello?" Sadie said, knocking on the open door.

Ethan's shoulders came into view as he leaned back from the kitchen sink. "Hey. Come in." A tea towel lay draped over his shoulder. He wiped his hands on it and greeted her. "What'd you learn from the professor?"

"Nothing yet."

Ethan frowned. "Then, what's the news?"

"News? I don't remember saying I had news."

"Damn it, Sadie. Were you tanked last night?"

"Don't get all judgy on me." Sadie's phone rang. "It's the professor."

"Hi, Nate," she answered.

"I've got news. Ariane spoke with Jane the day after your argument," he said. "Her investigator found Rebecca Morrow. She died years ago."

"Oh no!" Sadie said. "Jane would have been devastated."

"What's going on?" Ethan asked, shut out from the conversation. Sadie held up her hand to him.

"Who's that?" Nate asked.

"Ethan, the guy Jane's been seeing."

"There's more," Nate said. "Why don't the two of you join us? Ariane and I are heading to the house right now."

Ethan chose to take his own wheels and followed Sadie to the professor's place. After introductions, they took seats around the kitchen table, and Ariane told them about finding Rebecca Morrow. "We thought we might get more information from the in-care death investigation, but there wasn't one. The coroner concluded her wounds were self-inflicted. Her history of suicide attempts precluded further investigation."

"Who's Rebecca Morrow?" Ethan asked.

Nate, Ariane, and Sadie glanced at him and then at one another.

Ariane spoke first. "What do you know about Jane's dreams?"

Ethan jerked his head back. "Dreams? For the future? For a life without birthmarks? What are you talking about?"

"Shit! I thought he knew," Sadie said. "She'll kill me if we tell him."

"Tell me what!" Ethan said, crossing his arms.

Sadie addressed Nate and Ariane. "Jane's already pissed at me. If she really did take a vacation, when she comes back, if he knows, she'll never forgive me."

"And if she's in trouble?" Ariane said. "You don't think she'd understand?"

Ethan leaned across the table. "Somebody better tell me what's going on or I'm leaving here and going straight to the cops," he said, in a measured voice.

"I'll take responsibility for telling him," Nate said. "He might be able to help us find her." He didn't wait for anyone's agreement. "Jane may be in danger."

He started to tell Ethan what Ariane believed, but Ethan interrupted him.

"Jane told me about your theory. You don't expect me to believe it, do you?"

"How do you explain that she got those marks in the womb?" Ariane said.

"You're not helping your case," Ethan said.

"It's true," Sadie said. "When Jane curls up, the marks form rings around her body."

"The nature of Jane's dreams identify her as a Witness in the Inca culture," Ariane said.

Nate continued. "She dreams about the past, sees actual events as they transpire. We think she witnessed something that puts her in danger."

"You people are certifiable," Ethan said. He scraped his chair back and stood. "I'm leaving."

"She dreamed of you," Sadie said. "The car accident. The fire."

"Shut your mouth," Ethan said, flaring his nostrils.

"She saw the car weaving on the road. Saw the trucker pull you out from the wreck. Heard you scream. Saw your mom, in the front seat."

The colour had drained from Ethan's face. He stumbled back into his chair. After a moment he looked up. "That's not . . . possible."

"Isn't it?" Ariane asked, her voice a gentle question.

Ethan rubbed his face. "You're telling me her marks will be gone by her birthday and when that happens, whoever is after her will what? Kill her?"

"I'm afraid so," Ariane said. "Only her parents could have arranged for those marks. We believe they know what or whom she needs protection from, but we haven't been able to find them."

"We need to call the police," Ethan said, who looked to be gathering his wits.

"And tell them what?" Ariane asked, challenging him.

"Jane's missing. You said so yourself."

"The police won't waste their resources," Nate said. "Jane had a heated argument with her roommate and took vacation time that was owed to her. End of investigation."

"If Jane doesn't return in four weeks, they might take an interest," Ariane said. "We can't wait four weeks."

"Someone knows what Jane witnessed and who she is," Nate said.

"She dreamed about Rebecca Morrow," Sadie added, answering Ethan's earlier question.

"There's something else," Ariane said, addressing Sadie. "There is no Dr. Rick Kristan. He doesn't exist. Not here, not in London. There's no psychiatrist with that name."

Sadie blanched. She'd been a fool. Of course he hadn't used his real name.

"Kristan? Is this the asshole you've been dating?" Ethan asked.

Sadie swung her head around to Ethan. Nate and Ariane swung their heads to Sadie.

"Don't look so surprised," Ethan said, pulling his chair back up to the table. "Jane told me about your argument. I bloody well knew there was more to it."

"There is," Nate said, dragging his attention from Sadie. "Jane dreamed about Kristan. He's the psychiatrist who was treating Rebecca Morrow years ago."

Nate turned back to Sadie. "I'm a little confused. If you're dating Rick Kristan, why did Jane ask us to find him? Why not ask you?"

Damn it. Why hadn't she listened to Jane? Shame beat her shoulders into a hunch.

"It's not that simple," Sadie said, squirming under their scrutiny.

"Sure it is," Ethan said. "Let's go find him. Right now. See what he has to say."

"I don't know where he lives," Sadie said.

"Turns out you don't even know his name," Ethan said. "Who is he to you?"

Sadie's hackles rose. Ethan had no right. "Back the fuck off!"

"Don't you care about Jane? You know, your best friend? What if this guy—a guy whose name we don't even know—is the one who has her?"

Sadie flared her nostrils and turned to Ariane. "Can't Hunter find Jane through her phone? That's supposed to be easy to do."

"Who the hell's Hunter?" Ethan asked.

"Our investigator," Ariane said. "And that's the first thing he tried, but she's disabled it. He can't trace it, though he was able to confirm her signal had pinged off a tower on Granville Island a few times."

"She's in town!" Sadie said, buoyed by the news.

"Someone else is using her phone," Ethan said.

Nate and Ariane nodded in agreement. Sadie's enthusiasm fled. Jane's texts now made perfect sense. Sadie's phone wasn't the only one that had been compromised by Andy's app.

"Shit. Jane and I both downloaded an app to our phones. The neighbour down the hall developed it, sent us a link. Some kind of tracking app."

"Show me," Ethan said.

"Can't. Traded in my phone for a new one today. Andy's app isn't available in the stores."

"Andy's the app developer? Andy who?" Ethan asked, and she didn't much like the sneer on his face.

"I don't know."

"Do you know nothing about internet security?" Ethan asked, and looked away in disgust.

"Do you have Andy's phone number?" Ariane asked, her voice a gentle counterpoint to Ethan's simmering anger.

"I do," Sadie said, pulling out her phone. "I'll text it to you."

"It'll be a burner," Ethan said, shaking his head.

"Hunter can get his name from the landlord," Ariane said, disregarding Ethan's pessimism. "Jane also mentioned a Dr. Chadwick. Said he worked with Rick Kristan somewhere in London, England. Unfortunately, the only Dr. Chadwick we found died in 1999. Any records he had, including his office correspondence, were destroyed after the requisite ten years."

"Which brings us back to Rick Kristan," Nate said, looking at Sadie.

"Rick has something to do with this, doesn't he?" Sadie said. Jane's words came back to her. *He's in my dreams. That's not usually a good sign.* Guilt carved a chunk out of her pride.

Nate offered a sympathetic smile.

Sadie slumped in her chair. "I can't believe it. I saw him just last night."

"Where?" Ethan said.

"The Sutton. Downtown."

"You got his number?" Ariane asked.

"I do," Sadie said, straightening.

Ariane smiled. "Then Hunter can find him."

70 | Rick

What time are you clearing out today?" Rick asked the painters.

The older man checked his watch. "Another hour and we'll be done. Say, five o'clock?"

"I've got to go out. Lock up when you leave." Rick hated leaving them alone in the house and the barn unattended, but the hospital had insisted on a meeting to discuss the conditions of his leave.

He parked his car off the road at the end of the driveway, where the painters couldn't see it, and hiked back to the barn through the woods. Jane's behaviour after his last visit led him to believe she'd finally reached the brink. If she hadn't leapt yet, he'd give her another push. Excitement lightened his step. Soon he'd be free of the two biggest irritants in his life.

He fit the key in the padlock and opened the barn door. His upcoming trip to Europe would be the perfect topper, he thought, pushing open the inner door. As he approached the sound barrier, Jane spoke.

"Do you know what happens when I kill your brother?"

It seemed Jane did, indeed, need a little more motivation. "I'm not playing question and answer with you, Jane."

"History changes. When he dies, everything he's influenced from that point on alters in ways you can't possibly predict. But one thing I'm sure of is that I won't be here in this kennel."

"Even more reason for you to do your job."

"You won't remember kidnapping me, starving me," she said. "But I will. Did you know that?"

Was she threatening him? Lying? He took a moment to consider how that might impact him. He'd make a contingency. Write himself a note so he wouldn't forget who Jane was and why she was a threat to him. Even if he didn't remember the events of the last few days, his note would remind him to take care of Jane. Michael's death wouldn't change that.

Rick parted the curtains and dropped a bottle of water into her dish. "When's your birthday, Jane?" He left, not expecting an answer.

71 | Jane

Jane cracked the lid off the water bottle and took a drink. She had one day left and little faith that Sadie, or anyone else, could help her now.

A neat row of empty plastic bottles lined the back wall of her kennel. Including the one in her hand, there were six. She'd been there six days, if her guess that he'd brought her a bottle each day was accurate.

How long before the porta-potty overflowed? It had already begun to smell foul, despite the chemicals.

She picked up a dog bowl and checked the mark on her face, happy to see it still there in all its ugly glory. "Never thought I'd be pleased about that," she said, and her voice sounded gutted. She tossed the bowl, and it dinged off the side of the kennel, rolled on its edge, then gyrated once, twice, and settled upside down.

A strange disconnect had developed between her mind and her body. She attributed it to the lack of food. Her thoughts flitted around, unable to stick to any one idea for more than a nanosecond.

She pulled out her knife. An idea danced on the edge of her mind, like a word lost on the tip of her tongue. Again, she looked at the row of water bottles.

And then she jolted forward. It felt as if her brain had come back online.

72 | Sadie

Time had never crawled so slowly. Sadie checked her phone again. Ariane's investigator had had Rick's phone number for six hours—how much more time did he need? If Hunter were as good as his name, he'd have found him by now. And maybe Jane.

Guilt ate away at her. She'd practically handed Jane over to Rick. She'd been a fool. A greedy, stupid fool. And Jane was paying the price. There'd be no windfall in Sadie's bank account, no getting out of the business.

She paced another lap from the kitchen to the bedroom and back, and looked at her phone for what seemed like the hundredth time. Screw it, she thought. I'm not waiting. She punched in Nate's number.

"Has Hunter found him yet?" she asked.

"No, but he's on his trail."

"What does that mean?"

"Hunter's using the number you gave us to map Rick's movements. Most of his calls ping off two towers—one on Granville Island and another in Langley."

She was right. Hunter was crap. "If he can't narrow it down tighter than that, we'll never find him."

"He has a theory. The Granville Island area is too populated. Rick wouldn't risk holding Jane there. If he has her, he's holding her in Langley. It's horse country. Lots of barns and homes on large acreages."

"That's not reassuring."

"You're right. It's a big area with dozens of cell towers, but Rick's signal is bouncing off only one of them. Hunter's team is scouting the neighbourhood around the tower for potential sites. He'll check in again as soon as he has more information."

"What if Hunter's wrong and she's someplace else?"

"We're not giving up, Sadie. He's still monitoring Rick's number. Every time Rick uses his phone, we get a little closer to finding him."

"How long will that take?"

"Depends on how often he uses his phone."

Sadie hung up and phoned Ethan with an update. Icicles dripped off his thank-you.

A thought occurred to her as she disconnected. She could help Hunter find Rick. She thumbed a text to him. *Miss you. Call me.*

73 | Jane

Jane twisted her knife and worked a hole into the bottom of one of the water bottles until it was just big enough to jam the top of another one into it. She repeated the process until she had a chain of five bottles. She then went back to work on the first bottle, slicing jagged strips and bending them outward to act as grappling hooks.

Smiling, she admired her handiwork. After she checked to make certain the bottles wouldn't easily pull apart, she removed the second dog dish and got down on her stomach. She inched the chain of bottles out of the opening and held her breath as it reached the edge of the padded curtain. One more little shove, she thought, and thrust the bottle chain forward, but the lead bottle with the jagged hooks pushed the curtain away. She tried again, but each time she extended the bottles, she worsened the situation by moving the curtain farther and farther away.

The bottle chain wasn't long enough. She sat up, drank the contents of the sixth bottle, and added it to the chain. She tried again, but the bottle chain still wasn't long enough to overcome the excess of blanket that pooled on the floor.

In a last-ditch effort, Jane jammed her knife into the bottom of the last bottle to extend her reach even farther and shoved the chain as far as the tips of her fingers would go. The hooks of the lead bottle disappeared beneath the pooled blanket. "Yes!" Ever so gently, she pulled back on her knife. Inch by inch, the hooked bottle reappeared, having hooked nothing.

Jane exhaled in defeat. She retrieved the bottles and sat with her back to the kennel. "Wouldn't have done me any good anyway," she said, having taken up talking to herself.

She'd have to use the toilet again soon. The thought of lifting the lid and releasing the odour deflated her. The hanging blanket only made it worse, trapping the smell of sewage in her small cell.

"No. I won't let him win!" She dropped back to the floor. This time she tried the other dog-dish opening and started over again, attacking a different section of blanket with the chain of bottles. After a few more failed jabs, she felt anger seep in. Jane pictured Rick, a man she'd only seen in her dreams, and imagined it was him she was stabbing. She flung her arm in a wide, powerful arc and sent the chain of bottles skittering sideways.

Surprise halted her assault. She'd hooked the blanket. Carefully, slowly, she pulled her bottle chain back. This time, the blanket followed.

When the edge of the blanket drew close enough, she slid the remaining bottles back inside the kennel and yanked a handful of fabric in through the opening. She'd done it! The blanket she'd snagged covered the right half of the kennel. She needed to rest and hoped she had the strength to rip it down.

Even if hauling the blanket down didn't help her situation, she'd do it just to piss him off—at least she was doing something. And then she'd go after the blanket on the other side. Her gaze fell on the chain of bottles. He'd take those from her if he returned before she could finish. She lifted the mattress and kicked the bottles underneath.

"Now for you," she said, addressing the blanket. This time, she got on her back. She pushed the fabric out of the hole but kept a tight grip on it, and extended one arm out of each of the dog-dish openings. With the side of her face crammed up against the steel mesh, and her neck at a painful angle, she grabbed a firm handhold on the blanket, and heaved.

It held fast. She took a breath, adjusted her hands. "You won't beat me," she said, and gave the fabric a sharp jerk.

The sound of tearing cloth elated her. She gripped fresh handholds and jerked again. Rewarded with another rip of fabric, she yanked with enthusiasm over and over again. When the last of the blanket fell, she shimmied back inside the kennel, sat up and stretched her spine.

As she caught her breath, she examined the room beyond the blanket. Two metres to her right stood a cinder-block wall. A counter ran the length of the wall, and beneath it sat a row of wheeled bins, like an alley on recycle day. Styrofoam had been stuffed in high inset windows and duct-taped in place.

The door to the room, about four metres away, sat diagonally opposite the door to the kennel. She couldn't quite see it, but she knew from when Rick had opened and closed it that it was one of those hollow wood doors. Lightweight. She also knew it wasn't locked. It was the door beyond the wooden one—the outside door—that had a lock. She'd heard the metallic rattle of keys preceding Rick's visits.

At the sound of approaching car wheels crunching on gravel, she bolted upright and screamed for help, but the vehicle kept going. The sound of wheels faded off to her right. Coming or going? she wondered.

Sweat beaded on her forehead. She wiped it away, sat down and rested, and then she got busy. She wasn't going to leave the blanket there for Rick to tack up again. Foot by foot, she pulled the blanket inside the kennel. When its girth jammed the hole, she sliced off chunks, rearranged the fabric, and pulled more in. When she'd finally reduced it to rags, she retrieved the bottles and went fishing for the other blanket. This time, she didn't stop until she'd snagged it.

She took a breather, and then ripped that blanket down too. When she'd finished, she sat up and surveyed the rest of the room beyond her kennel. A kennel similar to hers but smaller and not bolted to the floor sat askew and pushed off to the side—making room for Jane's cage, no doubt. Against the wall on the left stood a stainless-steel dog-washing station. A handful of travel-style plastic dog kennels were stacked beside it. Dog leads and muzzles hung from hooks to the left of the interior door. The door Rick would traipse through, and she'd finally see his face.

Jane turned her attention to the blanket that now lay on the floor outside her kennel. "You're next," she said, and proceeded to haul in the blanket and cut it up. A hard lump in the fabric stopped her blade. She worked her knife around the lump and extracted it—a black plastic box, three inches long and an inch thick. Her nostrils flared. A wireless camera. He'd been watching her. Her skin crawled at the thought of it. She set the camera face down on the floor, stood, and drove the heel of her boot into it, shattering it into sharp splinters. Satisfied, she kicked the shards away, sat down, and resumed her task.

When she'd finished, the light beyond the Styrofoam in the windows had faded. She heard another vehicle approach and jumped to her feet. She shouted for help, but the vehicle continued, this time to the left, and silence returned. Rick? Was he meeting Sadie?

She settled into the mound of soft stuffing that now lined her kennel.

Tomorrow was her birthday.

She'd never been more frightened of falling asleep.

Visiting Dream

Jane cringes at the sound of a woman groaning in pain. She orients herself in the darkened space. She's inside Rebecca's room in the psych ward.

Rebecca's kneeling on the bed. She bites down on a face cloth and claws at the bedsheets. She's in labour.

The door to her room opens and Maria rushes in. She doesn't turn on the light. "It's time." She waits for the groaning to stop then helps Rebecca to her feet.

"We must be quick," Maria says, and supports Rebecca as she escorts her out the door. Jane rushes out behind them.

Maria uses a security card to unlock a door at the back of the ward. On the landing inside is an elevator and, beside it, a stairwell. An emergency exit sign emits a red glow. They take the elevator to the bottom floor.

"Another one's coming," Rebecca says, between short, sharp puffs, as they get out of the elevator. She drops to her hands and knees and Maria rubs her back, tells her to be quiet. She helps Rebecca put the cloth back in her mouth. Rebecca grinds down on it, and the groan that escapes is painful to hear.

When the contraction passes, Maria helps her up and supports her again as they rush down a hallway. Maria opens another door and white noise floods the hallway. They step inside. Pipes and valves twist in a complicated maze around tanks the size of dumpsters. The drone of the equipment covers the sound of their movement. Maria continues past the tanks to a mattress piled with pillows against one wall. Rebecca crawls into the nest.

The painful contractions go on forever. Jane wonders how any woman survives this. Rebecca rests between the painful bouts. As the night wears on, Jane worries they'll be caught.

Finally, Maria reaches for a couple of towels from a stack beside the makeshift bed. She has Rebecca lift her bottom and places the towels beneath her. Maria is gentle. She probes beneath Rebecca's gown as if she's examined delivering women before. Perhaps she's also a midwife, Jane thinks, as Maria encourages Rebecca to push.

Maria is on her knees before Rebecca's legs. "One more time," she says, pulling another towel close.

Jane remains steadfast by Rebecca's head, abashed at witnessing such an intimate moment. She offers comforting words neither Rebecca nor Maria can hear.

The birth happens remarkably fast after all the pain and agony. Maria is quick with the towel and all smiles as she lifts the tightly bundled baby to show Rebecca. A twisted umbilical cord dangles below the towel. "*Hermosa niñita*," she says. "You have a beautiful daughter."

Rebecca reaches for the child. "I want to see her," she says.

Jane leans forward to catch a glimpse of the baby so fresh from the womb.

The baby howls. Maria places the bundle in Rebecca's arms and cups her cheek in a reassuring fashion. Rebecca carefully unwraps the baby. Wide-eyed, the new mother looks up to Maria.

"No one will harm her now," she says. Tears stream down Rebecca's face as Maria helps her lift the newborn to her breast.

Jane is rooted to the floor, unable to look away from the blood-red ribbon that encircles the baby's body.

Rebecca whispers to the child, "Your name is Beth."

Jane woke with a cry in her throat.

74 | Rick

After his meeting with Vasul and the director of human resources, Rick drove to his townhome. Did they really imagine he'd be coming back after his leave? Morons. He'd be damned if he'd walk past the office that should have been his each day and enquire as to how she'd like her ass kissed. Someone less qualified than him? He'd sooner stuff his hand down a garbage disposal.

A six-month leave was about perfect. She'd fuck up by then, fall on her face, and the board would come back with their tails between their legs. Until then, he'd make himself scarce.

He poured himself a healthy shot and pulled out his suitcase. It had been a while since he travelled anywhere. He dug out his passport and made a start on packing.

A few hours later, heading back to Langley, he checked the time. It was almost 10:00 p.m. One way or another, his investment was about to pay off. With Jane taken care of, his future was secure.

At the house, he poured a drink and settled into his father's favourite chair. The painters would be done tomorrow, unless they were trying to bilk more money out of his mother. He'd have none of that and send them on their way by noon. Earlier if he could.

Though he considered himself highly disciplined, and took pride in his ability to delay gratification, at midnight he could resist no longer. He pulled up the video feed. But the screen was black. Damn it! The batteries must be dead. No matter. Morning would come soon enough.

His phone chimed. Even before he looked, he knew it would be Andrew. No one else messaged him at this hour. He looked at the screen. Sure enough, Andrew had sent him a text. *D-Day.*

Rick had pushed Andrew about as far as he could. The man was paranoid and impatient. If Jane didn't come through for him tonight and kill Michael, Rick would have to cut his losses and settle for eradicating only one of his two irritants. Not getting rid of Mikey would be a disappointment, but he could live with it. Jane was the bigger threat. She knew things that could send him to prison, and he wasn't willing to gamble on whether or not she had proof.

Excitement coursed through him. He'd waited twenty-five years and spent countless thousands of dollars. Today, he would finally gain the upper hand.

75 | Sadie

August 31

Sadie woke and rolled onto her back. "Happy birthday, Jane," she said, but her heart wasn't in it. She felt helpless knowing that Jane might be in trouble and there was nothing she could do about it. It was a crappy way to start the day. Though it was futile, a tiny spark of hope compelled her to check her phone.

There was nothing from Jane.

But Nate had texted. Her hands were shaking as she dialled his number. "Did you find her?" she said, swallowing the lump of anxiety that had crawled up her throat.

"Not yet, but this morning Hunter's team started knocking on doors and asking questions. They've got it narrowed down to four possibilities."

"Four!" Sadie said, exasperated.

"His men are watching three of them and Hunter's camped out at the place he thinks is the best bet. He says the place is unoccupied. The owner's in Palm Springs. The neighbours say she's a widow. Used to breed dogs on the property."

"Can he get in there to take a look?"

"Not without breaking in. He walked the perimeter of the old kennel, though. Said it was dead quiet. No sign of activity. No flyers piling up. There're two cars in the garage. One's the widow's Lexus. The other's a Land Rover, but Hunter can't read the plate."

"Damn it!" Sadie didn't even know what kind of vehicle Rick drove.

"He saw a painters' van pull in. They had keys. He hung around long enough to determine they were the real deal. Probably the ones keeping the place tidy."

"So that's it? He's done?"

"No. But he won't risk being seen snooping around and cause them to panic. He's catching some sleep. When the painters leave, he'll get a better look."

Sadie's nerves were a jangling mess. She trudged to the bathroom and then to the kitchen and put the kettle on. Her dishes were piling up again. She hadn't appreciated how often Jane must have washed up.

She made a coffee but the scent of it turned her stomach.

Her phone rang. It was Ethan.

"I found Jane's Rebel," he said. "Some asshole was selling in on Craigslist."

"How do you know it's hers?"

"I drove out to see it. Recognized the scratch on the gas tank. It's hers."

"How'd he get it? Did he see Jane? Is she all right?"

"He played dumb. Says he can get the transfer papers, but he was checking me out. Offered me a real good deal if I wasn't particular about them."

"Do you think he knows where she is?"

"Hard to say. But he knows that bike is stolen. I called the cops. They may not be able to look for Jane, but they can sure as hell seize her bike. Maybe something will come out of that."

"I'll call Nate and let him know," she said. "I have some news too. Hunter has narrowed down the search to a place out in Langley."

"And you were going to tell me this when?" Ethan said, frosty as ever.

"Lay off. I got off the phone with Nate a second before you called."

She heard Ethan inhale. "Sorry. I didn't mean to take off on you. I'm just worried about Jane."

"Yeah. Me too. Hunter says the place in Langley is quiet, but he'll snoop around when the painters who are there leave. I'll let you know next time I hear from them."

Worst birthday ever, Sadie thought, and headed to the shower. She let the hot water stream over her shoulders. If Jane ever came back, Sadie would be a better roommate. She'd do the dishes once in a while and stop complaining about Jane's obsession with tidiness. In so many ways, Sadie was her polar opposite. Yin and yang. It was a miracle they'd been such good friends. Maybe they each needed a little piece of the other to make them whole. Jane made her feel loved, worthwhile. She didn't have to pretend to be something she wasn't around Jane. She missed her more than she thought possible.

Sniffling back tears, she turned off the water and reached for the towel. She dried off, wrapped the towel around her head, and shivered as she stepped onto the cold tile floor.

She looked at the steamed-up mirror above the sink and stilled. A frown formed as she read the writing: *Send help 2 Highland.* It was signed *Jane XO.*

"Holy crap! Holy crap!" Sadie blinked back tears. Jane had left her a message, but what the hell did it mean? She swiped at her tears as she puzzled it out. And then she realized that part of Jane's message was missing. She slapped her forehead—she'd wiped toothpaste off the mirror before her shower. She'd destroyed part of Jane's message. "What the hell are you trying to tell me, Jane?"

Was she here? Sadie darted her gaze around the room. When she turned back to the mirror, the steam had started to clear. Sadie rushed out the door. She returned with her phone and snapped photos of the message before it was lost.

She sent the photo to Nate, Ariane, and Ethan, and then dialled Nate. "What does it mean?" she asked, as soon as he answered.

"We don't know," Nate said. "Ariane's sending the message to Hunter to see if he can make sense of it."

"I've got a call coming in," Sadie said. "It's Ethan. I'll call you back."

"Ethan?"

"I know what it is," Ethan said. "Highland Breeders. It's a dog kennel."

76 | Jane

Jane lay awake for hours. Rebecca Morrow was her mother. David Banner was her father. The knowledge that her parents had loved her and wanted her was the best birthday gift she'd ever received. She hadn't been abandoned, but how she'd landed in the Joyce SkyTrain station remained a mystery.

Why she hadn't figured out sooner that Rebecca was her mother needled at her. Jane had been blinded by her belief that she'd been abandoned. Discarded. Maybe she hadn't wanted to dig deeper for fear she'd find the woman who'd thrown her away.

The last mark on her face had faded with the dawn. She touched the newly clear skin with a sense of wonderment and new respect. Rick would kill her today, and now she knew why.

In the early-morning hours, she'd carefully sharpened her blade on the smooth concrete floor. The edge of it bit against the ridges of her thumb.

Sometime later, a vehicle drove by, left to right, but didn't stop. Again she wondered, coming or going? She no longer screamed for help. They couldn't hear her, and today of all days, she needed what remained of her energy.

When the next vehicle approached, it didn't carry on. This one stopped. Jane bolted to her feet and hid her knife in the waistband of her jeans. She heard the rattle of metal and then the swish of the outer door.

When the interior door opened, at long last, Jane saw the face of her tormentor. She found satisfaction seeing the scar she'd given him.

Surprise registered on his face, but he quickly covered it with a smile. "You've been busy," he said. "Shall I sing 'Happy Birthday'?"

"You killed my father."

"Your mother killed your father."

"I was there. I saw it. You murdered him."

"Thankfully, the police didn't see it that way. You're out of time, Jane."

"What happened to my mother?"

He tilted his head, studying her. "You have her hair."

"She had visions just like my dreams."

"Indeed. And if she'd put her talents to better use, you and I wouldn't be here."

"What happened to her?"

"She bled out a few weeks after you were born."

"Not suicide?"

"Her wrists were slit to support a suicide. It was easier that way."

"Easier for the hospital."

He shrugged. "Easier for everyone. Rebecca didn't want to live."

"And what about the baby?"

"There was no baby. She had a hysterical pregnancy. One of the hospital's physicians confirmed it. It's rare, but it happens."

His talent for justifying murder rendered her speechless.

But she couldn't afford to be speechless. She had to coax him close to the kennel. She dropped her gaze to the floor and stepped back. The thought of her knife in his throat made her hand itch. "Tell me more about my mother."

"I'd love to, but I have to finish packing." He turned to leave.

Jane rushed the door of her kennel. "What's going to happen to me!"

He stopped. "You won't feel a thing. Try not to worry about it." He left without looking back.

Jane screamed in frustration, heaving on the kennel's door.

She expended what little energy she had left and dropped to her knees. Her next paralytic dream would be her last. The terror of what he'd do to her left her shaking.

Hours later, a vehicle approached. Rick? Back to gloat, or to kill her? In the hours since he left her, she'd hatched a desperate plan. It was now-or-never time. She rolled onto her left side as if she were deep in sleep and rested her right hand close to one of the dog-dish openings. She'd removed the bowls.

The familiar rattle of keys preceded the opening of the outer door. Moments later, the interior door opened. Through the curtain of her hair, she saw a man she didn't recognize. Her breath faltered. A red gasoline can hung from one of his hands. It took every ounce of her being not to scream. His hardened features scanned the ceiling, where bits of ragged blanket dangled. The man cursed under his breath. Jane thought she heard Rick's name spit out in the mix.

She narrowed her eyes and concentrated to steady her breathing. He set the jerry can on the floor and turned his gaze to her sleeping form. She closed her eyes. Footsteps approached, tentative. Not close enough.

He retreated. She heard a rustling noise and then his footsteps approached again, surer this time. He was close, crouched in front of the kennel's door. She heard the scrape of something against the steel grate close to her face. A dull point poked her forehead and snagged her hair. He was trying to get a look at her face.

Absorbed as he was in his task, he didn't see Jane's knife. A quick jab through the dog-dish opening. Her knife pierced the tanned skin by his shinbone, and she drove it straight through his calf.

With a scream he fell hard against the kennel's door, his face a mask of pain. Jane sprang into action. She torpedoed her left hand through the second opening and clenched a fistful of his designer shorts. His eyes were wild as she stabbed him with her fighting hand again, this time in his thigh. He kicked at her trying to slither away, but Jane had a death grip on him, and with each swing of her knife, she inflicted more damage. A forearm, a knee, another shot to his thigh.

Her hand was slick with blood when she stopped. The screaming subsided. He'd curled into a heaving ball with his back to her, panting, his bloody hands covering his head.

Jane had him by his belt now. She dropped the knife back inside the kennel and rifled through his pockets. She found a ring of keys in the front right, a wallet in the back. She dropped both inside the kennel. He gasped as she shoved him along the blood-slickened floor. She extended her reach to pat down his shirt pockets and found another set of keys. They got dropped inside the kennel as well.

The man groaned. She adjusted her hold on his belt. "Roll over," she said.

"Enough," the man said, gasping.

"On your back," Jane ordered. When he didn't move, she yanked on his belt. He shouted out and rolled over, keeping his hands clasped around his head. Once again, Jane adjusted her grip on the man's belt.

"Now over on your side." He cried out as he rolled toward her. Jane found nothing in his remaining pockets. She pushed him along, as far from the dog-dish openings as she could. Then, holding his belt like a lifeline, she unfastened it and wove the tail end of it through the door's grating. When she refastened it, he was secured to the kennel.

Satisfied that he wasn't going anywhere, she scrabbled upright to examine the keys. Three on one ring and four on the other were possibilities. She reached to the mattress, where she'd prepared strips of fabric. First, she secured the key rings to the fabric. Next, she tied the fabric to her wrist. She'd had a lot of time to think about getting her hands on those keys, and dropping them beyond her reach wasn't in her plan.

Finally, she fed a sturdy piece of the blanket she'd cut from a seam out through the cage directly beside the lock. When the end of the fabric hit the floor, she walked it up the outside of the door's grate and pulled it back in on the other side of the padlock. She tied the two ends together, securing the dangling lock in place. It wasn't perfect, but it would help the lock stay put while she poked at it with the keys.

She sat back down. The energy she'd expended taxed her. Her quarry lay still, his arms in front of his face. His upper torso was bent around the corner of the kennel. His hips and legs lay in front of the door.

"You must be Andy," she said. He didn't respond. She counted six wounds. One on his arm and the rest on his lower extremities. Blood dripped from the gashes but didn't spurt. Probably wouldn't kill him. Not yet, anyway. But were his wounds enough to incapacitate him? She wiped her blade clean. She could finish him right now. That she was tempted to do it frightened her. Doing so would mean she was no better than Rick.

She abandoned visions of her blade buried in his temple and got on her back. When she shoved his legs out of the way, he sucked in air through his teeth, but he didn't fight her. Still, she wouldn't let her guard down. She wasn't as good with a knife in her left hand, but she didn't have a choice. Working a key in the padlock would require all the dexterity of her right hand.

She wrapped her left hand around the hilt of the knife and arranged the first key in her other. If he tested her, he'd see just how much damage she could do with her non-dominant hand.

"Don't fucking move," she warned, and she reached her right arm through the hole. The padlock was at the very end of her reach. She glanced at Andy one last time and then looked away, pressing her face against the cage to extend her reach. The key wouldn't go in. She turned it the other way and tried again. No luck.

She retreated and arranged the next key in her hand. Satisfied that

Andy hadn't moved, she repeated the exercise with the second key. It wasn't the one. The third key was also not the one.

She pulled her arm back inside the kennel and pushed back from the grate. Fatigue had set into her arm and shoulder. Her physical condition had deteriorated in the past few days. She rolled her shoulder, loosening the muscles, and turned her head to check on Andy. He stared back with cold blue eyes—steel daggers of contempt. He lay still, but his hands had crept toward his belt. Jane hammered a boot into the side of the cage, and he jerked back with a strangled cry. For good measure, Jane yanked on his belt, jerking him. He screamed.

When Andy was cowering again with his hands around his head, Jane got back to work. Four keys remained. She arranged the next key and again poked her arm through the dog-dish opening. Her left hand flexed around the hilt of her knife. She looked away from Andy and pushed the key toward the lock but misjudged the distance and knocked the lock sideways. She realigned it. The key didn't fit. She turned it around. No luck.

She retreated and reloaded. The next key also didn't fit.

Two keys left.

Two lottery tickets. Doubt started to nibble at her determination. What if she didn't have a winner?

No! She couldn't think like that. She pushed the thought aside and concentrated on fitting the second-last key in the lock.

She didn't see Andy shifting, and he caught her off guard with a knee punch to her right arm. She cried out. Before she could pull her arm back inside the kennel, he nailed her again.

With renewed vigour, he skittered to undo the belt that tethered him to the cage. Jane retreated inside, rolled onto her bruised arm, and blindly swung the blade gripped in her left hand. The flailing jab sailed cleanly through a two-inch opening and hit flesh. A wrist, she thought, or a forearm. A shriek registered.

She pulled back and swung again. This time her luck failed. The blade careened off the metal grate and twisted out of her grasp. Horrified, she watched her knife tumble to the floor.

Outside the kennel.

Andy drew his knees up against the door, leveraging his torso so his belt pulled taut. Jane tried but couldn't get purchase on the leather. The belt gave way with a snap, and Andy pushed away from the kennel. Jane lunged through the hole for his shorts and missed. She caught his sneaker, but he easily kicked out of her grip.

"Fucking hell," he said. He curled his fist around her knife and tossed it. The weapon clattered across the room. Then he lay on his back inches out of her reach. His breath came in shallow puffs. He rolled onto his side, away from her.

Jane's gaze fell beyond his back to the jerry can. She couldn't die like this. In silence, she surveyed her kennel. The keys were close. She retrieved them, cursing the unavoidable jingle. She moved with stealth to get back into position. Her arms shook now. She arranged her fingers again around the second-last key, shoved her arm up through an opening in the cage, and pushed the key against the bottom of the lock. It didn't fit.

She heard shuffling and turned her head. Andy, still on his side, was worming his way toward the jerry can. A bloody slug trail followed him.

She jerked her attention back to the key, flipped it around, and stabbed at the padlock. When it slipped inside, she caught her breath. With a turn of Jane's wrist, the lock fell open. Andy looked back. He had one hand on the jerry can.

Jane let go of the keys and worked the lock free of the hasp. The padlock dropped to the floor. She retreated into the kennel and reached through the opening, closing her hand on the lock. She scooted backward into the kennel and flung the lock against the back wall.

Andy was standing now, and he wore a chilling smile. She scrambled to her feet as he limped toward her knife. The seam of fabric she'd tied around the lock also tied the door to the frame, preventing her from opening it. She worked the knot with her fingers, glancing up at Andy as he bent over her knife.

The knot gave way and she bolted from the kennel and then halted midstride.

Andy held her knife as though he knew how to use it.

"Get out of my way," Jane said. He stood between her and the door to freedom. She stepped to his left.

He countered. "You're not going anywhere."

"You're full of holes."

"You think you can get through me?"

"You're leaking all over the floor. I only have to wait it out."

"Back in the kennel," he said, lunging at her with the knife extended. She took a step back, dodging his effort.

"That's it," he said. "Keep going."

He took another swing. She took another step back. His self-satisfied smile grew more confident.

She took one last look to gauge the position of the knife and then pivoted, turned, and delivered a perfectly aimed roundhouse kick. She heard the clank of her knife but didn't see it fall. She'd already pivoted again. Her next kick broke his jaw. He was out cold before he hit the floor.

Outside at last, Jane blinked as the daylight blinded her, shooting painful splinters behind her eyes. She filled her lungs with air that smelled of summer dust and sweet hay. Jane turned from the eye-watering glare and slid on loose gravel, losing her footing. Her hand shot out to the wood siding, and she steadied herself. She took a moment and then, with shaking hands, replaced the padlock on the outer door. She didn't want Rick to come across the building and think something was amiss. Not yet.

She had no clue where she was, or whether left or right led to Rick, but she wouldn't stop searching until she found him. With her knife back in her boot, she started Andy's truck and turned left. She soon found herself at a dead end in front of a garage and a large ranch-style house. There were no other cars in the driveway.

She sat in the parked truck for a long time. Whether it was the receding adrenalin or the lack of food, she couldn't decide, but weakness and a full-on body tremble overwhelmed her. When it subsided, she got out and walked around the house, looking in each window. No one appeared to be home.

The doors were locked, but a basement window had been left open. She kicked in the screen and entered feet first, dropping the few inches to the floor. She stilled to listen. If someone had heard her, they weren't making any noise.

A drop of water splattered into the depths of a nearby laundry tub. She darted to the faucet and gulped handfuls of water. Immediately, her stomach cramped. The water came back up as quickly as it had gone down. Weak in the knees, she rested her forearms on the sink and hung her head for a moment. Then she rinsed her mouth, and the cool water tasted better than anything that had ever crossed her tongue.

She tried again. One sip. Another. Satisfied it would stay down, she took a third sip and then straightened. She made her way through the basement and up the stairs and found herself in the kitchen. Kitchens meant food. She lunged for the bank of cupboards, flinging open one after another. Her hand landed on a box of Lesley Stowe crackers—the ones that she hated, with rosemary and raisins. She ripped open the box and gobbled them down two at a time.

Without a moment's warning, her stomach revolted. The fancy crackers made a reappearance before she could get to the sink. "Shit, Jane. Wise up." She rinsed her mouth once more. Would she ever be able to eat again?

She opened the fridge. On the shelves inside she found condiments, pickles, and salad dressings. The drawers held a few carrots and potatoes. A carton of coffee cream sat in the door beside a carton of chicken broth. Chicken soup was supposed to be good for you. Was it easy on your stomach? She hadn't a clue but chanced a swig of the salty water. When it didn't try to come back up, she took another gulp. She paused, thankful her stomach hadn't cramped.

A stack of mail sat on the counter beside the fridge. She flipped through it and took another sip of broth. The mail was addressed to Mrs. Audrey Atkins. Rick's wife? His mother? A sister? The address was in Langley. Finally, she knew where Rick had been keeping her. She tucked one of the envelopes in her pocket and carried on, broth in hand. Would they have a land line?

In the den, she approached a desk. Her gaze slid to the phone. She exhaled with relief. Help was just three digits away. She reached for the handset but hesitated. What if he'd rigged his phone so he'd be alerted if someone used it? He'd vanish, that's what. The thought that he might get away with what he'd done curled her lip and made her shudder.

She turned her attention to the desk drawers. They were filled with useless crap—pens, stamps, paperclips. A garbage can hid beneath the desk. She dumped it out on the desktop and sifted through it, smoothing out balls of paper and discarded flyers.

When at last she found something with his name on it, her knees gave out. She dropped into the chair behind the desk. In her hands was an Air Canada receipt with the name Roderick Atkins printed on it. Roderick. Not Rick, not Richard.

The lowlife was going on a vacation. Curiously, the address on the receipt wasn't in Langley but Vancouver. He had another home.

She took another swig of the broth and looked ruefully at the phone then shoved the receipt in her pocket and left the house by the front door.

Andy's half-ton had a GPS. She punched in Rick's address and wheeled the truck around. She'd borrow a phone at the first store she came to and call Sadie. There was no one she'd rather have as backup, and whether Sadie knew it yet or not, she had skin in this fight.

77 | Sadie

S adie had her phone to her ear and a hand on her hip. "How long is this going to take?" she said. Her impatience had turned to accusation. They'd known the name of the breeder for an hour already. The holdup was that Highland Breeders had closed down a number of years ago. The business's old phone number had been reassigned, there was no website, and nothing on social media.

"We're making headway," Nate said. "Hunter found the old business address. It's the place in Langley that he's been monitoring. He's there now, so we should hear any minute."

"Give me the address. I'm going out there."

"You don't know what you'll be walking into."

"That's my b-best friend. I'm going."

"We don't even know if she's still there. Give Hunter a few more minutes."

"I can't. What if something's h-happened to her?"

"A few more minutes. Hang tight."

Sadie sniffed back tears. "Who owns the place? Do we know anything about them?"

Nate asked her to hold on. Paper rustled. A moment later he told her the owner's name was Audrey Atkins.

"Who's she?"

"Don't know. She's a widow, in her sixties. She's out of the country. She might be a patient of Rick's. We're running down some possibilities. We're going to find him, Sadie. And we're going to find Jane."

"Hurry, please," Sadie said.

"Ariane's got her phone in her hand. The moment Hunter calls, we'll let you know."

Reluctantly, Sadie hung up. She called Ethan and relayed what she'd learned.

"Wait for me. I'm going with you," he said.

78 | Jane

Jane sped down Rick's one-lane driveway. Just before the cut-off to the kennel building, she came face to face with the shiny grill of a Cadillac Escalade. She stared through the windshield into the face of a man she didn't recognize with a determined set to his jaw. She cranked the wheel hard to the right, but the driver of the SUV countered, coming within inches of the truck, blocking her path. Jane glared at him.

He powered down his window. "You Jane?"

Panic seized her. She floored the Chevy. It connected with the Cadillac, but she had no momentum. The man behind the wheel of the Cadillac appeared unconcerned, as if she were a bug on his grill. The Chevy's wheels began to spin on the dry gravel. Shit! She jammed on the brakes, put the truck in reverse, and stepped on the gas.

The man in the Cadillac pursued her, never letting his vehicle get more than a few inches from her hood. She jumped on her brakes again and shoved her head out the window. "Back the hell up!"

"My name's Hunter," the man shouted. "Hunter Bishop. Ariane sent me."

Jane frowned. Hunter? Ariane's investigator?

The man stepped out of his vehicle and stood with his hands in the air. He maintained eye contact. "I know who you are, Jane. I'm here to help."

He could be anyone, Jane thought. Rick had her phone. He knew everyone she had contact with, including Ariane. This man could be another Andy; another of Rick's flunkies.

Jane put the truck in reverse again and pushed the pedal to the floor. The engine protested as she dropped back into drive and swung out to her left. The man anticipated her move and stepped into her path. She hit the brakes and skidded forward.

He banged his fists on the hood of the truck, startling her. "Let me prove who I am," he called out. "I've got ID."

"Get out of my way!" she shouted, inching forward.

The man banged his fists on the hood again. He then stepped back and raised his hands to his hips. "I'm not going anywhere," he said, shaking his head.

Jane stood on the brake and revved the engine, causing the Chevy's back wheels to spin.

The man didn't budge. He was maybe one-eighty, six feet. Not big enough to stop a truck.

"Do you have a fucking death wish?" Jane shouted.

"Like the guy down there in the barn?" the man asked.

Jane stilled. Her foot slid off the gas. Andy. Had she killed him?

"I'm a friend," he said.

Without taking her eyes off him, she reached for the chicken broth that she'd set in the console and took a drink. She could use a friend. If that's what he was. "Prove it."

He reached a hand into his jeans pocket.

"ID's not going to do it. Anyone can buy fake ID."

"Then tell me how?"

Jane frowned, thinking. If this really was Hunter, then he'd know Ariane pretty well. "What's Nate's favourite Peruvian dish?"

The man who called himself Hunter looked up to the sky. His chest expanded. Was he smiling?

"Picarones!" he shouted, and then he caught her gaze. "Peruvian fucking donuts."

Jane stared back, still unsure. Had she asked the right question?

"Ariane calls him Nathaniel," he said.

A friend, Jane decided, and the tension dropped from her shoulders. She took a deep breath and let it out.

Hunter walked around to her window. "You done trying to run me down?"

"Yeah. Listen, I gotta get out of here."

"No, you don't. That guy down there? That's self-defence, but you gotta stick around for the cops."

"I don't care about the guy down there. It's the one he works for that I want."

"That's a bad idea. Stay here and let the police sort it out."

"Can't. The guy he works for is getting on a plane to England. I've got to stop him."

"You go to the airport looking like that and you won't get far."

Jane looked down to her shirt. For the first time, she noticed the blood. She was painted with it.

"I'm not going to the airport." She pulled the receipt from her pocket and pointed to the Vancouver address. "That's where I'm heading," she said, handing it to him. "You can follow me if you want."

He stared at her hand, which was trembling. "You don't look in any shape to be behind the wheel. How about I drive?" He opened her door. "And we're not taking this truck. Come on," he said, urging her out.

Jane's hackles rose. She set her jaw. "I'll drive myself."

He gestured toward the carton of broth sitting in the console. "When was the last time you ate?"

She couldn't remember. She didn't even know for sure how many days she'd been locked up. Relenting, she stepped out, habitually shook her hair into place, and then reached back into the truck and grabbed the broth.

He opened the passenger door of the Escalade and she got in. He jogged around the back and then folded into the driver's seat. "Buckle up," he said, swinging an arm over the back of her headrest. He reversed to the cut-off and stopped. "Listen, this Roderick asshole might already be at the airport. I can make a call. I've got a friend with a badge. He can run interference, maybe delay his flight."

"Do it," Jane said.

"Have you got the keys to the kennel's padlock?" he said, as he punched a number into his dash-mounted cellphone.

Jane shook her head. She couldn't remember what she'd done with them.

A man answered. "What's up, Bishop?"

"Got a hot lead." He gave the man the Langley address. "Found my missing person. She flipped the tables on one of the guys who was holding her. Turned him into a sprinkler. He's in the outbuilding. In bad shape. Send an ambulance."

"I'll have a cruiser there in ten."

"They'll need bolt cutters. There's more. There's a second guy. He's got a ticket to Gatwick. AC854. Leaves in three hours. Name's Doctor Roderick Atkins."

"You got anything solid?"

"A receipt. A witness. If the ambulance gets here in time, you'll have an accomplice."

"All right. I'll do what I can. Stay put."

Hunter ended the call and tore off down the driveway.

"The guy in the kennel," Jane said. "You think he's dead?"

"Don't know. I smashed a window and saw him but couldn't get in. You did quite a number on him. How'd you manage that?"

"Dumb luck."

"Any of that blood yours?"

Jane pushed up the sleeves of her shirt. The blood had soaked through in places, but it wasn't hers. "No," she said. "How'd you find me?"

"Sadie got your message."

79 | Sadie

Ethan hadn't stopped moving since he arrived at Sadie's apartment. They were still waiting for an address from Nate. Sadie sat in a huddle on the sofa while his impatient footfalls picked at her nerves.

When the phone finally rang again, Sadie didn't recognize the number. "Hello?"

"Sadie?"

"Jane!" Sadie leapt up. "Where are you? Are you all right? Oh, god. I'm so sorry. Can you ever forgive me?"

"Only if you'll forgive me. I'm sorry too, Sadie."

"Are you okay? Did he hurt you?"

Ethan stepped into Sadie's personal space, eyes wide, nostrils flared.

"No," Jane said. "I'm fine."

Sadie backed away from Ethan and dropped boneless to the sofa. All the air left her. "We've been so worried. Are you coming home?"

"Soon. But first, I need to take care of something, and I want you here with me."

"Anything. Tell me where." Ethan kicked Sadie's shoe. She looked up. "Oh, and Ethan's here."

"Put me on speaker."

"Jane?" Ethan said.

"I'm here. I'm okay."

"Whose phone is that? Where are you?"

"It's Hunter's phone. He's Ariane's investigator. Rick has a place near Granville Island. We're headed there."

"What's the address?"

80 | Jane

Hunter pulled up to the curb across the street from Rick's place. Jane handed him back the phone. "Thanks."

"Still wish you hadn't done that."

"This is my fight, not yours."

"At least you waited until we got here to call them. This may be all over before your friends arrive."

Jane imagined how pissed Sadie would be if that was the case.

"Sadie and Ethan can take care of themselves."

"I hope you're right."

While Hunter enlarged the aerial view of Rick's townhouse complex on his GPS, Jane surveyed it from the passenger seat. The complex was set back from the sidewalk. Each of the townhomes had its own front door and a cement-slab porch. Curved footpaths of pebbled concrete led to each door, delineating a patchwork quilt of lawn. Rick's unit sat on the end. Jane reached for the car door.

"Not yet," Hunter said, holding out his hand to stop her.

"I appreciate what you've done, but you don't need to stay. I can take it from here."

"Can you? What's your plan?"

She looked down to her boot knife. "He's going to pay for what he did to me, to my family."

"I hope so, but that's not a plan." Hunter pointed to his screen. "I see two exits, possibly a third if there's an interior corridor leading to the underground garage. We can cover two of them."

He reached into the back seat, pulled a shirt from a duffle bag, and handed it to her. "Put this on."

Jane took the button-up shirt and slid her arms into sleeves that were far too long.

Hunter studied the screen. "It looks like the courtyards around back are fenced. Give me three minutes to breach the fence and get to the back door, and then you go to his front door and knock. As soon as he sees you, he'll head for one of the exits. Let's hope he goes for the back door. If not, he'll head to the parking garage, which exits here. If not, "he said, pointing to an alley. "We'll have to tail him in the car if he takes that route."

Jane rolled up the cuffs of Hunter's shirt. "How about you go to the front door. He'll open it for you. Then I'll take care of him."

"You think you have the strength for that? Because I don't. You're trembling, short of breath. And what if he's armed? Stray bullets could put other lives in the building at risk. You don't want to do that."

She paused. Starvation might have left her weak, but she had adrenalin on her side. Still, his warning reminded her that she no longer had the protection of her birthmarks. "All right," Jane said. "We do this your way, but if he opens the door, he's going to feel the bite of my blade."

Hunter pointed to the time on the screen. "Three minutes."

Jane nodded. Hunter climbed out of the Escalade and jogged toward the corner of the building. Three minutes? Might as well be three hours. At the two-minute mark, Jane left the vehicle and crossed the road. She reached for her boot knife, straightened, and held it by her thigh as she strode to Rick's front door. On his porch, she kept her head down, counted to ten. As she lifted her fist to rap on the door, she noticed the casing beside the lock had been splintered. She reached for the door and pushed. It swung in. She hesitated for a moment then slipped inside and closed the door behind her.

Her eyes adjusted to the shadows as she tiptoed down the hall. To her right, behind a glass-paned door, sat a figure behind a desk.

Confusion gripped Jane. She paused. It wasn't Rick sitting behind the desk—it was Cynthia.

Questions swirled in her head, and every one of them had the same answer. They were in on it together. Her anger boiled over, and Jane pushed open the door and stormed forward.

Cynthia looked up and raised a perfectly shaped eyebrow. "Jane?"

"You and Rick?" Jane spat.

Cynthia jerked her head back and curled her lip in disgust. "Don't be ridiculous." Cynthia looked Jane up and down and frowned. She wore a pristine cream-coloured suit marred by a single drop of blood on one lapel. "What's happened to you?"

Under Cynthia's scrutiny, Jane clawed her hair into place. "Is he here?"

A loud bang rang out from another room. Not a gunshot—more like something heavy hitting the floor. A shriek followed.

Jane turned.

"You don't want to go down there," Cynthia said.

Ignoring her, Jane headed toward the unmistakable sound of fists on flesh and froze on the threshold of the kitchen.

Rick sat tied to a chair, his face bloodied. A wall of muscle stood behind him, holding the chair upright. A second wall of muscle, a twin to the first, stood poised to land another punch but then pivoted, likely sensing Jane's arrival. The man stood six foot two, weighed at least two-twenty, and had a disproportionate amount of muscle in his neck and shoulders. His beanie and gloves were out of place.

His gaze slid behind Jane's shoulder to Cynthia, who'd followed her. Her enforcers.

Jane's attention was drawn to a nearby patio door. Hunter had stepped into view. He rapped on the glass. Three sharp, short cracks of his knuckles. He stood with his hands loose by his sides, shaking them out as if he were a boxer in a ring.

Sirens sounded in the distance. Cynthia tilted her head to listen. She spoke to Jane with a cold smile on her face. "If you have business with this scumbag, be quick about it. And don't damage the house. I own it now," she said, tucking a file folder under her arm.

Hunter rapped again. His nostrils flared as he glared through the door at Jane. Maybe not a boxer, but definitely a fighter, Jane decided.

Cynthia turned to her enforcers. "Finish this," she said.

The enforcer who stood in front of Rick bent to pick up a sledge-hammer. Without pause for thought, he swung at Rick's knee. Jane processed the horrific damage in slow motion. The sledgehammer connected with a bone-crunching crack. Long seconds later, a bellow unlike any human sound Jane had ever heard followed.

"Let's go," one of the twins said. He stepped toward the patio doors, opened it, and pushed Hunter out of the way.

"You have a nice day," Cynthia said.

Jane's gaze followed the twins, who flanked Cynthia as they hurried down the courtyard path.

Hunter stepped in front of Jane. "Put that away," he said, looking down to the knife in Jane's hand. She'd forgotten about it. She twisted toward Rick, whose groans bubbled up through mucus.

"Think, Jane," Hunter said. "Your DNA is already on the front door. Do you want it all over him?" he said, nodding toward Rick.

Jane searched Hunter's face. "He owes me."

"Oh, he'll pay. Those thugs just collected a down payment. But it'll be a whole lot less complicated for us if we're sitting in my car when the police arrive."

The sound of sirens grew steadily. "You think they're coming here?"

"No doubt the woman dialled 911 herself. Probably wants him hurting, not dead." Hunter skirted Rick's now unconscious body.

Jane allowed herself to be led out the front door and back to the street. But she never made it to Hunter's car. Ethan arrived, skidding to a stop at the curb on the wrong side of the street. He had his Harley on its stand and Jane in his arms before his helmet was off.

She felt herself collapse in his arms, a weakness she had no energy to fight. "I've got you," he said, holding her tight.

When they finally pulled apart, she looked around for Hunter and found him leaning back against his Cadillac. Ethan kept an arm around her waist, shoring her up as they made their way across the street.

"Ethan, I presume," Hunter said, offering his hand.

Their introduction was interrupted by Sadie's arrival. She screeched to the curb, barely missing Ethan's Fat Boy, and leapt out calling Jane's name.

Jane pulled away from Ethan and met Sadie in an embrace in the middle of the road.

Moments later, the street was ablaze in a kaleidoscope of lights. Hunter ushered them into his SUV. He had no argument from Jane, whose legs had started to shake. Fire trucks arrived first, followed by an ambulance, and finally, the police. Neighbours gawked out of windows and streamed outside, glued to their doorsteps. A few brave souls ventured closer to the action only to be turned back.

While they watched the rush of activity, Jane and Hunter filled Sadie and Ethan in on what had happened.

Hunter nodded toward an unmarked car that had just arrived. "That's my contact." He got out and jogged down the street. The aggressive body language between Hunter and his contact suggested his contact wasn't particularly happy with him. After some arm flinging, Hunter's contact hung his head. Hunter jogged back to the car.

"He looks pissed," Jane said. "What's going on?"

"Nothing I didn't expect. 'Shouldn't have left the scene, gonna pull your licence.' Same ol'."

Paramedics rolled a gurney up the path to Rick's door.

"What the hell did Cynthia do to him?" Sadie whispered.

"Not Cynthia," Hunter answered. "Her muscle. They pummelled the guy then kneecapped him, old style. Brutal."

"Jesus," Sadie said, shrinking into her seat.

Jane felt Ethan tense beside her. He narrowed his eyes at Sadie. "Is she your loan shark or your pimp?"

Sadie looked away.

A second ambulance arrived. Jane felt a prick of alarm. Was someone else inside? Hurt? Jane rolled her head in the direction of Rick's doorway, but the new ambulance blocked her view. "Who's the new ambulance for?" Jane gathered her strength and got out of the SUV to track the action. The others followed.

As Jane rounded the new ambulance, a gurney rolled out of Rick's house. She stumbled forward to put herself in its path, but Ethan swung an arm around her shoulder and held her back. An oxygen mask covered Rick's nose and mouth and a thick strap secured his torso to the gurney. When the stretcher passed by, Jane balled her fists, frustrated by the audience.

Ethan took one of her fists in his hand. "This time you walk away," he whispered. "There are other ways to get even. I promise."

Rick disappeared into the back of one of the ambulances.

"Jane? Look at me," Ethan said, drawing Jane's attention. He lifted her hair from the side of her face. "Your birthmark."

Amid the chaos, Jane had forgotten. She felt Ethan trace his fingers over the skin where the mark used to be.

"It's gone."

She allowed herself a smile. "You never saw it anyway."

Ethan wrapped her tight in his arms. She'd begun to tremble again. "Take me home," she said.

"Jane Walker?" she heard a voice say.

Ethan kept his arm around her as she turned to face the man. It was Hunter's contact.

Turned out Jane couldn't go home. The second ambulance was for her.

Epilogue

Six weeks had passed since Rick's arrest. In that time, Jane hadn't had a single visiting dream. She and Ariane had a bet going. If the dreams returned, Jane owed her a bottle of Pisco. It was a foolish bet. Ariane had been right about all of it. Jane was *una testigo*. A Witness. There was no cure, and no escape. In fact, Jane had already bought Ariane's Pisco. Eventually, she would dream again. She had to accept it and learn to cope with the responsibility.

After Jane had revealed the details of her visiting dreams, Ariane speculated that, in time, Jane's ability to interact with people and objects in her dreams would grow stronger and more consistent. It was a warning.

Ariane's time in Canada was drawing to a close. Jane would miss her. Nate would miss her, too—Jane could tell by the way he looked at her as if she were one of those picarones he loved so much.

Ariane had begged Jane to accompany her to Peru, but Jane couldn't. She wasn't yet ready to risk dreaming in unfamiliar surroundings. Ariane understood, and promised to set up video chats so Jane could meet some of the old families, learn from them.

Jane liked the idea of being able to travel someday. She had the means now. Turned out the Walkers had life insurance. Their combined million-dollar policies had been paid out on her twenty-first birthday. Those funds, which had been invested since their deaths, had grown beyond Jane's imagination. It meant she could do a whole lot of good in the Walkers' name, and that knowledge was enough to finally quell the sense of guilt she'd felt inheriting their estate.

Jane pulled her scarf tight against the bracing cold. She stood on a grassy plateau overlooking a creek. Mountains loomed to the east and Ethan warmed her back. "It's beautiful," she said.

Ethan hugged her tighter. "The house will go up right here. We can look out over this view every morning."

"Sounds perfect."

"I'll bring the trailer up in the spring and we'll make plans."

Ethan had made a deposit on the twenty-acre parcel. It was in the Sunshine Valley, two hours east of Vancouver.

Jane knew he was years away from building anything, but she loved that he was including her in his decisions.

The sky was darkening as he pulled to the curb outside her building.

"You sure I can't talk you into staying with me tonight?" Ethan said, as Jane dismounted.

She'd spent a few nights at his apartment and was getting acclimatized to trusting him with her secret. "Soon. Promise." They removed their helmets. He remained astride the bike.

"I like it short," he said, brushing Jane's bangs aside. She'd cut her hair into a jaw-length bob. In part, to help her break the habit of hiding behind her hair. The other part was her need for a fresh start.

Jane kissed him goodbye. He stayed there until she disappeared inside.

She continued past her apartment and knocked on Sadie's door.

Sadie opened it with a look of expectation. "Well? How was it?"

"Pretty. There really is a creek running through it." Jane looked past Sadie to her desk, where a textbook lay open beside her computer. "You want a glass of wine?"

"Sure. My head's full. Time for a break."

Sadie locked up and followed Jane back to their old apartment.

They'd mended their friendship after Jane's release from the hospital, but the wounds were still healing.

Sadie had been rocked to the core by Cynthia's ruthlessness. Rick's anonymous tip to the authorities had resulted in the freezing of Cynthia's bank accounts before Rick's cash payout materialized. For his efforts, Rick had lost a kidney and wouldn't walk for months—and never without a limp. His jaw was still wired shut.

Cynthia's lawyers had her accounts freed up within ten days and then sold the townhouse and pocketed the proceeds.

Rick had been smart enough not to identify Cynthia or contest signing over his house to her. Jane had no doubt doing so would cost him his other knee. Behind bars, he'd already be at the mercy of the other inmates, given his impaired mobility.

Ethan had piled onto Sadie's plate of remorse with a few choice words of his own. Her feigned naivety about the business she was in had infuriated him. Jane hadn't stopped him. Sadie needed to hear it.

Admitting to Ethan and then to Nate and Ariane that she was a hooker—actually saying the words out loud—was finally enough to get Sadie out of the business.

Cynthia forked over the hundred grand they'd agreed to and let her go, but Cynthia wasn't happy about it. Jane suspected Cynthia was biding her time, counting on Sadie to blow through the cash and crawl back to her. Jane was betting on Sadie.

They sat side by side with Jane's laptop between them. Her mind was on Pieter, as it often was these days. She and Ariane had talked at length about what Jane had done in her dream on the wintery night she'd helped Mary navigate the ice at St. Paul's Hospital. Hunter dug up local reports about the accident and the subsequent lawsuits. The Pieter she'd once known had never existed.

Jane's guilt over what she'd done ate away at her every day. Tears made a regular appearance. She hated the waterworks. They made her feel weak, as if Rick had broken something in her.

She'd explained to Sadie what had happened the day Pieter and Buddy were born. But Sadie's reality, her memories, had altered the moment Jane interfered with history. Sadie had only ever known Pieter to be in a wheelchair and Anna to be angry. She'd never met the man named Dylan; the man Jane knew and loved as Buddy. Buddy with the mismatched eyes and the larger-than-life smile. Buddy who called her Jaynee. She missed him and wondered if she'd ever see him again.

Andy had survived the stabbing. Jane felt zero guilt where he was concerned. He and Rick were, ironically, both behind steel bars awaiting a trial that was months, if not years, away. Jane took great comfort knowing where they were spending their nights.

As the credits rolled up on an episode of *Black Mirror*, Jane upended her wineglass.

"I've decided to change my name. Legally."

"For real?"

"Beth Morrow Walker," Jane said. "What do you think?"

"BMW? I like it. But how about you keep Jane in there somewhere," Sadie said. "I'd hate to lose her."

Jane took Sadie's hand. "You'll never lose her." Turned out their mantra of looking forward, never back, had a flaw. Sometimes you had to look back to see how far you'd come.

The End

Thank You

Thank you for reading *Blood Mark*. If you enjoyed it, please tell a friend or consider posting a short review where you purchased it. Reviews help other readers discover the book and are much appreciated.

—JP McLean

Excerpt from The Gift Legacy

Secret Sky is the first book in the thrilling, otherworldly The Gift Legacy series by JP McLean. Seamlessly blending paranormal mystery, fantasy, and romance, this beautifully written and deeply resonant adventure will swoop you into a vivid, new reality and leave your imagination soaring.

Secret Sky

When Emelynn Taylor accepted a stranger's gift, she couldn't know it would hijack her life. It strikes without warning, strips her of gravity and sends her airborne. Vowing to tame her gift, Emelynn returns to the seaside home where it all began. Here, she finds a dangerous world hidden within our own that will plunge her into a fight for her life.

Read on for an excerpt . . .

"CAN YOU TELL me your name?"

"*Emelynn.*" I closed my eyes to dampen the cresting wave of nausea.

"She's nonresponsive."

No, I'm not. I forced my eyes open. The man's face was a blur. "*My name's Emelynn,*" I repeated but, oddly, I couldn't hear my voice.

"Did you find any ID?"

Nearby, a siren wailed. Had it rained? The damp air smelled of worms and wet earth. I lost the fight with my eyelids.

"No, and no sign of her shoes or transportation either. Are you ready to move her?"

"Yes, she's immobilized and secure. On three . . ."

The world tilted at a dangerous angle. Flashing lights throbbed, breaching my shrouded eyes.

"Female, early twenties, BP's ninety-eight over fifty . . ." The man's voice trailed off as I melted into the pleasant reprieve of a quiet darkness.

I liked the soft, fuzzy quality of the darkness. I felt comfortable there, but loud voices and harsh lights dragged me back and dumped me into a boisterous room. The clatter hurt my ears. I desperately wanted to shush these people, but that would be rude. A hazy face pressed in, but my eyes wouldn't focus. The man behind the face flicked a sharp light in my eye. So . . . inconsiderate.

"Can you tell me what day it is?" he asked, as if I were an idiot.

It's . . . hmm . . . What day was it? And why couldn't I move? An overwhelming desire to curl up and go back to sleep tugged at me. The man finally let me close my eyes. I pulled against whatever held me in its grip, but I didn't have the strength to fight it.

"Let's get a CT scan, spine and head, stat, and run a panel in case we have to go in."

Even though my eyes were closed, the room was too bright—and noisy. A cacophony of electronic beeps, bells and sharp voices assaulted my ears. I wanted to ask everyone to leave me alone, but my voice wouldn't come. They jostled me and I dipped into that blissful darkness again—the one that pushed away all the noise.

The darkness soothed me until the man with the snap-on gloves interrupted the calm again, his sharp light piercing my eye like a knitting needle. "Can you tell me in what city you live?"

Did he think I didn't know? I almost said Toronto, but that wasn't right, was it? Didn't I just move to Summerset . . . or was that a dream? Why was I so confused? God, my head hurt.

"Any change?" he asked.

Was he talking to me?

"No. She's still hypotensive, but stable."

I guess not.

"Pupils are equal and reactive," he said, and then he sighed. "It's been six hours. Do we know who she is yet?"

My name's Emelynn," I said in defeat, knowing he couldn't hear me.

"No, the police searched the park. No purse, no ID."

"What was she doing in the park at that hour?" someone asked.

"The police haven't ruled out that she might have been dumped there, but she was wearing workout gear so she could have been hit while jogging."

"It would have been late for a jog in the park, wouldn't it?"

"Maybe she works shifts?"

Listening to the conversation exhausted me. Before I could figure out what it meant, the darkness claimed me again. If only they'd let me stay there, but they were relentless with their light.

This time when the stabbing light woke me, the thought that perhaps I was dying flitted through my mind. Was I supposed to go toward the light? Maybe I wasn't doing it right.

When the light retreated again, I slept fitfully and had the oddest dream. It was the dead of night. A powerful storm was gathering strength. Gusting winds blew across the crests of angry waves, creating whitecaps that seemed to glow in the dark. Towering cedars and firs rained needles as they bowed to the wind. The great, crooked trunks of old arbutus trees groaned and twisted, spewing glossy leaves into the breeze.

And I had a bird's-eye view of it all.

Home was here in the dream, somewhere. I sensed it calling out to me, drawing me toward its warmth and safety. I knew the small cottage so well but couldn't find it. The storm would stop if I could just get inside, but the wind blew me out over the treetops, farther and farther away. And then I was falling . . . falling . . . falling through the night sky, careening out of control, crashing through the tree canopy until that blissful darkness put an end to the terrible fall.

The pointy light woke me. "Can you tell me your name?" The man peeled back my eyelids and flicked that damn light.

"Emelynn," I said, relieved to hear the sound of my voice. But the relief was short-lived. My head exploded in agony when I turned away from the light.

As the pain hit a crescendo, I heard him remark "I'm losing her" and I surrendered to the peaceful darkness where pain didn't reach me.

"Emelynn," the man said, the next time he woke me with the flicking light. "Emelynn, don't struggle—we've immobilized your head. Do you know where you are?"

I squinted, straining to bring the face behind the glasses into focus. "The hospital?"

"Good. That's good, Emelynn. I'm Dr. Coulter. You've had an accident."

"What accident?" Car accident? I don't have a car. No, wait, I think I do have a car. Why was this so hard?

"You don't remember?" He pressed his lips into a thin line and furrowed his brow.

I tried, but the dream was all I could think of. "Did I fall?"

"We don't know. We were hoping you could tell us."

"My head hurts."

"You have a concussion. I can't give you anything for it yet. Can you tell me what you were doing in Sunset Park last night?"

"I live there," I said, but that wasn't right either. Why was I so mixed up? Sleep once again tugged at me.

He seemed to share my confusion. "We'll talk again later."

I folded into the darkness, and when it faded, it revealed an airport scene that looked vaguely familiar. I drifted toward a young couple with a little girl and watched as the man leaned in to kiss the woman.

"I love you," he said, pulling away.

My heart stopped when I saw the man's face.

He turned to the little girl and mussed her hair. "Be good for your mother. I'll only be gone a few days."

Oh, god, no. I knew what this was. I had to stop him. "No! Don't go!"

He put his big tackle box on the luggage cart beside the bag that I knew held his fishing rods. "I'll be back Tuesday. Don't forget about those peanut butter cookies you promised me." He smiled down at the girl, then turned and walked out to the float plane tied to the dock.

"No!" I cried, as he ducked into the plane, oblivious to my presence. "Please," I begged. Then someone called my name.

"Emelynn. Emelynn, that's right, look at me. I'm over here." A woman in scrubs moved her face into my line of vision. I blinked up at her.

"It was a dream, that's all, dear. You have a concussion. Your head is braced. Try not to fight it. You were thrashing in your sleep." She adjusted the blankets and checked the IV.

Pain returned with my awakening and ramped up quickly. It wasn't just my head anymore. My entire left side was on fire. A moan escaped my throat.

"I'll get Dr. Coulter," the nurse said, hurrying from the room.

Time crawled while I played a miserable little game of Which Body Part Hurts Most. There was no clear winner.

Dr. Coulter arrived at a gallop. He and the nurse succinctly exchanged statistics at a rapid-fire clip. BP? One oh six over sixty. Urine?

Clear. Orientation? Improving. With a clipboard in hand, he checked a number of beeping machines.

"Can you tell me your name?" He put the clipboard down with a clatter and pulled that damn penlight out of his breast pocket.

"Emelynn," I said, as he held my eyelid captive.

"Good," he said, distracted by his light-flicking exam. "Do you have a last name, Emelynn?"

"Taylor," I responded with trepidation. What kind of trouble had I gotten myself into?

He repeated the light exam with my other eye. "Very good," he said, and then he finally saw me, not just my eyes.

"Where do you live?" he asked.

"Cliffside Avenue."

He smiled warmly. "Glad to hear you've moved out of the park."

"Excuse me?" My head throbbed in time with the beat of my heart.

"During one of our earlier discussions, you said you lived in Sunset Park. I'm just happy to see that your memory is coming back. What do you remember about your accident?"

"Accident?" I mulled over his question, holding out for some clues. He wasn't offering any and my dreams were all mixed up with reality. Had I dreamt that I'd fallen through the trees or was that real? My head kept pounding. I drew my right hand up and followed the path of the tube sticking out of the back of it up to a dripping IV bag.

"Late Monday or early Tuesday?" he continued, bringing my attention back to his question.

"I'm sorry, I don't remember," I said, distracted now. "How long have I been here?"

"You came in on a 911 call at"—he checked the notes on the clipboard—"oh-one-thirty on Tuesday."

I tried to process the information.

"That's one thirty in the morning. You were found in Sunset Park. Do you remember why you were in the park at that hour?"

"The park is right beside my house." I tried to recall the details that would make sense of this scenario, but they escaped me, and the pain made concentration difficult. "I don't remember."

"Okay. Let's give it a few more hours. Memory loss isn't uncommon with this type of brain injury. It may be temporary."

"*May* be?"

"It's still early. We need to give it more time."

"It feels like I've been here for days."

"I'm sure it does. We've been waking you on the hour since you arrived. It's standard procedure for concussions. Unfortunately, your blood pressure is still too low and you've been unconscious more than not during your stay here in the ICU, so we're not done yet. How's your pain?" he asked. "On a scale of one to ten."

"Nine hundred," I said, closing my eyes. "What happened to me?"

"I don't know, but it was particularly hard on your left side." I heard him pick up the clipboard again. "You've got ten stitches in the back of your head plus seven or eight in your left ankle, and a whole host of contusions and abrasions, including some nasty-looking road rash on your face, but I don't think it'll scar." He flipped up a sheet of paper. "There's no evidence of sexual assault, but you sustained an injury to your kidneys. The blood has already cleared from your urine, so we'll remove the catheter in the next few hours."

I heard him set the clipboard down on the table again, and I opened my eyes when he took my hand. "I can give you something for the pain, but I'm afraid it won't help much," he said. "It's important that we're able to rouse you at regular intervals for the next six hours. Do you think you can hang in there?"

"Do I have a choice?"

He gave me a crooked smile. "I'll order your meds and check on you in a few hours."

The nurse returned with a needle and stuck it into the IV line. "I'll wake you in an hour."

A thick fog rolled in around me. I dreamt again, but not of the family at the airport or the terrifying fall through the tree canopy.

. . . I was nine or ten years old and beachcombing with my father. He had that tool in his hand, the one he used to break open fist-sized geodes searching for the crystals hidden inside. When I got close, he called to me and turned over a flat piece of shale. He laughed as I shrieked and ran away from the tiny crabs that scrambled to find fresh cover.

My heart quickened as the nurse woke me and the memory faded. She assured me it had been an hour. When she left, the thick fog came back, pulling me under.

. . . A blonde-haired woman in a wide-brimmed hat whispered my name. She held her hands palms out, inviting me to a game of patty cake, and I lifted my hands to mirror hers. She spoke in a quiet voice, repeating a haunting refrain while keeping watch over her shoulder, and when shadows approached, she vanished.

The nurse woke me again. I had dipped in and out of fog so often that my perception was all mixed up, making it difficult to sort out what was real and what wasn't. "What time is it?" I asked.

"Just after six in the morning," she said, pumping up the blood pressure cuff. "Wednesday." She paused to listen to her stethoscope. "You're in the ICU, and I'm happy to report that your blood pressure is improving." The Velcro made a ripping noise as she removed the cuff.

"Good morning, Emelynn," Dr. Coulter said, as he crossed behind the nurse to retrieve the clipboard. "Your vitals are looking better. How's your pain level?"

"It hasn't improved with time," I said, forcing a smile.

"Have you remembered any more details about your accident?" His expression was hopeful.

"No," I said. The lie came easily; I was good at lying. I'd been hiding my secrets for a long time.

Dr. Coulter raised his chin and glared down his nose. "Well, keep trying. You're out of the danger zone, so I'll give you something more for the pain now. Maybe you'll remember more after you've rested." He frowned in disappointment as he left my room.

He didn't believe me, but he didn't press me either, which was a good thing: I could fill the room with what I was withholding. Because unfortunately, I now remembered all of it. Every last detail.

Acknowledgements

No book shows up on publishing day without a long list of people who helped get it there.

I owe my gratitude to my editor, Eileen Cook, whose input added muscle to the story. My gratitude also goes to editor, Rachel Small, who polished the manuscript until it shone. Thanks also to editor, Ted Williams, who tidied up the pesky commas, hyphens, and misplaced letters.

And once again, I owe a big thank you to the design team at JD&J Designs for *Blood Mark's* intriguing book cover.

A big hug and thanks to Mickey Mikkelson of Creative Edge Publicity for his encouragement and stellar representation.

Thank you to retired social worker, Bill Engleson for sharing his insights. Thanks to Isabel Elgueta for her expertise with the Spanish language and the sweet Peruvian treat picarones. Thanks also to Frank Gay for the biker lingo.

The story improved immeasurably with the imaginative input from my early readers: Elinor Florence, Donna Tunney, Annie Siegel, and Dawn Stofer.

Thank you to the Denman Writers' Group for your input on the critical opening scene (twice!). My thanks also go to the supportive writers and friends at the Creative Academy.

And as always, my gratitude and love to the intrepid beta readers who never fail to provide valuable insight and direction: Jean McLean, Kathy McLean, Margaret Wigle, and Sue Cox.

And to the very first reader of all my books, thank you to my husband, John. XO

Any errors in this novel are entirely my own.

About the Author

JP (Jo-Anne) McLean writes urban fantasy and supernatural thrillers. Her writing has received honourable mentions from the Whistler Independent Book Awards and the Victoria Writers Society. Reviewers call her books *addictive*, *smart*, and *fun*.

Raised in Toronto, Ontario, JP lived in various parts of North America, from La Colorada in Zacatecas, Mexico and Tucson, Arizona to Calgary, Alberta, before settling on Canada's west coast. She now lives with her husband on Denman Island, which is nestled between the coast of British Columbia and Vancouver Island.

JP holds a degree in commerce from the University of British Columbia, is a certified scuba diver, an avid gardener, and a voracious reader. She had a successful career in human resources before turning her attention to writing.

She enjoys hearing from readers. Contact her via her website, jpmcleanauthor.com, or through her social media sites. Reviews are always welcome and greatly appreciated.

 Sign up for her newsletter ~ jpmcleanauthor.com
 Find her on Goodreads ~ goodreads.com/jpmclean
 Like her on Facebook ~ facebook.com/JPMcLeanBooks
    Follow her on Twitter ~ @jpmcleanauthor

Made in United States
North Haven, CT
06 July 2022